2 Sides Of the Same Coin: a very contemporary romance

Copyright © Tim Fulmer, 2010

Dedicated to the eternal clash of opinions.

Middle English *devel*, Old English *dēofol*, from
Late Latin *diabolus*, from Late Greek *diabolos*,
from Greek, slanderer, from *diaballein*, to
slander, set at variance, "throw across":
dia-, across + *ballein*, to throw.

Diabolein is destroying a vase in China solely for that idea.
Diabolein is people on the streets of Tokyo staring at mobile
phones instead of talking into them.
Diabolein is the blank tablet goal.

*language indeed is no longer satisfied to describe reality. a new
"symbolic system layer" is appearing. discontinuous time, two,
three months, six years one second. a "time" of glass. Very
overlapping. intoxicating blur. not about arrival.*

KBLHKBLHKBLHKBLHKBLHKBLHKBLHKBLHKBLHKB
LHKBLHKBLHKBLHKBLHKBLHKBL
ComMERZComMERZComMERZComMERZComMERZCom
MERZComMERZComMERZComMERZ

We are those who crawl … eat the dust.
We are still without bonds between us.

- Of who it is this motorcycle?
- It is a chopper.
- of who it is this chopper?
- It is of Zed.
- Who Is Zed?
- Zed is a deaf man, small... Zed is deaf.

grid n°1 grid n°2

[a]

Hey body of liquid gold, you are <u>not</u> special

ACT I

DIABLO: Now we got an argument dammit. Thank you very much!

PATTY: Why didn't you ask those poor people back there? Go ahead, ask 'em.

DIABLO: Hell you mean poor people?

PATTY: [mimicking DIABLO]: Hell *you* mean?

DIABLO: Know what?

PATTY: Yeah I got an idea. Circumstances constantly change - but how? Force majeure?

DIABLO: Hell's going on with you today? Wanna take over driving? You bored?

PATTY: Why didn't you ask directions from those people back there?

DIABLO: What?

PATTY: Poor people.

DIABLO: Oh dear.

PATTY [rooting around in her purse]: We're getting short on money too, the cash sort of money.

DIABLO: Everyone needs more money, on the continent at least. Round here [gesturing through the windshield at the snow-covered fields racing by alongside the ice-covered highway], it's one tough financial decision right after another, right up till your benefactors choose that favorite jeweled casket. Hah - at least they're stuck with *your* debt - can't take that shit with you to the grave, or back to the island, for that matter. Debt makes a terrible souvenir. Don't get me started on insurance, *auto* insurance.

PATTY: Please, you'll never stop with … Be quiet for a minute.

DIABLO: Sorry but I-I …

PATTY: Let's not discuss it. Hear me out - I don't intend to discuss money anymore.

DIABLO: Oh for Chrissake, Patrick has the money anyway.

PATTY: I told you I can't imagine Patrick's actually waiting for us in Duluth.

DIABLO: So your imagination's failed you again. Let me tell you how … or - wait a minute - what level are you working from here anyway?

PATTY: Level of what?

DIABLO: Transcendence.

PATTY: I answered your stupid metaphysical questions on yesterday's drive. I-said-I-answered-your-questions. I concluded you're crazy ... uncooperative … irritating.

DIABLO: Shouldn't be so abrupt with me. Just doing my job. I'm … I *am* cooperating.

PATTY: *Whoa*. We can't turn in here [gesturing at a large expanse of snow-covered asphalt crowded with gas pumps and eighteen-wheelers].

DIABLO: I need something to eat.

PATTY: I understand what you're doing. Take me for a fool?

DIABLO: Uh-huh, oh, in general not a fool but more specifically a … What do you think? What's this road-trip mean to you?

PATTY: Simple. Patrick's not waiting for us in Minnesota. I know it. He's probably dead - though *not* of old age.

DIABLO: Oh look at that little boy, that funny looking little boy [pointing through the windshield]. Looks like *he* solved the problem of old age.

PATTY: Watch out for that car. My God, you're mad! Hell are you thinking? We can't park here [gesturing at a handicapped parking space beside the entrance to the truck-stop diner].

DIABLO: Oh for that I'm *not* sorry. An old Pontiac Firebird like ours is definitely handicapped. … Yeah Patrick's probably dead - of old age though?

PATTY: What a mess. [Opening the car door] Freezing out here.

{a} When I talk about change I don't think of the sea (so I never describe a transformation as a 'sea change'). I also disagree with the idea of there being windows on other planets (don't you?). Nor can there be sewage in paradise (right?). No way. Out here on the continent we all share the fate of passengers when we awaken to the light of day, and I'm not sure if I wanna touch the sky to begin with.

Nothing's worse than the final word of the last line of a book's first poem - when the poet has time to joke about the presentiments of the forthcoming poem before the whole collection disintegrates into a series of poetic essays describing important social issues, crises, dilemmas, what have you (including some recipes for weird Indonesian cuisine). So let's try this:

Ladies and gentlemen, here's the first reason why the continent needs 24 hours of celebrity, why many of the TV channel networks require us to talk, for more than two years now, about the world's most outrageous celebrity and the basic operations of conspiracy that underlie his declaration of love at the edgy border between rebellious anger and full-on repentance. Ever attended a sci-fi convention? Men there often wear pleated pants, sometimes even flat-front trousers. It's a miracle more of them aren't in jail.

> DIABLO [shaking a handful of bills at PATTY.]: Where'd you get this money, all this cash?
> PATTY: From my work.
> DIABLO: Don't lie to me. Why are you hiding money under the car seat?
> PATTY: Why are you looking at me like that?
> DIABLO: Girl, don't you start with me! What are you planning to do with this money?
> PATTY: Well, what do you think about me spending the night with Patrick? That's not ...
> DIABLO: You're laughing at me - that's what. I'm sitting here watching you laugh at me, but you don't have a single idea of your own. All you do is laugh at people.
> PATTY: Jesus what's with you today?
> DIABLO: I swear to God I'll throw you into the trunk. I'm *not* looking back - to Nevada or anywhere else.
> PATTY: Thanks but I prefer to die like a dog on the side of road.
> DIABLO: Where'd you get that money? You suck dick for it?

PATTY: Okay you're right. Two thousand dollars worth of blowjobs in less than two days. I'm that good.

DIABLO [swerving the car to the side of the road.]: Get out of here *now.*

PATTY: You should see how much I earn when I let 'em stick me in the ass in Michigan or, better yet, Minnesota.

DIABLO: Get *out.*

PATTY: I'm not moving. You're a sad-looking sack of shit yourself, screaming at me over a bunch of worthless cash. How'd you turn out so ugly anyway? C'mon let's get the car back on the road. Want me to drive for awhile?

DIABLO: Yes.

PATTY: Man, these roads are icing up.

{b} I estimate humanity at more than one man. I estimate the soul as the body of total information (and a pathetic audience for my personal perceptions). The soul provides the internal life of my characters. I apologize if I die before I become aware of those souls.

My esteemed colleagues from Harvard University must hate me for publicizing this stuff here on the continent, hate me for writing (and publishing) the words 'millennial capitalism.' I've seen other writers threatened with prison after scribbling phrases like 'self-hatred,' 'dysfunctional family,' 'racial inferiority' - all such scary things, after all - those words couldn't be true, no, of course not, they must be symptoms of … or the lasting effects of terminal unemployment on a disgruntled writer. Those aren't society's problems. Those are the writer's problems. He's spreading lies. He's spreading hate. Bad things originate from that man. The rest of us are fine. He's the one who deserves prison. We need to protect ourselves from writers like that (it's white men who are the main problem). Thank you, God, for allowing the rest of us to get on with our precious lives.

Entanglement. Bomb-induced subway derailment. Why object to a vibrant economy like what we got here on the continent when most of our citizens lie there in bed eating microwavable mini-tacos, reading glossy research reports - with bags under

their eyes and recyclable bags in the trunks of their Cadillac
SUVs.

ACT II

DIABLO: This counter's a mess.

PATTY: Anyway, over the next two months…

DIABLO [smiling]: You know we could claim Patrick died of
cancer from smoking.

PATTY: I see you understand life's a bit more complicated than a
whole lot of money - on a good day at least, not a shitty day like
this. You're such a smoothie with these continental folks, putting
your four-dollar tip on the counter *then* complaining the place is a
mess *then* imagining other ways the pathetic bastard might've
died. Not old age - yeah. How's about cancer? Those are the
limits of life - disease and four dollars on a truck-stop counter.
Shit, where's my anti-itch ointment?

[PATTY roots around in her handbag.]

DIABLO: You should pay more attention to everyone out there
[gesturing through the diner's window at the many vehicles
moving in and out of parking spaces and pulling up to gas
pumps]. Those are the limits of life in general, right there, not
disease, no, but unreliable transportation.

PATTY: Hell's happening to you?

DIABLO: Well, at least we got *some* money. Most of them out
there don't have much beyond their credit cards. I enjoy
imagining they're all blind, flitting around like bats in a cave.

PATTY [preoccupied with putting ointment on her hands]: Uh-
huh. Never seen so many truck drivers standing around with their
hands outside their pockets.

DIABLO: That's right. One group of 'em has to pay off the other
half to keep the cycle moving - clockwise, last time I checked,
general direction of water in a flushed toilet.

PATTY [looking up]: Hold on - we're doing our own sorta giving-
slash-taking here. We gotta get some gas for the car and food for
our bellies. Where's that put us?

DIABLO [idly watching a TV behind the diner's counter]: Me and
Patrick agreed to this arrangement before we left Las Vegas.

We're square. Before that, Patrick paid off Captain Beginsu to ferry us over to the continent. Then *you* nailed his ass to a restroom wall with a damn pistol. Then *we* ran off with his shit. That's why we're square, whether or not we find Patrick again.

PATTY: Aaaaaah but that's *my* shit to worry about. Let's see how you enjoy the stochastic nature of travel.

DIABLO: I won't sit here debating the merits of chance, won't discuss money problems anymore either. I'm with you on both issues. That's why I said we're square.

PATTY: What *are* your problems then?

DIABLO [sarcastically]: Sir?

PATTY: Go to hell.

DIABLO [pushing away his finished plate of blueberry pancakes]: That hit the spot. Now let's go someplace where I can see a can of beer in my hands.

PATTY: I said go to hell.

DIABLO: Girl, I'm not crazy. I'm a genius. I know it takes at least *two* to play the game of chance.

PATTY: That's an idea, a grand idea. I think I'm vomiting.

DIABLO [standing up from the stool]: Not sure I agree with you one-hundred percent but I appreciate your approval.

PATTY: What?

DIABLO: Keep an eye out for state troopers [gesturing towards the parking lot]. Time for a fast performance in the men's room.

PATTY: What are you talking about? You were just in there.

DIABLO [walking away]: Man, that counter's a godawful mess!

PATTY [turning on the stool to face the AUDIENCE]: Please tell me what he's talking about. Yeah, uh, I imagined marrying Patrick in Las Vegas. Then this power-trip business. We, you know, paid off the [INTERFERENCE] and changed our names. That was a good idea. Why you need so much money anyway? I was gonna be his wife, you know, a woman who … anyway. Hell!

{c} Pardon me if injustice holds this story back, if wars and hunger interfere with my editor's impatience. So tell me, how in the world can love hate the *ghost* of love? Shit, that sentence has nothing to do with words. Writers should express themselves as cleverly as possible. We should write words that have mandatory meanings. Let me explain why I shouldn't be arrested, imprisoned, what have you, for writing the phrase 'millennial-postmodern capitalism.'

Cool. I'm not the only one who's embarrassed. We've heard the rumors, the speculation. Contrary to initial assumptions, Mr. Celebrity's trying to earn a living. Aren't you? Sorry if you gotta keep looking over your shoulder. Anyway, an accident in the middle of the night after leaving your house early in the morning is, well, you know, it puts your image at a disadvantage.

DIABLO: I'm not obsessing - I'm curious. Where'd you get that cash?

PATTY: From a bank.

DIABLO: What's it doing stashed under the car seat? That couldn't be just any bank. I know how financial arrangements work around here.

PATTY: Let's say I removed it from under Patrick's Italian silk sofa.

DIABLO: That wouldn't be the first time.

PATTY: And now let's pretend Patrick met me once before, on the island, before the two of you traveled to the continent. Something he told me about you I'll never forget.

DIABLO: Let's hear it.

PATTY [pretending to try to recall]: Oops, can't remember.

DIABLO: Honey, you're weird.

PATTY: My pleasure. *Whoa.* Now I remember. Last year, Christmastime, we were living on the island. Up to that point we had a healthy relationship, everything we wanted a relationship to be - exciting, both of us losing weight. We wanted to look good naked.

DIABLO: Well you're not ugly now.

PATTY: We wanted to be normal, a completely normal-looking, normal-acting couple. No sexual harassment. Nothing but normality plus lots of money.

DIABLO: And?

PATTY [after a long pause]: These snow banks out here, icy roads, snow plows help me imagine Minnesota as it might've been that Christmas on the island - one of the few times I felt like my entire life was behind me. The snow helps me imagine that feeling, the feeling that my heart's gonna cave in on itself.

DIABLO: That's everything you *pretend* to have done on the island. Fine. I don't care anymore where the money came from.

PATTY: There's a lot about me you'll never know.

DIABLO: In that case you're my personal hero. How does that suit you? Now lay off the reminiscences.

PATTY: Guess there isn't much joy in your life.

DIABLO: There's a lot about *me* you don't know either, beautiful things.

PATTY: Well I got a minute.

DIABLO: Go to hell.

PATTY: Are you afraid of me? You wanna kill me? Well, do you? Oh that's right. I forgot. You're the Devil. Your divine parents XXX & YYY are busy finding you a better career.

DIABLO: How's your life happier than mine? Seems to me all you got is driving around on the continent in the middle of a snowstorm in a shitty Pontiac Firebird that barely runs. Imagine someone's filing away this dialogue in a universal filing cabinet. Imagine they're looking at what we're doing right now. Imagine they're adapting our words to a theatrical piece or a screenplay. Wouldn't that make for a damn depressing movie?

PATTY: Depends on whether we got a psycho stashed in the trunk.

DIABLO: You listening to me?

PATTY: I gotta go to the bathroom. I'm pulling over at the next exit.

DIABLO: Great acting!

{d} Sometimes, in prison, it's hard to think. Suffering bodies sing strange songs in prison. Our bodies learn to expect anything.

I'm disappointed that battles over souls create our bodies in the first place. Got mirror images? Yeah they're misleading too. Ever try hanging a difference between the real and ideal? I should learn how to refrain from deception in the prison yard - I think it's the tireless energy of the sun.

Other onlookers have reported otherwise. For his entire career, Mr. Celebrity's made an exception to therapeutic anarchy. He's mocked the fashionable avant-garde artists. He's outcompeted risks, experimented with suspicions. He's based his performance on safety, not discomfort. He's made our production company a safe reliable bet based on a set of speakers from … uh, billionaires approaching him.

Consumers want to see Mr. Celebrity behave like a real celebrity at a real party. Here he comes now, approaching us, threatening us with the height of advertiser-friendly friendliness.

ACT III

DIABLO [talking to his reflection in the restroom mirror]: Change our names? Hell's she talking about? What *are* you, Patty, Patrick's alleged wife or *a* woman? Changed your name for that man? Shit, look at me - I'm here in hell. Where are you? *Who* are you?

PATRON [standing at the adjacent sink, head turned to DIABLO]: Awww God, where's my daughter?

DIABLO [ignoring PATRON, looking into the eyes of his own reflection]: Who *are* you?

PATRON: You seen my daughter?

DIABLO [turning to PATRON]: Who are *you*? You got a strong Michigan accent. Or is that Minnesota?

PATRON: This ain't a stupid joke - where's my daughter? Someone took off with her!

DIABLO: You stupid bastard. Why don't you let your daughter go? Just leave, get back on the highway. You gotta let the girl grow up. She's an adult now. She can take care of herself in a kidnapping situation.

PATRON: What?

DIABLO: Happy now, asshole? You never could raise a child properly. Now a maniac's run off with her. You weren't cut out to be a caring parent.

PATRON: What? Dad? That you, Dad?

DIABLO: Hah, your father's not here either. We left him several miles back at McDonald's.

PATRON: Which direction?

DIABLO: What's the problem? Today's circumstances are okay. Father's safe at McDonald's drinking one of his favorite bland milkshakes. I assure you he's okay. He does have AIDS however - though he's not senile. It's *not* the end. It's OK.

PATRON: You beat my girl, didn't you?

DIABLO: Can you be more specific?

PATRON: In what way?

DIABLO: Man, you're talking about possibilities. You're chastising me with possibilities. You're saying I beat your daughter or abducted her or something. Well, what's the biggest problem you can imagine? What's the difference between that problem and …

PATRON: I know you drugged, raped, beat my little girl. I know what you did!

DIABLO: Hey let's watch the language. No one here said anything about rape.

PATRON: Then what are we talking about?

DIABLO: You're pretty funny-looking standing there with your pants at your ankles and your dick sticking straight out like that. Gonna be the highlight of your day?

[DIABLO gestures at the PATRON's enormous erection.]

PATRON: Never underestimate the power of denial. I got no interest in anyone but myself.

DIABLO: That explains why your daughter ran away from home. Your fantasies …

PATRON: My coma's lasted more than twenty years. I'll probably retire in this here men's room shaking hands with Mr. Happy.

DIABLO: Gross! You'll excuse me. I gotta get back on the road.

[DIABLO leaves the men's room, returns to the counter where PATTY waits for him.]

{e} I know the blind are offended they don't see *too* much. I know bittersweet tears provide the salt of realism (demands of running water are endless). Well, may we please prove the nature of scientific theory wrong. In prison I'm hungry for any reason, yet I admit I'm rarely fooled by the eyes of imagination - I find evidence of truth in happiness *or* in dreams. I have a musical sense of solitude in prison. The same body convinces me I must be different from you. I study legs, long skinny legs, stocky legs, scarred and tattooed legs. I like to see different prisoners from different walks of life. Criminal dancers talk only to the guards with ample crotches.

Now we wait. On Sunday Mr. Celebrity meets with the local police to deal with, uh, you know, deal with how to move on from the despicable conclusion that he's not so perfect after all. Man, he's a human being - that's what his website says - so he acts a bit strange sometimes. (We remember he once passed out on the streets of a so-called urban ghetto.) Doing strange things is allowed *once* in your life. Anyway, if true, if he did behave strangely, how can we be sure that was *him* acting strange?

> PATTY [pulling into a rest area crowded with campers and RVs]: Here we go. You wait here. I'll be back in a sec.
> DIABLO: Seems like this bathroom behavior's making you feel proud.
> PATTY: Wait here.
> [PATTY walks into the women's room, enters the first stall, sits down on the toilet.]
> [Loud commotion in the adjacent stall.]
> VOICE: Today I left my job, told my boss to go to hell. That's something I'm proud of.
> PATTY: Then it's too late for me to offer you advice. I sold my soul before I set foot in here. I work for the Devil.
> VOICE: Your accent … You an islander?
> PATTY: So where'd you work before you ended up here?
> VOICE: I *want* to be unemployed.
> PATTY: *Where* did you work?

VOICE: I had a fast food experience.

PATTY: Oh I had one of those more than twenty years ago.

VOICE: I didn't fit in well.

[Loud commotion in the adjacent stall.]

PATTY: What the hell are you doing over there? What's that smell?

VOICE: Smoking pot. It warms me up on these winter days.

PATTY: You sure make a lot of noise when you smoke.

VOICE. I heard your whole life flashes before your eyes the moment you die.

PATTY: Yeah we've all heard that one before. Doesn't mean it's true. Anyway, birth, life, death - those are *not* accidents.

VOICE: I feel naked.

PATTY: Are you?

VOICE: I feel I need structure, discipline. I'm a total slut. Tell me, how could I *be* more pathetic? I wanna get nailed by the king.

PATTY: King of what?

[A fit of loud, phlegmy coughing echoes through the women's room.]

PATTY: What're you doing? What's going on with you over there?

VOICE: Nothing. Nothing at all. I'm choking on smoke and remembering what it's like flipping burgers all day.

PATTY: *Gross!* I gotta get back on the road.

VOICE: Good for you.

PATTY: No - okay for me. You need to feel better about yourself, less angry, less insecure.

VOICE: I'm already dead. That odor of burnt gunpowder proves it.

[PATTY wipes, flushes the toilet, leaves the stall, washes her hands, returns to the car.]

{f} In prison, space is no longer a problem for me. I suspend myself from the ceiling to adjust my heartbeat. I never stop. The heart creates its own roads away from reality. I love those circumstances. My social research begins whenever I meet a fresh prisoner. Lately we've seen too much of each other. At the end of a communication session I wanna slap that prisoner's hands. I sense my emotional stability has a subtle effect on his taste-buds

All refused to listen. I didn't tell anyone anything *ever*. I listened to advice from my lawyer-slash-agent. I tried to replace the direct consequences of my personal conduct with millions of dollars worth of sporting equipment, cars, clothes, and personal hygiene products. What do you recommend as an appropriate first reaction to bad news? I'm not hiding anything from you. I'm not a family man. I'm not hardworking or honest. I flirt with other women. I don't eat Wheaties cereal - it tastes unpleasant to me.

All refused to listen (unsurprising). Only two witnesses were there (also unsurprising) - the police and the media. When the rescue crews arrived with their unpleasant noisy machinery, we had a third witness. Everyone else was sucked into an information vacuum.

ACT IV
PATTY: Damn how long were you in there?
DIABLO: Don't know, a few months. Restroom's a mess too. Not sure who's in charge here. Janitor's an ungrateful son of a bitch though.
PATTY: Hell's your problem today?
DIABLO: Who's talking about anything? I was in the restroom long enough to come to my senses. I was *doing* shit in there. C'mon let's go.
PATTY: Vomiting your guts out?
DIABLO: Man, you're a sick twisted [INTERFERENCE].
PATTY: I'm an ordinary woman who's got nothing to lose. C'mon let's get outta here.
[DIABLO and PATTY leave the diner, get into the car, return to the highway.]
PATTY: Ever been to Duluth?
DIABLO: Oh my God.

PATTY: Well sorry.

DIABLO: Shut up about Duluth or I'll throw you into the trunk with the, uh …

PATTY: I see I've touched on a source of conflict.

DIABLO: Don't mention that word.

PATTY: Duluth - Duluth - Duluth - Duluth - Duluth - *Duluth*.

DIABLO [sharply swerving the car to the side of the road, nearly going into the ditch]: I can shoot, shoot, shoot you, then your children, shit, shoot all the little people out here on this icy highway! You want that?

PATTY: Get back on the road!

DIABLO: *No*.

PATTY: I'm sorry I, dunno, I was … I thought it would be great …

DIABLO: What? Well … *Well?*

PATTY: Why are we sitting here letting the engine idle wasting precious fuel?

DIABLO: You're such a superwoman, aren't you? How can we be together on this journey if you're such a superwoman?

PATTY: I get it - you're telling me to keep my mouth shut about Duluth. There's no need to turn back my neck.

DIABLO: That's brilliant.

PATTY: Yeah it's awesome.

[DIABLO maneuvers the car back onto the highway]

PATTY: I guess you decided not to park there after all.

{g} In prison, the material universe is no longer a restriction on my imagination. That means I can start letting this narrative live and breathe. The sun occupies space. No. The weather's ruthless. Yes - walls faced with madness often reflect the moon. Where should I hide my face when I wanna see more? I say let sunlight penetrate the integrity of our housing standards. Let respect for visitors not enslave the homeowner. Forget your complaints the moment you see me released from prison.

Though I won't suffer in the long term, it's too late for me to recover from the fallen forest and contribute a news story here. Instead, I flash my smile at the nation. What do I get in return? A large stock of superficial goodwill, a stale DNA sample, a late-

night joke or two, a television ad. I cannot publicize anything
without putting holes in my mind. Instead, I put this arm
[gesturing at my other arm] around my wife's waist. We return
home along an especially dangerous path. When we get there,
first thing I do is remove the tapes from the tape recorder.

> DIABLO: What a fanatic - the way you looked walking
> back to the car, like a damn Bible salesman.
> PATTY: I felt more like an insomniac.
> DIABLO: Tell me - did he have a big penis?
> PATTY: I'll speak to you later about *her* penis. Your turn
> to drive.
> [PATTY tosses DIABLO the car keys, walks over to the
> passenger side.]
> DIABLO: You're pretty uptight about sex.
> PATTY: I'm not your common whore.
> DIABLO: Why not? Around here you're a freak, a
> continental acting like she doesn't feel like she needs to
> feel better about herself.
> PATTY: I'm pretty cool for my twenty-two years. What's
> that [gesturing at a line of cars, pickups, SUVs,
> eighteen-wheelers parked alongside the shoulder of the
> icy highway]?
> DIABLO: Worthless gay parade.
> PATTY: How cute.
> DIABLO: Don't lie to me.
> PATTY: What do you see out there?
> DIABLO: I barely *can* see. Man, this snow's picking up.
> We should pull over too.
> PATTY [giggling]: I think you're the sexually frustrated
> one. You're afraid of the weather. You're afraid of
> Duluth. What a pussy.
> DIABLO: What I see out there's mostly white - like God
> glaring straight through this windshield.
> PATTY: Oh God, the whites of God's eyeballs. You *are*
> sexually frustrated.
> DIABLO: You better watch yourself. You're turning into
> a real bitch.

PATTY: Oh yeah? Jesus, calm down. This is continental life. That means more repetitive stuff will keep happening. That's the business of living around here - 'business as usual' they call it. More entertaining than domestic violence. I think you're kinda cute, Your Excellency.

DIABLO: That's the feeling I need right now - royalty, royalty in exile.

PATTY: I also think you need to jump my bones.

DIABLO: Shut up. You're making me uncomfortable. I can't concentrate on the road.

PATTY: Tonight at a luxurious Duluth motel you *and* Patrick will screw me till my eyes roll back in my head.

DIABLO: Shut up.

PATTY: I must be psychotic.

{h} In prison, insomnia bothers me. My latest variation on sleepwalking's an unimprovised dancing movement. I used to like sleeping on mountains of stones, in prickly bushes. So how can you expect me to drink this prison water without longing for bluish skies? Inside here, the mere *idea* of cold torments my body. I cannot stop touching this warm running water.

Got holiday plans? Some extra pounds on your package? Promises of employment plus baby fat plus candies ('sweetmeats' the prison guards call them). That's no scam. Long live our most absurd legal standards. For some young women, prisoners' faces become beautiful addresses. For others (the kind you find on film) - thank goodness they aren't stuck selling cosmetics and depriving their bodies of body fat. I giggle as the prison guard tries to escape from those Mary Kate-and-Ashley Olsen-brand panties. I'm not much when it comes to satisfying perverts - I never learned those moves - I lacked the passion for that kind of work. But I do know the street-corner gang named after the Devil kills *XXX* in the coldest of cold blood. [What's 'a competitive position' anyway - what's illegal about it?] I? with a child? Outside? I used this telephoto lens to shoot photos people can see with their naked eyes in a museum - I'm trying to discern the illegality of most of the things depicted in those photos. When did bold artistic expression become such a crime?

So despised, misunderstood … the prevention of dark and bizarre humor's now accepted as an American classic. Weird poster-sized public monuments to Michael Jackson and Rudolph Valentino - at least two dead children, including one who killed his own father - [Try looking out through the plane-stuff too.]

The title LANGUAGE HAS A FINE CAPACITY TO GO TO EXTREMES has a certain subtlety about it

1. Chickens or kindness
The Great Ones of the Past tell us to be patient for the quickening spirit of God. His divine contrivance soon will be accomplished. Only then will I be able to show you I got a good idea of what fleeing to New York City's all about. I predict it'll take us four days to undo everything here in Duluth - to see things in a way we've never seen them before (much as we failed to do in Nevada). That's when we'll regain the last metropolis of the continent - and consider our initial deeds of invasive violence sufficiently expiated.

The continent's a large spacious piece of land, well watered, richly endowed with hills, valleys, deserts. Nonetheless, only five gates afford direct access to that vast expanse, the five gates of our senses (ear, eye, mouth, etc.). Now, compare that geological condition with the design of our own island. See what I mean? We got a single very narrow gate each of us barely fits through. Not only that, we islanders kinda act the same. I mean, continental folks are not all of one complexion, nor of one language or religion. Over here, a burglar would never dream of finding valuable cash or silver beneath his own bed. Our island's a funnyish kind of place, not like what you'd think it was based on the photographs and videogames.

By now I hope the reader appreciates my lot, as an exiled islander, to wander throughout the continent. Fact is, I'm not much delighted to see and hear many things out here I never did much care for in the first place. I feel as sweet and useless as the winter wind. Main problem's that here on the continent society's delineated on the disordered state of … I see a black gulf stretching out before me - gulf of mistrust, dislike, revolt, desperate pride of oil slicks.

Ah old friend, quoth Cerberus, art thou come to Hellgate-hill again?

Once upon a time, a mighty giant islander named Diablo (or Diabolus, according to a previous generation of writers) decided to make an assault on the continent. He did so by swimming across the stretch of water that separates our island from the continent. Some geographers call that stretch of water a channel, others an ocean. In reality it's something in between those two extremes.

2. Making bricks out of straw

It's a queer thing claiming a man and a girl can't be good pals like two grown men, isn't it? The same could be asked of a writer and reader. So queer how most of our national writers talk sensibly while they write such rubbish. Yet they keep saying, "I'll do it somehow. I'll do it somehow. Do it somehow *better*."

"What's this?"

"Oh it's all right - I'll pay for that mistake too."

As a writing instructor I often administer what I call a "P.G. Wodehouse rescue package" to the manuscripts of first-time writers and students of literature. Otherwise the prose of those manuscripts would be far too smooth and absolute understanding far too impossible for the characters therein. Often in those double-spaced stories, mention is made of a 'growing sense of dread' or of death-defying stunts by students fresh out of college (like surviving a sniper attack from the roof of a Hollywood dormitory).

Main problem's that doubt and distrust are the offspring of 'slight investigation' - that explains the suspicious behavior of many of our national writers. They're trying to fit a whole set of encyclopedias into 800 pages without recourse to poetic compression. Reading their work's giving me the bends.

For example, on our car radio, here's a Christian radio station. Let's listen a moment. "You in the army of the Lord, *boy*. … Here in Heaven I'm your 'boss situation,' *boy* - I say flagellate yourself!" Now, if you could, glance up from the dashboard. [Pointing.] There's a transparent woman flying *inside* a pane of windshield glass (an image not altogether different from the special effect we remember in the first *Superman* movie). Perhaps that woman believes in the Lord. Perhaps the sound of my voice startles her. Boy, look at those transparent intestines. What could they *mean*?

In the distance, the church clock chimes nine o'clock. Dammit, you interrupted me. That's dreadful. I shudder, recoil from the sound as from a specter. My patience has its limits.

Here at Manskull Publishing Inc. I work in the Explanatory, Experimental, & Practical Department. My boss, Mr. Arthur Drinkwater, is what they used to call 'a man of letters.'

3. Down our Haight Street

I won't die in debt. I owe nobody anything. I paid for this overcoat. Pedestrians turn to look as I walk down Haight Street. I want them to believe I'm doing well. Indeed I know, on the continent, it's essential to buck up, behave as if everything's all right, as if to say, "Let anything come - I'm able to fight it off." On the island we can't trust our own parents, much less, you know, the… uh, …

By St. Mary, I'm glad to see you, old friend. Please let me take a seat. Thanks a lot for the energy drink too. [The two of us, Mr. Mind & myself, are sitting at a table in a Haight Street coffee shop.] The rest of the patrons are dressed for a bleak-tie dinner, well, uh … except for that guy over there in the corner [gesturing], the proverbial patient etherized upon a table. Mr. Mind looks quite French today, don't he?

You say Sophia's gone to bed?

[The sound of my voice startles Mr. Mind, whose ruddy face flushes purple at mention of Sophia.]

Excuse me?

[Lowering my voice] I wanna get this matter settled regarding Sophia.

Don't let's argue about it *here*.

Well don't keep me in suspense then.

That's enough - keep your voice down.

Well, I…

[Whispering in my ear] I know the enormity of your crime.

You want me to confess a crime?

[Harshly whispering] Not *here* in public, you idiot!

I begin to grow uneasy, impatient. I'm wondering why the effects of my misdeeds should be inexhaustible. Why can I not repair my error and be comforted? We all have a secret weakness, something queer or unmanageable in our characters that drives us into conflict with ourselves and society and provides the drama necessary to make daily life bearable, indeed, even meaningful. The saddest part of my own weakness is I fail to grasp the possibility of overcoming it if only my hands didn't tremble so much.

I hurry from the coffee shop, turning my steps homewards.

The door of the bedroom isn't closed. I push it open. Sophia lies in bed looking pale, tired, very young, defenseless. I tiptoe over to the bed, sit down beside her. I sense it would be criminal on my part to neglect such an opportunity.

Seems a pity to awaken you, Sophia, but don't you believe in friendship between a grown man and a little girl?

[Rubbing her eyes] What?

You're not offended, are you?

By what?

Were you having a nice sleep? [I rub my hands as if it were a very cold morning here in San Francisco.] I was saying it's a queer thing saying a man and a girl can't be good pals like two grown men.

No - er - I wouldn't, … uh, I never thought about it.

Not much fun traveling about on the continent alone.

Won't your brothers and sisters go with you?

They prefer something more exciting than traveling with their older brother out into the country. Anyway, your mom and dad ought to take better care of you. They should.

Oh, that's the way …

That's how parents treat their children on the continent - without kind regards?

Well, I…

You look ill. Have you been running up and down the stairs tonight?

What do you mean? Our house doesn't have stairs.

How would like me to map out a little course of reading for you?

Thanks but I think Mom can get most things I'm supposed to read at the library.

But I don't want you to be under that sort of obligation. [I take her arm, lead her to a chair.] Don't you want a bit of literary *fun* sometimes? [I hand her a book.]

[Turning to the AUDIENCE] I fear I can say nothing else suitable to this occasion. I'm doing most of the talking in our relationship anyway. Sophia's tired face droops sideways over the book. I'm trying to get the girl to read *A True Relation of The Holy War, Made by King Shaddai upon Diabolus, for the Regaining of the Metropolis of the World* by Minister Bunyan. Remember that book?

My reflections continue to revolve around a single point. I ruminate on last night's incident. How likely will Sophia repeat her midnight visit to the elm tree? If she does, should I resolve to undertake a new pursuit if it might signal disaster? Continental girls are queer. Sophia's no exception. Would her reappearance prove my actions are not *so* dangerous? How might I induce her to betake herself of a subterranean retreat?

[b]

La nature a fait son temps

{a} Diablo's existed for so long his copyright's expired (like Shakespeare and Melville).
   A little cage of silver wire hung from the bedroom's ceiling. For centuries Diablo had reclined in a single colorless-odorless-silent niche - slumbering in passive resistance - until a <u>sudden commotion</u> roused his soul. That moment he experienced a **mad craving** to enjoy sensual reality - to procure himself the sensations of a long journey - to enjoy the temporary arrangements of moving from place to place without fatigue or worry. Thus he yielded to an impulse to <u>seek further light</u>. *By candlelight, sky-blue takes on a greenish tone, while dark blue or indigo becomes black.* (The flickering candlelight causes the colors to alternate, much as the brain of a lizard causes its skin colors to crawl.) Now, many centuries later, having <u>drained the cup of sensual reality</u>, Diablo feels a **sick aversion** for sensations and perceptions. He's **fatigued**. He longs to return to that niche - so he <u>does</u> because he <u>can</u>.
XXX: Please, Diablo, reason with me.
DIABLO: You serious? You believe a machine thinks?
XXX: Well what's a machine?
DIABLO: An instrument for translating energy into action.
XXX: Would you agree an instrument must have a brain?
DIABLO: Beg your pardon? I said nothing about a brain.
XXX: A machine doesn't need a brain, right?
DIABLO: Well what *is* a brain?
XXX: A brain is an instrument for translating the energy of thought into action.
DIABLO: So a brain *is* a machine? Can such things be?
XXX: Indeed, it's one type of machine - a machine consisting of living cells. Other types of machines - telephones, computers,

automobiles - consist of dead matter. Nonetheless, they're all machines by *my* definition.

DIABLO: Very well, we're in agreement on that point. Some machines think, others don't.

XXX: Let's get on with the business of talking. So ... you recall Herbert Spencer's definition of 'life'?

[DIABLO is silent for a long time. He shrinks back from the doorway, standing a little to one side in shadow.]

XXX: God almighty - the only way to do this thing is to take the bull by the horns. Please come inside. Take a seat at the table. You recognize me?

DIABLO: How *can* I?

[Even in the candlelight, DIABLO cannot see the face of XXX.]

XXX: You've been here before, you know.

DIABLO: What?

XXX: In this candlelit room. You're compelled to return here periodically. That's why you cannot lock yourself in that niche and act like a prisoner forever. If you did, you'd never hear the end of it from *my* superior. Imagine that. Fact is, you cannot prefer to be left alone forever.

DIABLO: Yeah I know 'forever' is the operable word here. Fine. So let's get on with it.

XXX: Want something to drink? I have beer out in the car - tons of it.

DIABLO: I don't like drinking while preparing to travel to the continent.

XXX: Aren't you scheduled to make your first appearance in Nevada?

DIABLO: What do you mean 'first appearance'?

XXX: I mean your first destination is *not* the type of thing you'd talk about upstairs anyway.

DIABLO: I had no idea it's so bad up there.

XXX: Lately, yeah. Crazy shit's happening everyday - sometimes whole families - they're fighting like hell, frothing at the mouth, lunging at their wives, snarling. At this point, it's better to rip out society's back-straps, if you know what I mean. So tell me about your plans in Nevada.

DIABLO: Well it's not a tourist joint.

XXX: Good - since that's *not* why we're sending you up there.

DIABLO: I'm not planning on staying in Nevada the whole time. I wanna go further east, much further, but not too far. I wanna get near the exact middle of the continent - places like Minnesota or Michigan, maybe North Dakota.

XXX: We'll have to see about that… So what's in Nevada besides the gambling?

DIABLO: First vision I had was of a coin toss on the counter of a diner.

XXX: Any idea what the diner's called?

DIABLO: Not yet, no, … but if you gimme time to ponder, I could find out.

XXX: Ah it's unimportant right now. Go on.

DIABLO: I do know the diner's painted light green and orange, and inside they're remodeling it, painting the walls, putting in new booths - like that.

XXX: Gee that's nice.

DIABLO: It's a little town in the desert. I'm sitting at the diner's counter drinking coffee, smoking cigarettes, flipping a coin, jotting down the results - heads or tails - on a crumpled napkin - when a man named Patrick sits down on the stool beside me.

XXX: He's traveling through?

DIABLO: I guess. … Hey I got it - let's say he's on his way east, to Michigan or Minnesota, hoping to find a girlfriend … or a wife, an older woman. Their relationship's still hazy to me.

XXX: That's okay. So this man's never been to that diner before, right?

DIABLO: I doubt it.

XXX: Is there a witness around?

DIABLO: Yeah a waiter and a waitress.

XXX: No, I said *witness*. Forget it - doesn't matter. So who's serving you that shift?

DIABLO: The waitress. Anyway, like I said, the traveler introduces himself as Patrick.

XXX: As in 'father'?

DIABLO: What?

XXX: Go on.

DIABLO: He orders a glass of freshly squeezed orange juice, tells me he's driving a white Pontiac Firebird east from his parents' house in San Francisco. He's in search of the American dream.

XXX: Jesus Christ - get over it. The copyright's expired on that one too.

DIABLO: Sounds like a silly story, I know, but that's what…

XXX: Problem is we can't make any money on it… Okay, so does this Patrick own the Firebird or is it a rental?

DIABLO: Don't know. Never occurred to me to ask. …Ah, now I remember - the name of the diner is Melville's, yeah, Melville's Diner.

XXX: I've heard enough. So what's your second vision?

DIABLO: The second vision I'm still working on. Like I said, it's somewhere in the middle of the continent. But the *third* vision - that's the streets and subways of New York City. I'm accompanying a young husky-voiced woman. Thanksgiving, Christmas holidays.

XXX: At least it's not a casino or a tourist joint. So what kind of place is it?

DIABLO: We're sitting at a table in a diner, nighttime place, where… [trying hard to remember the details].

XXX: Why the obsession with diners? You moonstruck?

DIABLO: Yeah I know there's a lot of that. Not sure why. Anyway, when the waitress brings our coffee, she sets a vase of small flowers on the table. I take one of the flowers, hand it to the young woman whose name I keep forgetting.

XXX: Maybe the flower speaks to you?

DIABLO: You serious? You believe plants are conscious up there? What's wrong with you?

XXX: Please, Diablo, reason with me on this.

DIABLO [smirking]: Shit, I'd prefer not to.

XXX: Tell me - what *is* consciousness?

DIABLO [without hesitation]: A sense of awareness of one's self and one's surroundings.

XXX: Would you agree awareness implies a mental faculty?

DIABLO: Beg your pardon? I said nothing about a mental faculty.

XXX: Consciousness implies a mental faculty, right?

DIABLO: What *is* a mental faculty?

XXX: Ah forget it. It's time you get on with the business of living on the continent. That's why we're sending you up there - not for idle philosophical chatter.

DIABLO: Hey man, you brought it up.

XXX: Yeah, yeah…

DIABLO: By the way, I remember now that the young woman's name in Alphabet City is Mimi.

XXX: Back in the diner, what's the waitress's nametag read?

DIABLO: Let's see [squinting his eyes] … *Ginger Nut is serving you.*

XXX: What do you think of Ginger Nut?

DIABLO [grinning]: I think she's a bit loony.

XXX: Moonstruck, you mean. Does she live on ginger-nuts?

DIABLO: Don't know. She means no mischief. She's oblivious to everything but her own peculiar style of waitressing.

XXX [laughing]: Go on.

DIABLO: With what? You're getting me sidetracked here. My focus is on Mimi, not this stupid waitress.

XXX: Tell me a little more about the waitress, where she was born, for example.

DIABLO: I'd prefer not to.

{b} For each idea XXX offers Diablo, XXX puts a folded sheet of paper into a box that sits at the center of the candlelit table. Later, the two of them reassemble those sheets of paper into a compelling narrative.

SOMETHING SINISTER ABOUT THEM ALL. (A sinister feeling is one of **foreboding**.) Nothing's sinister about that cop's socks [gesturing to a cop walking down the sidewalk outside the diner's window]. There IS something sinister about a specific member of the executive branch of the continental government - something sinister about that strange elderly man over there patting his right trouser pocket inside the old-fashioned telephone booth with the folding glass-paneled doors - something sinister about city workers taking a break from putting up holiday decorations to enjoy hamburgers and orange juice at the diner across the street. It's WHAT APPEARS TO BE A SINISTER FEELING of unrest throughout the world. If it's a madhouse, at least it's fun.

Down the hatch Diablo went.

RIGHT BEFORE THE BEATLES a big bright red Xmas wreath hangs over the diner's cash register. Simple as that. No question about it. A big bright red Xmas wreath and magnificent appliances anyone might wanna use. Never a letup. Second week of December. No question about it. Simple as that. Big bright red Xmas wreath wrapped in red tissue paper with Santa Claus stickers. For a long moment I stare at it.

MARXIST UTOPIANS, BABY! Worldwide movements spring from worldwide conditions & causes. (Those are the pathways of human existence.) A cry of horror runs through our church. (That's the Holy Spark.)

Let's consider a story about an undercover cop, a bail bondsman, a Hollywood movie producer and what they did to each other last summer in Alphabet City.

PATRICK: What's this?

MIMI: A napkin. What's it look like?

PATRICK: Don't gimme that crap - I know what it is - a newspaper.

MIMI [laughing]: Take a look at the front page.

[MIMI hands PATRICK the paper, returns to eating her lemon meringue pie.]

PATRICK: What's wrong with you?

MIMI: Nothing. Just read it.

PATRICK: It's in *today's* newspaper, on the front page?

MIMI: Yeah that's what I mean.

PATRICK: Damn, but look at the picture on the *back* page.

[PATRICK hands the newspaper back to MIMI.]

MIMI [laughing]: *Whoa*. Story says the cops have no real leads. They can't imagine who did this.

PATRICK: Well you have to speculate on what comes next … what their actual goals are…

MIMI: Wonder what they mean by 'six times seven.'

PATRICK: Here - gimme the paper back. [Scanning the back page] no idea. Probably code for something. Says here 'they got their hands on a few.'

[PATRICK hands the paper back to MIMI.]

MIMI: Holy shit.

PATRICK: What now?

MIMI: Cut their heads off. Every one of 'em. That's what I heard they did in California.

PATRICK: I had no idea it was so bad out there.

MIMI: Hell no. The press will never hear the end of this, I'm sure. They'll fight like dogs.

[MIMI puts the newspaper on the table, returns to eating her breakfast.]

{c} You think it's possible to experience 'body'?

I think it's possible if I don't know what the word *means*. I mean, there must be one - right? - must be a body. I don't exclude that possibility.

Well, is the physical humor you put in your novels deliberate? Of course not.

Is that man one of the writers who inspire you to write [gesturing to a famous American writer walking down the sidewalks of Manhattan's Upper West Side].

Who?

That man over there.

Him?

No, no. That guy *there* - the one dressed like a dandy who's staring at a butterfly through his monocle.

He's an American writer?

Yes he is. He wrote [INTERFERENCE] and won the [N/A] award for his third novel [INTERFERENCE]. Tell me, have his books had an impact on your own writing?

Good question but I won't answer it.

Why not?

I don't think that man's writing is so strong as you believe.

How so?

It lacks the proper psychological logic.

How so?

I hope you don't mind if I take a stand on the issue and leave it at that.

Fair enough. Is psychology a key component of your own work?

Why do you ask?

Because you mentioned it as a shortcoming of his work.

Well, that man's main problem is he rarely allows his narrators to express specific concrete ideas. But more generally, psychology is a key component of every writer's work whether they admit it or not.

How so?

Everything seems to be going too slow. Am I not answering your questions right?

You're doing fine.

I don't know if I answered your question right.

I'm hoping you could elaborate on the importance of psychology to the modern novel.

What *is* this?

It's an interview, nothing unusual going on here.

With each question I answer, I feel like I'm harming myself.

This isn't supposed to be a traumatic experience.

Is this what critics call postmodern literature?

What?

Our conversation, this interview.

As I see it, this isn't literature at all. Nothing's being written down.

You mean to say literature *requires* the written word?

I believe so.

Tell that to my editor friends at *The New Yorker*.

Who?

Good question but I won't answer it.

Hour of the white logic

The name assigned to this case history is Morris Rozlamovat: career delinquent, intellectual pessimist, attic philosopher, driver by profession, former malnourished Elvis impersonator (I'm *not* kidding or trying to be weird here). These days Morris works as a dishwasher and janitor in the only transvestite club in Duluth, Minnesota - the Scope Bar - where a thousand snow-covered roads of romance and adventure converge on three whole city blocks of … a long list of offenses, introjections, and other remarkable incidents. In short, the content of individual consciousness can provide no adequate explanation for what I'm about to relate here (even while the phenomena of mental life can*not* be regarded as the result of accident or chance).

There are established ways of bullying a thin man, ways that are integrated within our daily lives. My favorite approach involves applying high emotional pressure (across narrow volumes) to break down a man's resistance to righteousness and suffocate him in the embrace of altruism. The following episode offers a case study. Here the thin man in question, Morris Rozlamovat, seeks an ANALYST who's energized to perform the sex act with his wife.

Of course, if the reader never sets foot outside that transvestite bar, he might conclude - much like many an innocent infant theorist - that every human being, male or female, possesses a penis. However Morris did (and still does) set foot outside - he must do so if … uh, as that's when he encounters, uh … look - this isn't Maui or Oahu. These are the dark tiresome nights of winter in Duluth, Minnesota [gesturing to the snow-covered sidewalks outside the bar]. When you leave this bar, *if* you do, be careful not to fall into the gutters and scrapheaps out there. Now look over here [pointing]. That's the bartender-confessor Dreyfus who wears a hat upon his three pointy horns. He's a bright-eyed open-faced gentleman in very good physical condition without sensory defects. And over here [pointing] - that transvestite dancer's the only one dancing at this late hour. Her Moorish-style dance moves are lively, obscene, not at all strange. And over there, alone at the table in the corner [pointing] - who knows that man's true business? C'mon, don't be shy, let's go ask him what he's up to. I hear he's been impotent for more than a decade.

Turns out that man at the corner table is another unconscious-acting average white class Polish-Canadian who's prevented from caring for the garden of his own impulses. He sits there at the table, alone, pristine, smugly stacking his mind with open questions, problems rather than issues, problems at work, problems with shit. In some case studies (not unlike this one), a heroic effort is made to violate all forms of treatment. The Polish-Canadian thinks, "If I could wear the bartender's painted robe, if I managed to see a woman sodomized, if I weren't so solipsistic."

Baffled and confused by the Cloaca Theory? Of course you're not. Earlier tonight, in the bar's restroom, you watched two patrons place their buttocks together and trade shots of flatus. That means you wouldn't mind inhaling on this hookah, right? I thought so. What we have, eh … my friend, to tell you the truth, uh, you see … I never talk shop with strangers at a bar. I don't like gossiping the way women do at their little gatherings. They talk about other women who happen to be absent. I prefer discussing more wholesome agreeable topics. A bit later, still sitting at the bar, your broad back turned towards the Polish-Canadian who remains at the corner table, you notice a tune running through your head, an unfamiliar verse from the Old Testament set to music. You turn around on the stool (the other direction, please), glance through the front windows, notice, across the street, a motel, and *look* - there *I* am at the front desk, with my red hair and Irish brogue, requesting two adjacent rooms for the night.

The motel's musty odors are hampering my concentration here. I need to ease this intense desire to urinate. Noticing nothing unusual in the hallway, I back up against the door to my room, fumble open the lock, eye the cup, crook the strap, and track the surface. I wouldn't mind seeing a prostitute sodomized by an animal right about now - but that won't happen in this motel room, not tonight. I'll show the proper respect for my destructive frame of mind. Besides, this annoying transmitter I'm wearing has put me into a solipsistic frame of mind.

I know nights and days are a kind of love-minus-love in a motel room like this one. I'm compelled to begin masturbating with you in mind, to entertain all sorts of erotic fantasies about … uh, I imagine that by telepathic suggestion you're giving me an impulse to have sexual relations with you. At first I feel anger - then I surrender to your erotic probing. Moments later I hear a faint knock at the door. It's Morris. I let him into the room. He's overflowing with threats, accusations, resistance to desire. He's got a voice like an Italian banana man. Yet, for all that, he cannot take his eyes off my erection. His general demeanor reminds me of a depressed Jewish woman well past menopause. Now he's swinging his fists at me. I know he's got only himself to be jealous of. I know undue jealousy in a man means he thinks he's got some deficiency in sexual power. I know Morris condones indolence and wastefulness in a lover. I know when Pharisee meets Pharisee then comes death.

I sense the episode's reaching its climax. I know Morris's behavior goes by a very uncommon name. He's proven himself a unique individual, however, and that strikes me as his own personal deliverance.

A great gift for Christmas perfectionists

There's no light whatsoever in the motel room. I push along the wall to the bathroom door. It's a queer thought that I'm burglariously entering the bathroom of my own motel room - but it's also an erotic thought: a burglar arriving to rob and rape you. Now, as my fingers touch the door handle, I sense the night's work has begun. Is it possible that on the other side of this door there should be light and life? Perhaps old Morris sits on the toilet or preens before the mirror. I imagine his skinny face, his gray locks tucked beneath that knitted nightcap, his dark contorted eyebrows. I haven't come to hurt or rob you (I'd shout at Morris) - I've come to help you, so help me God. To protect you (Morris) from that good-for-nothing-brute (referring to the reader, of course). Morris, I won't leave you to your fate. I promise to protect you if you give me a chance to share in your inheritance.

Like so many other continental folks, Morris struggles with a drinking problem. He's dogged by dark twists of fate that add a Kafkaesque dimension to his life. It's all he's got of religion - a plea to prevent *me* from treating him and his life with excessive irony. Thank you, Morris, for your passion for fundamental truth, but I come here to the continent (and that includes Duluth) to treat everyone with irony. Count yourself lucky. I have your best interests at heart.

If *you* (the reader) were here this morning with (Morris? and) me, how would you explain the unusual dark red rings around the bathtub. I still cannot. Until last night I worshipped reason. I believed there was logic in things, in events, pure logic, a white logic. All was so clear to me that I lacked the will to die. But how to explain the red bathtub ring? That's why I've decided to shut myself in this motel room for the next fifteen days or so - to answer that question once and for all.

Phantoms compounded of meat and wine appear in my daydreams. Blue mice, pink elephants, black rascals crawl over my skin. Insects crack jokes in the funny papers. The general effect is of a great masked ball with transparent disguises.

Today I begin a diary of my sad and tragic life - an analytical deep-psychological diary stockpiled with minutiae. Like I said earlier, I'm no longer resolved to kill myself. Instead I'll become a writer *in private* - a diarist. I'll become the judge of my own numerical strength. I'll modify the pictures as I see fit. I'll anticipate the day of my death, again traversing the horrible paths of memory and sorrow - yet I'll expect everything to go off quite respectably this time around. Why not? Truth will at last shine forth triumphant. I'll prove Jack London wrong: life's so-called truths *are* indeed true. His problem was he was drunk all the time and suffered from an over-accentuation of the homosexual component of his libido (like most alcoholic writers). Poor ole chap. So many things tried his patience and squeezed the sap of good nature from his veins. I'm reminded of Raymond Carver.

In one notorious passage of the diary I dismiss women as barren amusements, while in another I describe the pursuit of the very bodies of witches. Over time the diary bears literary fruit. Rather, let us say the diary starts materializing 'via the rectum.' Each sheet of the diary is numbered. Each sheet begins with fierce words of jealousy and concludes with a parting injunction (business first, pleasure afterwards, as we islanders never like to say).

Mmmmm … on the other side of the wall, a love scene … a girl giggling with a queer-sounding man. Mmmmm … those sounds mean nothing.

Then one morning, in the mirror, I notice I've become lean, lank, cadaverous. There I stand, readers - the misanthrope, the latest understudy of Duluth's most notorious funeral director. I know *he who runs must read*. I know the best solution to loneliness is belonging to a series of corrupt churches.

Mmmmm … that means nothing.

One day I take a break from writing the diary to read the newspaper. But when I turn the newspaper over on its side - what new and bitter disappointment: Duluth's most respected animal rights activist is an amateur taxidermist in his spare time. Once again, proof there's nothing new under the sun. Once again, my expectations have tricked, outwitted themselves. Once again, I lose power over speech and motion. I fall into imaginary fits of epilepsy. Ever hear of a patient who couldn't get proper medical attention? Let me see, the average fee for bringing medics to this part of town is … Great Scott, how hardhearted is the medic who expects his fee so promptly.

It's blackmail.

No.

It's the infamous imposture of robbery.

No.

Take all the money you want, murder me, you hulking beast of a homosexual!

No - I don't want your dirty money [waving a flimsy 20-dollar bill in my direction]. I won't kill you either.

[To my astonishment, you leap onto the pile of cash that covers the bed and begin tearing bills in half.]

The dark red rings around the bathtub seem … lawless, inexplicable, solipsistic (explain that one). This brings me to the final point I need to make here. Tonight's prostitute is much like the statue of Venus de Milo in that she's lacking arms. That's the problem with continental prostitutes (in Duluth anyway). They so easily scatter to the four points of the compass when a cop car rounds the corner.

[c]

COIN TOSS

OPENING ACT

PATRICK: Mind if I use the restroom first?

DIABLO: There's no light in there.

PATRICK: Why no lights?

DIABLO: Don't know. Stopped working for some reason.

PATRICK: You sure?

DIABLO: Jesus, nobody around here listens to me! If I didn't want you to pay attention to me, I wouldn't say anything in the first place. Doesn't the fact I'm repeating myself make it clear I'm indeed certain there are no lights in there? I guess the cook doesn't wanna pay an electrician to repair the lights. Maybe the electrician stiffed the waitress on a tip.

PATRICK: That's real humble of you.

DIABLO: C'mon - go take your piss or flip the coin [pointing at a peso piece lying on the table]. I'm tired of waiting. Feels like I'm caught between two fires - loyalty to the laws of chance and the desire to watch you piss in the dark.

PATRICK: I'm sure you'll manage.

[PATRICK gets up, starts walking towards the diner's restroom.]

DIABLO: Oh, hey Patrick, you break that mirror in there, I'll kill you. Nothing personal.

PATRICK [shaking his head]: Man, you're obsessed with mirrors in public restrooms.

[WAITRESS arrives at the table with a coffee refill.]

DIABLO [turning to the WAITRESS, gesturing to PATRICK]: You think that guy's an annoying customer?

WAITRESS: What's his name?

DIABLO [grabbing a pack of cigarettes off the table, glaring at the WAITRESS]: You're an idiot.

WAITRESS: Feel better now?

DIABLO [laughing]: I feel better now. You owe me ten dollars for that comment.

[WAITRESS walks away from the table. PATRICK returns from the restroom.]

PATRICK [speaking to DIABLO, gesturing to the WAITRESS]: I'm gonna mess that bitch up, not you. Hell you looking at?

DIABLO: Tonight?

PATRICK: Made the arrangements - right over there in the motel [pointing at a multistory building across the street from the diner].

DIABLO: Feel better now?

PATRICK: What?

DIABLO: That waitress is fifty years old. Her thighs will rip your head off.

PATRICK: I feel better. I like to call her Mother. So tell me, what prostitute ever calls you Mother?

DIABLO: Remind me again - that waitress is a prostitute?

PATRICK: Earlier I saw her rubbing the back of that guy at the counter [gesturing to a man sleeping at the counter].

DIABLO: What's her name?

PATRICK: Veronica.

DIABLO: Damn, what a wonderful name to associate with a whore.

PATRICK: She's got loose nuts with a rubber too.

DIABLO: Meaning?

PATRICK: She's mature and shit. She expects a nice meal, doesn't lay nonsense on you all the time. She can change a tire. Get what I'm saying?

DIABLO: *Enough.* C'mon, let's get back to this coin. Flip the coin. … Say, doesn't it feel like this table's on a slight decline?

PATRICK [ignoring the coin on the table]: I got other girlfriends too.

DIABLO: That waitress is your girlfriend? Damn. You mean you told her "Veronica, I love you"? I love sexy talk. You're cute as hell, Patrick.

PATRICK: Go to hell.

DIABLO: Inconsiderate bastard. ... I understand the motel's got the best of both worlds.

PATRICK: You mean are there any logs in there?

DIABLO: I *know* there are - I seen 'em - biggest pair you can imagine. Gorgeous transvestites with dicks that put mine to shame.

PATRICK: Best of both worlds doesn't mean I wanna broaden my horizons with gay porn.

DIABLO: Forget it. I'm offering you hard bodies. All you got for me is semantics.

PATRICK: And blasphemy.

DIABLO [grimacing]: Forget it. Flip the coin. I wanna broaden my horizons too.

ACT II

PATRICK: Wanna rent a movie?

VERONICA: Tonight? I thought we were going to the motel.

PATRICK: We are, but we can rent a movie to watch if you want.

VERONICA: I don't need to get a room for the night just to watch a movie. I can do that in my apartment.

PATRICK: You used to work as a clerk in an adult video store, right?

VERONICA: I still do, on the weekends. C'mon, let's go.

PATRICK: You mind if my friend joins us?

VERONICA: Well, if you wanna blame someone for your perversions, blame yourself, not me.

PATRICK: I'm not twisting your arm to do it - only a suggestion.

VERONICA [clocking out]: Okay I'm officially finished for the night. Let's do it.

[PATRICK and VERONICA exit the diner, cross the street to the motel.]

PATRICK: I don't understand why my friend can't come [gesturing over his shoulder to DIABLO who sits at the table smoking cigarettes, drinking coffee, looking out the diner's window, watching PATRICK and VERONICA as they approach the motel].

VERONICA: Let's say I'm *not* his ex-girlfriend.

PATRICK: No shit. He's not your type? ... You're doing this tonight on your own recognizance. Don't be an asshole and try to overcompensate for your performance before it's started.

VERONICA: Christ, I'm a waitress *and* I work in a video store. I got no illusions about what I do, none that are important to me anyway. Trust me. You got no reason to be jealous.

PATRICK: You sure you don't wanna rent a video?

ACT III

VERONICA: You unlocking the door or what?

PATRICK: Gimme a second. Someone's jammed gum or something in the lock.

[PATRICK and VERONICA enter the motel room. PATRICK flips on the lights, turns on the TV. VERONICA sits down on the bed.]

VERONICA: What's on TV?

PATRICK: Looks like a some kind of porno movie.

VERONICA [studying the TV screen]: Oh yeah I've seen this one. It's *My Cat and Eight Wells*.

PATRICK: You smell something?

VERONICA: Shoe polish, I think. ... Man, this place is a pit. We're more than half an hour late too [shaking her wristwatch at PATRICK].

PATRICK: What are you talking about?

VERONICA: Nothing. You said this wouldn't take anything longer than twenty minutes, right?

PATRICK: Hell's your problem tonight? What's the hurry?

VERONICA: Hurry? That's life.

PATRICK: Life?

VERONICA: What are you looking out there for? I'm sitting over here.

PATRICK [opening the curtains, then turning away from the room's window]: You better be in the mood to suck dick tonight. I'm paying good money for it. I don't wanna feel like I'm humping a dead body.

VERONICA: What's the fuss?

PATRICK [sitting down next to VERONICA on the bed]: Noticed how many of the prostitutes raised their prices recently?

VERONICA: In Duluth?

PATRICK: All across the continent. Used to be islanders risked coming here specifically for the cheap sex. Now it's … like - you'd think the whores we're being paid to have sex with a diseased corpse or something.

VERONICA: Damn, now that you mention it, you're right - the price hikes are terrible.

PATRICK: What's your problem tonight?

VERONICA [picking up a magazine from the nightstand, paging through it]: What's the deal with you islanders anyway? Don't you guys got nudie booths and sex shows over there too?

PATRICK: I doubt we'll ever have nudie booths on the island.

VERONICA: Why not?

PATRICK: You know why - it's a legal issue. Except for nourishment, islanders aren't allowed to insert things anywhere into their bodies and receive payment for it in a public space.

VERONICA: Any opening?

PATRICK: It's the Aperture Laws.

VERONICA: Can someone jerk you off?

PATRICK: Depends on who and where the act occurs.

VERONICA: Whatever.

PATRICK: Can we *not* talk now and get with this performance?

[VERONICA begins removing her waitressing uniform.]

ACT IV

DIABLO [gesturing to VERONICA who's resumed her waitressing shift]: So what kind of show was it?

PATRICK [lighting a cigarette]: First of all, she let me insert things any place on her body.

DIABLO: That's the strangest craziest thing I never heard of. Any opening? How much you pay?

PATRICK: Ten dollars.

DIABLO: Man, that's a bargain.

PATRICK: Yeah I think so. Not only that, she used filthy language in front of me.

DIABLO: I tried to watch but didn't see anything.

PATRICK: That's too bad. When I opened the curtains I could tell we'd be impossible to see from down here. Next time I'll get a room on the first or second floor.

DIABLO: You see any internal organs?

PATRICK: Excuse me?

DIABLO: Did you see *inside* her?

PATRICK: No. I can do without that stuff.

DIABLO: Anyway, sounds like you had a great time for ten dollars. Using filthy language in front of customers - that's classy continental behavior. Don't know whether I should feel sorry for them or try to hurt them more deeply. ... I remember once - it's been several years now - I met a transvestite dancer at a bar that used to be right here, in this exact location, before it went out of business and became this diner. The two of us went across the street to the same motel. No kidding. That place has been around forever - with the same clientele - islanders picking up continentals.

PATRICK: You know what I can do without?

DIABLO: What?

PATRICK: All the drinking that goes on in there.

DIABLO: What?

PATRICK: Yeah the alcoholics wetting their beds. That sorta thing.

DIABLO: What are you talking about?

PATRICK: Me and Veronica got involved in a series of vignettes with this broken-down alcoholic, a writer or something. He joined us because he had a lower IQ than ours and ...

DIABLO: You mean there were *three* of you in one room?

PATRICK: Not the whole night - just for an hour or two. But the guy did nothing except pass out in the bathroom.

DIABLO: That's not cool. He didn't put on any quality movements?

PATRICK: He was catatonic. If it hadn't been for the snoring I might've assumed he was dead. Veronica tried having sex with him anyway - without his knowing - against his will - on the floor next to the toilet.

DIABLO: Ooooh, they don't call that rape over here.

PATRICK: They call it something.

DIABLO: Continentals choose the least intellectual way to commit a crime, don't they?

PATRICK [gesturing to the mug]: Your coffee still hot? I hate cold coffee.

DIABLO: Take it if you want [pushing the mug across the table to PATRICK]. So what happened next? A herd of wild animals? Lasagna?

PATRICK [lighting up a cigarette]: What are you talking about?

DIABLO: Continental folks do crazy shit during sex, don't they?

PATRICK: It comes down to how much you're paying.

DIABLO: That's the thing about the continent. Everything comes down to money over here. *Everything.* No matter what it is, you can make it happen with money. It's like you give them enough money, they'll figure out how to murder their mothers and get away with it so they can spend all that money you gave them. Doesn't have to be hard-earned money either. You could steal it from somewhere. Doesn't matter.

PATRICK: In a way, money simplifies things, doesn't it?

DIABLO: Takes so much of the confusion out of life. You know what your proper goals should be - get as much money as you can, everything else falls into place - it's an immutable law.

PATRICK [patting his stomach]: You hungry yet?

DIABLO: I ever tell you about the time I had sex with three different continental guys?

PATRICK: How many?

DIABLO: Three. Three independent contractors who were dissatisfied with their cocks and wanted an islander's expert opinion.

PATRICK: Oh my God, you sucked their cocks in a row? How'd that go? Man, what'd it cost?

DIABLO: It was different - more important. As they saying goes, "Don't try to suck any oath from the system via the car-park." What I mean is we didn't have sex but we fooled around a lot.

PATRICK: You're still a virgin?

DIABLO: Ummm ... Lower your voice.

PATRICK: *Hey.*

DIABLO: Isn't it ironic? I love gatherings of people but ...

PATRICK [in a hushed voice, leaning across the table]: But you hate people.

DIABLO [also whispering]: Not *all* people. It's the only way I keep my long-term sanity on the continent. That's why I prefer to masturbate people and have them masturbate me. It's not a big deal.

PATRICK [leaning back, exhaling cigarette smoke]: *Manually* masturbate - what's that? ... [Laughing] I've been a smoker for twenty years. I guess I manually smoke.

DIABLO: Your lungs are paying for it too.

PATRICK [laughing again]: Your dick's sure not paying for it.

DIABLO: Wait a minute - you're making me out to be a hatemonger, like I wanna watch a whole continent of people go extinct. That's ridiculous. I'm no merchant of death.

PATRICK: At least I'm confident you won't anally rape my mother.

DIABLO: Yeah, she's dead.

PATRICK: Excuse me?

[VERONICA approaches the table holding a pot of coffee.]

VERONICA: What are you two laughing and arguing about?

DIABLO [turning to VERONICA]: You rent videos? I'm looking for All-Grain Screwing Volume Six and Ass Worship Business End.

VERONICA: What's your problem?

DIABLO: By the way, you know Patrick loves you?

PATRICK: Hey, man, you're way outta line here.

VERONICA: You guys want refills or not?

DIABLO [winking at VERONICA]: I love you.

VERONICA [stepping back, then throwing hot coffee on DIABLO's face]: I love you too, bastard!

PATRICK [slapping VERONICA hard across the face]: Your tube needs cleaning or what? Look what you've done to him [pointing to DIABLO who's holding his scalded face in both hands, moaning in pain]. You've lost complete managerial control here. You're responsible for this.

VERONICA: Responsibility? What responsibility? You forget you're on the continent. I don't give a shit if he's your friend or not. I'll knock these boots against his ass if I have to.

PATRICK: Super - you're blunt but you *don't* have a point. You'll go the whole nine yards on Diablo, play field hockey on his crotch. What do you care, right? He's just another islander to you. All you gotta do is cross the street, request a room, polish off the rest of the idiotic aviation industry.

VERONICA: What the ...?

PATRICK: You know what I'm talking about - big black cocks with pearly white gates.

VERONICA [swinging the empty coffee pot at PATRICK's head]: Both you assholes can leave *now*!

PATRICK: Gladly [pulling DIABLO up from the booth, supporting him]. You're a blood clot in a pool, Veronica - you're not even free pussy when it comes to drinking stale shit from a toilet!

VERONICA [walking towards the counter]: I hope you both find humiliating ways to die in the street.

PATRICK [helping DIABLO across the diner towards the exit, calling back over his shoulder]: My retarded cousin's nothing compared to your embarrassing pussy!

VERONICA: I'm not listening.

[PATRICK and DIABLO walk across the street to the motel.]

ACT V

DIABLO: Did that man working at the front desk speak Russian?

PATRICK: I don't know. Who cares?

DIABLO: You'd think he might speak at least a little English, living on the continent and all.

PATRICK: How's your face?

DIABLO: My lips and jaw are so large I can't talk about it.

PATRICK: It looks very large in the mirror too. Look.

[PATRICK takes DIABLO by jaw, turns his head to look into a mirror that hangs on the wall of the motel room.]

DIABLO: What are you doing?

PATRICK: Showing you yourself in the mirror.

DIABLO: Chicken ... *Chicken!*

PATRICK: What now?

DIABLO: Where's my coin?

PATRICK: In your pocket, I guess.

DIABLO: No, I mean the coin on the table back at the diner. That specific coin.

PATRICK: Dunno. Maybe it's still back there. Maybe Veronica took it as a tip.

DIABLO: God I feel so oppressed. How can I talk about the way I feel? I come over to the continent to uplift people and this is what I get [gesturing to the reflection of his swollen face].

PATRICK: What are you doing?

DIABLO: I'm pointing at myself in the mirror.

PATRICK: I mean what are you complaining about? That was hardly a shocking abuse of authority. She was acting like your typical continental type - out of control, lacking power. Can't you see she's sick, been that way since childhood? She's the latest breed of sheep is all.

DIABLO: You let her suck your dick. You stuffed your penis in her mouth.

PATRICK: Great story, huh?

DIABLO: Oh my God, you're still a virgin?

PATRICK: Not according to your mother.

DIABLO [laughing]: Veronica's no good for you.

PATRICK: I'm not scared of her.

DIABLO: You know what I see in that mirror?

PATRICK: The reflection of a couple islanders down on their luck?

DIABLO: I see the reflection of *Return of the Jedi* from the television set.

PATRICK: Wouldn't you know it - in Duluth everything's ass backwards.

DIABLO: What can I say? Getting beat up by a continental slut's a strange thing for me.

PATRICK: I'd say it's one of the most bizarre things I've seen in the eleven years I've traveled here.

DIABLO [coughing]: Are we allowed to smoke in this room?

PATRICK: This is the continent - you can smoke pretty much anywhere. They can't stop it.

DIABLO: Oh yeah, where?

PATRICK: All over but especially here in the Midwest - Michigan, Minnesota, Iowa, hardcore continental types of places. Real intense.

DIABLO: And to think you got first dibs on those women.

PATRICK: Yeah there was Sophia … Patty … Veronica.

DIABLO: Good choices, all of them - except for Sophia. She was too young for you, even by continental standards.

PATRICK: Patty's the one who …

DIABLO: Oh yeah I know Patty. She's my favorite. That winter in Minnesota, the two of us driving around in that old Pontiac Firebird trying to find you.

PATRICK: I'd give anything to watch that video, see who said what to who in that Firebird, you guys swerving all over those icy roads.

DIABLO: You kidding? We nearly broke our wrists trying to free my dick from a little boy's frozen mouth.

PATRICK: I can imagine.

[The telephone rings.]

DIABLO: Who the hell's calling our room? Who knows we're here?

[PATRICK walks across the room, answers the phone.]

ACT VI

PATRICK: What are you doing calling here, Veronica? How'd you get this number?

VERONICA: Hi, Patrick.

PATRICK: Be quiet.

VERONICA: Having sex in the bathroom?

PATRICK: That's your job. I'm serious. This isn't funny. Diablo will be scarred, if not for life, at least for the next several months. How can he show his face around Duluth looking the way he does?

VERONICA: He has to learn to stop with that drivel. We don't tolerate that kind of talk around here.

PATRICK: What are you talking about? This is the continent. Everything's tolerated so long as it doesn't put a dent in your bank account or screw up your credit rating. I feel nauseous just talking about it.

VERONICA: You sure you don't wanna come back to the diner?

PATRICK: Why?

VERONICA: ¡Jesus! Time off, Patrick - relaxation.

PATRICK: Time off - shit - no way - not yet.

VERONICA: You islanders - always looking for arguments to dictate your behavior.

PATRICK: And next week - the end of the world.

[VERONICA hangs up the phone.]

[d]

COIN TOSS CONT'D

ACT VII
[Phone rings again.]
PATRICK [answering]: What now?
VERONICA: Tell Diablo he forgot his coin over here.
PATRICK: He knows.
VERONICA: Tell him to come get it.
PATRICK: Anyone tell you how much you sound like Dr. Seuss when you're drunk? - the tone of your voice, I mean.
VERONICA: I'm not drunk. I'm working.
PATRICK: Continental folks are great liars, best in the world, hands down.
VERONICA: C'mon. Did I tell you I saved the napkins Diablo writes 'H' and 'T' on? You guys can pick up the coin tossing game right where you left off. I know you're thinking how much you wanna get back to that game, right?
PATRICK: That's what I'm thinking?
VERONICA: Yeah sure.
PATRICK: Okay *now* what am I thinking?
VERONICA: People smiling, dogs running, rainbows …
PATRICK: Listen - if we come over to get the coin, will you stop with this coffee-throwing shit?
VERONICA: How's that different?
PATRICK: What I mean is - you won't kill yourself at the end of the night or hurt either of us with a screwdriver in the neck or a garden implement. Got it?
[PATRICK hangs up the phone.]

ACT VIII
[PATRICK and DIABLO have left the motel, are walking across the street to the diner.]
DIABLO: Man, it's getting cold again.

PATRICK: Does it bother you?

DIABLO: What?

PATRICK: Walking around in circles.

DIABLO: *What?*

PATRICK: That's what we're doing here, back and forth, diner to motel, motel to diner.

DIABLO: Such is the stochastic nature of continental living. I've been trying to illustrate that fact with the coin toss but you're not paying right attention. It goes like this - if you … ah, let's take this up when we get back to the diner. It helps me having the coin there as a prop, helps me explain how chance works.

PATRICK: I can't wait.

DIABLO: Say, how would you feel if I got you a professional, you know…

PATRICK: A professional?

DIABLO: Hooker.

PATRICK: Man, what's your problem?

DIABLO: My problem's you got a secret you don't wanna tell, so what we got here's a little game of show and tell - like you're waiting for me to give you the secret codeword or gesture or something.

PATRICK [turning to DIABLO]: Look at my face - I'm not thinking anything bad about you.

DIABLO: Ever feel prickly things on the back of your neck? You believe in magic?

PATRICK: Go to hell.

DIABLO [rubbing his hands]: Man, it's getting cold. Snow's in the forecast. … You sure you're not tired? You look tired.

PATRICK: No, I'm fine.

DIABLO: You know how you feel when you're sitting there and all the water's run outta the bathtub?

PATRICK: No. I take showers.

DIABLO: You sure you're not tired?

PATRICK: I'm sure. In fact I don't remember ever feeling this wide awake. Everything looks different. Something's crossed over inside me. There're no going back.

DIABLO: Back to the island, you mean?

PATRICK: To my old life.

DIABLO: That's the island, right, the sun, the surf, palm trees - that's Honolulu. You mean you can't go back there? You nuts?

PATRICK: I can go wherever I want. I know it sounds crazy, but I got a knack for this continental shit. What I mean is, on some level of existence, Minnesota or Nevada suit me just as well as Honolulu. It's the same to me.

DIABLO: I'll give you a dollar to eat that snow off the ground.

PATRICK: *You*, on the other hand, pride yourself on being infantile.

DIABLO: Continental women love that shit.

PATRICK: That's crazy coming from guy who got half his face burnt off by a waitress earlier tonight - a waitress we're about to see again, by the way.

DIABLO: Shit, I've always been crazy. Being here in Minnesota is the first chance I get to express myself. Back in Nevada, well, I didn't feel the *need* back there in the desert. Maybe the desert's …uh, the desert's in the middle of nowhere - but Minnesota - cold weather, the snow - I mean, Minnesota's the true middle of the continent. Make sense?

PATRICK: You're quite an individual, Diablo.

DIABLO: Takes all kinds.

ACT IX

VERONICA: Decaf or regular?

DIABLO: Why bother asking?

VERONICA: And a glass of orange juice for you, Patrick?

PATRICK: If you got it fresh-squeezed, sure.

VERONICA [pouring the coffee]: Mind if I join you guys on my break [sitting down in the booth beside PATRICK].

PATRICK: So tell us a little bit about this place.

VERONICA: *This* place?

PATRICK: Right where we're sitting.

VERONICA: Okay. Where to start? … Duluth's one of the oldest cities on the continent. Almost any place you go in the city has history and a story behind it, even this diner, the land it sits on.

Would you ever guess it was once a transvestite nightclub, and before that, an Italian restaurant run by the Midwestern branch of the Mob?

DIABLO: Midwestern *branch*?

VERONICA: That's right. Over there against that wall [pointing to an expanse of light green and orange wall], a guy got a bloody hole in his head.

DIABLO: I heard about that. I know about the layers of history. I used to be a geologist by trade. That explains my familiarity with this city in particular, you know, iron ore mining.

VERONICA: Lots of generations of continentals have lived and died in Duluth.

DIABLO: I'm sure - but now look at them [gesturing to the snowy sidewalks outside the diner window]. They don't see each other. They see only what they wanna see. They don't know they're dead. It's ridiculous.

VERONICA: What are you talking about? There's hardly anyone out there this hour of the night. I see one person, over there [pointing].

DIABLO: Well *I* see them, dead-looking people, zombies.

VERONICA [turning to PATRICK]: Please tell him to stop with the dead people stuff. He's creeping me out.

PATRICK: You tell him. … Say, could you serve us some wine in a glass, not a mug, but a real glass of wine?

VERONICA: We don't have a liquor license.

PATRICK: What are you talking about? I don't see any cops out there. Since when did not having a license prevent anyone from doing anything on the continent?

VERONICA: If the manager saw me do that, he'd fire me or at least dock my pay.

PATRICK: Where *is* the manager? Far as I can tell, it's just the three of us here and that man passed out at the counter.

VERONICA: That man passed out *is* the manager.

PATRICK: C'mon, just one glass for each of us - for making a toast to Duluth and getting a bit drunker. How about it?

VERONICA: Where would I get wine at this hour?

PATRICK: In the back, in the kitchen, in the restroom - I don't know. Didn't you used to hide liquor bottles in the toilet tank?

VERONICA: No, but I heard the Mob hid their guns in there when they wanted to make a hit.

PATRICK: I think you saw that on TV. You're getting memories mixed up with entertainment. I notice that happens a lot over here.

VERONICA: Where's your woman friend tonight?

PATRICK: You mean Patty?

VERONICA: I don't know her name.

DIABLO: Patty's around, … around the state somewhere.

VERONICA: State?

DIABLO: This is the state of Minnesota, right? Well she's somewhere around this state.

PATRICK: I think he means she's away on business.

VERONICA: Oh.

DIABLO [to VERONICA]: You got a flashlight I could borrow. I need to use the men's room. This coffee's making me nauseous.

VERONICA [running behind the counter]: Gimme a sec.

PATRICK: Glad I stuck with the orange juice.

ACT X

DIABLO [vomiting in the restroom stall]: Certain words and phrases keep drifting through my mind.

PATRICK: Spit 'em out, c'mon, clear 'em out of your system.

DIABLO: One thing I know is we gotta leave this place.

PATRICK: Go back to the motel for the rest of the night?

DIABLO: No, I mean leave Duluth, leave Minnesota.

PATRICK: Okay. It wouldn't be the first time we drive off in the middle of the night.

DIABLO: Besides we have appointments to make in Alphabet City, right?

PATRICK: Yeah but we're ahead of schedule so there's no hurry.

DIABLO: So what. I wanna get outta here *now*.

PATRICK: I guess that means we can hook up with Patty somewhere down the road.

DIABLO: Call her on my cellphone, tell her to meet us in a couple days in Ohio. Tell her we'll get back to her on exactly where.
PATRICK: Sounds like a serviceable plan. Where's your phone?
DIABLO: Back on the table, I think, next to the coin.
PATRICK: Okay I'll take care of that now.
[PATRICK leaves the restroom.]
DIABLO [wiping his mouth with a paper towel, turning to face the AUDIENCE, grinning]: I'm feeling much better now. Where the hell did Patrick go?

[Ax raised over his head]

Dedicated to every reader who believes the letters "ugly" and the story of "late" is growing.

Nothing's allowed but anything can happen - thus certain dark *hidden* stuff floats to the surface of the narrative… What's your problem? I love this flick - the opening scene sets up everything that follows. The schlocky murders are *not* the problem. I love this flick. "Oh, Africa, brave Africa." That line was so funny. "Don't touch the clock - I'm on a diet." What did she mean by *that*? The protagonist was supposed to be an abstraction - right? - an illusory creature, a mannequin-type thing, like his head was on a stick or something. What about his past? Let me put it this way - the protagonist's 'insides' don't exist for most of the movie. You're a lawyer - you ought to know - (you own this publishing company) - you can do anything you want *and* act stupid. As for me, I'm uncertain the editors are gonna let me get away with revisions this time. That's *my* problem. This time I don't wanna fit in with the other writers. Something horrible's happening inside here [pointing to the general area of my spleen]. I feel so lethal I think this mask of sanity is slipping off. Now, the holy man (Tsadik) was a kind of devil (Dybbuk) - that's why the cops took him away. But the protagonist, he was responsible for driving God too far underground. That's *his* problem. Excessive sunlight's whitened the dark secrets too - that's the problem with the mathematical formulae (mystical numbers). Like I said, you're a lawyer so I think you ought to know. My problem's I wanna clean your vagina, as they say, I want oysters on the half shell, a thousand roses, a single chocolate truffle: the bestiality of evil. Now, in the film, the protagonist's the only character to have a real relationship … with God? It's sure funny seeing how the difficulties worked themselves out in Duluth. Shit - something keeps buzzing in my ear. Yeah? You're a closet homosexual with lots of cocaine? Your nose, those nostrils look ... wonderful - nothing else to say. I think the antagonist is the Jungian shadow of the protagonist. Got it? - Two sides of the same coin.

Not quite blonde are you? Not quite brunette either. Well, you can get thinner ... look better. Balanced diet, rigorous exercise - you know the routine. When I see a beautiful girl on the street, I think two things. Wait - where are you going? You look ... wonderful - there's nothing else to say. Nice schlocky colors. (Oh the decorations.) Are you dating anyone - a holy man perhaps? I can't understand why the voice of reason was *not* the girl next door. Fact is, I'd love to support a child-hero next door. Fact is, I loved the girl next door. What was her trick anyway? She was playing God. Simple. She used Scotch tape. Those invasive close-ups of her crotch provided a mysterious connection to the hard-edged world of scientific research. Myself, I'm not an evil son of a bitch. I'm a child of divorce. Leave me alone - and cool it with those anti-Semitic remarks. I wanna talk a little bit more about Diabolein.

[e]

The play's the thing

1. *When economic necessity allies itself to vice (or, This tramp would like to sell her secrets for more than two dollars an hour)*

Diabolein is pure luck.

Diabolein is both sides of being and becoming.

Diabolein is a series of battles on the surface of a planet.

Diabolein is two sides of the same coin plus a single alphabet.

Diabolein is a genetic template scrawled on *this* perforated sheet of blotting paper.

Diabolein is a board game in a gaming parlor in a mansion on a Polynesian island.

Against one wall of the gaming parlor stands an Egyptian mummy-case. On the other walls hang stuffed flinty-eyed birds. On the floor lie rugs made from the skins of wild beasts. Out on the balcony, a view of cloud-colored vertical lines rising from the continental horizon line. That's right - even if the laws of material evolution won't allow it, the point here's to create something new and strange, atmospheric, something difficult in extremis.

- a knock at the parlor door -

"I wonder who *that* is ..."

The man sure looks professional, though his hands are trembling. Patrick leads him over to the bed. Mother, gasping for air, speaks what will be her last words: "Out of evil shall come ... uh, shall ..."

"Mother, you would know, wouldn't you?"

The professional-looking man removes a sterile syringe from his jacket pocket, holds the syringe point up, taps out a bubble. Patrick swabs the inside of Mother's elbow with alcohol.

"How can I thank you?"

The man steps back from the bed with the empty syringe held away from his body.

"You can't ..." [Mother's faint voice sinks below the surface of self-awareness - ... newspapers would report she died from pneumonia brought on, no doubt, by exposure to the this autumn's cool weather.]

Patrick pulls the parlor's blinds closed.

The man disposes of the syringe and leaves.

This would also be a cruel autumn, with winds and temperatures pitched perfectly for well-crafted earthly wrongdoings.

"What are you thinking about, Patrick?"

"Last time I felt ... profound sadness"

"Felt *what*?"

"Her pain was trivial, right?"

"Listen to me - never take that shirt off. Never let them see you bear the signs of an islander."

As Patrick leaves the gaming parlor, three successively louder explosions shake the mansion to its foundations.

Diabolein is competing claims of humility before God.

Diabolein is a society of idealized absolutes gone Mad.

Diabolein is a meddling intellect that disdains to dwell upon Uniqueness.

Thus the latest tale of political independence unfolds.

2. *Battle of Praise Hills - therefore it's ours to keep*

In the opening act - a country-style mansion (a chateau named Elsinore) on a bluff overlooking the eastern shores of the island - everything inside as the playwright imagined it - every trifling object comparable to an Oriental masterpiece - every curio not to be confused with a knickknack or a trinket - the servants sweeping and dusting off those incomparable objects -

In autumn - October - continental military forces begin firing at the island from across the channel.

"Is that a declaration of war?"

"No, not exactly hostilities. Rather, we're on the *verge* of hostilities."

"When shall the real hostilities begin?"

"In the second act. For now, let's have a few diplomatic preliminaries." ("Talks" the media calls them.)

[Autumn puts us in a revolutionary frame of mind.]

Later, that same autumn - November - continental military forces attempt to invade the eastern shores of the island -

Chaos ensues - submarine-torpedo attacks - massive oil slicks - naval blockade -

[Hospitals in the island's capital city overflow with a sudden inexorable surge of casualties.]

In the second act, before vacating Elsinore in the face of an invading army, Patrick shows off his unique style of genius by burning everything inside the mansion as the playwright imagined it - every trifling object, including the servants sweeping and dusting off those objects, including a little basket filled with important cards and letters, including the Diabolein board game itself -

"Come. Come. Be generous, ole chap. Give it up. Be kind enough to seat yourself in your favorite great blue easy-chair while we take a look around the place. Consider yourself at home."

"Was that a declaration of war?"

"To the knife."

"Then we will *make* you make *us* give it up."

"With pleasure."

"Ransack at your will - we shall be interminable, odious."

"Au revoir, Mademoiselle."

Even while the playwright reminds us death treats everyone equally (watch him dig those open graves), military battles remain whirls of excitement and suspense. ("Conflicts" the media calls them.) Who will win that battle over there [pointing at the horizon]? What are the Vegas odds our local platoon will surrender in a fortnight? How far will the islanders go - what sacrifices will they make? - to prevent us from blocking their bid for independence?

3. *The keys are in the locks - therefore it's mine to keep*

Patrick realizes here's a chance to do 'good action,' a chance to achieve artistic satisfaction - a worthy purpose no doubt, as grandiose and purposeful as gliding through the blackness of self-justifying denial. Forced to leave the island in the face of an invading army, Patrick makes a dramatic exit on the last cross-channel ferry bound for the continent.

Every fiber of Patrick's body is alive and tingling as the Battle of Praise Hills rages around him. He takes in the various sights scarcely aware of what they mean, yet the view fascinates him and he's pleased to take such pleasure in it. The channel's clogged with warships, battleships, this ship, that ship, out-of-place freighters, motorboats, waterskiers. Scores of fleeing islanders ("refugees" the media calls them) are wedged into the ferry, their faces expressing burning impatience, blank oblivion, indignation, unexplained animosity, perplexed despair, unmoored desperation, self-recrimination, hallucinatory clarity, disorientation. Patrick leans forward over the railing, ready to leap into the channel, feeling himself on the verge of plunging into a cold unknown stream at the last possible second to avoid a migraine attack.

"How blind I've been, how modest, impassive - yet here at last is contiguity with greatness. I've never lived till now. The typical islander's deadpan approach to life is supposed to be funny, even wise, but now I see it for nothing but negativity. Look at these downtrodden refugees, their obsequious sorrow, their … uh, I can't grasp any of it. Why can't we interpret these insults against us? In response to such violent outbursts, why aren't we willing to dance on the very edge of taboo? - tell me *that*."

While the other refugees prepare themselves for the possible shock of explosion, Patrick stands aloof from the strife. He pretends the entire event lies outside the scope of his experience - the reverberations of battle resounding in the unexplored depths of (his being?) - refugees cowering beneath their faded striped umbrellas -

"I'll not be at war with myself. I'll no longer pretend to kill myself out of grief for my dead mother. Instead … uh, instead I'll join the IUF [Insular Underground Forces], swearing myself to secrecy - and though true subversion is by definition a difficult thing to pull off, I'll remain 'in between,' fixed nowhere, and that'll be a good thing, a dramatic thing, a subcultural product of the moment. One must be willing to let things be - then act decisively. Otherwise, uh … well …"

Man, this is shaping up to be a long three-day weekend.

4. *Light housekeeping over gas jets*

Having disembarked from the ferry, Patrick's confronted by the first great vital fact of continental life: the twin abstractions of exchange: cash & credit. His face burns. Darting pains pierce his legs and feet. Each building, each object he sees in the city has a unique degree of roundness, transparency, solidity, and opacity. The terrain is Martian.

Rows of grubby-looking taxis, their tailpipes spewing exhaust, shuttle refugees from the ferry-house to hundreds of lodging-houses located throughout the city. When's the last time he set foot on the continent? Patrick hurries over to the nearest taxi to meet his fate: a cabdriver with little vials of medicine lined up on the dashboard.

Patrick and the cabdriver speak back and forth - do they not? - across the laminated distance between them. Outside the taxi: treeless streets - a hallmark of continental urban planning - the incongruity of rows of white-box dwellings, the props, set, wardrobe, flapping banners, cracked domes, torn tents, the bizarre wreckage of - *Welcome to lodging-house 4AB-T1.* Your belongings are piled over there on the radiator. The out-of-tune piano is free to all to play (diminished chords mostly). Around here, you do as you please - except if you go outside: be careful not to cross the property line. Otherwise, you're free to take advantage of all the continental freedoms you islanders turn your haughty little noses at (though with the corresponding risks of breadlines, foreclosures, bank failures, and terminal infantilism). You know what *that* means [pointing through the upstairs window at the casinos, whorehouses, and shopping malls across the street].

For one thing, this narrative's more than bifurcated. For another, rather than the less familiar device of a nervous breakdown, we've installed an epiphany here in the midst of wartime catastrophe.

Still woozy and weightless from the cross-channel transit, Patrick creeps through the lodging-house. What of these shabbily dressed refugees passed out on the floors and slouching against the walls? The entire scene lies so far outside the scope of his experience Patrick cannot feel sympathy for any of these scoundrels and tramps. He steps to the nearest window, stands there staring down at the triangular intersection below. Right there, on the sidewalks and streets of the largest westernmost city, continental folks and malcontented islanders jockey for position to watch the big news screens. The relentless hyperrealism of those streets is bizarre, surrealistic. Yet, now that Patrick's become an adopted son of the continent, he feels an overpowering sense of relief. Fact is, more than half the island's population could be dead this very moment. Death's little more than a bad excuse for most of those islanders' so-called 'wise passivity' anyway. "Now death's overtaken them without their having to pursue it." Only a maze of tangled and broken threads remains of their past.

Why can these two communities *not* keep to their own spheres? Why must they rub up against one another? Why must they mix?

Patrick ejaculates into the curtains with a shudder.

5. *Boxing the compass*

A young heavyset woman in a yellow sundress, not quite blonde, not quite brunette, descends the ladder from the garret's skylight-room. At the bottom rung of the carpeted ladder she pauses, glances at Patrick with a pair of large black eyes. A flush appears on her cheeks.

"I hope you'll enjoy my hospitality. I have a thing for islanders."

"You mean you won't mind me climbing over you every morning?"

"Won't mind at all. I'm in my comfort zone here in the lodging-house. I hope you don't mind my regular ministering to these sebaceous cysts" [gesturing to her torso and neck].

"I guess not."

Patrick appreciates, above all, the curve of her bright red lips and the manly bear hugs. She has no true identity. She's a vessel. Her name's Patty. She'll be coming along for the ride.

6. *18 inches on Diablo*

"Casting agency looking for man to play fits of drunken rage"
- "Grim comedy of errors" - "Unflinchingly violent" - "A farcical
look at man's relationship with God"

Patrick rips the poster advertisement from the retaining wall.

He's sick and tired of this coastal city. He's ready to travel
inland, eastward, *that* direction [pointing to my right] - towards
the desert, where authority figures can't raise their eyebrows at
bored islanders seeking after the bizarre.

So Patrick steals a car and drives off in the general direction of
Nevada. Look - there he goes [pointing to my right] - and there's
Patty riding shotgun.

[f]

Abbie Rose

I been most everything ... I got power to assume a pleasing shape ... to create the very cunning of a scene ... It's no real pleasure in life ...

Do I happen to know anything scandalous about his personal history? Do I know what's happened to him, what's become of his body, which accounts are true? Did he vanish - evaporate - - go into hiding mumbling to himself and knocking things over in the dark (that sepulchral mumble!) - perhaps he fell overboard - or in April took ill, died - or … - indeed, these are the raw materials you need for a contemporary romance filled with striking figures and heightened circumstances.

Nobody's business but my own ... I got nothing but I got my principles ... Besides, it don't kill me to march alone ... To this day, it's difficult imagining Diablo as an established factor in my life. (He reminds me of that old joke - Why's so-and-so so *un*like a leopard? - He's always changing his spots.) In the wake of the chaos that was the Battle of Praise Hills, I never hoped for a romantic conclusion to our friendship. Fact is, Diablo was an unacceptable companion of my own nomadic wanderings. Yet one thing's certain: no one who knew him deigned to call him anything but Diablo - Diablo the coin collector.

That was his job as far back as I can remember - to carry a pocketful of coins (and sometimes peanuts) - a solitary sojourner crisscrossing the continent - from LA to Hoboken then back again. I imagine he wandered alone for forty-odd years before I met him in Nevada - a deliberate sort of gentleman (though without knapsack or walking cane), who dispensed an amazing hodgepodge of learning without inflicting philosophical platitudes on the nearest pedestrian or displaying the superficial bohemianism we associate with such behavior - not the shoulder-clapping/thigh-slapping sort either, nor the type of man to have exotically disturbing tendencies and unspeakable birthmarks (though he'd lost two fingers from his left hand). Nonetheless, he was a bit wilder than your average local artist - more the likeness of a solid man with a square beard, big balding head, and ... uh, his nose betrayed him as a [INTERFERENCE].

I had the good fortune of being chummy with Diablo in those early post-Praise Hills days - I say 'good fortune,' though he leaves me with the singular impression of making me shiver that first hot afternoon, standing there, in the full blaze of the desert sun, waiting for something meaningful to happen between us in that dusty diner parking lot.

The days (and nights) wore on in Nevada - first a series of small desert towns, then Reno, finally Las Vegas. Diablo struck me as a rather queer gentleman. His eyes, seemingly loose in their sockets, gave him a ghastly, even luminous, look. He was a conscientious reader of the local weather reports. He had a theory on the effects of desert sunlight on the Caucasian race. Worst of all, while I hankered for two half-glasses of the clearest gin every morning, he made a point of never touching any drink stronger than beer.

However, it was the corrupt Las Vegas casinos, the malevolent prostitutes, the impartial solicitude of greedy escort services, the rabid barking dogs, and ultimately our general bad luck that left us wanting someplace further inland, someplace secluded, where the locals paid little attention to tomorrow's strange visitor and we were unlikely to encounter the eyes of a nature stronger than our own. I wonder now if they *all* scream - the gamblers who've lost their souls to the roulette wheel, the alcoholics who study young boys with latent suspicion, the [INTERFERENCE]. I screamed the first day I lost five thousand dollars in five seconds. The effect was vertiginous - as if I were leaning backwards over the parapet of London Bridge to get a better view of Tower Bridge (and I've never visited London).

Novelty - love of pleasure - *Right*? Not exactly. If you recall, after fleeing the island during the Battle of Praise Hills, I spent some time living as a refugee in a lodging-house in one of the largest coastal cities - before striking off for Nevada. Fact is, when you've become satiated with the artificialities of urban life, the only genuine reaction is to go towards the natural, the wild, the primitive. In my case, rather than drive north, wandering alone in the Arcadian gloom of evergreen forests, gazing into the deep ultramarine of crater-lakes eighteen miles across, I turned my gaze east - towards what I knew, from the maps, was the Nevada desert. But what I found was Las Vegas.

Sure, if I wanted, I could write an entirely different sort of story, much less romantic, a bit less impressive, describing the stale untruths of several equally destructive possibilities. But I'd rather mention one of those Las Vegas prostitutes - Penelope - and her (pimp?) (associate?) (accomplice?) named Mr. Riordan.

There we stood outside the entrance to the city's largest casino, the four of us, Penelope handcuffed to Mr. Riordan's wrist, myself feverishly entertaining foolish gambling notions, Diablo baring the summit of his balding head. What were we watching? A procession? A parade? A black mass? One after another: itinerant peddlers - timorous wayfarers from the continental 'outer worlds' - silent peasantry hoisting rudely carved crucifixes over their heads - clergymen in cassocks and shovel hats - hundreds of unemployed homeless with their trademark earthenware mugs of sparkling mineral water. - If *continental folk refuse to change their principles, why should I change mine?* So little of Diablo's life was spent in his own country. No wonder he was the first among us to appreciate the futility of chasing after pleasure - rather, let those pleasures come chasing after you - *let them lose their self-possession* - why be in such haste?

I would stay but ... I would stay but ...

Before that scene, I recall me and Diablo wandering about in one those vacated Nevada desert towns - a true ghost town just for you, kind reader, if you thought such towns existed only on Hollywood back-lots. Diablo's face lit up when six snarling dogs of various breeds came bounding forth to greet us. He wasn't afraid of the curs or the diseases they carried. As we walked around, Diablo recited a monologue chronicling the history and vicissitudes of the place and the wild animals to whom its buildings belonged. The daylight was fading, giving way to the troubled countenance of desert twilight. What do I know? That may have been my imagination. I recall peeping through the doors of an abandoned house - - that's right: the comfortable yellow glow of muted sunlight in the vacant internals of an empty house - irregular silhouettes of furniture - dishes on the washboard washed up - stove perhaps warm to the touch - box-like compartments - cubbyholes - worn staircase - casements ajar - a peasant's deathbed. What do I know? He drank too much. Diablo thought me crazy - and I was, a little, and I still am, a little (though 'godforsaken' would be overstating it). I followed Diablo into one of those houses. What's that hanging from the kitchen ceiling, some ... er, say, you see that ...? - what do you mean? Diablo lifted his fist, bringing it down with a sudden crash on the dusty dining room table.

Fact is, I cannot abandon the feeling Diablo's now very far away from me here in Alphabet City, on other continents working out new patterns of harmony in space. Fact is, I got ample time here in my Alphabet City flat, with these palsied fingers, deep-cut wrinkles, with little strength left for real work, to think about Diablo and the past we shared. Why not? I spend long careless hours with my dreams, with Bach, Schubert, and Mozart, with these eccentric expressions of jealousy and nostalgia. (On second thought, for 'eccentric' read 'erratic.')

I recall me and Diablo stretched out naked on a freighter's deck, hands clasped behind our heads, beads of sweat glistening on our foreheads, trickling down our cheeks. *Abbie Rose* wasn't impressive as freighters go - nothing about it appealed to either of our tastes - but it would take us to our destination - back across the channel, of course, *to die at home at last ... a few more weeks few more months ...*

[g]

Foreign affairs and other people's business

1. New scenes, old faces, a flood of humiliating metaphors

You heard about Captain Fiction, right? A bit later I'll mention Costa Move - and Joey Scattergood - well, what about Doctor Swoboda? - you heard about him? That's right - his name's Swoboda - he's a professional *egotist* (*not* an egoist) and therefore disqualified from participating in Diabolein: he's *forgotten* that everything he now possesses or ever can possess is <u>received</u> from something/somewhere else: the material things coloring his existence (including his thoughts) imply a <u>source</u> external to those material things (and thoughts). Problem is Swoboda's forgotten how to <u>obey</u> that source - he's forgotten it exists - he's forgotten <u>humility</u>. Fact is, no word exists in this language that corresponds to the idea of *Diabolein*, just as none exists corresponding to the idea of <u>transcendence</u> (God knows what He does with that shit).

Heavy stuff, I know - therefore *karma*.

Egotists forget things.

Continental folks tend to forget things.

- tend to *forget* <u>no devils outside humanity</u>.

[Turning to face the AUDIENCE]: If the reader's made it this far, she's read lots about me and Diablo, right? Well, if you can, read a bit further (<u>patience</u> is the watchword here) - try to look beyond our madcap antics and appreciate how the two of us are part of a tradition, a <u>received</u> <u>tradition</u> from which we cannot escape - it's impossible for me to justify that claim.

Islanders try to remember things but tend to fail.

As for the Battle of Praise Hills [gesturing out the window] - well, is that truly a civil war, as the continental government claims (to this day), or a battle driven by nonpolitical motives?

In the island's capital city, traffic still moves to and fro on tires of rubber and metal.

Banks still handle our funds.

In the schools, egotistical teachers teach their children to forget things - parents are so delighted with their children learning how to forget - they can't remember having felt so happy - when all's said and done, the child receives a diploma to hang on the wall.

Traffic moves to and fro on tires of rubber and metal.

Banks continue to handle our funds.

[The latch of the front gate clicks open.]

Welcome - welcome to Elsinore. It's just me and my dying bedridden mother who live here.

Last night's rains have washed off most of the paint, leaving the walls well scrubbed and ... Hello! Come inside ... *whoa* watch your step. Imagine your having such bad luck on your first day! Can't let that happen now can we? ... Here we go ... I know our mansion has a rather rundown cluttered appearance but that shouldn't bother you. Mother and I live the simple life out here. We don't miss too many things about city life. ... Anyhow, we'll begin our tutoring session forthwith. First I must give Mother her quote-unquote brunch. Take a seat in the gaming room. You'll see, on one of the gaming tables, I've laid out some books you might care to glance at.

[The teenage girl enters the gaming room, takes a seat at a table, begins looking through the books.]

[A few minutes later I take a seat across from the girl in my favorite great blue easy-chair.]

All right ... sorry for the delay - but we can't neglect Mother's appetite now can we? She's a faithful old soul - even if she does overrate the importance of my favors.

So, I know you're here because you wanna learn how to play Diabolein. Fair enough, that's my specialty and life's work. However, I must warn you the required preparation and training are ... well, we can get to the disclaimers later - I sense a certain impatience in you - believe me, that's a good thing.

First off, I'm glad to hear you wanna study philosophy in college - not science, law, or medicine - certainly not business and finance. That's very good, means you won't replace worship at the temple altar with worship at a laboratory bench.

Secondly - this is a disclaimer - you should understand that what you're about to embark on is, let's say, dangerous, even subversive. But of course you must know that, otherwise you wouldn't be here. What I mean is, even if Diabolein's not illegal on the island as it is on the continent, it's sufficiently frowned upon that the training must be done in secret if you hope to complete it.

Bottom line's this - <u>you must be able to keep a secret</u> - under duress, especially under duress. I hope I'm not scaring you - you'll be scared like you cannot imagine soon enough, once the training's underway - but you must understand the revolutionary nature of Diabolein. I never use the word 'revolutionary' lightly.

Okay [clapping my hands] the good news is, with Diabolein, if you want, you can grow up to be a truly remarkable woman - that's what Diabolein's about, its practical aspect: <u>becoming your own creator</u> - though only if you remember how.

[The gaming room's windows rattle.]

Don't let those explosions frighten you - that commotion out on the channel's still rather far off. We're safe here.

So tell me, what's the earliest thing you remember?

2. Stains

Boo!

So, what's the first thing happens when you try to remember things? - *fear*. Thus <u>courage</u> becomes the watchword in the second phase of Diabolein training.

Happiness and suffering are self-created. Why bother creating either?

Yeah, me and your uncle had some wonderful chats the other day about how to help you overcome fear. We were sitting on a park bench right outside your high school.

[The expression on the girl's face changes. Her lips are quivering. Her neck turns crimson, swollen, seemingly too large for her collar. She averts her eyes, then lowers her head, clutching one of the Diabolein training manuals in her lap.]

Once the training's complete, no one can order you about - but until that time, you'll have to take orders from me. That's a fundamental paradox of the Diabolein training - you must submit to your tutor to learn how to be free. In the olden days they called it the 'guru principle.' Fact is, so long as that principle offends you, so long as you're frightened of that principle's implications, you cannot progress in the training.

I see you got a bit of a stain on your dress there [pointing at her right breast]. Could you please go into the other room and wash that stain out?

[She looks at me mutely, then rises from the chair. I follow her to the door of the washroom, look inside, … see her standing at the washbasin preparing to remove her dress.]

Because I say you mustn't - that's why.

[I return to the gaming room, gaze out the window at the many battleships on the channel.]

The continental navy has set up some sort of blockade - but they're allowing the ferries through. So it's *not* a blockade, right? - typical continental nonsense.

3. Slough of despond

About evil? - *the social and personal habits that result from forgetfulness.*

Isn't the wonderful thing about morality that it makes us feel righteous in our superiority to other people's social and personal habits? Fact is, once you've overcome the fears of your own imagination and memories - and that's no mean feat - you must next overcome the fear of moral judgment. That means transcending morality.

Heavy stuff, I know - you might end up in prison - but if you do, you won't feel ashamed about it - how could you? - you won't have a social conscience by then.

I get the unpleasant impression the smile coming to the girl's face is somewhat forced.

4. A strange light with cool new variations on darkness

You heard about Captain Fiction, right? Well, what about Doctor Illuminatus - you heard of him? That's right, his name's Illuminatus - he's a professional seer and therefore qualified for participating in Diabolein: he <u>remembers</u> that everything he possesses now or ever can possess is <u>received</u> from something/somewhere else.

Illuminatus belongs to a very old family of worth and distinction. He's indifferent to yet entirely in control of his life. Look at the garden behind his house. Look at the immediate neighborhood. Look at the neighbors themselves, how everyone dresses in spotless white.

Isn't Illuminatus a remarkable man? His spacious one-story house has more than a dozen rooms, a long wide veranda with wicker chairs and benches, and faded green shutters.

[The gaming room's windows rattle.]

[h]

ECCE DIABOLUS (or, No crime's without political dimensions)

ACT I
["Duke of Earl" by Gene Chandler plays on the car radio.]
PATRICK: Here we are on the road!
DIABLO: Yep, that's where we are all right.
PATRICK: So which way we going?
DIABLO: East.
PATRICK: That's cool. Never been east.
DIABLO: That means we'll eventually arrive on the East Coast, you know, New York City. No way around it. We've flipped the coin. Now we must stand staunchly by the results.
PATRICK: Great word - 'staunchly.'
DIABLO: The watchword of Diabolein. Am I right?
PATRICK: Diabolein has lots of watchwords. I guess 'staunchly' could be one of 'em. Why not? I always say everyone's right.
DIABLO: Imagine that - New York City .
PATRICK: It'll be ladies' night every Monday night of the week.
DIABLO [wincing]: Up yours, you two-bit son of a bitch.
PATRICK: I'm serious - I can imagine it too. I can *see* it right here [tapping the middle of his forehead].
DIABLO: Just remember, something invented in the head soon becomes grafted to the lower body.
PATRICK: Jesus - watch where you're driving! You nearly sideswiped that semi [looking over his shoulder].
DIABLO: *You* take it easy - driving's serious business. I'm not having an accident on account of you. … Speaking of Jesus, you notice how the further east we go, the more men have beards and grow their hair long?
PATRICK: I don't care. I won't miss Duluth - that's for certain. Man, I'm getting sick. I feel a cold coming on [wipes his nose on the back of his hand].

DIABLO: Not the flu is it?

PATRICK: Problem with Duluth was the boredom.

DIABLO [shaking his head]: You're constantly talking about boredom. What's the difference? Boredom's your hobby. You need boredom to make sense of your life. Other people get on with what they're supposed to be doing - you, on the other hand, do nothing in order to proclaim your boredom.

PATRICK: Well put, but you don't get it at all. I mean, there's boredom and then there's capital-B Boredom. Duluth falls in the latter category.

DIABLO: You learned that from those existential philosophers, huh?

PATRICK: The concept's straightforward, nothing philosophical about it. Without a steady series of intellectual or physical challenges, you get bored. Simple. At that point you compensate for the boredom by turning to bizarre sideline pursuits. Sure enough, that's what happened to me in Duluth. You saw it. I started spending more time at that motel doing weird shit to take my mind off the uniformity of existence.

DIABLO: Uniformity of existence? If I push you out the door right here [leaning across the seat], you can hitch the rest of the way to New York. How's that for a series of challenges?

PATRICK [sneezing]: We got any Kleenexes or decongestants?

DIABLO: Shit…

PATRICK: Anyway, we need to be moving on regardless of my boredom. Our work's done in Minnesota.

DIABLO: *Your* work's done. My work's never done no matter where I am. That's why I'm never bored.

PATRICK: Jesus, have it your way. I always say everyone's right.

ACT II

 ["Locomotion" by Little Eva plays on the car radio.]

PATRICK: I like this old music.

DIABLO: This satellite station plays only songs that were popular before the Beatles screwed everything up.

PATRICK: I never get tired of old music no matter how much I hear it.

DIABLO: Goes to show those satisfactions are permanent.

PATRICK: So what do you think - continental military forces have taken over the island by now?

DIABLO: No idea. Media blackout's not my closest friend.

PATRICK: It doesn't matter as far as we're concerned. I mean, even if the Battle of Praise Hills never happened, we'd still have found our way back to the continent. … If your job's spreading Diabolein, why the hell would you need a battle or war to incite you? Get my drift?

DIABLO: Incite me?

PATRICK: Forget it.

DIABLO: The way I see it, for all the differences between the island and continent, the one thing both sides agree on is suppressing Diabolein. That's the fundamental thing islanders and continentals have in common. They don't wanna confront Diabolein. That's why people like you and me are on the run no matter where we are.

PATRICK: Human nature. Two sides in constant battle, going back and forth, back and forth. They hate being reminded they're in fact two sides of the same coin and victory lies in tossing the coin aside. The point isn't demolishing your enemy but demolishing the need to have any enemies in the first place. But that requires some form of detachment.

DIABLO: Both sides share the basic misconception that there are two kinds of people in this world, while in fact there are *three* kinds of people. Three is the perfect number here. The two of us - we're examples of that third kind.

PATRICK: Virtuous, evil, and observer.

DIABLO: What?

PATRICK: Those are the three kinds of people, as I see it.

DIABLO: Virtuous and evil, good and bad - yes - those are two of the kinds. As for the third kind, well, you're right we're observers. But more than that we're judgment - right? - we're judges. We're judgment against the other two kinds of people, judgment against good *and* bad. We're outside the ethical bullshit the other two kinds take so seriously.

PATRICK: Fact is, they can't bear to look at us - if they have the ability to *see* us in the first place.

DIABLO [laughing]: Yep we're *that* ugly.

PATRICK: There [pointing to a billboard] - pull over that truck-stop. I need to take a leak.

DIABLO: Where?

PATRICK: Next couple exits, I think.

ACT III

["Book of Love" by the Monotones plays on the car radio.]

PATRICK: Over there, park over there [pointing]. … Man, this Firebird's on its last legs. Listen to the engine rattle.

DIABLO: Every car makes its own tune.

PATRICK [getting out of the car]: Go ahead and order me a hamburger and coffee.

DIABLO: Okay.

[PATRICK enters the truck-stop diner, walks into the restroom.]

PATRON [standing at neighboring urinal]: Ever notice how in a restroom one bastard goes in before another comes out?

PATRICK: It doesn't matter.

PATRON: Aren't you ashamed?

PATRICK: Of what?

PATRON: Being in a loony bin like this.

PATRICK: Loony bin?

PATRON: Before you came in I saw one guy take a shit on the floor back there [gesturing to the far corner of the restroom]. Isn't that crazy enough for you?

PATRICK [zipping up]: I dunno if that's crazy. It's odd though.

PATRON [zipping up]: You don't understand. The same guy's still in here, jerking off somewhere. Isn't that crazy enough for you?

PATRICK [looking at the PATRON's reflection in the restroom mirror]: This doesn't look like a padded cell to me - looks like a run-of-the-mill men's room. You familiar with the saying 'a rolling stone gathers no moss'?

PATRON: Yeah sure.

PATRICK: Look at me - look at *my* reflection.

PATRON: Okay. I am.

PATRICK: It's funny the world we live in. It's so easy to think everything's going crazy, everything's out of control. You get stuck in a rut and everything seems to move right on by you and you get frightened, start saying everyone's crazy. But here's the thing - maybe you're the one who's nuts for letting yourself get stuck in a rut. Maybe you're the one who's stagnating. Maybe *you're* the two-bit whack-job.

PATRON: What gives you the right …?

PATRICK: I'm trying to help you.

PATRON: By calling me crazy?

PATRICK: I'm not a monster. No need to treat me like one.

PATRON: You think you can just judge me and walk away?

PATRICK: What? I'm always 'walking away,' as you put it. That's how I exist - on the move. That's why I don't get trapped in a rut. … It puts me ahead of the curve.

PATRON: I don't know you. You're a random stranger.

PATRICK: That means I'm unbiased, unprejudiced, fair. What better person to have cast judgment on your life? I don't give a shit about you one way or the other. I don't care about what you've done or what awaits you. I'm simply looking at you here in this mirror [pointing at the reflection of the PATRON].

PATRON: But you just met me. How can you know?

PATRICK: I *observe* you right here and now. That's enough. Like I said, I'm trying to help you. Rather than feel threatened, it'd make more sense if you welcomed my judgment, right?

PATRON: Why are you doing this if you don't care about me one way or the other?

PATRICK: Opportunity presented itself. Remember, *you* started the conversation, not me. Only reason I came in here was to empty my bladder. If you hadn't said anything, none of this would've transpired. But you did say something - and here we are [gesturing to their two reflections in the mirror].

PATRON: I think I ought to be going.

PATRICK: Is there a problem?

PATRON: Nah, I'm done here.

PATRICK: Poor choice of words.

PATRON: What?

PATRICK: We're never *done* anywhere anytime. That's your problem. You're not moving properly. You're not agile. Like I said, you're stuck in a rut.

[PATRON leaves the restroom.]

PATRICK [turning away from the mirror to face the AUDIENCE]: Am I that ugly? It's not about money here. It's about sending a message. Sometimes the truth's not good enough. Fact is, truth's an ugly frightening thing.

[AUDIENCE applauds.]

[PATRICK leaves the restroom, joins DIABLO at the diner's counter.]

DIABLO: Why so serious?

PATRICK [putting a quarter in the mini-jukebox]: Requests?

DIABLO: I don't care so long as it was popular before the Beatles came along and screwed up rock 'n roll.

[PATRICK makes a selection. The jukebox plays "Since I Don't Have You" by the Skyliners.]

PATRICK: What the hell's going on here? This place is too crowded. We're never gonna get waited on.

DIABLO: I ordered.

PATRICK: Yeah sure.

DIABLO: Why are you depressed?

PATRICK: Depressed - what are you talking about? I have a bad head cold is all. I feel like shit. Nothing depressing about that.

DIABLO: Smile or something.

PATRICK: What did you order?

DIABLO: A Three Musketeers, a ballpoint pen, a couple flashlight batteries, some beef jerky ...

PATRICK: Go to hell.

DIABLO: I ordered what you asked for. Nothing's wrong here. Relax.

PATRICK: What about their speaking English?

DIABLO: I'm sorry?

PATRICK: I saw this continental guy on TV once and he could count from one to ten in English.

DIABLO: I missed that.

PATRICK: You think it was some kind of trick or something?

DIABLO: Yes, it was a trick.

[COUNTERMAN arrives with their order.]

PATRICK: Oh this hamburger looks beautiful.

COUNTERMAN [smiling]: Thank you, sir.

PATRICK: You're number one with me. You're the greatest - the last beautiful free soul on this planet.

COUNTERMAN [blushing]: It's been a long time, ain't it. *Enjoy.*

PATRICK [turning to DIABLO]: What did you say?

DIABLO: You seem to know a lot of weird guys.

PATRICK: That creep's not a friend of mine. He's just horny. That's why I like you - you're different.

DIABLO: You want a knuckle sandwich?

PATRICK [making an obscene gesture]: Keep your smartass mouth shut.

ACT IV

["Runaway" by Del Shannon plays on the car radio.]

PATRICK: I'm not adding up to anything, am I? Not making any sense here.

DIABLO: No.

PATRICK: That's because I'm running a fever. I feel like total shit today. So hot in here - and sweaty. Anyway, I was saying she left a suicide note that read "All's not lost - I believe in reincarnation" and, uh, she left ... uh, ...

DIABLO: Did you hear that?

PATRICK: What?

DIABLO: A new rattling noise I never heard before.

PATRICK: How about a smoke?

DIABLO: Yeah sure. Thanks.

PATRICK: So how's your leg?

DIABLO: Hurts a little.

PATRICK: Your stomach?

DIABLO: Empty as a basketball.

PATRICK: Your love life?

DIABLO: Still looking for that perfect woman with the midnight qualities.

PATRICK: Lots of those in New York City. So when do you think we meet up with Patty again.

DIABLO: Hard to say.

PATRICK [looking at a road atlas]: Looks to me like somewhere in Ohio or Pennsylvania.

DIABLO: What do you think is the logical explanation for her taking a trip with no luggage?

PATRICK: Why not?

DIABLO: You think she'll threaten suicide again?

PATRICK: Not if she's planning a suicide attack.

DIABLO: But the audience for that shit left twenty years ago.

PATRICK [turning to the AUDIENCE]: I hate to think where that puts me.

[i]

Do they have **to know?**

1. *Fixed groups of associations*

INVESTIGATOR #1: Am I to understand that over a period of seven months you trained yourself to juggle four balls in the air and simultaneously read a newspaper placed on a table in front of you?

PATRICK: That's right.

INVESTIGATOR #1: Why would you do such a thing?

PATRICK: I got the idea from Houdini - that's all.

INVESTIGATOR #1: Why'd you set out to do it?

PATRICK: I needed some new intellectual and physical challenges. I was bored with my life, tired of living … wherever. So I took up juggling to keep myself from getting stuck in a rut.

INVESTIGATOR #1: Then you added reading to the juggling act?

PATRICK: At some point juggling became so automatic, sort of reeled itself off like a spool of tape, so I decided to make the task more challenging by adding reading to it.

INVESTIGATOR #1: You succeeded?

PATRICK: I did. I haven't forgotten either. I'll prove it right here if you bring in some balls and a newspaper.

INVESTIGATOR #1: That's unnecessary.

PATRICK: Wanna give me an IQ test or something? You still believe in the value of a CAT scan? Doesn't anyone around here *walk* anymore? Lain in your lettuce yet?

INVESTIGATOR #1: What? - no.

PATRICK [pressing on his temples]: *What* then? I'm getting hungry, by the way. Maybe you could pop a couple slices of stone-ground whole wheat into the toaster.

INVESTIGATOR #1: Write all food requests on this Post-It note.

PATRICK: That's not exactly what the housekeepers around here call health food. Shit, make it German potato salad and Boston baked beans.

INVESTIGATOR #1 [turning from PATRICK to face the AUDIENCE]: Don't get me wrong here - I'm not an all-knowing expert or a member of the Authenticity Police - but why can't we let guys like this die in peace?

2. *Something less repellant than those strange inanimate objects*
INVESTIGATOR #2: So where did you first meet Patrick?
PATTY: In San Francisco.
INVESTIGATOR #2: Where?
PATTY: In the basement of a place called the Randonnay.
INVESTIGATOR #2: What goes on there?
PATTY: Daydreaming.
INVESTIGATOR #2: How do you mean?
PATTY: You've never daydreamed?
INVESTIGATOR #2: Of course I've daydreamed, but I don't go to a special place to do it.
PATTY: Well, how good are you at controlling your daydreams?
INVESTIGATOR #2: How good am I at daydreaming? Dunno. Never thought much about it. A few years ago I imagined I was a vacuum cleaner salesman.
PATTY: For example, when I'm reading a story I see the things described just as plain as if they were right out there [gesturing away from her body].
INVESTIGATOR #2: I guess I'm not that good.
PATTY: What do you think daydreaming is *for* anyway?
INVESTIGATOR #2: It's using your imagination to fulfill a wish rather than doing the work to make the wish come true in real life.
PATTY: A form of laziness, you mean?
INVESTIGATOR #2 I guess it is in a way - laziness or maybe cowardice. Anyway, if we could, let's return to this place you mentioned - the Randonnay. So that's where you first saw Patrick?
PATTY [pressing on her temples]: As I recall, yes.
INVESTIGATOR #2: Can you tell me about that first encounter?
PATTY: Across the room I saw this tall white figure with piercing black eyes and long black hair.

INVESTIGATOR #2: He was wearing white clothes?

PATTY: I don't know his true race, but that night he *appeared* white - that's it - incredibly *white* - with incredibly *black* eyes and long *black* curly hair. I've never seen such a stark contrast before or since in a, ... uh, in the same person. For a moment I thought I was experiencing a religious hallucination - but I decided against that interpretation. Instead, I decided this great black-and-white figure had sprung fresh from the ground.

INVESTIGATOR #2: So, ... okay ... go on.

PATTY: He studied me for awhile, from a distance, not moving. At first I was frightened, but I got up enough courage to run over to him and introduce myself.

INVESTIGATOR #2: Other people were around?

PATTY: Lots. It was a party atmosphere. So the next thing I noticed, once I got right up to him, was his long fingers and the tiny blue capillaries just below his eyes.

INVESTIGATOR #2: How long were those fingers?

PATTY: Unusually long, to be exact - and he had tentacles for arms.

INVESTIGATOR #2: What?

PATTY: I'm kidding. Jesus - this room's so *cold*. Can someone please bring me a blanket?

INVESTIGATOR #2: We're almost finished with the questioning.

PATTY [shivering]: Please ... I'm cold!

INVESTIGATOR #2: If you could, continue describing that first encounter.

PATTY: He stood there silent, rubbing his hands as if cleansing them of dirt. After awhile, the silence between us became unbearable - similar to intestinal sensations, and when I spoke, he had to stoop over to hear my words against all the commotion.

> "With that long black curly hair and those tremendous fingers, you're a real regular devil, you know that?"
>
> "Why are you so small? You're underweight. Maybe you should put that operating gown back on before the hospital staff return with a broom in their hands and their heads in a bedpan."
>
> "Can I tell you who you look like?"

"You just did - the Devil."

"Clever move. Can I tell you what *else* you look like?"

"Jesus, now I *know* I'm being patronized."

"Hey, c'mon - I'm looking for some company tonight."

"You sure I'm the right one? You look like you're running a temperature."

INVESTIGATOR #2: You don't need to recount the entire conversation verbatim.

PATTY: What the bloody hell are we doing here?

INVESTIGATOR #2: So what happened after that initial conversation?

PATTY: He took me back to a lodging-house where he was staying. We spent the night there, sharing a mattress on the floor, like the rest of the refugees.

INVESTIGATOR #2: An islander refugee camp?

PATTY: That's right. As I recall, in our particular room, there were ten men, three women, six children.

INVESTIGATOR #2: Was that the first contact you'd had with islanders?

PATTY: No, not at all, but it was the first time I slept with one.

INVESTIGATOR #2: Have you ever visited the island?

PATTY: No. Whatever contact I'd had with islanders came from living in San Francisco, where there's a big islander subpopulation, as you know. That's all. I ate at their restaurants, went to their neighborhoods, not much else.

INVESTIGATOR #2: But not long afterwards, you found yourself enjoying Patrick's company, right?

PATTY: Sure. Like so many islanders who spend time on the continent, Patrick grew bored with our cultural emphasis on financial transactions. I think from his perspective most of us continentals are irate taxpayers who mope around in a haze of window-shopping and TV screens. Patrick couldn't stand it. He found [INTERFERENCE] so degrading and [INTERFERENCE]. That's why he was impatient to find ways of invigorating his life and stimulating his intellect.

INVESTIGATOR #2: That's why the two of you decided to take off across the continent on a road-trip? - because you felt degraded?

PATTY: Nothing was holding me in San Francisco. The city was a mess. Refugees crowded the streets. Broken glass everywhere. You remember how chaotic things were in the West Coast cities after the Battle of Praise Hills. It was crazy. When Patrick said he wanted to go east, I asked if I could come along - he said sure, why not? So we left.

INVESTIGATOR #2: In a stolen car?

PATTY: I didn't steal it.

INVESTIGATOR #2: Why go to Nevada?

PATTY: Dunno. You'll have to ask Patrick that one.

INVESTIGATOR #2: How long did you stay in Nevada till you continued eastward?

PATTY: Three weeks, first in small towns, then in Las Vegas.

INVESTIGATOR #2: Did you see Patrick meet with anyone - islanders, for example?

PATTY: He met with quite a few people when we were in Las Vegas. I imagine some of them were islanders - hard to tell sometimes. I didn't pay much attention.

INVESTIGATOR #2: What did he talk to those people about?

PATTY: I was never around to listen.

INVESTIGATOR #2: He forbid you from being present at those conversations?

PATTY: I just never heard what they were talking about.

INVESTIGATOR #2: Was there any particular individual he seemed to favor over others?

PATTY: Diablo.

INVESTIGATOR #2: You were first introduced to Diablo in Las Vegas?

PATTY: Yeah. I got to know him quite well. He was Patrick's advisor. Coffee was his favorite beverage. Great smile, great enthusiasm for life - and what an imagination! He was adept at convincing you he had a heroin habit.

INVESTIGATOR #2: Are you aware that Diablo's an islander?

PATTY: That's a point of controversy. He's such a good method actor, no one's sure whether he's an islander or a continental ... or what's going on there.

INVESTIGATOR #2: No - you're wrong about that. He *is* an islander. We have the documentation to prove it.

PATTY: Well I'm sure you'd never want to claim him as a continental even if he were one, what with his *apparent* criminal activity.

INVESTIGATOR #2: You dunno what you're talking about. He's an islander who's been hiding out on the continent, living a life of crime for more than a decade. We know about his so-called 'redecorating networks.'

PATTY: Then why are you interrogating me if you know so much about him? What a waste of time! You must also know he hangs an old Kentucky rifle over the fireplace mantel.

INVESTIGATOR #2: So, the three of you - Diablo, Patrick, yourself - traveled east from Las Vegas?

PATTY: Yeah, in two cars. Diablo and I drove that old Firebird. Patrick drove a different car, a Toyota, I think.

INVESTIGATOR #2: Why that arrangement?

PATTY: Mostly to stimulate the intellect, keep our bodies feeling alive. We set up a sort of race to answer the basic question, Who can reach Minnesota the fastest?

INVESTIGATOR #2: Who did?

PATTY: That's where things get hazy - for me, at least. ... It was wintertime. The further east we drove, the heavier the snow got. We got as far as ... uh, I think we reached Colorado or somewhere in Kansas.

INVESTIGATOR #2: Our records have all three of you turning up in Minnesota.

PATTY: Yeah, of course, like I said, Minnesota was the goal from the outset. But between Nevada and Minnesota, the sights, sounds, and smells become hazy - to me at least.

INVESTIGATOR #2: So why Minnesota?

PATTY: Christmas shopping - shit, I dunno - maybe to stimulate the intellect, keep our bodies feeling alive by braving the rigors of a northern Minnesota winter.

3. *Living history's not a new technique*

INVESTIGATOR #1: If we could, I'd like you to take us back to when you first decided to break off your relationship with Patty and Diablo.

PATRICK: Those are two different things, two different breakups.

INVESTIGATOR #1: Then let's take them one at a time. Which came first?

PATRICK [pressing his temples]: Patty - leaving Patty behind, me and Diablo leaving Patty.

INVESTIGATOR #1: Okay.

PATRICK [pressing temples harder]: Dunno. A lot of what happened between Minnesota and here in New York City is hazy. Keep in mind I'm your typical islander. I'm not a packrat like most of you continentals - I don't covet my memories or keep books of snapshots. I value my psychotic tendencies. Half the time I can't separate reminiscences from wishful thinking.

INVESTIGATOR #1: Well, try.

PATRICK. Okay, so somewhere in, … east of Minnesota, … Indiana, I think, we ditched the Firebird at an Interstate truck-stop, replaced it with an SUV of some type.

INVESTIGATOR #1: You stole an SUV?

PATRICK: We sure didn't buy the damn thing. Anyway, that Firebird was on its last legs. So we took this SUV, and … [laughing] … weird thing about that was whoever owned the SUV was using it as a moving van [laughing louder this time]. In the back there was all this weird stuff like you might find in a museum or something. I remember driving and Diablo in the back going through this loot - a World War One gasmask, a fake Thompson submachine gun, a Roman gladiator's breastplate, a real powdered wig, few dozen cartons of cigarettes, a large bottle of carrot juice, a mangled saliva-drenched cigar. Other stuff too, I imagine, whips, corsets, garter belts, lots of leather straps, VHS tapes, a nice Catholic girlfriend. As we drove, Diablo started throwing the shit out the back windows [pressing his temples, eyes squinting]. What a waste of time.

INVESTIGATOR #1: I don't need this detail.

PATRICK: Well, I don't understand *what* you need.

INVESTIGATOR #1: Okay, go on.

PATRICK: Our original plan was to rendezvous with Patty in Ohio. But I think somewhere outside Cleveland, near the Pennsylvania border, we pulled over to another Interstate truck-stop to get something to eat. ... Now, *this* part I remember like it was yesterday.

"I'll take two hotdogs with everything, an order of onion rings, a black coffee."

"I'll take the same but leave the hot sauce off the hotdogs, please, and add a hot fudge sundae piled high with whipped cream and sprinkles."

[COUNTERMAN walks away.]

"Damn, I can't believe it's snowing this far east."

"Going east has no bearing on the matter. Fact is, we're pretty far north. I wouldn't be surprised if we have to deal with snow all the way to New York City."

"So now it's waiting time, huh, wait until Patty shows up?"

"Yeah we could wait - or we could push on through."

"Leave Patty behind?"

"I mean, she'll make it to New York City. So I'm saying there's no

reason we *have* to meet up with her before the city."

"Fair enough. But she'll get pissed off about it."

"She has our number. She knows how to reach us. It's not like she's

never gonna hear from us again."

[COUNTERMAN arrives with the food.]

INVESTIGATOR #1: That settled it? You kicked her out like that.

PATRICK: Pretty much. No reason to make a big fuss about it. We ate the hotdogs and ketchup-covered onion rings, got back on the road. Then around Buffalo we hit a major winter storm, forcing us to stop for the night.

INVESTIGATOR #1: So let's fast forward to New York City.

PATRICK: Fast forward to 'stalled in traffic on I-95'? Don't you wanna hear about Diablo?

INVESTIGATOR #1: What?

PATRICK: About what happened to Diablo?

INVESTIGATOR #1: You mean you severed your relations with Diablo *before* arriving in New York City? That's odd. In your affidavit you said the breakup occurred *after* the two of you arrived in the city.

PATRICK: I've talked to so many people recently, I don't know what affidavit you're referring to. On top of that, I have great difficulty keeping all your legal terms straight. Affidavit ... deposition ... uh, testimony, what have you - I've heard those words used a million times, but this whole experience is one long drawn-out conversation to me. I'm not clear where one dialogue ends and the next begins.

INVESTIGATOR #1: So earlier when you said you split with Diablo in New York City, you were lying?

PATRICK: Uh, no, not at all. Can you *accidentally* lie? - not by my definition. Like I said, my memory's spotty on these things - it's part of my insular upbringing. We don't take tradition and progress as seriously as you do on the continent. We don't think data processing's the wave of the future. That's why we don't expect much from the past to help rationalize our plans for the future. We acknowledge up front everything's got a built-in arbitrary nature.

INVESTIGATOR #1: If we could get on with the questioning - I'm not interested in hearing your personal theories on society. So then, describe how you split with Diablo.

PATRICK: He's still alive, you know.

INVESTIGATOR #1: I'm not interested in hearing you speculate on something you cannot know about. So, do you remember where you split with Diablo?

PATRICK: In a small motel outside Buffalo, New York. But then psychopaths are consummate liars, right?

INVESTIGATOR #1: I see you're no longer interested in cooperating with me today. Fine. We can take this up tomorrow. I'm in no hurry. I get paid one way or the other.

PATRICK: That's kind of a sticky wicket, isn't it? Getting paid one way or the other.

INVESTIGATOR #1 [turning around to leave the cell]: We'll continue tomorrow morning, and you better be more cooperative!

PATRICK: You think I'm psychotic? Why don't you mind your own damn business?

[INVESTIGATOR #1 says nothing, leaves the cell.]

PATRICK [turning to face the AUDIENCE]: I tried but I can't get through to the man. I'm dealing with a real pro here. He needs to do his legal things to keep his job. But I wonder why his robes are streaked with blood and his major arteries are clogged.

[j]

The dream's always stays the same.

Everyone! [to the AUDIENCE] - novelists! moral philosophers!
social scientists! clinicians! jurists! deputy sheriffs & district
attorneys! - before you listen to me plead insanity, please look
over there [pointing]. You'll notice a large mirror's attached to the
back wall of the auditorium. A Franklin stove's also attached to
the wall. A dart board's attached to the wall. Feel free to attach
some of your own things to that wall. Let's put lots and lots of
stuff on that wall. Let's let deadly ants crawl up that wall. Then
let's brush off the ants and beautify the wall. Some of the
decorations will be askew, I know, but that's a consequence of the
crowding of impenetrable material objects: a sad fact of our
social reality. Car owners are furious about that fact. The size of
their respective garages limits the number of cars they can park
inside. Too bad they don't have the slightest respect for their own
imaginations - - but that's a different (separate) issue from our
social reality. The topic of *this* entire story? - a love story? - yes,
a very contemporary romance about opposites attracting and
repelling each other eighty-thousand times (before I run out of
useful things to say).

Back in the motel room I can't believe Patty forgot to eat
her jelly donut. Such deformation of character! I'm calling
the Duluth police. You watch - the officers will bring their
BB guns too. Patty's barely *what?* eighteen? nineteen?
twenty? It's uncanny - her birthday was yesterday. Now
she's vanished. "Precocious" I say over the phone. "Let me
tell you that girl's capable of far more than any law
enforcement officer can hope to imagine." Now she's gone
off in the middle of the night, got on a bus to some broken-
down place never to set foot in Minnesota again (didn't like
it much here anyway.) I slam down the receiver. Next I'm
hearing a sound enter my head, the sound that precedes the

sounds of approaching sirens, the businesslike sound of the local radio station playing rock 'n roll oldies. After that, the sound of exhaled cigarette smoke ruffles the pages of an upscale men's clothing catalog. I stub out the cigarette, stand up, shuffle over to the room's window, look out at the parking lot and the barren autumn landscape beyond. This time of year Minnesota grows very cold late in the evening. That explains the headaches, the slips of the tongue and cognitive slippage, the names of material objects forgotten (replaced?) by [INTERFERENCE]. Napkin holders. Candlesticks. Vases. A smudged mirror. A hundred acres of prime real estate permanently deformed outside this cracked misshapen window. "Metalworking" I say aloud to myself. "Who's being buried here?" an imaginary voice asks me. "Zhivago" I reply. "Oh I see" they answer - while the radio blares "Lucille" by Little Richard.

> The faux funereal atmosphere's like an advance warning of what's to come. I wanna say something wise about gambling, something expeditious yet cautionary - but that's my first mistake. As I look out over the casino floor, downright indecent thoughts begin racing through my head, thousands of thoughts (as Horace puts it). But don't be angry, kind reader, if, at least for now, I don't repeat them all. Those thoughts don't know a thing about theory so they're unimportant here. Instead I listen to combative discussions erupt over chance and probability before scores of gamblers hurtle towards the tables. Then I look up. Buzzards lazily circle us eying a pile of delectable dead carcasses. Then I look down. On the pit's perimeter countless rattlesnakes [INTERFERENCE]. Dammit this is Apache territory. Injuns are trailing me! You pull out a knife (or shot glass), you better know how to use it around here. I can't keep up. Diablo's much too quick for me. He bets more money than I thought humanly possible. Before can I stop him he sits down at the nearest

roulette table, places ten purple $500 chips on black. That's when the air flows right outta me. That's when I wish I were a debt collector for this casino or at least a descendant of a rich king or prince from olden times. When do we scoop up *our* earnings, Diablo? Where's *my* funnel? Oh that's right, gambling doesn't work that way. Don't reckon I have much choice in the matter. Instead I imagine, beneath these luxurious floorboards, huge infernal engines chugging out number after number as if by black magic.

MIMI: Thanks for coming up to me like that. You're one hell of a storyteller. But I wonder, how much of it's true, and why's it so out of order?

PATRICK: It's in the order my memory works.

MIMI: You got early-onset Alzheimer's?

PATRICK [pointing out the cab's window]: Looks like the snow's changing to rain … or sleet. Weird weather for Thanksgiving. It's getting dark so early too. This can't be typical for New York. It's not how I imagined it.

[MIMI's cellphone rings]

MIMI [to phone]: We're on our way, should be there in ten-fifteen minutes. Yep, that's right. We're coming up from Alphabet City. Okay, see you soon.

PATRICK [to the cab driver]: Could you turn up the radio. I like this song.

[Cab radio plays "One Hundred Pounds of Clay" by Gene McDaniels.]

PATRICK [to MIMI]: I'm impressed the city's cab drivers listen to rock 'n roll oldies.

MIMI: That was my dad on the phone. Sounds like we'll arrive just as they're pulling the turkey from the oven.

PATRICK: Amazing timing.

MIMI: I think you'll like the apartment. It's a classic Upper East Side place. Across the street there's a police station.

PATRICK: Whole family's gonna be there?

MIMI: Father, brother, and sister - actually stepfather, stepbrother, and stepsister. My brother and sister are much younger than me. I'm the only islander in the family.

PATRICK: You were part of that old adoption program, to help reduce the island's population, right?

MIMI: Yep.

PATRICK: So where's your real mom?

MIMI: She's dead, died a long time ago on the island. Met her only once. Don't remember my grandparents.

PATRICK: Your mother had other children?

MIMI: Dunno much about my mother. Like I said, I met her only once, and that was after the stroke. She wasn't able to talk, spent her time in a convalescent home watching TV and reading magazines. The one time I saw her, she mistook me for one of our neighbors. Not a pleasant experience. Anyway, I think you'll like my stepfather, although I gotta warn you he comes from a military family.

PATRICK: How about your stepmother?

MIMI: They're divorced so she won't be there. She's a big-shot architect here in the city. We don't get along so well. She's thinks I'm throwing my life away even though I've never felt happier.

PATRICK: Why stress yourself out about it? Parents want only what's best for their children. You could have it worse. Look at the poor guy [pointing out the window] changing a tire in the pouring rain.

MIMI: Was that thunder? Weird. Never seen anything like this weather before. I get the feeling something's about to happen.

PATRICK: Something's always 'about to happen' [air-quotes].

MIMI: Like over there [pointing]. See? - appears to be a street protest.

PATRICK: Oh yeah. Is that a convoy of military vehicles?

MIMI: Seems to be … one angry-looking crowd.

PATRICK: 'Unruly' is the word I'd use. I bet a few people get trampled to death tonight, big teenage boys mostly.

Patty: Protests are common in the city this time of year.

PATRICK: Seasonal affective disorder?

MIMI: You'd think everyone'd be in a holiday sort of mood.

PATRICK: No, that mood officially kicks off tomorrow, the day *after* Thanksgiving. For now they're obsessed with finding new ways of terrorizing each other.

MIMI: You're saying the protest is one big hoax?

PATRICK [to cab driver]: Why's it so hot in here?

MIMI: Leave him alone.

PATRICK: Yeah you're right - look at him up here behind the wheel. He's a bloodthirsty warrior in his chariot.

MIMI [laughing]: Those sunken cheeks and bloodshot eyes. We'll be there soon.

PATRICK: I hate winter, not just here in New York but everywhere. In Duluth it was so cold and dark all the time.

MIMI: It's brighter above the clouds.

PATRICK: Assuming they let you fly.

This [INTERFERENCE] isn't a simple case of amnesia, nor is it glaucoma. Yet you tell me a kind of stained magnificence hints at alien forgotten behaviors here. Well, you're right. Nothing's left to worry about, reader. We got things under control. Nothing's more clear-cut than the impact of ridiculous accusations on a writer trained in patience. So pop those rich brown waffles into the toaster. Pour yourself a cup of muddy brown coffee. Feel that blast of hot air. Let's eat a quick breakfast. We're hungry. Two or three hours have passed but we still got time - to think and plan. That's the worst part of this job, nearing the end of a story, the part that keeps me awake at night, makes me feel uncomfortable - as if finespun linen were knotted loosely round my neck. (Problem's every alphabet eventually exhausts its possibilities: when a drama's combatants tire from delirium or mania (as they must), they start to miss something inside themselves - the dust of distance gets beaten right out of them: they realize there's *white* between these words.) Anyway, I notice Diablo's turkey sandwich is still untouched. Well, take your hands away from the plate and exercise your imagination. Add some pepper to the stuffing. I don't care if you eat Thanksgiving Day leftovers for breakfast. Simply chew the food then spit it out. Happy holidays, Diablo! By the way, what's that explosive thing you got strapped to your saddle-roll? And what's your full name again? When I saw you through the window I got frightened - yeah I'm kidding!

A bitter wind drives the angry choppy waters across the channel. Why are the waters angry? Who so many whitecaps? And why's the wind so bitter? Why do waves slap so hard against the sides of the ferry? What kind of idiocy could *that* be [pointing at the (bulging?) gray sky]? Well, Patrick blames the water's anger on the battle raging round him. The gunships, warships, battleships, enormous orange fireballs. Indeed, soot-speckled historians (who exposed themselves to us in the past) would call this the Battle of Praise Hills. Yes, continental forces first came ashore at Praise Hills, very near where Patrick and his mother once lived in that hideous mansion with its twisted gables, oak-bannistered stairways, wavering apparitions, and clutter of empty wine and ale bottles, the mansion called Elsinore (since burned to the ground (with a euthanized mother inside)). Continental forces just rolled across the beach right up to Elsinore's smoldering ruins. That's how the invasion went down. So what's new here? Haven't islanders and continentals fought this battle before, balancing their figures over and over again only to fall from God's natural grace? Dunno. Stop asking me those questions and ladle some soup into my silver bowl. God, I wish I were born deaf!

[k]

Um, horse tranquilizer.

1. *Germany is* not *Hamlet*
MOTHER: Just consider how they spell words like 'duty' and 'integrity.' You *know* the continentals, Patrick. I don't have to tell you. … If you're in close contact with 'em, like your father and I were for so many years when we worked in San Francisco, you see their obnoxious charm, well, … a virus, an emotional virus - not biological - infecting their own and islanders as well. They should apologize for that charming disease rather than punish *us*, but they refuse. They're that stupid. I see it all the time right there [pointing at the TV from her bed]. Is it a question of money?
PATRICK: You always have the right answer.
MOTHER: How many cigarettes you smoked today?
PATRICK: One too many.
MOTHER: For all you smoke, for all that smoking and partying - blame the continentals for that too.
PATRICK: It's hard to take you seriously in this state, Mother. Here you are, on the verge of dying, yet you feel you must do this, uh … cruel rant against continentals.
MOTHER: A final list of grievances, quite good, yes, a list - while all around us, out on the channel [gesturing to the windows], the military's closing in, cordoning off [labored coughing].
PATRICK [shaking his head]: I got grievances too. More than ever, this planet needs the proper scale to show everyone, continental and islander alike, what can and cannot be accomplished in a single lifetime. The fact there's no scale makes me very sad.
MOTHER [laughing]: Listen to yourself. Scale? *Today* is history - tomorrow's history - yesterday *was* history. That's the only scale you got, only scale that matters. Today will be remembered for its battles won, battles lost, each day, what's unknown, what includes another wonder. *Today* is history, Patrick - you own it.

History lasts longer than a thousand-year occupation of a tiny island. If the continentals are to blame for other problems too, the so-called Great Criminality, or the [coughing]. Remember this - continentals have been trying to invade this island for centuries - every single time repulsed. Their leaders bet their political livelihoods on taking over the cities and shores of this island, and in the end they make *us* pay for their pathetic ambitions. *We* are the ones arrested for blocking their military, the ones thrown in jail for terrorism - while every year a few more continentals succeed in setting up schools, businesses, science labs, 'culture centers' all around us. That's what continentals do in the face of a culture that doesn't share their aspirations - destroy it, either outright with a military or mischievously through business dealings. At the end of the day, continentals cannot develop into a more enlightened society. For most of our lives, your father and I [coughing] learned that. But for you, Patrick, *today* is world history.

PATRICK: Jesus, Mother, I graduated from the local seminary with a degree in theology.

MOTHER: Ah, of course, I forgot. You're already infected … behaving like an educated continental, like {//-redacted-//}.

PATRICK: You know you're not allowed to mention that name even in the privacy of your own home!

MOTHER: Ah, of course, I forgot - the death penalty. Shhhh! What? They're gonna take me out, shoot me [laughing] while I languish here on my 'deathbed' [air-quotes] complaining of pancreatic cancer?

PATRICK: You know my stand on this. I'm trying to do a job here - that's my contribution - teaching young islanders there's more to life than school education.

MOTHER: Well, you're right.

PATRICK: Yet all you can do is say how behind everything lurks the evil influence of the continent. What islander can ever be worthy to you?

MOTHER: No, no, no, no - You can do whatever you want. You're an adult.

PATRICK: You're not treating me that way.

MOTHER: I *want* you to reach out to our youth - I do - that's why I support you. I want you to save our children from [INTERFERENCE] of a bogus adulthood. What I'm saying is social problems continue to plague us and I see the process [gesturing to the TV]. Anyway, I understand you're not like me or your father, not a person *literally*, but, uh, your view's right, I suppose. Maybe it'll turn out I'm the one who's wrong compared to your diplomas. I'm the vermin, rodents … fleas. I, uh, … you make some good points [leaning forward to kiss PATRICK's forehead].

PATRICK [recoiling from the bedside]: Jesus Christ, Mother, you're out of your mind! *You* yourself suggested I go through the education and get the diploma to help blend in better and disrupt continental values from the inside out. Remember that phrase - 'inside out'? You decided your and Father's approach failed, so it was time for a new kind of rebellion, subversion, whatever.

MOTHER: No, Patrick, I think not. Your father told me this little, … Isn't it, uh …?

PATRICK: You'll never learn. At this point in you life, you're better off that way anyhow - stuck in a rut. I don't know. When you ... were better.

[MOTHER yawns.]

PATRICK [glancing at his watch]: It's eleven. One of my students will be here soon.

MOTHER: If your father and I'd made more money, not thrown so much away [yawning] might be evidence the continentals are giving up on destroying the island, focusing on destroying themselves instead. So future generations … aren't … you're … done for.

PATRICK: Enough! You're not making any sense. I don't care to hear what you're saying.

MOTHER: You're too kind. So how many students are you tutoring these days?

PATRICK [standing up, stepping back from the bed]: At the moment, ten, ten students.

MOTHER: You think it's safe bringing them here to Elsinore?

PATRICK: Yeah sure.

MOTHER: *How* can you be sure?

PATRICK: Let's talk about this later, okay?

MOTHER: Let me understand - you earn money from your tutoring work, yet you're not doing what I asked you to do?

PATRICK: *Asked* me to do? I took … I, uh, I can assure you I'm doing fine.

MOTHER [pointing at the TV]: I see the military's out there in the channel.

PATRICK: Was there ever a time they weren't?

MOTHER: I want you to help our people - my people - the islanders, generations of islanders - the people I …

PATRICK [shaking his head, smirking]: You sound like Moses.

MOTHER [starting to sob]: Not me! That's not what I'm good for … not working, not working.

PATRICK: Forget it, Mother - I'm not feeling sorry for you, so cry if you want.

MOTHER: You're certainly not Moses!

PATRICK: And you're certainly hysterical.

MOTHER: Please bring me my brunch before you start the tutoring.

PATRICK: Yes, of course.

MOTHER: I forgive you.

PATRICK [turning around from the bed, walking to the door]: No, you don't forgive me at all. You keep pushing on me. One day, if you're not careful, you might just kill me.

MOTHER: I push on you because I love you.

PATRICK: You push on me because you love your *idea* of me.

MOTHER: I have that idea of you because I've learned from my mistakes and know what it takes to become the best possible person.

PATRICK: You don't realize there's more than your own way to recover from mistakes and become a better person.

MOTHER: Your problem's you don't realize I speak from a place of genuine authority.

PATRICK: Your problem's you can't see beyond your own ego.

MOTHER: Nor can you, Patrick.

PATRICK: I guess we're screwed.

MOTHER: I guess I can't forgive you after all.

[PATRICK leaves the room to get MOTHER's brunch.]

2. *E 10th & Avenue B*

MIMI: So you killed her?

PATRICK: She was in a great deal of physical pain from the cancer.

MIMI: But did she *ask* you to put her out of her misery?

PATRICK: In so many words, yes.

MIMI: How many words?

PATRICK: By the time she died, Mother was so at odds with the world around her, not just the continent but the island too. All that physical pain … I don't think it made any sense for her to go on living. Only thing she had going for her was the TV, cartoons, and breakfast cereal.

MIMI: Sounds like the recipe for a nervous breakdown.

PATRICK: She'd been through a couple of those many years before. This time around it was a recipe for that ultimate personal disaster known as death.

MIMI: That's why you killed her? I mean no disrespect - I know you're a brilliant genius and all - but you murdered your Mother because she was bedridden?

PATRICK: Not *me* exactly. I had one of the many nurses or nurse assistants who've attended to Mother over the years inject her with a high dose of barbiturate mixed with a synthetic morphine derivative, to kill her instantly and minimize the physical distress.

MIMI: Assisted suicide.

PATRICK: Or lethal injection - depending on how you look at it. Afterwards I'd hoped to sell Elsinore. But before that could happen, as you know, the continental military attacked the island, triggering the Battle of Praise Hills and forcing me to get the hell out.

MIMI: What's Elsinore?

PATRICK: Our family's mansion - if it's still standing. I have no way of knowing.

MIMI: You *named* your house?

PATRICK: Father did, named it like a pet - pretentious bullshit, right? - named it after the castle in Shakespeare's Hamlet.

MIMI [laughing]: You're the worst tourist in the world.

PATRICK: Let's stop talking about me and pretend you're my beautiful girlfriend. I won't tolerate anyone around here looking at you [gesturing to the crowds walking through Tompkins Square Park].

MIMI: Were they - just now?

PATRICK: Sure, why not?

MIMI: Seeing what? Seeing *here* [gesturing to her breasts]? They can see below there too [gesturing to her crotch]? You mean I can't let my ass out to dry?

PATRICK: I know this neighborhood used to be crawling with prostitutes.

MIMI: If you looked in the right places, sure. That was years ago.

PATRICK: I may've grown up on the island with my dick in my hand, but I *know* you can find bloody prostitutes around here. Prostitution's good. Children may wanna grow up worshipping that pussy.

MIMI: Thank you.

PATRICK [standing up from the grass]: Okay, I retract that bit about pussy. C'mon, let's go.

MIMI: Where now?

PATRICK: What are you deaf? - for a walk.

MIMI: We just sat down.

PATRICK: Can't get stuck in a rut now can we?

MIMI [standing up, brushing offer her pants]: So did you have your father murdered too?

PATRICK [putting his arms around MIMI's waist as they begin walking down 10th Street]: No, he was assassinated before I could consider that option.

MIMI: Assassinated?

PATRICK: That's what they call it when someone very important is murdered.

MIMI [stopping in her tracks]: I thought that's what they call a crucifixion. By the way, do you know where you're going?

PATRICK: Let's follow this street, see where it takes us. It's called sightseeing.

MIMI: I know where it takes us - to the other side of the island.

PATRICK: Sounds good. ... C'mon let's go. I wanna see all of Manhattan's dirty inanimate objects.

MIMI [sighing]: You know karate?

PATRICK: The name's not familiar, no, we never met. Ah, I know, bad joke. No, I don't know any martial arts.

MIMI: Don't bother learning. My lower back's been killing me all week.

PATRICK [patting a trouser pocket]: I got a strong horse tranquilizer you might wanna ... ah, okay - another bad joke. Horse tranquilizers are serious business around here.

MIMI: What are talking about?

PATRICK: Just bullshit.

MIMI: Let's talk about something else. Like why you came to New York City.

PATRICK: I came here to shoot black wind ten years on a machine.

MIMI: They don't allow that in the city limits.

PATRICK: Shit, they don't allow anything on the continent - but I know anything's possible.

MIMI: But not *that*, what you just mentioned.

PATRICK: Okay I won't hold it against you.

MIMI: So why'd you come here?

PATRICK: To get a better price for my dead cat.

MIMI: C'mon!

PATRICK: I wanna rebalance the continent in favor of insular culture over mindless fun.

MIMI: How?

PATRICK: Let's talk about this a bit latter, okay?

MIMI: How do you like the city now that you're here?

PATRICK: I love it. I'm having a real good time. I feel like a big fat cock after screwing a black girl on a swing in the countryside.

MIMI: What the hell's *that*? I'm not sure knowing you is the real thing. In your world, everything derives from killing or sex.

PATRICK: That's the story of our people, no?

MIMI: What were you doing before you arrived in the city?

PATRICK: I was trying to steal a ... a, uh ... I took my hands from his uh, and ... discovered throats are full of emptiness. Then

I turned to avoid that look in his eyes - but now I see those eyes on fire again … like the medics said would happen, … uh, and you know the last thing I said to him as he lay there dying in that ridiculous bunny rabbit costume?

MIMI: What?

PATRICK: "Keep the door open, you stupid rock man!"

MIMI: Are you Irish?

PATRICK: That's right - Ireland - in the original.

MIMI: Plus English humor?

PATRICK: Jesus, Mimi, I'm trying to talk about something too strong or higher, … rather than strangling people and making fun of foreigners for not exchanging their money.

MIMI: I wanna know - I'm curious - how many people have you killed in your life?

PATRICK: I cannot answer that.

MIMI: How many have you crucified?

PATRICK: An insufficient quantity.

MIMI: If you were in a movie, I bet the dream sequence would be warped.

PATRICK: If I were in a movie, I'd commit suicide. Don't hold it against me.

MIMI: It'd be a classic film, I'm sure, absolutely incredible.

PATRICK: Everyone would have the acid and happiness for you too.

MIMI: You islanders are crazy.

PATRICK: I got no idea what you're referring to.

[1]

Above the elbow crushed right into one of the bookcases (Or, watch out where you take things from before you decide on where to take them to)

Shit, I'm *not* in the proper mood to analyze any singular human experience. Let's take a break from writing and editing. Let's explore Buffalo's museums, attend to its theatres and marketplaces. Let's wipe the perspiration and caked dust from our brows and pretend we're homesteaders moving in for the night. There's plenty of land around here. The beef's always better at the beginning. I'm fascinated. I enjoy the theatre, the detachment of being in the audience. I can watch a drama without participating in it, without allowing it to influence me. That's a wise perspective. A man who watches what goes on around him will surely make his mark. That's why I enjoy watching movies. I'm an idealist. I enjoy collecting and recombining my thoughts rather than expressing them. I don't need to talk much about myself. *Whew!* The air inside the auditorium's getting cooler. I see Diablo's bleeding from a stab wound up on stage. I shake my head free of that [INTERFERENCE], yet my neck's stretched out farther than is humanly possible. I gotta see what's gonna happen next. Something always 'happens next' - the question's whether what happens makes <u>sense</u> to the audience. Of course, that question involves notions of <u>causality</u>.

> Why am I laughing? Funny, thinking about that final breakfast at our favorite diner in downtown Duluth - the wilting bouquet of fresh zinnias on the table, the dining area's pink businesslike wallpaper, the blueberry flapjacks, sliced mangoes, and Diet Coke with very little ice. Such were Patty's favorite culinary deformations. Oh my God, she's spilling Diet Coke down the front of her dress. Look at that! Now the sweet liquid's all gone. The coffin lid's closed, nailed shut. You can climb down from the

windowsill [pointing at the AUDIENCE]. I always said if I
had a sister I'd name her Patty, short for Patricia. She'd be
skinny, her hair cut short like a boy's. She'd be my
understudy, for awhile, till she learned how to live on her
own - like a daughter, I suppose, a daughter who's lost her
taste for hard candy. She'd be a wonderful dancer too,
ballet, tap-dancing, you name it. She'd go without food
sometimes - to remain skinny. Dancers must be rail-thin in
their little outfits resembling bathing suits. Funny, thinking
about Patty leaving Duluth all by herself, heading to New
York City for some fast-paced action and eclectic dancing
styles. What's going on in the big city anyway? The streets
are downright narrow, the cars much too small, the heights
of the buildings straining upward against the downward
displacement of traffic (Bernoulli effect: road rage or
murder?). It's hard speaking about New York City now,
even as a physicist. I know I laugh too much, doctor. Thing
is, I thought Patty'd be halfway to Moscow by now. But she
twisted an ankle, never fully recovered, had to give up
dancing for world travel and apologetic [INTERFERENCE].

    Dreams, piles of preposterous dreams we've
memorized from the only songs we know by heart,
provide much needed relief from the smoky yellow
false sunlight, the dark squatting shapes - and the
towering yet crumbling walls of sound. First of all I
can hear the slot machines. Then I hear the moans of
gamblers calling out to God & Mother (the drone of
bagpipes?). Then I smell the odors. Burning plastic?
Mix it up - mix it up, man! Over *there* [pointing] I
see a brightly lit coffee shop, a sushi bar, a pizza
parlor, a French bistro, a German beer hall, a soul
food outlet. But I'm not hungry for generous portions
of smoked beef tongue and caviar from Provence.
Liquid crystal screens attached to the casino's
mirrored walls display a succession of kingdoms and
empires whose names I cannot bear to repeat here.
Perhaps I owe this place the courtesy of staying outta

their business. Perhaps, as I watch Diablo rear up and head to the nearest craps table, I should console myself with the thought that our lives will turn grander the further east we travel. Yet nothing I perceive here can stanch this flow of downright indecent thoughts. Why's that? It's all lies and nonsense. Who do they think they're bluffing? Everything on the continent eventually ends in gambling and drunkenness.

PATRICK: This is quite a Thanksgiving Day spread, intimidating. I feel like we got a hostage situation here - held hostage by our appetites.

FATHER [laughing]: You're somewhat funny. Please, sit down, dig in. Hey, everyone [calling into the living room], dinner's begun!

[MIMI, BROTHER, and SISTER enter the dining room, take their seats at the table.]

PATRICK [to BROTHER]: Why do you stare at me like that? I'm not the bearer of such disturbing news, you know.

MIMI [to PATRICK]: Ignore him. He threatens everyone. That's his thing. Plus he's got a filthy adolescent mouth.

PATRICK: That's okay. I like the looks of your brother. He's a brown-eyed handsome man.

BROTHER [to MIMI]: Your boyfriend's annoying. Plus you're taking sides with him, aren't you? - like the two of you are joined at the hip or something.

MIMI [to BROTHER]: Yes, he *is* my boyfriend - you got a knack for the obvious. Maybe you could introduce yourself and since you think you're so special, sum up yourself as a person.

BROTHER: One of my teachers at school told me I'm a good kisser for my age. How's that for a summary?

MIMI: You're an ass, you know that? Pass the stuffing, Dad.

FATHER: Okay, everyone, what should we drink to today?

BROTHER [ignoring FATHER, turning to PATRICK]: You got a whole worldview, right? - like the rest of the islanders. You won't settle for anything less than the ideal [rolling his eyes]. Well, whatever you *do* settle on, let's hope it's something we can laugh about tomorrow.

FATHER: That's enough! Your attitude's not helping the situation. It's time to make a toast, people. Here everyone [pointing to glasses around the table], try the single-malt scotch.

MIMI: I hate that stuff.

SISTER: Me too.

FATHER: How'd you know? Make the toast with a glass of water or a Sprite.

SISTER: Mimi let me take a sip of beer once.

FATHER: Okay.

MIMI: Why's it so hot in here?

I wish I knew some intriguing French medical terms for non-causal influence, wish I had whole lists of such terms - outrageous medical terms. But I'm unqualified. I haven't the skills. (I'm a theologian, a philosopher, a physicist - in that order.) Besides, outrageousness is the sole work of the devil. That's why he keeps his hair cut short like a little boy's. His job's to distract, and for better or worse the devil's favorite tool is drama. This story would be incomplete if I didn't mention that fact. One paragraph stands in opposition (or responds) to the previous or following paragraph. Within each paragraph, each sentence stands in opposition to the previous or following sentence. Within each sentence, each word stands in opposition to the previous or following word. And within each word, of course, each letter stands in opposition to the previous or following letter. *Whew!* By the way, that process is not dialectical - nothing *ever* overcomes or surmounts something else here - every opposition shares the same ontological plane. I know that's technical but I gotta mention that fact too, so the reader understands my editorial decisions, both good and bad. I hope I inspire you to do what I've attempted to do. I hope by the end of this story you've lost interest in drama and instead prefer to explore the depths of existential boredom. I must admit drama's a damn nuisance (even while it makes me rich and famous).

PATRICK [to BROTHER]: So what do you do for fun?

BROTHER: Play handball and collect fire trucks.

PATRICK: You play darts?

BROTHER: In bars, yeah, when I have a fake ID. Why?

PATRICK [turning to SISTER]: How about you?

SISTER: You got a strong islander accent, don't you?

PATRICK: So I'm told. What do you do for fun?

SISTER: I'm taking dance lessons, ballet.

PATRICK: Where'd you get that colossal-looking T-shirt?

[The chandelier begins flickering.]

FATHER: This is a freak Thanksgiving thunderstorm. Never seen anything like it. First I thought we were getting an early snowfall, but now the winds are picking up and the rain's coming down in sheets. I bet we lose power soon.

PATRICK: Glad I'm not the only one surprised by this weather.

FATHER [turning to BROTHER]: You okay? Want an aspirin? If you're tired, you can go to bed.

MIMI [grabbing BROTHER's arm]: He's still alive - I feel a pulse … barely.

BROTHER: The scintillating conversation makes me wanna light the kitchen on fire.

MIMI [to BROTHER]: You're not gonna try to kill yourself, are you?

BROTHER [leaning back in his chair, rubbing his eyes]: Tell us, Mimi, where'd you get those bruises on your neck and that scar on, uh, on your … ?

PATRICK: So does the family have a pet?

SISTER [smiling]: We have a dog, a pit bull terrier.

PATRICK: Where is he?

SISTER: At the vet, sick with rabies. I think they're gonna put him down.

PATRICK [exhaling loudly]: Who lives up there [pointing to the ceiling], in the attic?

BROTHER: There *is* no attic, moron.

MIMI [glaring at BROTHER, turning to PATRICK]: The cleaning lady used to live upstairs but she's deceased.

FATHER: Acute renal failure.

BROTHER: That was her fault [pointing to MIMI].

MIMI [ignoring BROTHER]: Dunno what's up there now. Storage room, I guess. How can it be *my* fault [turning to BROTHER]? She shot herself through the mouth. I didn't pull the trigger. She was in excruciating pain so she off'd herself.

FATHER: That's right. She should've never taken those black-market fertility drugs. Now let's drop it. So, you got any plans for tomorrow, Patrick? It's the biggest shopping day of the year, you know, Dark Friday.

> Soldiers are yelling and screaming even louder (into the moaning wind no less) than the blanketed refugees who cower from the white puffs of gunsmoke on the decks of the ferry. Dammit - just once can't these soldiers act like real men, throwing their heads back, grinding their teeth down, blowing their bleeding runny noses into scraps of Belgian curtain lace? Look at Patrick lifting up his chin to catch sight of San Francisco far off the distance. Yep, that's the continent [pointing]. That's what awaits you, Patrick, not the plush carpets of Paris, Amsterdam, and Madrid, not the pungent aromas of a Kodiak herring fishery, no, but the absurd pleasures of passing out in a pile of frozen horse manure. A little backbone's all it takes over there - plus lots of money. You call that life? Why not? Glancing back and forth at the refugees' half-frozen faces, then retreating into the shadows, next watching a half-naked boy with mittened hands dance his last steps in the numbing wind, Patrick finally thrusts his fists deep into the pockets of his poncho to remove, in succession, a knife, a cord, and a shiny piece of chocolate.

[m]

A passion for bad weather cannot stop our love affair.

1. *I believe in death, delete, chaos, greed and dirty.*
["Fools Rush In" by Ricky Nelson is playing on the car radio.]
DIABLO: So you killed her out of a weird sense of comic-book realism? You sick [INTERFERENCE].
PATRICK: That remark's stupid. Stop barking threats at me! Come back when you're ready to talk and you know how to submit the proper questions.
DIABLO [adjusting the dashboard heater, lowering his voice]: Man, it's getting cold in here again.
PATRICK: Anyway, I don't care. She needed help so I gave it to her. As Father used to say, "Every autumn, a chicken-humping eagle's coming."
DIABLO: I don't give two shits about what your father said. Fact is, I've lost more than a decade of my life to this continental bullshit. I've lived the snake hours, the scoundrel hours, beat to the fire - I know this ain't no country club. What I *can't* believe is you killed Patty for … what?
PATRICK: I didn't personally kill her, you know.
DIABLO: Like what then?
PATRICK: For all the pain, suffering, vile things the continent inflicted on her - you saw it happening.
DIABLO: Killing her made our lives better? You're not alone here with the repercussions of your decisions.
PATRICK: Yet you think you're the only one who's *right*.
DIABLO: So why lie to me about meeting up with her again in Ohio, Pennsylvania, wherever?
PATRICK: Hey, man, you wanna party tonight?
DIABLO: Dammit, please don't change the subject or put your mouth on restriction. Let *me* ask *you* the questions [pointing at PATRICK].

PATRICK [rolling his eyes]: Tell me straight out - you wanna hear garbage. Well, I'm in no mood for it. Got lots of homework. Can't you close your mouth and drive? After Diabolein and the rest of the training, you still believe in poppycock, but life's too short to be angry all the time asking for explanations. Try reading *Mein Kampf.*

DIABLO: Here's the deal. New York's three or four hours away. We got the time to sort this shit out. That's what we're gonna do.

PATRICK: I'm not apologizing.

DIABLO: I'm not asking for an apology. At this point it's pointless. I wanna understand the why and wherefore. Did you kill Patty out of boredom? What were you trying to prove?

PATRICK: First off - have you forgotten - she was a continental, *and* she was a social parasite. I saw it myself: every night thousands of continental social parasites flow through the boundaries of those West Coast cities. They got their own refugee problem over here.

DIABLO: I know. Black, brown, yellow, whatever.

PATRICK: You forgot she joined me in the beginning because she was bored herself hanging out doing nothing in San Francisco. She stalked islander refugees at those lodging-houses hoping to find a companion, a mate, … someone who … who'd take her on the road, offer her an adventure. So that's what I did. Was it a mistake? - no, not at first. But I soon realized she wasn't interested in learning Diabolein or teaching it to continentals. She wanted to feel special hanging out with subversive islanders.

DIABLO: When did you realize that?

PATRICK: Somewhere in Nevada, … in Las Vegas. Of course you were addicted to those casinos. What did you care, right?

DIABLO: Did she have money problems?

PATRICK: Who knows. That's not the point. Once we got to Minnesota, it should've been obvious to you that her head was in the wrong place. What was the point of that automobile hide-n-go-seek game? It was her idea, remember? - to go driving around the state in the middle of winter to what purpose even now I cannot grasp.

DIABLO: I admit that was weird. But once we settled in Duluth, she ... uh, she helped us.

PATRICK: In reality she screwed that up too.

DIABLO: So this is all by way of saying she deserved to be murdered?

PATRICK: Should I've killed her father instead, bash his head in with a fire extinguisher like I saw in a French movie once?

DIABLO [lifting his two index fingers off the steering wheel]: This does not relate to *that*.

PATRICK: Anyway, I didn't pull the trigger. I hired a drug dealer at the motel to shoot her on his way to collecting his monthly welfare checks.

DIABLO [adjusting the dashboard heater]: Does it seem stuffy in here to you?

["I Will Follow Him" by Little Peggy March begins playing on the car radio.]

2. *E 10th & Third Avenue*

MIMI [whispering]: So you killed him?

PATRICK: Yep.

MIMI: How long did it take?

PATRICK: I didn't personally kill him. I hired a refreshing skinhead-type to make his head explode like a piñata.

MIMI [giggling]: Took you how long to realize the two of you were enemies not friends?

PATRICK: Don't remember.

MIMI: Then what are you doing here in New York?

PATRICK: What do you think?

MIMI: You're making me a little jumpy.

PATRICK: I'm happy. I feel lucky to be in New York. So I had at least two people killed on my trip out here - well, *I* didn't kill them - that must count for something. I may be manipulative but I'm not arrogant. Here's further proof [unbuttons his shirt to reveal a large swastika tattooed on his chest].

MIMI: Now that *is* odd [pointing at PATRICK's chest] - an African-American male with a swastika tattoo. How'd you come by that?

PATRICK: Remember, only this body's black [pointing at his chest], not *me*. Same goes for you - only your body's white, not *you*. One of the key lessons of Diabolein is we are *not* our bodies - rather, our bodies are our instruments. *We* are eternal non-empirical control points.

MIMI: That info's important for me to hear right now?

PATRICK: You bet. So I got the stupid tattoo - yeah I know it's stupid and ugly - to further enhance my disgust for this body. You should do the same, Mimi, feel disgust for your body rather than celebrate it.

MIMI: I do. Look at *this* [unbuttoning her shirt, lifting up her bra to reveal something very strange and impractical].

PATRICK: Nice. Anyway, I think the reason I'm here in New York is to … one of his … yes.

MIMI: C'mon, man. You're not indebted to me, not yet anyway.

PATRICK: Of course that's stupid. I'm not your neck on the phone with some farmers possessing a donkey. Nor am I married to you.

MIMI: You wanna smoke? When was the last time you glanced down at your feet?

PATRICK: When I stomped on Diablo's head.

3. *So, but where to start?*

["He's a Rebel" by the Crystals play on the car radio.]

DIABLO: Right after your mother died, the continental military bulldozed your house?

PATRICK: I burned the place down. There's nothing back there for me to return to, nothing I care about. That's the main reason I plan to make New York my new home, Alphabet City neighborhood to be exact, where an islander friend named Mimi's been living for, oh, five or six years.

DIABLO: Your mother was an important part of your life?

PATRICK: She was always there. By the time she died I suppose I took her for granted, but … yeah, she was a constant presence. If there was something she needed, I was never too far away.

DIABLO: You lived with her?

PATRICK: Most of my life. The older she got, the more she required of my time. I cooked her breakfast, lunch, dinner every day. I combed her hair, brushed her teeth, gave her sponge baths. Every night I read her a book.

DIABLO: You miss her?

PATRICK: Yes and no. On the one hand, she was a valuable advisor. But near the end, her condition was so bad I don't think she intended to live much longer. The pain was too great. She was bedridden. She could barely hold up her side of a conversation without the pain causing her to be in a constant state of rage and agitation. What kind of life's that?

DIABLO: Over here it counts as life.

PATRICK: But as you know, on the island things are different. Euthanasia's something that … Anyway, one thing I learned from the whole experience is that extreme pain causes you to identify with your body again. Here's Mother, who practiced Diabolein on the mental level every day, for decades never identifying with her own body, seeing it as the instrument of a higher self - but when the pain got bad, she regressed to a state where she was so upset with her body she couldn't reason, much less practice Diabolein.

DIABLO: That shouldn't shock you.

PATRICK: I need to pee. Could you pull over at the next exit?

DIABLO: That's all you got to say about your mother?

PATRICK [smiling broadly]: Hello. I'm Forrest - Forrest Gump!

DIABLO: Go to hell.

4. *E 10th & University Place*

MIMI: You're a lot like me, aren't you?

PATRICK: Sure. When I'm tired, I sleep. When I'm hungry, I eat. When I wanna go, I leave.

MIMI: Congratulations!

PATRICK: God's listening - that's the first thing I wanna say.

MIMI: C'mon, let's pick up the pace. We gotta reach the river before the sun sets.

PATRICK: I can't wait to see the shores of New Jersey.

MIMI: God doesn't listen to anyone in New Jersey.

PATRICK: I need to pee. Is there someplace we can stop around here, sandwich shop or something?

MIMI [pointing to a parked car]: Right there's the gutter.

PATRICK: Who do you take me for - a lowlife sucking freak?

MIMI [laughing]: You said you needed to pee.

PATRICK: Don't get me wrong. I love long walks. But where the hell, God, am I supposed to piss around here?

MIMI: In the lower third of Manhattan.

PATRICK: I gotta say there's more trees in these parts than I imagined - and wall-to-wall parked cars.

MIMI: Damn, son, now that we're no longer strangers tell me something about the Battle of Praise Hills. Seems so far away from us here on the East Coast.

PATRICK: I watched it from the deck of a ferry. A big pile of dog shit. You couldn't tell where the sky ended and the end of the world began. It was an obnoxious experience.

MIMI: Wish I'd been there.

PATRICK: Maybe you were.

MIMI: Were you scared?

PATRICK: Don't know. You working tomorrow?

MIMI: Got the day off.

PATRICK: You gonna shut yourself in?

MIMI: If that's my destiny, yeah.

PATRICK: If not?

MIMI: I'll jog to the end of the world.

PATRICK [laughing]: Run, Forrest, run! First try to save yourself time to vacation somewhere, *then* never return.

MIMI: I don't care if I'm on a trip.

PATRICK: I gotta say I almost love you. Why are you so good to me?

MIMI: You're my guy's why!

PATRICK: Whoa. Even if that didn't rhyme, we'd have a problem here - that homeless guy's trying to grab your sleeve.

MIMI: Who?

PATRICK: All of Manhattan knows I'm your gay friend - at least till we reach sight of the Jersey shore.

5. *E, E, E, E, E ...*

["Blue On Blue" by Bobby Vinton plays on the car radio.]

DIABLO: Your mother didn't care about you joining the seminary?

PATRICK: No - she had nothing against the religious life.
DIABLO: But did she realize what it'd entail? - lifelong virginity.
PATRICK: What's normal anyway?
DIABLO: Dying of cancer for one.
PATRICK: Does it feel stuffy in here?
DIABLO: You're getting sick again, aren't you?
PATRICK: What counts as healthy anyway?
DIABLO: No coughs due to colds.
PATRICK: That's it?
DIABLO: Foot doesn't hurt.
PATRICK: These shoes are comfortable. I can't wait to do lots of walking in New York.

6. *W 10th & Avenue of Americas*
MIMI: You're not a killer, right?
PATRICK: That's right. I have a worse condition - I'm a writer. That's why I'm so obsessed with lying.
MIMI: You don't *look* deceptive. So everything's hidden in your handwriting, huh?
PATRICK: Yep.
MIMI: Well, I think the basic joy of reading a story's not knowing what happens in the next sentence.
PATRICK: Or paragraph.
MIMI: Good stories aren't about facts. They're about memories and dreams.
PATRICK: We all need stories to remind ourselves who we are. I'm no different. Next time we meet I won't remember this conversation.
MIMI: Thank God.

7. *Your brains out*
["Next Door to an Angel" by Neil Sedaka plays on the car radio.]
DIABLO: Funny, I don't *know* how long Patty's been gone.
PATRICK: It's like her body's in the trunk or something.
DIABLO: That must suck.
PATRICK: Shit, I don't know how long Mother's been gone either.
DIABLO: What are some things you know for sure?

PATRICK: Most of us live for revenge …
DIABLO: … whether we admit to it or not.

8. *W 10th & 7th Avenue*
MIMI: How'd you say you killed him?
PATRICK: Can't I let myself forget that for now?
MIMI: Make up your own truths then. You're a storytelling liar.
PATRICK: Well, first tell me - what would you kill for?
MIMI: It's easy. You … uh, you …

9. *Hold up a photo of your bloody face*
["Hurts So Bad" by Little Anthony & The Imperials plays on the car radio.]
DIABLO: This is your car.
PATRICK: That's why I'm driving it.
DIABLO: I'm trying to have a little fun here.
PATRICK: Guess what - it's too early in the narrative of our lives for you to know I killed you.
DIABLO: What?
PATRICK [swerving to the side of the road]: Plus I don't want your money.
DIABLO: What then?
PATRICK: I want my life back!

10. *W 10th & 9A*
MIMI: Here it is, end of the line.
PATRICK: So where's New Jersey?
MIMI: Across the river. First we gotta cross this street … then you'll see it. Those trees are sort of blocking the view.
PATRICK: Ah forget it. I don't care. Holy shit - what's that way down there [pointing to the south]. *That.*
MIMI: The Derek Jeter Nine-Eleven Memorial Office Building Complex.
PATRICK: Then let's go this way [pointing northward].
MIMI: All right. I got friends in the Meatpacking District. I suppose we can crash there if it gets too late.

PATRICK: I love walking around like this. I'm getting my life back in order.

MIMI: It's that easy, huh? You … uh, you … what?

[n]

Unruly passenger

This strange throbbing in my left arm's celebration enough for ending your life, Diablo. I don't have to close my eyes to remember the pain. I'm not bewildered or distraught. I don't require an outright acquittal here. I was in the motel room typing (somewhere near Buffalo, New York) when I heard you scream in the bathroom. Did you hear the typewriter from inside there? You were unconscious by the time I reached for the doorknob. I didn't know what'd happened. I can't see through walls. I can't witness every event that precedes death. When I opened the bathroom door I didn't see any blood from a stab wound (at first). Something wasn't wrong with you or the knife that lay at your side. You *were* breathing. You *were* thrusting your face forward. Your cheeks shivered. You tried to bring a hand up to your throat. You were in a great deal of pain. Your face had turned yellow-white. You couldn't get any words out. That's when I decided to send you over to the other side. That's when I reached out for your neck - and squeezed. That's when your face turned smooth, untroubled, and your eyes closed. That's when I loosened my grip from your throat, wiped the perspiration off my forehead. How long did we lie there on the bathroom floor? I didn't blame you for my outrageous (wild?) unpredictable behavior: it was rooted in the tragedy of your failed suicide attempt.

That final morning (in the motel room) I stuck a note for Patty beneath the coffeemaker. I didn't wanna wake her before I left, didn't wanna risk arrest for attempted murder *before* next Wednesday. I needed the extra time to attempt a dramatic escape. That may sound strange now, but everything changed the moment I closed the motel room's door behind me. (My whole body was shaking so hard.) Not actual attempted murder, you understand, oh God no, but [INTERFERENCE]. Thinking back on my childhood, dunno why Mother loved dressing me and my sister alike, in matching coats and mittens. Those cold Duluth winters! Every night Mother in the kitchen chopping vegetables for soup. Father, a high school English teacher and local choir director (his snubbed nose barely stretching out beyond that scrawny neck and bald head), cheering right behind Mother when he wasn't contemplating the great questions of living and dying in northern Minnesota. Oh my God, looks like Patty's spilled tomato sauce down her dress. No wonder I can't help staring at her. We got one hair-raising episode after another here [AUDIENCE laughing]. Father used to tell Patty she was so full of life and energy. He was right. Just look at the way she slammed those kitchen cupboard doors - a force like that carves letters into tombstones.

In the casino lounge, thick smoke settles around me and the video poker terminals. No point rushing the story. Even here I can't escape the sound of money draining from slot machines - one five-hundred-dollar jackpot after another, and lesser payouts that leave the patrons desperately begging for more loss. I find Diablo sitting alone in a booth drinking glass after glass of Chardonnay. His face is ruddy, sun-blistered. Sweat trickles down his cheeks. He looks ridiculous dressed in jeans and a yellow cowboy shirt. "You're not exactly Alan Ladd now are you?" He flips me off. I pinch his neck fat. He punches me in the thigh. I pull up his shirt to expose his ribs. "Yep still flesh and blood." He flips me off *again*. "But next time you slap a woman, I beat your face in, Diablo!" I know he's got a helluva temper. But I can look for trouble too. Plus I make no promises I cannot keep. I step away from the booth, look out over the casino floor, try to spot Patty. That's when I feel my joints lock up, when I feel like a white man stranded in the Nevada desert. Wiping the sweat from my forehead, I realize most of these games require very little skill. You pull a lever, punch a button, wait

for the Hands of Providence to knock you about a bit
- then start all over again. If glass explodes around
you, ricocheting bullets fill the air, paneling cracks
and splinters, you don't care. You're gonna prove
yourself to the laws of chance one way or another,
earlier if not later, *once* upon a time. It's the repetitive
nature of gambling that turns me off (like weekly
television programming). I hate getting stuck in a rut.

FATHER [to PATRICK]: You been in the city for how long - three
months?

PATRICK: Yeah. I'm a regular fixture around here.

FATHER: Ever think about where you'll be ten years from now?

PATRICK: No.

BROTHER: I often think about where I'll be.

FATHER: Which is?

BROTHER [laughing]: Lying face-down in my own feces.

MIMI [to PATRICK]: There you have it - my brother's unique
brand of self-deprecating humor.

PATRICK: I kinda like it - makes me feel at home. Does he know
any magic tricks.

BROTHER: Excuse me - you can direct your questions to me
[pointing at his chest].

PATRICK: Well, do you?

[BROTHER refuses to answer the question, looks down at his
plate, starts picking at a piece of turkey.]

FATHER: Patrick, my one piece of advice to every islander is this
- the trick on the continent is making yourself invisible. You
gotta pretend the war's over but no one knows it yet.

PATRICK: That's how natural selection works around here, huh?

FATHER [looking up at the flickering chandelier]: *Whoa* the
storm's getting worse. If we lose power, Mimi, be ready to light
the candles.

MIMI: Where?

FATHER [to MIMI]: You gonna play along with me here?

A vase of flowers, a pair of candlesticks, an Academy Award
statuette, and the steady ticking of a clock are all reflected in the
wall mirror. What's their purpose? What seems to be the trouble

here, Diablo? I keep thinking about you taking your own hands
away from your throat. Were you choking on something? I
thought you said you didn't drink alcoholic poison. How old are
you anyway? - then act your age! Why are Korean soldiers
crowding into the room? - I'm joking. Remarks like that, while
seeming random or surrealistic and humorous, result from a non-
convulsive form of epilepsy. That's nothing to be ashamed of -
that's why I don't treat the condition. Besides, nothing's more
clear-cut than the impact of ridiculous accusations on a writer
trained in patience. I smile at myself in that mirror. I know what
I've done. My lips aren't trembling. It might be my true calling in
life is to assist people in dying. Each spring tulips and azaleas
bloom. In the fall chrysanthemums blossom. (Plus there's no a
constellation I cannot name.) Around the corner from the motel I
find an Episcopal church shaded by magnolias. So jot this down
on your yellow legal pad, doctor: the problem's I never know
where to start a biography. I refuse to admit it's impossible to
recreate every event that occurs in someone's life. I need a bigger
cup of coffee. Big deal! *You* [pointing] need to brush your teeth
(like they do in Greece and Turkey).

FATHER [to PATRICK]: What's your profession?

PATRICK: I went to seminary school.

FATHER: What's that prepare you for?

BROTHER: You never heard of the blessed trinity, Dad, and altar
boys and Catholic school girls?

MIMI [to BROTHER]: Jesus, let it go! I'm sorry [turning to
PATRICK] - Dunno how many times I'm gonna have to apologize
for my brother's shit.

PATRICK: No kidding, tell him to calm down.

BROTHER: Hey man, I'm sitting right across from you. Make your
requests to *this* face.

PATRICK [to BROTHER]: Okay - what if I belt you in the mouth?

BROTHER: A proper display of affection, uh? - on Thanksgiving,
no less.

FATHER [to PATRICK, pointing at BROTHER]: Compared to you,
his life's been pretty small, I guess. We never leave the city
much. It's made us sorta conservative … except for Mimi, of

course. She loves to experiment - that's her islander blood speaking.

PATRICK: I think conservatism's a very bad habit.

FATHER: Political conservatism?

PATRICK: Any belief that limits your conception of what's possible in life.

MIMI: Great way of putting it, Patrick.

BROTHER [rolling his eyes, giggling]: You're a criminal addicted to melodrama and bullshit posturing. You know [laughing louder], just because you know how to read between the lines you're not any better than the rest of us.

PATRICK [to BROTHER]: Thanks for not laughing *too* hard.

BROTHER: I know, I know - everyone's got an agenda. Sometimes you just gotta say what the fuck, right? The way you see it, on the continent we're addicted to sales and marketing. We're so backward and pathetic. Shit [shaking his head] - excuse me if I don't sound pretentious as hell.

FATHER [exhaling]: That's enough!

PATRICK: What I meant to say was conservatism makes us self-important and unwilling to compromise. That's how we get a world of judgmental pricks who wage war and violence.

BROTHER: Oh, I get it. I'm the super-villain in this scenario.

PATRICK: You're sure not much of a role model, acting like you run the whole universe.

BROTHER: Who the fuck *are* you? You went to seminary. So what? Tell me, where'd you lose your virginity?

MIMI: Shut up! Patrick's been around and seen things you only read about in your books. Your problem's you can see the world only through those books.

BROTHER: My stroke books, you mean?

MIMI [to PATRICK, gesturing at BROTHER]: Clearly I'm too obscure for him.

BROTHER: What do *you* know, Mimi? If this new guy wasn't here, you'd still be stalking islanders. Your life's a nightmare either way. Every day's nine hours of agony. No wonder you have those bruises around your neck. No wonder [laughing] you ripped the phone out of the wall and hid in the crawlspace last week.

MIMI: I was upset the other day. I got so sick I thought I was gonna die.

BROTHER: But now everything's okay. You've organized everything so you won't be bored again. A mysterious islander arrives in the city and a missing piece clicks right into place. You realize you're Sylvia Plath.

PATRICK [turning to BROTHER]: If you must know, I lost my virginity to a medical secretary. Good enough for you? Anyway, Mimi's right. I arrived in the city on my own terms. That's how I plan to live here. What's wrong with that?

BROTHER [to SISTER]: Go in the kitchen and get this guy a toasted bagel with cream cheese. That'll shut him up.

SISTER: Can I be excused. I gotta do my homework.

BROTHER: What are you talking about. Today's holiday. You don't gotta do crap.

FATHER: Let her do what she wants.

SISTER: Okay, first I'll eat pumpkin pie, then I'll go study.

PATRICK [turning to FATHER, pointing to SISTER]: Very unusual - someone so young yet willing and able to make compromises.

What kind of idiocy could *this* be [gesturing to the military vessels crowding the channel]? Is Patrick encountering the end of his dreams here? - *What* dreams? Without Mother's support how can he continue as ... what? - radical philosopher, theologian, spiritual trainer, wilderness guide? He's nervous. Where'll the money come from? He's not qualified for pure financial pursuits. That's right. Patrick's the man standing over there at the ferry's railing (his eyes insensitive as solid walnuts) contemplating suicide. He imagines a sonar screen and a boat maneuvering in a circle around his sinking body. Could there be a more diabolical fate? He imagines handkerchiefs strewn about the deck. The mourners would share the same pocket of sky - like specks lost in the blue heavens. Shit, why hire a corps of sobbing cheerleaders and vivid recollections? Patrick's a loner, a dissenter. What *me* worry? He's optimistic about killing himself. Drowning leaves no trace of disappointment or self-consciousness - it's a small human sacrifice, hardly different from dropping anchor or doing a bad fish impersonation.

[o]

A new world, material without being too real (or, The Swastika Holding Company)

1. *Market & Drumm*

PATTY [letting out her breath]: This city's so insane. Look at the people milling around Market Street, blocking traffic. Barefoot children and homeless people passed out against streetlamps, sign poles, and stacked bags of potatoes. What's their true purpose? I'm guessing they're refugees from the island.

PATRICK: You don't have to remind me. I'm walking to the end of this street, getting on a bus, heading east to Nevada.

PATTY: Clearly you're not from around here. You walk to the end of this street, there's no bus station.

PATRICK: Shit.

PATTY: I'll show you the way. We're not far from where we can catch a bus out of the city.

PATRICK [pointing to the high rises along Market Street]: Are those buildings occupied?

PATTY: What do you mean?

PATRICK: Are those buildings empty and isolated or are people scurrying around inside them, climbing up claustrophobic stairwells, hiding behind opaque curtains and intricate machines?

PATTY: Why not? A couple suicides, famous retired movie stars in pancake makeup, lost lovers, drag queens, authoritarian assholes, forlorn plutocrats, hierarchies of humiliation - the standard ruins of corruptible dreams … uh, and more smashed up things.

PATRICK: So this city won't have a happy ending?

PATTY [laughing]: Nope, but the details will be in tomorrow morning's newspaper, with quotes from the people hired to clean up the messes in those buildings.

PATRICK: Suits me. Like I said, my main concern's getting outta this city. I'm sick and tired of those lodging-house refugees. I got things to do, people to meet - I promise.

PATTY: In Nevada?

PATRICK: Yeah in Nevada, where the desert's plain as day except in Las Vegas. I can imagine the meaning of it.

PATTY: What else?

PATRICK: What do you think? This latest round of nonsense will resolve itself in the end - *all* of it - the lying, cheating, stealing - all of it. I'm gonna live the rest of my life as I see fit. They've run me off the island, destroyed my house, left me with nothing but a suitcase and a compulsion to wander. Don't worry - I'm not gonna hurt *you*.

PATTY: Is that an invitation to come along?

PATRICK: You get me on a bus to Nevada, you're automatically my companion.

PATTY: I never spent much time with islanders outside their neighborhoods.

PATRICK: Here's your chance.

PATTY: What else?

PATRICK: I'll teach you Diabolein.

PATTY: The underground board game?

PATRICK: Board game? That's a fraction of what Diabolein's about, merest fraction - the outer aspect of Diabolein. Fact is, I can teach you the inner aspect too. Diabolein's a vital process, a living dynamic thing, quite the opposite of a thirty-year mortgage.

PATTY: You know Diabolein's illegal over here?

PATRICK: It's illegal on the island too. That never stopped anyone from learning and practicing it.

PATTY: You think that's what this new war's about - the continent stamping out Diabolein?

PATRICK: Shit, nothing stamps out Diabolein, not even the smell of antiseptic. This war, or battle, is like the rest - about establishing an identity. Islanders and continentals find their identity in their hatred of an opposition. … But Diabolein - that's the message of the *third* perspective.

PATTY: What do you see from there?

PATRICK: You see the other two perspectives - polar opposites of good and evil locked in their futile struggles for domination. You see one side, the 'good guys,' [air-quotes] behaving as if they could destroy the other side, ' bad guys,' [air-quotes] to produce a world that's good - and they would call it peace. But the whole charade *cannot* end. Reality's not designed that way. Those two perspectives share a willful ignorance of the third perspective of amoral detachment. There you have my standard intro speech to Diabolein recruits.

PATTY: At least it's more than the latest gadget to keep off the rain.

PATRICK: Diabolein's a living dynamic thing - so don't think I'm gonna stay in Nevada forever. No way. Think of Nevada as an episode in a series of continental episodes.

PATTY: But then what?

PATRICK: Further inland, further east. Maybe we'll pick up more people along the way, maybe not. Maybe we'll create a new world, maybe not. Maybe we'll *find* a new world, maybe not. Maybe we'll arrive in Manhattan or Long Island. Shit, maybe we'll experience what Thomas Pynchon calls 'the orbiting ecstasy of true paranoia.'

PATTY: But then what?

PATRICK: The series never ends - reality's built that way. We're pioneers moving westward, well, eastward in our case, far east as possible before we encounter another insurmountable body of water.

> PATTY [leaning back on the bed's pillows, idly staring ahead at the greenish dead eye of the TV]: Problem's this place has got just as boring as San Francisco and Nevada ever were.
>
> PATRICK: This motel room?
>
> PATTY: All of it - the motel room, the diner across the street, Duluth, the snow and ice. Whatever happened to the 'emergence of unutterable possibilities' [making air-quotes] you and Diablo talked about on our drive out here?

PATRICK [leaning back on the bed's pillows, lighting a cigarette]: Those possibilities are *here*. You're not paying close enough attention. Where's your capacity for wonder? First, stop complaining. After that, be patient. Third, learn to control your daydreaming.

PATTY: No dreams, huh?

PATRICK: What's key is learning to *control* and *focus* your dreams. Any kind of idle daydreaming saps away your energy, leaving you in the state you're in now - frustrated, bored, desperate, acting like ninety-nine-point-nine percent of the people on this planet. You're ashamed of the fact your deepest desire is dying young.

PATTY [throwing up her hands]: Was this all a mistake? - coming to Minnesota with you guys.

[Telephone starts ringing.]

PATRICK: It's Veronica calling from the diner. She gets restless on the nightshifts when she's got no customers.

PATTY: Then what? We go back over there, hang out in a booth the rest of the night flipping coins and drinking coffee with her and Diablo?

PATRICK: Man, you're in a bad mood. Wanna order some room service, a bottle of wine or a Heineken and a ginger ale delivered on a linen-covered silver tray? I'll order one of my favorite freshly squeezed orange juices.

PATTY: I think it was *all* a mistake.

PATRICK: If you think that, it's a failure of *your* imagination. You're being tossed to and fro between ecstasy and misery. That may be human nature, as they say, but it sure as hell ain't Diabolein.

[Telephone stops ringing.]

PATTY: Besides, wine gives me a headache.

2. *Market & Fremont*

PATTY [grabbing PATRICK's arm]: Stop - turn left here.

PATRICK: Looks like more of the same buildings.

PATTY: What'd you expect?

PATRICK: A new world - the edges of things harder, more real, chromed, peach-toned, waxed shiny.

PATTY: Anybody tell you that you got big hands?

PATRICK: It comes from clutching big coins. I got big elbows too from leaning on lots of diner counters and booths. You think these are big [making fists], you should see the hands of my associate Diablo.

PATTY: He comes from the island?

PATRICK: He comes from an unchanging conception of himself. I predict we'll encounter Diablo in Nevada. You watch. He carries a pocketful of coins for flipping and tossing on diner counters.

PATTY: To what end?

PATRICK: Think of it as solitary illumination in the middle of the night - a clean well-lit diner. When Diablo announces 'heads' or 'tails' you hear the breath going right outta him - not a single word there but a horrific-sounding whisper and frost on the insides of the upper-story windows.

PATTY: I remember gambling in Las Vegas in the winter of '94.

PATRICK: Please don't remind me of your past.

PATTY [shaking her head, smiling]: I can't believe I'm gonna be traveling the continent with a subversive islander.

PATRICK: Perhaps it's too much too soon?

PATTY: No way. I can't go on much longer living in San Francisco. I'm ready for a change. I *need* a change, … a second chance.

PATRICK [laughing]: For what? What's there to change? You don't have a job or a single asset to your name.

PATTY: But I'm bored. That's reason enough to change. I'm ready to take a tumble on the grass, as grandpa used to say. At this point in my life I can't imagine my parents giving birth to me at all. I'm so different from them.

PATRICK: Ever sat inside a speeding ambulance?

PATTY: Not yet.

PATRICK: That's one way of describing Diabolein. Another way of describing it is 'getting your foot stuck in the rabbit hole.' A third way, 'strange amalgam of delight and dread.'

PATTY: I hope this isn't another promotion about transcending society's imposed boundaries and facing the horrors beyond.

PATRICK: Do you know what 'beyond' is? Did you know that in the beyond all things touch?

PATTY: Oh, another mode of meaning behind the obvious? No doubt you got an irritating habit of telling scary stories about the inexhaustible variety of life. You've read lots of John Ashbery poems and Don DeLillo novels.

PATRICK [laughing]: No doubt you got an irritating habit of using words without first understanding their multiple implications.

PATTY: Then scare me - right here. Let's see what you got.

PATRICK [unbuttoning his shirt to reveal a large swastika tattooed on his chest]: Check this out.

PATTY: That's odd, downright disturbing. Aren't you worried a symbol like that dates you? I know a company around here that sells swastika armbands but they're going out of business. No one on the continent displays swastikas any more, even as holiday decorations, much less as symbols of superiority. We put that stuff behind us.

PATRICK [smiling]: Along with the rosary, Hopalong Cassidy, the Warren Commission, and the American Legion, huh?

PATTY: Hell of thing, isn't it, one crazy bastard changing everything like that?

PATRICK: The so-called bad guys drive history. You know what that means, don't you?

PATTY: We're cast in the role of bad guys here - our shining moment.

PATRICK: That's right. Not just the two of us but everyone associated with publicizing and disseminating Diabolein. They'll describe us as 'evil,' 'immoral,' 'corrupting,' though in fact we're neither good nor bad. We're outside that opposition. Yet those who are confined to good and evil cannot imagine things any other way, so each side slots us into the role of enemy. That's why islanders and continentals hate us equally, even more than they hate each other.

PATTY: Hell of a thing, one crazy bastard changing everything like that. Reminds me of Plato's cave metaphor.

PATRICK [pointing at the TV]: Hey, look - one of those old Warner Brothers westerns. This station's running a whole series this week.

PATTY: Listen to yourself - raving on about a stupid TV series. I never thought I'd see the day.

PATRICK: What makes you so sure a TV screen isn't broadcasting the truth?

PATTY [taking a swig from the Heineken bottle]: So is this a special green beer bottle, best of its kind? Can't this stupid bottle count as truth? Am I paying close enough attention to what's right here in front of me? Is that a capacity for wonder?

PATRICK: You got a death wish, right? You don't wanna be here to learn Diabolein. Is that what's going on?

PATTY [raising her voice]: I got a wish to get on with my life is all. Whenever I disagree with you, you accuse me of being suicidal. Makes no sense!

PATRICK [sighing, stubbing out his cigarette in the ashtray]: In some sense, we're all suicidal: we dream of changing into something we're not. Anyway, you're too far inside now ever to go back. Even if you returned to San Francisco - and I doubt that's possible - you'd fit in *worse* than before. Right now you're caught in the middle of a transformation process. The more you fight it, the more you think everything's conspiring against you, though it's not. So let it happen. Don't be proud. Sometimes life does the striving *for* you.

PATTY: How long does the transformation last?

PATRICK: That's up to you.

PATTY: How can I accelerate it?

PATRICK: Stop complaining, be patient, don't get carried away with grandiose daydreaming. Focus on what's achievable, then build on that. Let grandiosity take care of itself.

[Telephone starts ringing.]

3. *Fremont & Mission*

PATTY [grabbing PATRICK's arm]: Stop. There's the bus station [pointing off to her right].
[Traffic light turns green.]
PATRICK: Great. Let's go inside, get our tickets, be on our way.
PATTY [letting out her breath]: I admire your vast ambition.
PATRICK: That's true. The continent's vast. If Diabolein has a chance of conquering it, we cannot lose our capacity for wonder.
PATTY: You mean everyone's gotta have a dream?
PATRICK: Yeah but the problem's that ninety-nine-point-nine percent of the time your dreams are far too grandiose relative to your present circumstances. That means one of two things - either you destroy yourself in the failure of achieving your unrealistic dreams, or you retreat into a world of self-absorbed daydreaming, never achieving anything practical. In the world of Diabolein, there isn't a Jay Gatsby or Emma Bovary anywhere in sight. Over here [pointing to his forehead], we're in control of the realization of our dreams. We don't create drama unless it serves a purpose. This isn't the 19th or 20th Century. We don't belabor progress or get nostalgic for youth. We're practical. Diabolein's pure creative science.
PATTY: Sounds like science fiction or new-age fiction.
PATRICK: I'm sorry but I fail to see the fiction. If you must put Diabolein into a literary category, I'd call it a contemporary romance - with emphasis on the word 'contemporary.' It's like nothing you've read before.
PATTY [pulling at PATRICK's sleeve]: C'mon, let's get on the bus. Nevada here we come!

[p]

Stamp Act's repealed!

It was Diablo's birthday. Was he frightened when I opened the bathroom door? Why be scared of a hat? I mean, what happens on or after your birthday makes a lot of sense once the threat of statutory rape's gone. Diablo's no longer dangerous to himself or others. I'm glad I know where he is. He's got no shortage of company. So tell me the story you told the police. Let's go back to the beginning of this convoluted drama. Tell me the truth. Let's relax a bit. I didn't perform mouth-to-mouth resuscitation (never seen it done in person). I tried to speak to Diablo, tell him he was on the verge of dying. But I began to feel dizzy, nauseated. My vision blurred. Nothing was wrong with me. Nothing was wrong with him. But there *is* something wrong with you, doctor, you and your colleagues trying to outdo one another in your expressions of moral indignation. Yet no one's at the controls there! There's no sign of a pilot in your gondola. Don't you forget I've seen you at close range. I'll remember every crease and pockmark on that face of yours. I've been keeping track. I got plenty of storage room underneath here. (Boa constrictors swallow their prey whole without chewing.) I can even smell urine and fresh-baked bread. Anyway, I was feeling light-headed when I opened the door and began screaming as loud as I could to wake up Diablo. I also felt an ache in my back, a heaviness in my heels - I saw a blackness where constellations were. Then I dropped hard onto my knees (afterwards no longer able to move).
Speaking of which - Oh my God! Hello? Duluth police? Yes, I'm calling to report a missing person - excuse me, an *injured* person - a rowdy cross-dresser named Patty, my alter-ego. She just turned eighteen maybe nineteen or twenty. That's right. "Precocious" I say aloud, before hanging up the phone, clearing my throat, dialing a second number, ordering a piping-hot pizza. You heard right - I

discover Patty passed out on the bathroom floor. Plus there's lots of blood in there. At first I think she's scraped her wrists across something (a razorblade disguised as stained glass) while straddling that huge white porcelain bucket we once called a toilet. Excuse me, doctor? Er, yes, yes, of course, I'll try *not* to speak faster than one word per minute. I should've known you smoke. You're careless. Anyway, Patty had suffered multiple head injuries. She lay there in a daze, her eyes - *what?* - vacant? - yeah, as if she were making a rapid sort of mental calculation. That was my first impression. After that, I watched her bring those fingertips up to her mouth, and her last smile had a great charm about it, believe me. Her face was paralyzed, yet with a forefinger and a thumb she was able [INTERFERENCE]. Now, I'm not sure, but I left her lying there on the floor bleeding to death because, well, because Patty frightened me. (God, I hate the word 'because' - now I've used it three times in one paragraph!) I could've strangled her, put her out of her misery, assisted her in completing that suicide. But she was very young and had a chance of surviving if the ambulance arrived on schedule.

Casino's aren't complicated - their mission's to encourage you to donate money to your favorite charity, to do whatever your heart desires - but *only* that . All things considered, you feel gambling's for the best. That's why the low ceilings make you feel claustrophobic and the mirrored walls persuade you that some things are more delightful the more they're retold. Everybody wants to be something, but most folks ain't what they ought to be. That's right. Take a look at this row of dark squatting shapes [pointing]. That ancient Civil War veteran (he bears scars from Shiloh *and* Antietam) - look how he leans against that slot machine making awkward wood-plucking motions. Been here the whole night. He's forgotten about rejoining the wagon train. He thinks he sees sparkling clear water running through his grimy hands every time he turns the faucet. Fact is, he's dying of thirst. He'll never make it outta here alive. All things considered, it's for the best. Next, check out that guy [pointing] - a former Mexican ranch-hand. He did great deeds in his time. Now he's a masterpiece of [INTERFERENCE]. He doesn't even speak Spanish. Like I said earlier, everything on the continent ends in gambling and drunkenness.

PATRICK [to FATHER]: I was married once before.

MIMI: He has a son too.

FATHER: Yeah? Where's he live?

PATRICK [clearing his throat]: He's in a special care facility for the mentally deranged. Holy shit! - not to change the subject, but where's that blood coming from [pointing to the carpet beneath the table]?

[Everyone except SISTER moves their chairs back from the table.]

MIMI [to SISTER]: Oh my God, you're bleeding! What's wrong?

SISTER [in a daze]: Dunno. It just started and won't stop.

MIMI: You're having your first period, aren't you?

SISTER [hyperventilating]: I guess. What should I do?

MIMI: C'mon, let's go to the bathroom. We'll deal with it in there.

[MIMI and SISTER leave the dining room.]

FATHER: You here that banging sound?

PATRICK: Sounds like it's coming from the kitchen.

FATHER: You smell that … burning?

BROTHER: Get the extinguisher!

FATHER [to BROTHER]: Did you light the kitchen on fire?

BROTHER: I was kidding earlier. Dunno what's going on. I don't light random things on fire. You're confusing me with the new cleaning lady who leaves the iron on.

FATHER [standing up, walking into the kitchen, yelling over his shoulder]: Without rules there's chaos.

BROTHER: Jesus, why do I feel like I'm trapped on the stage in a bad play?

PATRICK [laughing]: You are. Watch this … [turning to face the AUDIENCE]: What's up?

BROTHER: You mind telling me what's going on?

PATRICK: That's another dimension [pointing]. If you had children of your own, you'd understand.

FATHER [returning from the kitchen]: Isn't that what the poet Keats called 'negative capability'?

PATRICK: What?

FATHER: Another dimension.

PATRICK: I have no idea what you're talking about.

BROTHER: Can both of you stop trying to humiliate me? Doctor, if you're so sure of your indignation, maybe you wanna confront something more robust than abstract moral oppositions, like lots of encounters with lots of serious people in serious situations. Maybe you wanna chew on their skin and sinew while they attempt to make sense of their own lives. Maybe you wanna see (spread out before you) a galaxy of jungle adventures more threatening than what you ever imagined. Once we've established the cause of evil, defensive actions serve to illustrate its effects, right? Well, I don't wanna see any of that distracting shit. Even if it's entertaining (and I hear footsteps coming up the stairs), even if it 'makes sense' (and that's what I wanna talk to you about) - still it detracts from what's important here. Instead, let's look at what's right *there* [pointing] - incandescent light falling on a vase of flowers. C'mon, let's have a closer look. The flowers' petals appear to be made of porcelain. - Write that down on your yellow legal pad. Join the club. I'm not tired. I'm reasonable - I get tired only in the mornings. You're the one who's tired. What's your name again? Man, you're in a sorry state - or maybe that's normal. Maybe you sleep during the entire six months of your digestion (like a stupid boa constrictor).

> As the captain eases up on the throttle, and the ferry docks at the ferry building, Patrick's mind shifts into a higher gear. Even on the continent, life's real work will be mental, not physical. He'll survive without a menial job, without misfortune. He'll become the centerpiece of his own story. Patrick looks about himself, inhales a long breath, tightens his jaw, stands there on the deck stiffly erect, defiant, oblivious to the plight of the other refugees who prepare to

disembark in what for most will be a strange and startling city. The booms and masts of docked boats tower over Patrick. Deckhands, fishermen, laborers, dockworkers, tradesmen, bug-eyed military personnel all crowd and patrol the docks. Packing crates are strewn everywhere. Watch out for those puddles of brown water! From the light poles hang stuffed effigies, paper signs pinned to their chests. Prostitutes with muscular calves clutch at each other, giggling, shouting, wildly pointing at refugees who lean over the ferry's railing begging for a prostate biopsy. It feels like ten years have passed since the ferry left the island behind. It feels like Patrick forgot to cross his fingers. The world has gone mad for sure. A terrified refugee grabs Patrick by the arm, holding him back from the gangway. Patrick turns around and unleashes a violent beating on the man, raining down vicious blows on his head, while the rest of the refugees surge forward, desperate to disembark on the pier and run for their lives. Pistol fire rings out. Women lift up their skirts. Patrick appreciates the sex and violence. This ain't no Presbyterian churchyard.

PATRICK [to MIMI]: You got rabbit ears on your TV. Don't see that a lot.

MIMI [to FATHER]: Why's it so hot in here?

FATHER: It's cold and damp outside.

SISTER: I'm hungry. I wanna order a pizza.

FATHER: I'm not surprised. You didn't eat breakfast or your Thanksgiving dinner.

SISTER: I never eat breakfast. I'm trying to lose weight.

MIMI: I'm gonna turn down the heat, okay?

FATHER [to PATRICK]: I got an unusual question for you, Patrick.

PATRICK: Okay.

FATHER: Tell me, what do you know about murderers?

PATRICK: How do you mean?

FATHER: You ever read a murderer's confession?

PATRICK: No, not as far as I know.

FATHER: Do believe in hypnosis?

PATRICK: Sorry but where are you going with these questions?

FATHER: Remember earlier we mentioned the cleaning lady who shot herself?

PATRICK: Yeah.

FATHER: Well, it's more complicated than that. When we found her dead, there were torn-up photos scattered around the room. The other strange thing was old newspaper clippings tacked to the wall.

PATRICK: Was there a note of some kind?

FATHER: There was. It read, "I'm trying to kill myself."

PATRICK: Sounds pretty self-explanatory. I thought you said something about acute renal failure earlier.

FATHER: I did. She overdosed on medicine *and* shot herself. The scene has a haunting quality about it, right?

PATRICK: And a confusing quality. What's any of this got to do with murderers?

FATHER: Not more than two hours before we found her dead, two doctors and two nurses were found brutally murdered at a local hospital.

MIMI [returning to the room]: Please don't go on about your theories, Dad.

PATRICK: No, that's okay, Mimi. He's got me intrigued. What concerns me most here is grown-ups need explanations, even when the threat of dying (killing?) is gone. I'm not unhappy about that hat [pointing to my skull] - which means I *am* happy about it. Do I remember the other grown-up visitors who thought I looked *un*happy in that hat? Well, that's debatable. Ideas occur to me when I'm busy. That's how I get more and more ideas faster and faster - by getting busier and busier. Soon I feel dizzy, nauseated. The motel room blurs and darkens around me. Furniture and windows vanish. That's how busy I get - so busy that nothing's wrong with me. I'm not screaming. I'm concentrating. - - Then you're beating me with your fists, pounding on my back. I grab you by the shoulder, try pushing you away. Moments later you begin coughing, choking on something, crying out in pain. Something unusual is caught in your throat. You look unhappy. You shake with fear. I loosen my grip from around your neck. I wipe the perspiration from my brow. Nothing you say or do can improve my opinion of you, doctor, nothing short of your choosing another career. I'm such a reasonable person.

I'll tell you why I'm laughing about an incident I can't quite place - but I warn you, the Irish version of the story's yet to come. Damn, what's going on here? *I'm* supposed to be the one with funny ideas in my head. You gotta be putting me on. I can't remember the last thing I see before I fall asleep. No, no, *you* tell me - would *you* happen to know the time of my arrival at the final frontier of my mind? I've covered so much ground here. I'm getting impatient to meet my maker (reader?). That's right, I'm referring to the front page of the Bible, down to the very day and month of creation. But let's not bother about that now. Let's pretend, on that particular morning, Patty died for her country. Let's carve her name on a monument rather than a tombstone. Like I said earlier, I was a young boy when my father died on the continent. (I can barely see his face now.). So Mother had to raise me by herself. (I never learned how the two of them came to marry in the first place.) Anyway, it's funny going off to fight a war when you don't *have* to. But there he went, Father on a ferry across the channel, first to San Francisco, then on to Nevada perhaps or Chicago, maybe as far as the East Coast. I suppose he didn't manage his affairs too well. I know he didn't talk to Mother much by phone, computer, or by letter (the old-fashioned way). Being away from home for so long, he had affairs with many local girls. Indeed, I can imagine a large silver cup sitting right there at his feet.

There [pointing] I see Patty. She's the woman wearing a baseball cap, a sleeveless Harley Davidson T-shirt, no bra, faded blue jeans, and flip-flops for sandals. Her lips never move. She's walking around the casino like she owns the place. She's looking for trouble. I wanna take care of her but I can't speak. All

I can do is listen to the wall of sound. I got no cash, credit cards, or ATM cards. I can't call Mother because she's dead. I can't sell my son because that's illegal. Finally me and Patty drag Diablo away from the tables, drag him outside, discard him on the sidewalk. "I lost my money!" he cries out to us. "Please, I lost all my money! - No wait!" He begins going through his pockets - only to find a crumpled up empty pack of cigarettes. "Oh thank you, Diablo. That's a nice roll of money." He begins grabbing for something in the air, phantom gambling chips, or credit cards and ATM machines. He looks like an idiot. His hair's disheveled. His nose is running. He keeps saying "No … no … no … NO!" Patty and I start kicking Diablo in the sides to make him feel better, more relaxed. It's pure pleasure breaking those ribs, bruising those organs. *Muy* beautiful. Finally we hail a cab, tell the driver to take us to our hotel. The driver turns around, asks if that guy's okay? I say he's fine. He's visiting Las Vegas for pleasure.

Having exited the ferry building, now set loose on the streets of San Francisco, Patrick can resume his insular buffoonery. He starts walking up Market Street. First thing he'll do is put on a high-styled wig and starched white hat and search out a lodging-house. After that? - back to business as usual. What he gives with one hand he'll take away with the other. He's got the spins. The high-rises tilt at forty-five-degree angles. He feels like a character in a 1930s movie. The basic problem's Patrick can't keep track of time in a sequential fashion. How prepared is he psychologically to deal with the damage the continent's prepared to inflict on him? Better make a cheese, lettuce, and mayonnaise sandwich, better have faith in God (rather than believe in yourself). That's what Mother said. God's the one who'll latch the shutters closed when he's finished mocking your life. Patrick begins eating the sandwich. Again he's got no idea what he's listening to. Gasoline-powered generators? A freezer unit? Again he wishes he were born deaf. How much easier it would be to disregard convention - nor would he be able to argue with himself (or the doctor) over and over again.

[q]

Inconspicuous as a tarantula on a slice of angel food (or, Edge of its voluptuous field)

{a}
INVESTIGATOR #1: It's time to start.
INVESTIGATOR #2: What?
#1: Cutting through the sentimental fog.
#2: Superb.
#1: You take Patty in room 9A. I'll take Patrick in 9C.
#2: What do you think - thirty minutes?
#1: Tops. We know punks are punks, not shamans or clowns.
#2 [laughing]: Indeed. Panoramic realism will reveal its advantages here - everything spread out before us for our own amusement and selection - we become the scissors-and-paste guys.
{b}
#1: It's time to start.
#2: What?
#1: Imagining a small open window at the top of a long peach-colored cinderblock wall in a long interrogation room.
#2: Okay, I see it.
#1: Outside that window the rain's stopped, the clouds are low, the sky's gray.
#2: Right. Now I'm crawling out that window onto a sidewalk alongside the precinct house.
#1: A sense of portent and foreboding churns in your belly.
#2: I feel nausea as I continue crawling along the sidewalk …
now opening the rear door, crawling into the backseat of a squad car parked at the curb.
#1: You hide yourself on the floor so the uniformed cop can't see you when he gets in. He starts the car, maneuvers into traffic.
{c}

#2: It's high time I sit up in the backseat, startling the uniformed cop.

#1: Everything about you is serious and efficient.

#2: I don't like the cop or the way he drives, don't like his tan skin, black hair, buttoned-up uniform.

#1: Ten minutes go by. You're getting antsy waiting for the cop to pull over and ask why you're here and who you are.

#2: I don't like the squad car, its dingy ceiling, ancient air vents, stale odors of soy sauce, its radio blaring country music. The dashboard lights make my eyes ache.

#1: Ten more minutes go by. You check your watch. You check your cellphone for messages. The car's interior begins to have a strange effect on you.

#2: I said I don't like the car's cramped interior. I try to stand up but bump my head on the ceiling. I sit down again, start drumming my fingers on the armrest.

#1: You're eyeing the door. You sense the door's responsible for the strange effect the car has on your mood. You draw away from the door, to the opposite side of the backseat. But you keep your eyes on that door.

#2: Yes, the door has special meaning. It's part of an allegory, a symbol of some sort. I notice the door's been unlocked the whole time the car's been moving. I realize all I gotta do is open that door to free myself.

{d}

#1: The cop swerves to the side of the road, slams on the brakes.

#2: I start to wonder if it was a good idea leaving the precinct house in the first place.

#1: The cop turns around. For the first time you notice his face is bruised and disfigured. He begins questioning you. *Why didn't you call the police after you heard about Diablo's murder? Why'd you go see Patrick later that night? Did you deliver something to him or one of his female friends? That night, had Patrick already befriended Mimi?*

#2: I glance in the rearview mirror, looking into my own eyes. I realize that's a two-way mirror, and cops lurk on the other side of my reflection watching the uniformed cop interrogate me from the front seat of the car.

#1: You're getting antsy, waiting for the cop to finish the questioning and ask why you're here and who you are. You start drumming your fingers along the back of the front seat.

#2: I don't like that rearview mirror at all. I wanna smash it. I'm getting suspicious of myself.

#1: Then you get angry. You tell the uniformed cop his line of questioning's ridiculous. You've known Patrick, Mimi, and Diablo for hardly a week, and besides, that acquaintance is purely coincidental: your apartment's adjacent to Mimi's - that's all. You never met or heard of a second woman named Patty.

{e}

#2: The cop attempts to strike me across the cheek with a heavy object. He starts screaming. *Go to hell, you liar!*

#1: You give a loud weary sigh. You understand this drama's very much beside the point now that Diablo's dead.

#2: I keep my wits about me. I'm not distraught or confused. I swing open the back door, crawl out onto the sidewalk, roll onto my back, look up at the sky.

#1: There she is, leaning against a wall - Mimi.

#2: Her arms are crossed over her breasts. She's shaking her head at me.

#1: She's annoyed.

#2: She's wearing black jeans and a loose navy blue sweater. Her face is covered in pancake makeup.

#1: Something's not right about Mimi. She seems to be expecting something weird to happen.

#2: She tells me the NYPD are looking for Patrick. They wanna take him in for questioning.

#1: You roll your eyes like you don't believe her.

#2: She starts screaming at me. *I'm not making any of this up! Look at me!*

#1: You tell her you don't know what happened between Patrick and Diablo. You don't care. You're an innocent bystander, an accidental acquaintance. There's no way you could rat anybody out if you wanted to. Shit, you don't even watch the evening news.

#2: She continues screaming at me. A crowd of onlookers forms on the sidewalk outside Tompkins Square Park. *I'm not a terrorist, for Chrissake! I didn't paper the walls with those fliers!*

{f}

#1: You watch the squad car pull away from the curb. You feel stranded, vulnerable, overwhelmed, preoccupied. You feel like Lee Harvey Oswald.

#2: I stand up, decide to walk into Tompkins Square Park.

#1: Mimi follows, screaming at the top of her lungs. The crowd of onlookers disperses, then reforms behind Mimi as she follows you through the park entrance.

#2: I hurry to the other side of the park. I haven't done anything wrong. No one should suspect me of anything or feel the need to inform me of my rights. My behavior's routine.

#1: Mimi continues to follow close behind, screaming.

#2: At the other side of the park I find an unmarked car at the curb, with a driver behind the wheel. Its engine's idling. I open the door, get inside.

{g}

#1: As the car pulls away, you watch Mimi continue to yell and gesticulate in your direction. Soon she's vanished from sight.

#2: I turn around to discover it's *you* behind the wheel. I smile at your reflection in the rearview mirror.

#1: I also smile, laugh slightly, tell you we're returning to the precinct house to interrogate Patrick.

#2: I promise I'll be more careful next time about climbing into the backs of squad cars parked at the curb.

#1: I maneuver the car through the thick traffic of cabs and delivery vans.

#2: Outside the car's windows, the rain's stopped, the clouds are low, the sky's gray.

{h} *This is* not *happening.*

Why's traffic so bad? There's some kinda protest or demonstration up ahead. Amateur night at the local abortion clinic, eh? Yeah, those red hats stand for hatred. Well, I always say everyone's right - even the deaf mutes working at the filling stations. Hah, hate tastes great. Anyway, let me remind you we're due a full moon. Tonight? Yeah, so help me find something sharp. For stabbing? Exactly. Some sort of thrusting object to put us beyond the bounds of prudence and good taste. Now, pull over to the left there and park [pointing]. Right *there* [pointing]? Yeah, that's right. But we're several blocks from the precinct house - what's the point of walking? Doesn't matter. We're already late for the interrogation. Trust me on this - I need to buy a book I saw last week in that bookshop [pointing]. Jesus, you don't look like a man who's interested in first editions, and anyway, this is no time for browsing bookstores. We got police matters to attend to. We're *on* duty! I know, I know. But the book I'm gonna buy will help us understand Patrick's psyche, help us question his motives. Man, I can't believe what you're telling me - you no longer trust your own instincts. No, *you* don't understand. When I want sensitive information I ask for it like a man - I don't grovel for it. Christ [throwing up his hands], you've lost all sense of reality.

{i} *Dictionary of Rare & Peculiar Diseases (or, the Metaphysical Fallacy of Laboratory Science)*

Today's an important date today. You get to reveal some of your best-kept secrets today. Think you can handle that, Patrick? No problem - consider me a neutral observer. My right hand hasn't seen my left in thirty years - that's what Diabolein's all about: the best of everything's good enough for me. So tell us, Patrick, where's Patty? Dunno [looking around himself] - this is a big interrogation room - she could be anywhere in here. - - We know she's dead. What we wanna know is where you put the body. I [laughing] … uh, I … let's say I carried it up the golden ladder to the place I wanna get to. - - Where'd you learn Diabolein? From my mother and father. Where are they? Dead. And what are you doing on the continent? Spreading the word of God. Truly? That's right - but I must be a little bit confused. I've heard these questions many times before in similar interrogation rooms. What's today's date anyway? What astrological sign are we laboring under here? Didn't Karl Marx say drawing up a program for the future's a reactionary thing to do?

{j} *Something attacked the city - (a patron of the arts?)*

Are you familiar with what a restraining order is, Patrick? - - Just because something *isn't* good doesn't mean it's bad. Consider the so-called benefits of formal schooling. Shit, consider the benefits of slavery. Just because something sounds awkward doesn't mean it's poetry. I promise no repeat of the Trenton Incident. Just leave me be, here in New York, and nothing will come of it.

{k} *Hair Department head*

What's the first thing you can remember, Patrick? - - Swinging doors, a jukebox, a barstool - no, wait, uh, wild dogs running in packs at night, …uh, first thing I remember. The Las Vegas Public Library. - - How can that be - didn't that branch burn down? Okay, sorry, I'm a bit confused today. Fact is, I don't know what's the first thing I remember. A bar of some sort, a nightclub. Islanders say a bar's the best friend a guy ever had. Well, I like to see people drink. I'm an islander: I enjoy my vices by proxy. Oh yeah? *I* like to see people looking happy - that's why I buy things. Me? - I like to see people laugh. As for your earliest memories, Patrick. Yeah, yeah, I'm trying [rubbing his temples]. You gotta understand I was born the one and only rebel child in a family meek and mild. Not only did I drink, I played the horses, I played the wheel, I, uh, I like to see people drink. You mean to say you gambled? Sorry, did my behavior imply that?

{l} *Property & People 'R Precious (P&PRP)*

What are the goals of Diabolein, your motives? - - What do you think? - to take the edge off one's passion for life. Why do that? - - Why else? - to provide yourself access to alternate realities much larger, more all-encompassing than our social reality - to see the bigger picture we once called 'God' back in the olden days, God The Great Pretender. Man, I'm getting tired of these questions. I'm no gossip columnist. I'm a heartless thief - and *this* [pointing to the nearest wall] my collage. I'm like Balzac here. I'm breaking new ground. This ain't no bildungsroman. This is blasphemy and a bit of obscenity.

{m} *Okay, I'll try it just this once.*

How long's Diabolein been around? - - At least since the early 1950s, since rock 'n roll and film noir and U-2 planes and the great What's-It, before the Kennedy assassination and the Beatles - shit, dunno exactly. Diabolein's never wanted to outlaw or demonize certain behaviors. We simply strive to lose interest in those behaviors - lose interest in *all* behaviors. We strive to overcome striving. We're not optimists, nor are we self-important and power-mad. We embrace paradox and contradiction to help us escape from the world of our senses. We want nothing to do with humanity and its highly limited social realities. Now please leave me alone!

{n} *Too real is this feeling of make believe*

But where does that attitude lead you? - - Where do you think? - to the brink of madness - the straight & narrow entranceway to the higher realities - the bigger picture - to glimpse the higher purpose of humanity in the larger scheme of things. Got it?

{o} *Never to be forgiven, or forgotten*

Sounds clever, cynical, unpatriotic, conceited, forever closed off from the rest of us, the flawed ones trying to make sense of our daily lives - - Oh my God it's unpatriotic, though far *more* than that - misanthropic. Now let me outta this interrogation room! I told Mimi I'd meet her tonight for one of our regular Manhattan strolls. Where *is* she? Where do you think? Alphabet City, where most of the islander transplants live around here. That's no secret I *know*. You must also know what she's doing, so leave her out of this line of cold distracted questioning.

{p} *Secret symmetries of individualism and egalitarianism are served*

What do you mean how do we make ends meet? Me and Mimi walk wherever we wanna. Isn't that sufficient contemporary debate? I know continentals like to see themselves as optimistic people. That's their basic failing - an obsession with humanity, a belief that a pursuit of happiness is basic to social life. What? Diabolein's 'sinister motives'? Yeah, right, unpatriotic to its core. Your orbiting sensors didn't pick up on those involutions, huh?

{q} *An alphabet within an alphabet*

How could it *be* a conspiracy? Tell me, how would such a conspiracy work? Remember, most islanders despise Diabolein just as much as you continentals. Everyone hates Diabolein because everyone's obsessed with their own humanity. They cannot *see* beyond their own humanity - by definition, in one sense, though something else becomes visible in another sense.

{r} *Daisy chain of terror, suspicion, and uh, ... and ...*

Ever consider the serial regularity of an alphabet? Oh yeah? Good for you. So what comes after 'Z'? That's right 'A,' letter 'A' for 'armed men.'

{s} *Daily jostle of a nondescript life*

{t} *They just sit there or stand there.*

{u} *While I make it happen*

What? A pilgrimage of islanders to the East Coast - yeah it crossed my mind. But tell me, why am *I* the only one sitting here answering your prismatic questions? You think I'm suspicious? There's nothing left out there for me to explore.

{v} *His education or lack of it*

So you carried out a series of mercy killings?

{w} *Posthumous history*

{x}

{y}

{z}

{A}

[r]

Something black in the green part of your eye

The wall switch for the light's on. That's good. I thought you said you don't drink, doctor. Then why do you act so outlandish in the dark? Why are you laughing at my descriptions of killing Diablo? I got a better idea - why don't you pretend to sleep while I smash your skull in? - or how about more golden brown waffles instead? Never mind the cook's ridiculous accusations that we're abusing our breakfast privileges. Outside the motel room's windows (sorry, I mean clinic's windows), the sun's dropping lower in the sky. That means the shadows are lengthening across the even surfaces of our day-to-day lives. Soon we'll need night-vision goggles. Distant mechanical sounds (helicopter?) … distant video images are [INTERFERENCE]. But the threat's gone. I'll take my hand away from your neck. Holding my arm up is no accident on your part. That's *my* fault. Don't look surprised. That's one decision I'll never regret. Please, go ahead, take hold of my hand. Later you can ask me questions about what happened between us. Don't panic. You're gonna die first - *then* me - it's normal. What's happening makes a lot of sense. I know I look silly, but I feel an ache in my back, so don't drop to your knees beside me. I'm too sick to blame you. How long have we been lying here anyway? Let's return to the very beginning. When did I enter this hospital? Look over *there* [pointing] - a ladder and a chest lean against the room's wall. I've watched them every evening at the same time leaning there for the past (four?) months. My life's taken on a strange simplicity. That explains why I remember to wipe the perspiration from my brow.
PATRICK: So why are we here?
MIMI: In this life?
PATRICK: I almost electrocuted myself this morning. Why are we here in this store? This is no place for a two-time felon. Where's the blasphemy and pornography? Where's the connection

between obscenity and antisocial behavior?

MIMI [laughing]: We gotta pick up some wine for tonight's Thanksgiving dinner and some flowers.

PATRICK: You're good at maneuvering that shopping cart. Anyway, I'm not worried about those security cameras [gesturing to the ceiling]. It's impossible to police the imagination. We're all criminals in our own heads - that counts for a lot. I just raped that twelve-year-old boy over there [pointing] - to prove our thoughts exist in a separate indestructible realm.

MIMI: You sure dream big.

PATRICK: Hell yeah. That's how dreams come true. I got a political-religious dream.

MIMI [laughing]: Like Martin Luther King?

PATRICK: I'm a black man, aren't I? Anyway, I never listened to King's entire speech he gave that day, so I don't know what his specific dream was. I only know he *had* a dream. My point's if you're gonna have any dreams at all, you gotta sustain 'em by exercising your imagination like you do your body. You gotta go to the gym and lift weights. That's called creating art, painting a picture, shooting a film, writing a novel.

MIMI: So what's your political-religious dream?

PATRICK: In a nutshell - solve the world's problems by detaching from those problems without trying to solve them.

MIMI: Detach? You mean let sleeping dogs lie?

PATRICK: You don't get it. The point is *not* taking sides, not getting involved in arguments and drama, no fistfights, no wars, no progress, no decline - no up and down, no back and forth. You want peace, then you gotta learn *not* to care. The moment you take sides is the moment you create conflict. Trying to make our world a better place only introduces more evil into it.

MIMI: You're sounding like an infomercial. So why's the world designed that way?

PATRICK: Dunno. But what it means is every time you try to make an improvement, you step on someone else's toes, and they say, why you gotta step on *my* toes? Why am *I* the one suffering and making sacrifices so *your* dreams come true? The moment

you try to change things, improve things, there's an *I* and a *you*.
That's conflict. That's good versus evil.

MIMI: So your dream's teaching everyone not to give a shit? You
sure know how to kill a girl's dreams.

PATRICK: Tell me, Mimi, what's this fucking war about?

MIMI: You've lost it. Now you're using the F-word in the middle
of a supermarket.

PATRICK: In the detergent aisle, no less. Well, if you think God
gives a fuck about the word 'fuck,' you're fucked.

MIMI [shaking her head]: Okay, tell me, what's this war about?

PATRICK: It's about the continent and the island thinking they
know what's best for each other and the rest of the planet.

MIMI: So who's in charge here?

PATRICK: Exactly my point. No one can know who's in charge.
Neither side has access to an absolute criterion of what's right and
wrong. Yet they behave as if they do. They pretend they're *right*
and people die as a result. Then afterwards both sides clamor for
peace. Whole thing's the stupidest thing I ever saw. It's a media
war, how each side sees itself portrayed in the media - if only
both sides could learn not to care.

MIMI: Then what? How'd you raise kids in a world like that?

PATRICK: Who's talking about kids? I'm talking about 'supreme
indifference' - got a nice ring to it. If humanity dies out, so be it.
I've seen the postmortem photographs. I got no trace of drugs in
my system. Who's talking about kids?

MIMI: I am. I'm pregnant.

PATRICK: I think you got water on the brain.

MIMI: What's that mean?

PATRICK: It means I've been down roads like this many times
before - right down the hatch - all the way to premature labor.

MIMI [pointing to her abdomen]: That's where life begins. I'm
serious.

PATRICK: No. Life begins in tide-pools. Anyway, if my dream
came true, people could still have kids. What's stopping them? -
nothing.

MIMI: I guess life here on the continent seems a little strange to
you.

PATRICK: Not any stranger than on the island. Both sides think they're so different from each other, but their differences are the most superficial. At the end of the day, both sides are fundamentally identical, and nothing scares them more than facing that fact.

MIMI: Why?

PATRICK: Because then they got nothing left to live for. Their lives lose meaning when they got no dark powerful forces to defeat. … Listen to that [pointing to the ceiling] - this store's playing rock 'n roll oldies.

MIMI: What song?

PATRICK: Dusty Springfield's "I Only Want To Be With You." Tell me, Mimi, is *this* film based on a true story?

MIMI: This film?

PATRICK: Right. *This* film. You've seen the darkness too. So tell me, are you ready to work with me on this story?

MIMI [laughing]: I hear your voice calling out my name.

PATRICK: Laugh all you want - but courage is about facing the unknown. It's not about liberating Kuwait and staying to fight Saddam.

MIMI: Yeah, I heard your voice calling out to me, … but now I hear only one thing, the phrase 'apple core.'

PATRICK: C'mon, let's buy this shit, go to your folks' house, have the Thanksgiving dinner, and get this show on the road. I know our film's based on a true story, the story of eternal life - which begins tomorrow when we leave the city and head back west.

MIMI: I *am* pregnant, you know - with *your* child.

PATRICK: Okay, so that's eternal life. Fucking expensive though. Too bad I'm prohibited from opening a bank account on the continent.

MIMI: Didn't stop the pilgrims.

["I Get Around" by the Beach Boys begins playing on the supermarket PA system.]

[s]

Mental filmstrip

MIMI: That's the Hotel Gansevoort [pointing]. There's a swimming pool on top.

PATRICK: Who gives a shit. I'm tired. We're getting a room there or what?

MIMI: No. We'll crash with some friends of mine who live around here … if I can remember where.

PATRICK: And if you can't?

MIMI: We sleep on the street.

PATRICK [feigning concern]: Oh my gosh. Are you sure anyone lives around here? We walk all this way and now …

MIMI: What?

PATRICK: We're gonna miss out on the bar-top dancing? What the hell are we doing here anyway?

MIMI: Good a spot as any.

PATRICK: Man, I'm tired and hungry. See this drool dripping from the sides of my mouth? You'd think we might be able to find at least a frozen turkey in these parts.

> {a} On the continent, much as on the island, the same social patterns hold sway generation after generation: there's no twilight of the gods (or idols), never will be: nothing ever changes - *if* by 'nothing' you mean the fundamental patterns of human community. On the other hand, if you're referring to the more superficial patterns of trends and fads, well, everything's changing - nothing stays the same (including that mildew stench and those crack vials in the gutter [pointing]).

MIMI [shifting her weight from one leg to another]: It's getting kinda chilly out here.

PATRICK [snapping his knuckles]: I guess so. But cold weather keeps the heart pumping, you know. Say, let's go talk to that guy across the street [pointing], the big security guard wearing the earpiece. Maybe he can put us up for the night.

MIMI: I doubt it. His main job's holding the door open for slutty ladies and keeping everyone else out.

PATRICK: What door? I don't see anything but shadows and bricked-in windows. A beautiful autumn evening like this one - the guard's gotta be in a good mood. I bet he lets us into whatever he's guarding.

MIMI: I'm tired. I don't like going into dark strange alleys any more than you do.

PATRICK: *Look* - now he's talking to that black guy in the red dress and stilettos. Holy shit, he's letting him into the club, bar, whatever. What do we gotta do around here?

MIMI: Let's exchange our clothes. How about that?

PATRICK: You think I can fit into your skirt?

MIMI: Dunno. Let's find out ... just change here ... in this alley.

PATRICK: Can the guard see us from over there?

MIMI: Only if he wants to.

PATRICK: Why the hell would he care what's going on in a dark alley across the street, right? What could be going on over here except a master dismemberer with butchering instruments?

MIMI: They don't have those around here anymore. Rents got too high.

> {b} *Look* - over there [pointing across the cobblestoned
> street to an animated billboard]. That's Fex Urbis, my
> favorite kung-fu movie house. That's me, third in line,
> wearing white Levi's and a tight black T-shirt. Next to me,
> that's my girlfriend - a beautiful Brazilian ex-nanny with a
> pixie cut and a French manicure. Let's watch in horror as
> the wound in her neck begins spurting blood onto the nicely
> polished sidewalk. She's clutching at her throat with both
> hands.

PATRICK [shouting over the pounding-pulsing music]: So what *is* this place?

MIMI: Entertainment's nonstop around here. That's normal.

PATRICK: I can barely hear you. We've digressed into something ... uh, into ...

MIMI: A tranny bar.

PATRICK: Why do those FBI guys keep the chubby dancer blindfolded the whole time they screw her?

MIMI: They can't be disturbed. It's part of the performance.

PATRICK: That dancer has bad skin.

MIMI: I'm a friend of a friend of his.

PATRICK: He gives out financial advice, right?

MIMI: He's a high-paid personal-injury lawyer.

PATRICK: He's too fat to be a full-time dancer.

MIMI: Most of his extra weight's muscle.

PATRICK [grinning]: That's all you got to say?

MIMI: He spits up blood too.

PATRICK: I remember a time when only black chicks did that.

MIMI: Those days are pretty much gone forever.

PATRICK: You think they serve food here?

MIMI: I doubt it. But five thousand dollars would sure buy lots of drinks.

PATRICK: Think they mind if I take incriminating photographs with this cellphone?

MIMI: Just be discreet about it.

PATRICK: By the way, did you notice the bartender has a small crescent-shaped scar under his right eye? I wonder how that happened.

MIMI: Don't be so wary. Let's wait, see what goes down. C'mon, we'll sit at that table over there [pointing]. I'm tired of standing.

PATRICK: I hear you. My feet hurt in these high-heels.

> {c} In the wee hours of the morning I'd sit there alone at a counter in a Howard Johnson's eating ice cream sundaes. The hostess (who had an eerie resemblance to Sarah Jessica Parker) would be strung out on methamphetamines. The waiter, a preoperative transsexual, would talk with anyone who'd listen about boxers and comedians and jazz musicians. The jukebox would play "Folsom Prison Blues" or something similar.

MIMI: You never told me how Diablo died. Killed in an auto accident?

PATRICK: Let's say I smashed his head through a cosmetics counter.

MIMI: So you're not all fun and games *if* you're telling the truth.

PATRICK: You should see me bend over to pull pants on my legs.

MIMI: I guess I will later when we return our clothes to each other.

PATRICK: You look great in my tracksuit, by the way.

MIMI: My lip gloss and blush look good on you.

PATRICK: I need lessons on how to bat these false eyelashes.

MIMI: With practice you'll get the hang of it.

PATRICK: Are there any possible side effects from cross-dressing?

MIMI: For one evening, no. But if you make a habit of it, well, …

PATRICK [laughing, wiping the back of his hand across his mouth]: Maybe I'll place a personal ad.

MIMI [frowning]: Those are creepy. They attract desperate maladjusted people.

PATRICK: Isn't that the point?

MIMI: So add it to your to-do list.

PATRICK [snapping his fingers]: Done. What's next?

> {d} Hey gorgeous, *I* didn't break that empty beer bottle against the fruit-punch machine. Not that it matters. I did lose the keys to your father's liquor cabinet however. Uh oh, Gorgeous isn't much happy about that. My God, look at her standing there in that down ski jacket. She wants a serious relationship.

MIMI: For some reason I keep fantasizing about the bartender. I got a crush on him. I like his freckles and the small bump on the bridge of his nose. I wonder if he enjoys the color Rothko Red as much as I do.

PATRICK: I hear he's got a passion for art history and the great master painters. He's a serious obsessive-compulsive too. His apartment's stuffed with to-do lists and perfectly clean Chinese takeout containers.

MIMI [taking a gulp of beer]: So?

PATRICK: How long we gonna stay here? I feel like I've lost a significant percentage of my hearing.

MIMI: You're hopeless.

PATRICK [leaning forward]: You're crazy.

MIMI: I bet that bartender ends up a spinster.

PATRICK: Are his testosterone levels are screwed up?

MIMI: He doesn't like modern art. He doesn't see how abhorrent he is.

PATRICK: So you've changed your mind - you despise him now?

MIMI: God, why can't he be a girl? I want a female version of him.

PATRICK [frowning]: This is getting complicated. I'm having a hard time following. You want a woman, not a man?

MIMI: How long we known each other?

PATRICK: Not long enough. Let's see, I arrived here about three weeks ago. Most of that time was spent getting interrogated, and then … uh …

MIMI: Don't say anything else. Your mouth's disgusting.

PATRICK: Okay, I'll keep my mouth shut. So how long we gonna stay here?

MIMI: Wanna go back to my place right now?

PATRICK: Absolutely. I'm tired of wearing your clothes.

MIMI: Let's go.

PATRICK: We're gonna walk all the way back to Alphabet City this time of night?

MIMI: Nope. It's times like this they invented cabs for.

{e} Every damn time I stepped inside the doors of that ten-thousand-square-foot loft I'd see the same things - same people in the same clothes reflected in the same floor-to-ceiling mirrors. Gucci suits. Yves Saint Laurent cocktail gowns. Pucci scarves. Five-inch patent leather stilettos. Mink-lined boots. In the bedroom, 600-thread-count bed sheets, floor-to-ceiling lacquered doors.

MIMI: What do you think of my apartment?

PATRICK: That's your cat over there?

MIMI: He's got feline leukemia.

PATRICK [turning around]: Okay, I'm leaving.

MIMI: What?

PATRICK: Keep your diseased cat away from me.

MIMI: He's not contagious.

PATRICK: Maybe not, but if he's killed once, he'll kill again. You should take him to a vet.

MIMI: It's a 'she,' by the way. Want something to drink?

PATRICK: Sure [walking towards the kitchen behind MIMI]. I remember once I saw a rabid pit bull get loose on a playground. It was horrible.

MIMI: Pit bull?

PATRICK: Pit bull terrier. Staffordshire bull terrier.

MIMI: What?

PATRICK: A damn dog - ah forget it.

MIMI [standing at the open refrigerator]: What do you want?

PATRICK: What do you got?

MIMI: Not much it turns out. Sorry.

PATRICK: Got any hard liquor in that liquor cabinet [pointing]?

MIMI [removing a key from around her neck, unlocking the cabinet]: Yep, look at that - pepper vodka.

PATRICK: Great. Let's do shooters.

MIMI: Russian-style drinking, huh?

PATRICK: You could call it that. But if you had tequila, it'd be Mexican style. And bourbon ...

MIMI: We need a chaser?

PATRICK: Nope. Let's pretend we're raving alcoholics. All we need's a single shot, unmixed, served at room temperature.

MIMI: Okay, here goes.

PATRICK [toasting]: We got the whole summer ahead of us. Here's to Diabolein. Down the hatch. So where's the sixty-inch flat-screen TV?

[PATRICK walks into the living room.]

MIMI: Give me a sec, all right? I need to visit the bathroom.

PATRICK: Okay. Do your thing.

MIMI [minutes later, returning from the bathroom]: I ran out of Xanax. Man, the bathroom's a war zone too.

[The doorbell chimes.]

PATRICK: Who could that be at this hour?

MIMI [walking to the door]: It's Tara coming by with beer.

PATRICK: How'd she know we're home?

MIMI: I called her on my phone when I was in the bathroom.

PATRICK: Good timing.

[MIMI opens the door.]

TARA: Hi, Mimi!

MIMI: Hi there. Come in. My friend Patrick's here too.

[Introductions are made in the living room. Everyone takes a seat. Bottles of beer are opened.]

PATRICK [smiling with feigned excitement]: Now what?

TARA: Let's not get carried away.

PATRICK: Should I call the police - or child welfare?

TARA [frowning]: Why would you do that?

PATRICK: You look very young. So what's that on your face, Tara?

TARA: A couple bruises. It's innocuous. I'll be all right in the morning. People don't die as easy as you might think.

MIMI: C'mon, guys, let's have some real conversation.

PATRICK: Shouldn't you see an innocuous doctor?

TARA: I'll be fine. Head and face wounds always bleed profusely. But you should see Ashley.

PATRICK: Why?

TARA: She's laid up in the hospital with a concussion, a broken femur, and, uh, some internal bleeding.

PATRICK: You sure you shouldn't see a doctor?

TARA: I hate doctors. That's how this happened in the first place. We were demonstrating outside an abortion clinic when we were attacked.

PATRICK: Oh, I see. Next thing you know, they're attacking you with box cutters. I've heard the safest thing you can do is agree to an abortion.

MIMI: C'mon, guys! Can't we talk about, uh, I dunno, something …

TARA [pointing at PATRICK]: You're one of those islander refugees, aren't you?

MIMI [cutting off PATRICK]: Yes, he is, but he's cool. C'mon, Tara, he's joking around.

TARA [glaring at PATRICK]: Why the hell would I wanna drink beer with you?

PATRICK [shaking his head]: So far nothing's happened, but you act like I've joked about killing your mom or something. You're the one who's getting carried away. Okay, Mimi, you wanna change the topic. Well, Tara, tell me about your varsity lacrosse team.

[TARA says nothing, looks down at her drink.]

MIMI [to TARA]: Patrick here's traveled all the way across the continent to be here.

TARA [turning to PATRICK]: So why *are* you here?

PATRICK: It's a very long entertaining story, as they say, with many stop-off points and plot twists, including separate Nevada and Minnesota episodes.

MIMI: The cops have been hassling him all week.

TARA: Why?

PATRICK: No big deal. Their questioning's concluded now that I've convinced them I'm insane but harmless.

TARA: Why are they monitoring you?

PATRICK: Why else? - I'm an islander. I might be up to no good.

TARA: Are you?

PATRICK: I wanna start a new life on the continent. Besides, it's *their* problem. They attacked the island, forced me out. I never asked to be a refugee.

TARA: You're on their no-travel list?

PATRICK: Me and hundreds of other islanders. But now that I'm cleared of suspicion I can get on with my life.

TARA [growing more interested]: What kinds of questions did they ask you?

PATRICK: What you'd expect - stuff about Diabolein mostly.

TARA: I have some friends who are into that. Myself, I don't see what the big deal is. ... Say, I have an idea. You guys wanna do some drinking at an airport bar? We can take the subway there. Easy enough.

MIMI: But why?

TARA: Something different. Plus it's open all night.

MIMI: So are lots of other places around here.

TARA: I like having those bleary-eyed travelers around me.

PATRICK [standing up]: I'm up for it. Why not? I qualify - I'm bleary-eyed. Might as well continue our urban roving. We've covered half of Manhattan. Let's take in the airports now.

MIMI [rolling her eyes, putting her drink down on the coffee table]: Let me first change outta this skirt.

> {f} You happen to know the secret shortcut to the baggage claim area? - - Ask that woman over there clutching the Coach suitcase. Her [pointing]? The one in the Michael Stars T-shirt who's recovering from her first Botox injections.

TARA: What do you think?

PATRICK: Can't remember how long it's been since I set foot in an airport. I'm impressed. I feel like a little kid on Halloween going into a haunted house.

MIMI: You afraid to fly?

PATRICK: No, but the continental government's afraid to let me fly.

TARA: You're on their no-fly lists too?

PATRICK: No-travel list, no-fly list. I bet I'm on all their lists. The idea's to keep me confined to the island. It works until they attack the island and drive me out. The inconsistent policies of the continental government never cease to amaze me.

TARA [adjusting a diamond pendant hanging above her cleavage]: You're blessed.

MIMI: With islanders that's the only thing that matters - blessings - and luck.

PATRICK [shaking his head]: Can't explain it, but islanders manage to survive wherever they go. Even when a place doesn't feel right, we're flexible enough to fit in. Let's say we don't like pale green walls or minimalist interior decorating, let's say something isn't quite right. Well, it doesn't matter. We survive anyway.

MIMI: To me, as an islander, it feels more peaceful the further I go east. That's why I don't plan to leave Alphabet City.

TARA: I forgot you're an islander too, Mimi. Guess that goes to show how well you guys adapt and blend in.

PATRICK: Still, certain things give us away.
TARA: Like what?
PATRICK: We're genetically incapable of ...
MIMI [laughing]: *Shhhh!* Don't reveal our secrets.

[t]

Only so many hours in a universal work day (Or, Transubstantiation: giving a thing a name that belongs to something else)

PART I

Hey Patrick, for a most of the story you've been quiet about your son. Perhaps you're concealing something from [INTERFERENCE] and them [pointing to the AUDIENCE]. So tell us, how old's your son? What's his name? What hospital did you say he's serving time in?

Oh, believe me, Diablo, I worry about my son. I know this hospital's incredibly boring for a boy with such wily wandering qualities and multiplicity of the mind (*metis*): a boy so unstable though only in *appearance*. I'm serious. That's how we raised him, me and my ex-wife, to be serious - though with a strong sense of humor. Seriousness is important if you stand a chance of making headway with Diabolein.

How old's your son? What's his real name? Can he sing a theogony like Hesiod? Can he piss poetry like Pindar?

I forget my son's real age, prefer not to mention his name here in the presence of the medical prophets. Indeed I recognize this hospital on the outskirts of Las Vegas. Why, look at those austere rows of one-way windows, the plastic blinds, stucco walls, fresh paint and posters, plastic carnations on Formica [INTERFERENCE] … molecules bonding together … at various times in the past … in a variety of ways … now one thing … then another. You get the impression no one ever comes in or goes out of that building.

What *type* of hospital?

A special mental hospital for dissident thinkers and political opponents of the regime, not mere crazy people - a whole other dimension, with sleazy moments of tenderness and faces flushed red, like a Sam Fuller film or something. Ain't it the architectural antithesis of a casino?

So what are we doing here today when we could be gambling and slaughtering sheep? My whole body hurts.

First off, we're having a birthday party for my son. That's why we're skipping the gambling. In a sense this will be my son's longed-for homecoming - the beginning of a golden age on the hospital grounds - weaving, sewing, carpentry, cereal boxes, spaghetti dinners, so on.

After the party winds down?

We give voice to the ancient Greek Gods. We cry out to those waiflike gods. We *do* slaughter sheep in another sense. We put my son forever out of his misery [patting his right trouser pocket].

What's that you got there?

Rather not put words on it except to say 'symbols of power.'

Is that your boy running over *there*, the one with the ratty blonde hair and baggy pants and Popeye forearms [pointing]?

Indeed it is [laughing, blushing]. That action sequence proves my son's quite the romantic. He's playing his favorite game called Boogeyman. When he knows I'm due for arrival, he hides on the hospital grounds, in the bushes or behind a sculpture, waiting to leap out at me when I pass on the sidewalk. Often he brandishes a golden staff and a lyre pretending to be Hermes. After I notice him and jump back in surprise, he turns away, in another direction, consistent with his latest conception of the various voices of God. Among the patients, he's distinguished by a strong sense of control over each and every unreliable appearance.

What's that dog yapping at his heels?

A pit bull terrier named Buck. The doctors assign each patient a dog to symbolize faith in and misguided commitment to socially mediated philosophical truths.

Did you say your boy suffers from the spiraling efforts of epilepsy?

Oh gosh, I never said 'suffers', did I? How can you suffer if you're outside social reality looking in, if you're detached from society? Sure, his mind's on fire, but he's got complete control over each and every vocal cord. You'll see. God has spoken to me through my son - I'm *not* deluding myself. God is the mind on fire.

What else do the two of you do for fun? I can't help but be amused as your story spins out of control.

Real fun, you say? Something wider in scope, more temporal and topical than inanimate objects scattered across a lawn? Well, when he's confined to his cell, I tell my son make-believe stories about make-believe places and make-believe people. Those figures of speech allow his mind to wander through a long series of obscure transformations, culminating in grand condensations of character and setting - plus a musical accompaniment of rock 'n roll oldies (before the Beatles ruined everything). My son's favorite locale is [clearing his throat] Hollow Earth, a quaint place ruled by the iron- and ham-fisted Captain Beginsu.

Oh yeah, you mentioned that man earlier in thhis story, much earlier. I remember the place too - a sort of Inner Earth knockoff, right?

But so much more, with many other distortions, characters, and protean playthings - Costa Move, President Dr. Rikmansuort, Joey Scattergood, Mr. Riordan, Morris Rozlamovat, Doctor Swoboda.

Those names ring a loud bell in my head. … Costa Move - the guy who gulped Christ's blood and gnawed on his flesh, right?

Look [pointing, laughing] - there he goes! My son's got a fine running form, akin to a javelin-wielder. Anyway, speaking of the Eucharist and similar ceremonial benedictions, you ever heard the resounding voices of Greek Gods yielding to the flesh of Greek boys? I got the notebook evidence right here [patting his left trouser pocket].

My, Patrick, sounds like you know how to have *real* fun with your son. God bless you! So why's he committed to a hospital - in Nevada of all places?

Must we get into that here?

Where's the boy's mother?

Must we? To prove murder, you must first prove intent. Anyway, the story's a long one, with many twists and turns. You should see what it looks like on paper - the imbrications of sentence and paragraph … uh, … or no - rather, a literary mosaic pleasant to the touch when read aloud while puzzling the reader with its lack of a single proper meaning - a literary method more metrical than semantic. Dammit, please stop pulling at my sleeve, Diablo!

Okay, sorry. You mean your story's following up on an ancient oral tradition?

That's why I make explicit mention here of Polytropic the Great Liar.

Who the hell's *he*?

Urban legend claims he's the originator of Diabolein. I first learned about him in seminary school. The point is - who's to say who's a liar if we're all agnostics? Get it?

Where are we going with this [gesturing towards the flagstone walk]?

Let's follow my son back into the hospital. His ass is showing - how quaint.

PART II

Now that we're safe inside our institute's canteen [loosening a ring of keys from his belt], can you tell me your son's real name?

Andre.

How puzzling and deceptive. That's why you're proud to say he's a liar?

If you prefer, yes, though in fact my son's a creator. He fashions something out of nothing. If you call that mere artifice, well, you better take it up with every mother-form on this grinding green planet. My son uses his imagination to invent things.

Around here we call that lying, Father, commonplace and unnoticed till you raise it to the level of an art form (*techne*).

Tell me, doctor, before we discuss the fate of my lying son and the hallowed arts of deception, where did you take my companion Diablo? Must I remind you to put down that ratty old copy of Kraft-Ebbing and pay closer attention to the deviated realities at hand?

Problem's you appear to be provoking the patients with your talk of god and the devil. That's the issue here - your persistent use of emotional facsimile [air-quotes]. Plus you're a chain-smoker.

Got a nicotine lozenge?

Nope [puffing out his chest], but I got a travel-packet of antacids [patting his jacket pocket]. Anyway, this institute makes a point of ignoring the nihilistic logic so typical of you islanders [turning his back on Patrick, walking over to the vending machine, pressing a button, triggering a coffee pour]. How long you intend to stay at our institute?

As long as it takes to put my son out of his misery.

Always the joker. I wonder, why does that comment bespeak such failure on your part?

Excuse me? I'll blow your head down!

That's enough, Father! Stop picking your nose!

Now I have a joke for *you*, doctor [laughing]. There's arsenic in that there coffee [pointing].

Aw c'mon now. Gimme a break. Don't you islanders have a conscience?

Sheep were made to be slaughtered - get used to it.

PART III

What's that [pointing to the air]?

The pungent odors of hair gel and avocado soap predominate throughout this particular corridor. Also notice how the floral patterns on the patients' knickers clash with the linoleum.

I'll take note of nothing. I wanna know when we're returning to Las Vegas. Not only should I gamble one last time before we depart, Patty's no doubt wondering where the hell we are. I told her we'd have lunch together. Imagine her shock when she learns we're at a local hospital murdering your son.

Jesus, Diablo, we'll return to the city after the doctors stop patronizing me with their manila folders. Patty will have to be patient.

I feel like we've been airdropped deep in enemy territory. This whole place makes my stomach surge. I'm scared shitless.

You might wanna wipe off that cushion before sitting down [gesturing to the sofa in his son's room]. And you [pointing at his son lying in bed], stop squeezing those blackheads! ... Okay [turning back to DIABLO] you sure none of the doctors followed us down the corridor?

I'm sure. C'mon, let's get on with it. We got a long day of driving tomorrow.

Okay then [facing his son]. The purpose of our visit, Andre, is to take drastic action, to find a final solution to your [INTERFERENCE] problems. All you gotta do is sit back on your bed, relax, let your body go limp. I'll take care of the rest. ... Trust me - it's okay. Main thing's to relax. After I clean my fingernails, I'm gonna grab you by the throat before you can blink and squeeze the life right outta you. I'm stronger than you are, Andre.

[INTERFERENCE]

[Turning to the AUDIENCE, laughing] Fact is, putting my mother and son out of their misery has only whetted my appetite for euthanasia.

PART IV

PATTY [turning away from the bus's window to look at PATRICK]: You like surprises?

PATRICK: Sure, but there's nothing surprising about this bus taking us straight to Nevada.

PATTY: Not directly. First we go south to LA, then cross over into Nevada, which puts us in the Las Vegas area.

PATRICK: That means we're gonna breathe some of the dirtiest air in California.

PATTY: It was our only choice if we wanted to leave San Francisco immediately - 99 south to uh [looking at map] to Bakersfield, ... no wait, to Pasadena, and ... let's see ...

PATRICK [gesturing out the bus's windows]: Man, this freeway's tied up in massive knots of traffic. Loveliest thing I ever seen . Like polyester - some people can wear it and still look elegant.

PATTY: Clearly the entire state's dealing with an islander refugee problem, not only San Francisco.

PATRICK: When will the authorities learn?

PATTY: So, tell me the godawful truth - there *is* a specific reason we're heading to Nevada, right?

PATRICK: How do you mean?

PATTY: Tell me the truth, Patrick.

PATRICK: I'm looking for some fresh faces. I'm sighting down the barrel of a gun, aiming to shoot that crop-dusting plane or that U-Haul [gesturing out the window].

PATTY: Looking for fresh faces, huh? I don't buy it.

PATRICK: Why are you wearing that headscarf?

PATTY: It's a disguise. You'll see I got a thing for costumes.

PATRICK: Like Halloween?

PATTY: Year round I like to dress up and play roles.

PATRICK [laughing]: You know what they say - if you want catharsis, go to the theatre.

PATTY: Oh yeah, the all-the-world's-a-stage stuff, huh?

PATRICK: More than that. Can we ever know if we're truly lost, if we're way off course?

PATTY: Simple - never make an arrival unannounced. So tell me, who's expecting you in Nevada? Who's there?

PATRICK: Dunno. You tell me. I never been to Nevada. I'm imagining desert vistas, casinos with steam-cleaned carpets, concrete shopping centers, fast-food drive-thru, uh, law-enforcement agencies, hardware stores, uh, bulldozed fields covered in searing hot asphalt.

PATTY: You got most of it right. Still, you gotta tell the truth. We have to trust each other if we're gonna travel across the continent.

PATRICK: All the way across?

PATTY: Whatever.

PATRICK [throwing up his hands]: Okay! I'm not afraid of you. There *is* someone just around the corner in Nevada - my son, Andre.

PATTY: Holy shit, you got a son? What's he doing on the continent?

PATRICK: The storyline's a convoluted one, filled with lots of guilt and startling admissions.

PATTY: Your son's a grown man?

PATRICK: Yes and no. He looks like a grown man but acts like he's younger than fifteen.

PATTY: He's a citizen? He's got a visa?

PATRICK: Very special circumstances brought him here. He's sick with a rare familial genetic disorder. Continental doctors petitioned the government to let him get treatment at a special convalescent hospital in Nevada where they can study him.

PATTY: How long's he been here?

PATRICK: Most of his godforsaken life.

PATTY: Where's his mother?

PATRICK: Covered in asphalt. Andre was a source of friction between me and my ex-wife. She left us several years ago, disappeared. I was sorry to see her ago. She was a terrific decorator. Last I heard, she's buried in a cemetery on the island. Died of black lung disease - chain-smoker.

PATTY: You got pictures of your son?

PATRICK: Not with me, no. The surveillance tape footage burned up when I set fire to our mansion before leaving for the continent.

PATTY: Surveillance?

PATRICK: That's right. Over the years, Andre's roommate at the hospital secretly and illegally provided me with tapes of my son's lengthy failed recovery. Hey, why are you scribbling this down?

PATTY: I'm keeping a travel diary.

PATRICK: This is personal stuff. What if it gets into the wrong hands, a rogue publisher or something?

PATTY: Your son has a roommate?

PATRICK: For many years he's had the same roommate - Costa Move. He's crazier than my son, believe me. That guy's got a different kind of genetic disorder that involves drinking the blood of dying or recently killed animals.

PATTY: That's firsthand information you'd rather forget?

PATRICK: It's not from anonymous phone calls if that's what you mean.

PATTY: This is shaping up to be quite a story.

PATRICK: Beautiful, isn't it? - like something you'd see on a New England postcard.

PATTY: But it needs lots of work.

PATRICK: What does?

PATTY: You getting hungry?

PATRICK: Not yet. Want a cigarette?

PATTY: I'm imagining warm peach cobbler with vanilla ice cream.

PATRICK: I hope you're putting that in your travel diary too.

PATTY [taking PATRICK's hand, squeezing it]: I realize there's lots for us to do. This is a difficult situation. Yet there's nothing like a child to help lift one's spirits. Oh shit, I just realized we left our sleeping bags at the bus station in San Francisco. We got nothing to sleep on tonight.

PATRICK: Who cares? We'll deal with it. What we lack in strength, we'll make up for in lovemaking. Plus, I like surprises.

PATTY: So few of us still enjoy surprises.

PATRICK: Boo!

PATTY: Thank you so much for the wonderful welcome.

[u]

Hard-driving thriller (or, Stuck between a casino on one side and a McDonald's on the other)

I

DIABLO [leaning back on the bed's pillows]: I'm a big boy now. I can flip my coins right here for the rest of the night. No reason to go downstairs to the casino - save that experience for tomorrow.

PATRICK [lying down on the blue oriental carpet, looking up at the hotel room's ceiling]: Man, I feel slo-mo explosions right behind my eyes. If only I could sorta lurch forward into a healthier future … sounds fading out, replacing this headache.

DIABLO: Tantrum coming on?

PATRICK: It's not the flu or an ulcer or cosmic narcissism.

DIABLO: You practicing abstinence?

PATRICK [pointing to a green oxygen cylinder leaning against the bed]: Anything left in that?

DIABLO: Nope. Patty used up the last of it.

PATRICK: Where is she anyway?

DIABLO: She's out on the town spiking the football, as we used to say.

PATRICK [laughing]: Squeezing air out of a dying man's lungs …

DIABLO: … lying on a narrow bed aneath a crucifix.

PATRICK: How the hell's she avoid getting pregnant?

DIABLO: Once is all it takes and afore you know it - a lump the size of a grapefruit.

PATRICK: Well, *I've* been practicing abstinence.

DIABLO: I had no idea. Should've given it more thought.

PATRICK [opening and closing his mouth]: No one ever does.

DIABLO: Very embarrassing answer.

PATRICK: And irrelevant at this point.

II

PATTY: What's that you're holding?

PATRICK: This? - a martini glass.

PATTY: No, *that* [pointing].

PATRICK: A pile of human bones wrapped in a blue oxford-cloth shirt.

DIABLO [pointing at the bones]: Let's pretend that man's name was Mr. Riordan.

PATTY: What did he do?

DIABLO: Let's pretend he was too heavy for his height, round-shouldered, with a long fleshy nose.

PATTY: So?

PATRICK: So he was a little past his expiration date. By the way, what do you get when you cross a laptop with a wheelchair?

DIABLO: An old-fashioned school desk?

PATRICK: A suburban dentist in a freshly pressed oxford-cloth shirt. Get it?

PATTY [waving her hands]: Where'd you get those bones?

PATRICK: From the examination table of a local convalescent home.

PATTY: The doctors gave 'em to you?

PATRICK: You like surprises, right?

PATTY: Is that what this is - a nasty surprise?

PATRICK: Oh honey, don't be scared. We'll give them bones a proper burial. We got funeral plans and an autopsy report.

PATTY [shaking the hair out of her face]: I'm gonna throw up.

DIABLO [turning to the AUDIENCE]: That's rather unpleasant news. Perhaps she doesn't realize Mr. Riordan was on a respirator in the ICU for many days before we pulled the plug.

III

PATTY: What *is* this place?

PATRICK: An old-fashioned CIA computer room.

PATTY: Disguised as a resort suite?

PATRICK: Why not? It's the perfect front.

PATTY [catching her breath, then biting her fingernail]: I'm not sure.

PATRICK: How are you feeling?

PATTY [blushing]: Guilty.

PATRICK: About what?

PATTY: Where's Diablo?

PATRICK: Downstairs gambling. So what are you feeling guilty about?

PATTY: My mother was a stripper, for God's sake, and I don't know who my father was!

PATRICK [wincing]: You mean you were born out of wedlock?

PATTY: The idea scares the crap outta me.

PATRICK: Why? There's scientific precedent for it.

PATTY: God, this is horrible. I'm gonna be sick.

PATRICK: Again? Guess that explains the constant vomiting.

PATTY [rushing into the bathroom]: Excuse me - it's panic time!

PATRICK [turning to the AUDIENCE]: What's up with all of you?

IV

PATRICK: This is Las Vegas, Patty, nobody cares. Gamblers and prostitutes aren't supposed to procreate. That's basic biology. If you cross the two, the resulting child [INTERFERENCE].

PATTY: Is a mutant, right?

PATRICK [laughing]: I'm never having sex with you again.

PATTY: That isn't funny.

PATRICK [standing up from the bed]: You sound mad. *Arrgh* I'm feeling dizzy. What time is it?

PATTY: Shouldn't we rescue Diablo from the craps tables before he loses all our money?

PATRICK [walking over to the window]: Jesus, what did that bastard tell you?

PATTY: About what?

PATRICK: Our travel plans.

PATTY: He said the two of you are gonna visit your son in the hospital and I'm supposed to have everything packed so we can make a run for it when you return to the resort.

PATRICK: Make a run for it? Did he say *where* we're going with our luggage?

PATTY: No.

PATRICK: That's a problem, isn't it? What kind of chance operation is Diablo running here?

PATTY. Don't ask me. I'm along for the ride.

PATRICK: You're helpful. Just look at those lights down there [pointing out the window at the Vegas Strip], the traffic, the waterfalls, the swimming pools and enormous atriums and banks of glassed-in elevators, the parking lots attached to Spanish-tiled condos, the 7-Elevens, the sprinklers on timers - I could go on and on and on. Instead, let's imagine all that illumination bringing our dead friends back to life and abolishing unfair labor practices. I'm floating on air.

V

DIABLO: How's it possible to be so uncomfortable? Tell me, *how* did I get here - to Las Vegas?

PATRICK: If you recall, we met at that roadside diner in the desert where you asked me to flip a coin.

DIABLO: No - before that, before we settled on a mission - if only I could remember.

PATRICK: What?

DIABLO: *Before* we met. It was dark, pitch dark.

PATRICK: Yeah that sums it up for everyone.

DIABLO: If only I could remember.

PATRICK: Why are you so uncomfortable?

DIABLO: There's no way I can leave this hotel without settling on a destination.

PATRICK: Then flip the coin! Where the hell are you taking us anyway, what address?

DIABLO: Me? It's the coin speaking [holding up the peso piece]. That's chance. I'm unwilling to leave before this coin's luck changes.

PATRICK: If the coin's not working, what do the gambling chips say? Shit, what's the *map* say [pointing at an atlas opened on the floor]?

DIABLO: Las Vegas is a pit stop, a minor annoyance to be shrugged off. We're not meant to put down roots here.

PATRICK: So let's roll. This isn't an Olympic-level sport run amok. I'm curious, what's that place *there* called [pointing]?

DIABLO: Area 51.

PATRICK: What about Patty?

DIABLO: She's rundown, scrawny, seems to be allergic to everything - even the desert. Plus, how'd she get that jagged scar across her face?

PATRICK: Pretty gruesome, huh? I imagine her T-cell count's off the charts. Anyway, she's coming with us, right?

DIABLO: Tell me, what do we *know* about our friends?

PATRICK: Douche bags.

DIABLO: You sound mad.

PATRICK: There's an insistent pounding in my skull.

DIABLO: You should call that a hangover.

PATRICK: I call it a bad headache.

DIABLO: Lots of caffeine will do the trick, plus Nicorette gum.

PATRICK: Lots of caffeine *caused* it, you moron!

DIABLO: You should've got hooked on other stuff. Anyway, I'm optimistic. I vote for taking Patty with us.

PATRICK [rubbing his eyes]: I feel like shit.

DIABLO: Thanks for noticing.

VI

PATRICK [feeling the pulse in PATTY's neck]: Did I wake you? Oh, I'm sorry. I'm not gonna hurt your head or neck. Mind if I take a close look at the surface of your body?

PATTY: Knock yourself out.

PATRICK: Mind if I take a blood sample to see if you have an over-reactive immune system?

PATTY: Whatever you need.

PATRICK: You're pretty confident.

PATTY: I've done nothing wrong.

PATRICK: Who was that valet parking attendant?

PATTY: Mr. Hooper. He works at a cable TV network.

PATRICK: I've heard otherwise. He parks cars for a living.

PATTY: From who?

PATRICK: Diablo. He's been keeping tabs on you.

PATTY: Where the hell is he?

PATRICK: Downstairs. One last gambling session before we hit the road.

PATTY: Are you threatening me?

PATRICK: Why threaten you?

PATTY: Honest to God I have no idea what you're talking about.

PATRICK: You think maybe Mr. Hooper could, uh, procure us a second car, a Toyota, for instance, or an SUV.

PATTY: What's 'procure'?

PATRICK: Jesus Christ, I'm sorry if I overestimated your, uh, your [INTERFERENCE].

PATTY: You treat me like shit, then expect me to steal a car for you - *that's* threatening me!

PATRICK: You sound mad.

PATTY: You don't have the balls [walking towards the door].

PATRICK: Don't slam the door on the way out. I got a terrible headache.

PATTY [turning around in the doorway]: You think you're one hard-nosed son of a bitch, but I know better.

PATRICK: It's obvious you've done your homework. The implications are clear.

VII

DIABLO: I've changed plans.

PATRICK: Any idea why?

DIABLO: To hell with Mexico. We're going east, … the Colorado Rockies and beyond … Iowa, Minnesota, Michigan [pointing at the atlas].

PATRICK: Wherever we go, it's fine with me - but LET'S GO!

DIABLO: You sound mad.

PATRICK [shaking PATTY by the shoulder]: Wake up, Patty, wake up. We're leaving.

PATTY: What's the difference?

DIABLO [dabbing at his mouth with a handkerchief]: What makes you think we're just a couple crazy islanders?

PATTY: Why go to the trouble to think at all, right? Doesn't matter what the hell we decide to do. This is some kind of sick joke, isn't it?

DIABLO [turning to the AUDIENCE]: I rolled the dice and crapped out. So what?

[v]

ALLUVIAL GOLD TOO SOON -

DIABLO [to the AUDIENCE]: Y'all know me. I never wear a life jacket when I'm out here on the water. Y'all know I know how to survive an invasion. Don't be surprised if I capture the minds of you and your ... [INTERFERENCE]. Not easy being a bad blue [INTERFERENCE] around here. The Age o'Solar swallows us whole. Alluvial gold comes too soon. We must act quickly to return this performance back to a per-pay basis. C'mon, spectators, act happy! If you treasure your necks more than 300 U.S. dollars, you might find a whole new boss in these alphabetic factors - 1 to 2 to 26 - assuming I catch your [INTERFERENCE] afore she's deleted 10 more factors. What do you care? You wanna survive initial linguistic establishment? You wanna play it safe? Then make yourselves widespread throughout the battle. I want no volunteers. That's right, captains of language - on this island of text I advanced myself 10,000 U.S. dollars to choose heads *and* tails. Whole thing afore the Age o'Solar swallows us whole.

PATRICK [to the AUDIENCE]: Let's be reasonable about the choppy waters, okay? This ain't the time or place for some half-competent type of post-thing. I'll not stand up here, watch the audience drown. See him [pointing], the little refugee boy spread-eagled in the aisle?

DIABLO [turning to PATRICK]: That's psychological. Your tears are [INTERFERENCE]. What? You shouted *incoming!* with your hands on the Independence Day start-up button.

PATRICK: And you almost drowned in the channel. So tell 'em what happened.

DIABLO [turning back to the AUDIENCE]: Submarine torpedo-attack on the 2nd of October. Our leader returned to the island with ... Imagine an explosion on the 11th, right there in the channel, crashing 12 minutes long. You don't *hear* the first attack for half an hour yet you know when you're *water-long!* You turn the back clock to the end. I know our mission's secret. No editor can solve that problem. These episodes aren't listed overdue for a week. Anyway, at first light, our leaders will begin rebuilding the strong framework, and it'll be like pushing the old square peg into the old round hole. You'll see the different names scrawled on the calendar - Battle of Waterloo, Hiroshima, Nine-Eleven - yet the idea will remain the same. Those screaming refugees, man, they're pounding on the sides of the boat, hollering (like rollercoasters?). Sometimes it's gone ... other times it won't reappear ... one time the ferryman's on your right side staring straight into your left eye. Re: the ferryman: no living eyes - black eyes - doll eyes - when he works, he don't live, and when he bites your arm his eyes flicker black turning white flickering back and forth ... a coin toss ... terribly high ride there inside your inner ear. Teeth clean bite through, oceans of red - pounding, hollering, tearing you split to pieces. That's how you know the end of the first dawn's attack - dead, bloody. But how to immortalize thousands of refugees when you don't recognize a single one? Continental administrators set our average survival to 6 hours on that Thursday morning. Then I run into an old friend on his way to Duluth, Akron maybe, a crazed crew member. That's him over there [pointing]. I wake him up. He's good as above subversion, a young man, lots younger, bites his own arm in half above the wrist.

PATRICK [turning his back to the AUDIENCE] : Roll tape!

Ginger Nut-Mother murder (or, *Happy like a kid, stressed as a framework)*

envisioned by the insular poets of the Crowned Original *tutti quanti* - dedicated to a lover executed on homicide - composed under report-ratio tension: to let verbs be done tactile, to go down into verbs so low life's unthreatened by them, to make way for the celestial punishment of virtue, to hinder thinking in the round, subdividing lives into agreeing disorder. *Find yourself there!*

1 <u>Great blows of campaign-marketing</u>
as the new small refugees of bad dreams, these metaphors only
come out at night - on our island - assuming *Mother* lies in bed:
first hear breathing, scrapings of the throat, saliva one swallows,
the concentration that aspires. A hand tightens about the kerchief,
eyes fix on the printed script where *she* starts to read:
There was nothing Time ago afore History. everyone apparent
ignorant of dear smallest stature in its first lebensjahren, when,
like a gehauchter kiss on a girl's face, the orange veil of evening
shrank ... first fires of pagan worship lit silent as speech ancien.
the search for tradition, for a great line registered on every cold
stone, to erase family history, to cover shame with ... *you* sensed
an auto+biographic background, some short - bad - fairy tales -
very short stories. hermetic, obscure, vacuum.
2 <u>I am an unconscious instrument elsewhere</u>
a scientifically understandable body as it were, romantic poet of
the K&K times who lives at the price of 'wear without repair,' on
the straw, became blunt, went away ... dying. *I* took the life *I*
tried to ruin long before through Morphiumabhaengigkeit, as if
I'd gotten in such short intense experiences enough insights
(alone by the First World War). In effect, dominated by false
pursuers, *my* literary glory run to self-destruction. Drink, enter,
borrachera ... borrachera, single 16 springs, condemned to
perpetual relegation - door unopened to the drinker who enters.
Nonetheless considerable degrading.
3 <u>Hazlo without fear</u>
Sloppy-horse was a movement wanted to be different from the
others: put an end to the bulk-heading, celebrate reverence in
insular uneasiness: an international petition d'intellectuels and
d'artists: campaign against abandonment animals, scholastic
abandonment,1848 abandonment, all forms of abandonment. Via
the margins of schizophrenic [INTERFERENCE], script writers
would find, in the childhood of art, a spontaneous freschezza, a
luccichio of knives. STILISTI TRAPS vis-a-vis 10 lines of
chairs along the black/orange file. Labyrinths of alleyways
would crisscross the roots of pine trees. Silence.

4 Bump-of-Stroke, aka Freiwillige the Exile

I knew *my* first prison experiment at fifteen: track of an exceptional sensation. On the shores of the continent *I* saw great crowds churned from their jobs - orange green, red glassworks, confused colored balconies, arches, cimborrios, belvederes, galleries of blinds. still later an arch, another, the lock, a third bridge, far, farther …

COIN TOSS

OPENING ACT
PATRICK: If I don't return to the island, tell Mother I love her.
DIABLO: Your mother's dead, Father. I heard she died in the Battle of Praise Hills.
PATRICK: You heard wrong. Let go my sleeve!
DIABLO: What's the most you ever lost in a coin toss?
PATRICK: Sir?
DIABLO: The most. Lost sometimes. The coin toss.
PATRICK: Don't know. Don't care.
DIABLO: Flip a quarter against the change. Extend your arm. Call it.
PATRICK: Call it?
DIABLO: Yes.
PATRICK: Call it what?
DIABLO: Call it.
PATRICK: I need to know what you wanna call it.
DIABLO: It should be called. I won't call it for you. Won't be fair.
PATRICK: I'm not up for that.
DIABLO: Call it - there's room for improvement here. You cannot know the whole sweep of your life. You know what date-design is?
PATRICK: No.
DIABLO: In 1967 a forty-two-year journey began. Here you are today in a diner on the continent. Whether you run, or hightail it, I say *attention*.
PATRICK: Behold I *know* I'll reach the opposite coast.
DIABLO: Everything.

PATRICK: What's that?

DIABLO: You stand to win everything - *attention*.

PATRICK [flipping the coin]: All right. Heads. What's that tell you?

DIABLO: You're not of the pocket. You don't mix with continental folk. You're directly of insular design. What it is, it is, you don't need to do this or that. You say the same things once again.

PATRICK: Then what do I say next?

DIABLO: You say Do Not Do This.

PATRICK: I do not *need* that?

DIABLO: Good.

PATRICK: That's the best I can do.

DIABLO: *Attention*.

PATRICK: From the way you're standing there, I gather you're [INTERFERENCE]. I know you know what's in the future of that coin.

DIABLO: Call it again.

PATRICK: I'm not gonna flip or call her again.

DIABLO: Call it.

PATRICK: The shape of that coin suggests this day exists just for me one final time. Now it's *your* turn to flip it.

DIABLO: I was here when the coin behaved the same way on the same counter ten years ago when Elvis Presley was on the airwaves in one hundred-degree desert heat.

ACT II

PATRICK: You're gonna disturb *me* now - after what I've endured to make it this far?

DIABLO: That depends. You *see* me?

PATRICK: Although you … Do I?

DIABLO: Yes - *me*.

PATRICK: Uh … accounting for …

DIABLO: I gave you the Mexican coin, the peso piece, but that's ridiculous me not selecting the right coin for you.

PATRICK: I asked are you gonna disturb me now?

DIABLO: That depends. You see *this* coin?

PATRICK: I'm guessing you planned my future if you clapped my eyes on that coin. Don't worry. I'm not the man who made that toss.

DIABLO: I know. I can see. Everything's unique.

PATRICK You're *in* so you're not blind to this world.

DIABLO: And you're the guy designed as the island's last badass warrior. Ultimo hombre.

PATRICK: I won't describe myself as such.

DIABLO: How'd you describe you?

PATRICK: I don't understand. I don't know if the dreams [INTERFERENCE]. Waiter [gesturing in the waiter's direction], call the transponder, indicate a bag of cashews!

DIABLO: *Attention.*

PATRICK: Yes?

DIABLO: How'd you find me here in this diner in the middle of the desert?

PATRICK: When I entered I wasn't looking. Then I saw you sitting at the counter. I know your name won't be spoken. Not this way. No way. I don't understand anything else though. I'm simply passing time at this diner.

DIABLO: I'll be more polite - how'd you find your way into these travels?

PATRICK: Look at me - I'm immobile. Coffee wore off. I passed out at the counter. Slept about three hours. I wake up. Here you are sitting there.

DIABLO: But this place is a hard one, man. You cannot stop what's coming, not all the **experience** that awaits you. Your vanity either. A coin held up is what happens to a horse you bet on, your favorite horse. Soon you're seeing a man about a horse.

PATRICK: That's linear.

DIABLO: Sure not cyclical.

PATRICK: Probably not me but I believe it's linear.

DIABLO: This counter's a mess.

PATRICK: How much should I bet? What's the danger compared to what?

DIABLO: An epidemic, that's what. I found cancer in those odds. I won't return to the racetrack. Waiter, more coffee, BLACK!

ACT III

PATRICK: Something else wrong?

DIABLO: What's that?

PATRICK: Anything wrong now?

DIABLO: You're asking me is something wrong with anything?

PATRICK: Existence of anything else I mean.

DIABLO: Now you're asking me to express the meaning of anything?

PATRICK: Well, I'm ordering more food before the diner closes.

DIABLO: Let's see about the closing.

PATRICK: The waiter *said* they're closing.

DIABLO: Now is *not* the time when you or anyone else closes. I'm saying you better stay seated *now*.

PATRICK: I don't wanna talk with you, not in a sense that works for you.

DIABLO: Remember, you came to *me*. You know I know where you're going - to a city near a river where the sun sets on a dog's dead.

PATRICK: Makes sense.

DIABLO: No coins remain on the counter. No tip. Where'd you put it - in your pocket?

PATRICK: It should be on the counter right there [pointing].

DIABLO: Then let's consider history. Let's say I give you back the coin and you let her go and you're responsible this time and you get a better deal in return. Well, I cannot guarantee you'll save yourself since neither of us knows the outcome. So what'll you do? What *are* you doing, honey? - something dumber than hell!

PATRICK: What would *you* do?

DIABLO: I'd leave a message to the counterman on this crumpled napkin. You hear me? Lord, I cannot provide you any more statistical information.

PATRICK: You cannot tell me what ... *what?*

DIABLO: Look at the coin! A cast-iron bone's sticking outta your hands. I don't mean a stick.

PATRICK: Let's pretend it's the trigger of a gun.

DIABLO: Big talk. Keep the coin in your pocket as the journey progresses. How many personalities are in you now, besides the shooting of a waiter who dies in a hospital?

PATRICK: What are *you* pretending to do?

DIABLO: I pretend I'm retired from the crime of greedy living.

PATRICK: If you say so. If you follow the rules of chance that gave you that peso piece in the first place.

DIABLO: What do *you* do in the first place? I need to know.

PATRICK: What can I say? Medical *por favor*. I'm getting older, not much better.

DIABLO: Where will you live?

PATRICK: No, no, *no* - you don't understand - at *all*.

FINAL ACT

DIABLO: If you think you know what's gonna happen, accept your case and there'll be no indignities. Flip the coin.

PATRICK: Go to hell!

DIABLO: You got any idea how stupid you're acting?

PATRICK: You mean the stochastic nature of conversation?

DIABLO: Let me tell you something, Father. You cannot deal with chance. Your insular principles to combat money, drugs, credit, infantilism, anything like that - they cannot conquer chance. I keep a little cash right here [patting his right trouser pocket], pocket change stolen from six special customers. A stranger might say principles don't much respect me, but *I* can deal with chance. ... Waiter, please validate my parking ticket!

PATRICK: Your attempt at humor is a fraction of a television series. I'm wondering if ...

DIABLO: You got any idea how stupid you are? I mean *what* you are. Any idea?

PATRICK: You mean the stochastic nature of conversation?

DIABLO: For your sake I hope that's not a question.

PATRICK: Then what's *your* real name?

DIABLO: That's not a real question either.

PATRICK: It is up to a point.

DIABLO: Why are you so damned impatient? Did I say things would start off easy?

PATRICK: My persistence isn't random at all.
DIABLO: Imagine three years ago you said the same words at the same diner. So what's the most you ever lost in a coin toss? Here - give me your hands! Let me show you how gambling works in Nevada.

The insistent thing at its contingency

In a diner, at the end according to midday, a soak speaks a kind of reversed pride, extremely:

This morning I'm a bit badly with the belly, though not the least bit over eggs and hash browns. Afore biting into either, I sharpened these black plastic hooks, made a tssssss tssssss. No longer memory if I were Abel or Caín.

I, El man, iconoclasta of the evident thing. I, simulator of small uncertainties, humorist by certainty, astonished at the daily. I, friend of parabolas & secrets, descreído of dogmas, matador in the free-speak of all possible sonetos. With such-//-such lucky verse - each of these steps a fall while yet a simpler means whereby a typesetter maneuvers through the tunnels of one's dreams. Of fuí that of that? What summit is *that* goal?

Astonishing to return to the multiple nuances of our natal excitation. At present I'm calm though *that* will pass soon enough (...) when the island's bamboo blooms, ... famine, death and destruction never far, far (...) away. an attack launched upon the sky. buildings singed to a fine crême. five syllables one line one, seven one line two, five one line three. Why in the shade of sudden reflection? Richness lies not in the destination rather in the voyage away from Mother's island

> towards the west or south, a fifth from iron doors
> to ports yearning for distant latitudes
> over the sprinkled stones of streets asleep in ivy
> La Paz at night enamored
> a clock's blood measured in Sumatra
> vague hours at a garden gate in Combray
> elementary plains alive with flag or blind prank
> the flat immensities of sand, ferns, snows

towards the inverse towers between two skies
in the city of Cambaluc, capital of the Great Khan
where to scatter my explosive tenderness through
fabulous cadence.
Oh, how I yearn for those madnesses!

NOMADS OF ALL KINDS HAVE A SPECIAL RACIAL TRAIT

ACT I

PATRICK: I wanna work nights in the east *or* west of the continent.

DIABLO: I get you a job anywhere, anytime.

PATRICK: You get me a *used* job?

DIABLO: Anytime, anywhere.

PATRICK: God you're …

DIABLO: No - that's your area. You know continental folk are full of superstition. What's to say? Armed creatures, lowlifes decaying on the roads selling their glass for song - lowlifes in dark hallways, dark alleyways, in casinos, in contexts where you're the squarest of people. That's why I won't call you a murderer or drug addict *yet*, not a screw-head who wants to screw it all up. Man, I hope you drink your fair share of wine.

PATRICK: Sounds like you ought to be home, not here in a diner, dressing up to go out with your boys to the casinos.

DIABLO: Shit, I'm waiting for the day this desert truly shines.

PATRICK: What desert? I'm waiting for the rain to wash the waste off *that* [gesturing beyond the diner's window to the streets of Las Vegas].

DIABLO: The idea's to increase your brainpower for some real fun here. All the king's men won't put it over on you again.

PATRICK: I'm healthy as I feel.

DIABLO: You mean established health?

PATRICK: Look at me - - organized - - organized. That's hardly a joke. … O-R-G-A-N-I-Z-E-D ...

DIABLO: Then you mean established health - with small signs of desire to follow that cop on the glitzy sidewalks [again gesturing to the streets].

PATRICK: I'm no boogeyman. I got little more to do with flipping a Mexican peso piece on the counter.

DIABLO: That's change for a nickel yet more than a penny. Flip that coin, Father.

PATRICK [flipping the coin]: See you later, copper!

ACT II

DIABLO: I'm no cop, man.

PATRICK: If you are, it's entrapment.

DIABLO: Someone's made this city ... toilet-empty.

PATRICK: I feel it too. The days go on. They end. My whole life aware of new places I should go. But I won't devote my life to more attention. My life needs a female companion like other men.

DIABLO [pointing to a wall calendar]: June 29th. I got doubts. Too many continentals don't sit well with their bodies these days, too much abuse for too long. From now on they won't be doing fifty push-ups every morning or fifty pull-ups. No pills, more bad food, destroyers of their bodies. Yet they'll also have complete organization, every muscle established strong.

PATRICK: How about my driving record? Clean?

DIABLO: I can make it clean, real clean, clean as your conscience, cleaner than what's outside these windows. So let's watch the continentals come out tonight - whores, skunk-women, queens, fairies, Baptist buggers, drug addicts, sick, the corrupt. They're everywhere. You'll see - back East I kill 'em in the Bronx, Brooklyn, take 'em down in one fell-swoop in Alphabet City. Don't care, don't matter to me. Some of 'em won't even spies take. Don't matter to me.

PATRICK: Sorry to hear your life's throughout only bars, in cars, sidewalks, stores, everywhere - nothing avoided. I *am* a people of God. You have *your* doubts. But *I* am a people of God. Life takes another turn. I continue on a regular basis once again, with a difference of one day later. In a long continuous chain, change does occur.

DIABLO: You want a used job? Whether to work or not to work -

that's a question.

PATRICK: Look at it this way. An islander refugee takes a job on the continent. He goes to work if that's what he gets [gesturing to the streets]. It's never what you *do*. Ten years of nights I got one and the same sensation. Know why? This must be what I want. Is someone forcing me to sit at this counter? Other people, they find a job, do their work. One man lives in Brooklyn, another in Boston. You got a lawyer here in Las Vegas. Another dude's a doctor in Minnesota. He dies but the other man recovers. People are born - so let's envy their youth. C'mon, man, powdered eggs get drunk on nothing. We got choices here.

DIABLO: That's the dumbest shit I heard coming from an islander. What do you want - what *I* know? I'm supposed to be the devil. That means agnostic to you. Dunno what the hell you're gonna say next.

PATRICK: Listen you screw-head, people can't subvert anymore against scale - vagina, dogs, dirty shit. People can't stand up for what they want.

DIABLO: You see the large cup-44 standing on that waitress? [pointing] Yeah you see it. Large cup-44 will do what it does to a woman's chest. You should see what's inside the other cup.

PATRICK: I see it. My whole life's pointed in the direction of this diner. Never had a choice.

DIABLO: Shit I got lots of bad ideas in my head too, bad insular designs.

PATRICK: Faster than you, son of a … I saw you deserve hell. Damn.

DIABLO: Like you, I'm here on the continent to [INTERFERENCE] … more steps. It's your move.

PATRICK: More bad designs.

DIABLO: Don't screw up what you *are*.

ACT III

PATRICK: You talking to me? You talking to me? You talking to me? Hell are you talking about? I'm here with a cup of coffee, a cigarette. What are you talking about?

DIABLO: Bad design.

PATRICK: Okay let's pretend you're the devil. That makes sense. We meet at the crossroads of history in a city in the middle of the desert. No wrong paths taken.

DIABLO: Bringing you to a city like this is about as exciting as saying 'Let's boogie.'

[Waitress's cellphone rings.]

PATRICK: The answer is?

DIABLO: What you wanna say?

PATRICK: I can't sleep nights.

DIABLO: Then stay awake. Continentals never shut down porn theaters and casinos. They build more.

PATRICK: Or they expand. I ride through the night - metro, bus. If I'm gonna travel I gotta pay for it.

DIABLO: What's the point of traveling? Need a sideline? A prostitute?

PATRICK: I want a good job, work long hours. What prostitute are you talking about?

DIABLO: Disgust your whole life, everywhere, bars, in cars, sidewalks, stores, everywhere - can't be avoided. If you're truly a people of God, you must be a wanderer.

PATRICK: Let me tell *you* something. If you end up in hell you're gonna die in hell like the rest of 'em.

DIABLO: You see that waitress's large cup-44?

PATRICK: That weapon's expensive.

DIABLO: It's OK. She's got money.

PATRICK: She's a real monster, a boogeyman. Brings any man to a stop one hundred meters.

DIABLO: If you want, I'll let you place a round in her engine. How's that for a business broker?

PATRICK: I understand now what's similar about you and continentals. You're distant, cold. Continentals fail to convince women of the necessity of marital union.

DIABLO: Damn. Go on. The night's ending.

PATRICK: You're less a devil than a demon. You come to this diner. I see you here. I see the people around you. I see the phones, things on the counter, the tables. None of that frightens or impresses me. I saw you when I came in, saw your eyes, saw you're unhappy. You think what you want. If you wanna call me good company you might even convert me to a friend.

DIABLO: I'll tell you why this place is a filthy mess. Our energies are going in the wrong direction. When two strangers like us meet at a diner, they link together, enter into something between them before one of them's pushed on to the next in a series of episodes. Otherwise I don't have the right to speak with you and tell you what to do. I'd never have the courage to talk with you. When I came in, I knew I was right. See it? - walking contradictions, partly truth, partly fiction, and on their knees in pain - worthless people. So do me a favor. Learn to desire fewer problems. Okay?

PATRICK [flicking cigarette]: How?

DIABLO: You know … remember me. I'm no drug dealer, never pushed. But who else can I talk to around here? Don't know how you feel. So I - I - I want you to imagine a tropical island. You'll feel better or, uh, or a virus, a virus for 24 hours. It happens. You gotta find a job, undercover work. Let's say you wanna be, oh, ER support, or an afterlife manager, few days or so - cup after cup of coffee. I say down or up, anything at all, we, uh … Oh, okay, okay. You're getting the check right? I sent the waitress flowers. Yeah, okay. Can we get back in touch tomorrow or the next day? Ok. No, I … Ok. Yes, of course, good.

PATRICK: I … What *is* it? Stop pulling at my sleeve!

DIABLO: Twelve years on the island I never had a passport. Now in the wake of Praise Hills we're here on the continent. One city after another awaits us, one diner after another, one motel, one [INTERFERENCE]. We can do whatever we want. You can come in her mouth, put it in her ass, come on her face, your dick so she can blow, whatever - be a man with her. No harsh words. She's a master of the middle of the bridge. She can change her pantyhose there.

PATRICK: I'm not what you think I am. Of course you never know with life, but I say, Got a life? - not on the other side of the continent, in that woman's Alphabet City apartment. My future wife isn't … I'll murder the bitch.

DIABLO: Oh dear, we don't want that.

[PATRICK punches the DIABLO in the stomach, kicks him in the shins, leaves the diner.]
PATRICK [turns back to the AUDIENCE]: There you have it, the first episode. Confused? Well, yes *and* no.

A Panegyric to the medium brown eminences

THAT GOD FORGIVES ME TO REVEAL IT IF ONLY FOR A LITTLE WHILE

those wild continentals mislaid in the meanders of their quasi-psychotic ramblings buckled, ficellé, threaded, tallied, quadri, chrome, glossed, famous, linké: escaping the wire of historical-theoretical death.

those bastards there carried us a hard blow THEIR BODIES GOLD WITH THE ABSOLUTE FUSIONNEL OF SECOND GASOLINE, chests armored in medals inlaid with iperrealiste plastic substances, glances dark, carbonaceous (Turkish? yougo? Rumanian?). This morning they're blôttis. (subscription néc.)

all good journalists must handle the adjective with great virtuosity. introvertidamente ironic Доктор Геббельс?

[w]

For time out of mind - 哎那之後呢？

If, as Belgian Heliowatts states, Stockhausen seems strange to any computer lover, Fisherman Lincolnshire must be stranger.

Watch this: words "sign Conet" at the final stage of signing will signal the arrival of Glockenspiel Girl (GG). She's a well-to-do short thirty-year-old intelligently dressed girl (never has any adventures, never anything unexpected). She's accompanied by evidence of minimal folk song transmissions. She says (to me - now I'm telling you): "For proper corporate callback on your iPod radio-phone-linkup, you must achieve the right 'introductory experimental sound' by using the shiny brass yellow knob in the exact middle [gesturing *here*]. Usage failure - i.e., failure to do so - will mean discomfort in a hole through the ground (though not a nasty dirty wet hole) - meaning discomfort."

Hold it - turn to the radio - *on* with your ears, man, I LAUGH. How can I avoid the cost of public consumption in this public space? I LAUGH. I ask every scrap of history "Is *it* going after *that*?"

Glockenspiel girl tells me ordered numeric one-time keypads are the key to a breakthrough discovery - "Alleged" is a key word here - rare media-core of "alleged."

"Apa itu akan kemudian, eh?"

Yuehanzuoen road-freight - Thaemlitz electrical ontology - surreal voice recordings of Ethiopian music - fragments of electronic eavesdropping on the city's mobile phones. I'm on my way to Aquarius Records in San Francisco. I'm on a mission to learn the purpose [of the uselessness of watching Project Mayhem on a third-generation digital TV] -

I don't speak a total shit auto + biography or something.

Living conditions: Multi-Level Hollow Earth with best rooms on left-hand side (lots of these)

Favorite Alias: Doctor Linguistic Junkie / / Sinister Super Hankie //Mr. Morris Parker

Official Arrival Date: July 4, 1950

Official Initial Access Point: Half Moon Bay, the [Pacific Rim]

Life in: San Mateo County, California, Continental U.S.

E-mail: N/A

Occupation: Student star-machine / nature philosopher/ The poet & the humor / / psychonaut/ psychopath/ "Free Computer Guy" / Hack Outreach / edge researcher /God descended from "Silly" / G-artist / Nature Lover Associate Editor / Internal Revenue Intelligence (IRI) Central Evolutionary Incentives (CEI) / Reckless Political Guidance (RPGs) /

Incoming Higher Education: End the great powers of the Third World Phase (TWP) [time position 1948]

Outgoing Lower Education: Doctorate of Hollow Earth Linguistics [time position 1971]

Relative Religious affiliations following International Religious Merger (IRM): 51% servants of God (Indians incarnate) / 7% - 5% Pantheism / 3% divine units of Aunt Helen / 2% - 2% (?) Orthodox + Catholic / 2% Catholic - Protestant / 2% Magan / 2% Sophistic / 2% Buddhist (put Muslims here too?) / 2% The 2 Holy earth-mothers / 2% of the Jews (turn Shinto on its head?) / Rosicrucian 2% / 2% Rastafarian / 2% Not likely people (NLP) / 2% Sweet Sweet Jane / 2% Other than Confusion / 2% Hollow Earth / 2% Unexpected Parties / 2% 3 Ways to Make Napalm, 2% etc.

In Hollow Earth, Hobbits™ lived in a ditch - no, no, they lived in dirty holes stained with urine, with worms on perfectly ugly textures. Sitting in their ditches, Hobbits™ ate their food with the barest of hands. Those odors - like odors from a final hole in the sands of time - were convenient for locating (not cannibalizing) Hobbits™ when the inner winds blew just right.

Hobbit, hobbit very well - this Hobbit's name is Captain Beginsu.

What are Hobbits? Who owns the trademark? How can I license the technology? I suppose Hobbits require a description. They speak in vowels. Let's say I'm a Hobbit today. Shit I think I need a painkiller prescription. Anyway, fold-away stairs are available to Hobbits in these ditches. Sophisticated chairs too. Meadows line the gardens along the Lower River over there [pointing outside the ditch's windows in the direction of what the Big Stupid People on Surface Earth dismiss as Hollow Earth]. The ditches Hobbits live in are comfortable, perfectly good quality, with green grass ball centers, round doors, windows, wooden walls, pantries, wardrobes, sloping carpets, tiled tube-tunnels linking rooms providing heat. Hats and coats of many a jaded Hobbit hang at the door over here [gesturing to a bunch of worthlessness].

Everything in Hollow Earth is dangerous. Last week my sickly Hobbit neighbor lost his arm in an arm-wrestling championship. Soon [gesturing from the stage] we'll see if the audience out there loses something from their minds - fades out, I mean, explosively forgets - Is it going? Eh God I hope so.

Captain Beginsu - top-drawer Hobbit mind of the Third World Age (TWA) - adventuresome - bit callow if less elderly - lower than half the height of a Barbados child, more enchanting than ever ('special,' that is). Cover your abdomen, Captain - with light-colored clothing (thick warm green-yellows to match the material of your head). Tennis shoes. Captain Beginsu is, I mean, (this is) a hand waving, laughs, an intelligent face - long fingers - good-natured humor - deep brown?

This evening began with a screenplay on the establishment of my great green shoulders.

In Hollow Earth I work as a Hobbit waiter at the Russian Cow Milkbar. Afterwards I squeeze a gun in your mouth, tell you the first step into eternal life is you must be dead for a very long time. Me & Captain Beginsu are fast friends. Strangers tell me I look a lot like or should learn from Captain Beginsu. I need sleep. I need a painkiller prescription. Starting to see things (hallucinate?). No - that revelation's useless here.

"This gun's employed at the back of your throat, Captain

Beginsu. Truth in death."

In my own case I imagine the silencer has holes drilled in it so the shot noise expands with the gases, creating a small laconic boom as the metal ball moves forward faster 'n faster (accelerating?) through the course of the gun's drilled pipe. That design allows gases to avoid slowing down the speed of the ball's sound. Something like that. Sounds technical anyway. (Hobbits prefer scientific research over telling a good story.) You drill holes the wrong way, man, that gun explodes in your mighty Hobbit hands.

"This dialogue is not *that* dated, Captain Beginsu. You're a legend you can't grow out of. You're famous. You're the flimsy material history books are made of."

I hear my dialogue, see my pale cheeks in the mirror, wanna kill myself. I'm thinking you're not a writer. You're a vampire - or a screenwriter.

Me & Captain Beginsu are dressed to the height of fashionable systems. Pairs of black tights too tight across the ole jelly mold. We requested tight pants too tight in the groin to protect us from the randy gangs of Hollow Earth boys. A kind of design operates here. Our pockets are full of Deng Xiaoping. Got me?

In 10 minutes me & Captain Beginsu won't own this high-rise building. Take an angry 98-percent solution of nitric acid, add several times more the amount of sulfuric acid to the ice bath, pipette drops of glycerin: you got nitroglycerin - we both know that. Don't get me started on putting sawdust into nitro, otherwise we're on our way to plastic explosives. Hobbits mix their own nitro into cotton balls, adding Epsom salts if they want that sulfate tingle. Successful? Some Hobbits use paraffin mixed with nitro - takes up the slack from an ensuing explosion. Don't work for me though.

In Hollow Earth money's not everything you keep in your trouser pockets. You hear glass breaking? That building's turning on its edges, highest building in the world, strong cold winds everpresent. Not so quiet after an explosion now is it? Get the feeling a big enough explosion in Hollow Earth turns our planet inside out? You *call* this a planet?

You got that feeling mastered - I'm telling you to experience it *now.* That's why you're one of the monkeys up there on the surface. I give little pushes to the lever - this lever does mechanical work - I draw back that lever and push the button way over there (*you* try to reach it).

Explosion happens. You understand anything you want. You die. That's 911 floors ninety floors up, overlooking edges off roofs, towering over streets speckled with carpeted pedestrians having sex in the sidewalk position (shitty views too). Breaking glass in the windows below us, window frames blown out from building sides, black cabinets filed with refrigerators right below us midair.

Ask me how the nerve gas works in 10 minutes.

"Apa itu akan kemudian, eh?"

Please gimme that, Captain Beginsu, gimme that sexy anesthetic darkness.

WOULD YOU PAY FOR IT?

When he came out (Jesus) to the surface, met by a man ... had devils long time ... / s comet rips the sky / He (unclean spirit) long tormented him - *it* is bound with chains - ties - though he brake the bands ... Jesus asked him: What's your name? He said: "Legion." ... I must die. / (read Luke Rome 6 summer kuuta - 6 am).

Jackson hung on meat hooks so heavy his back straightened up a bit. This hook he hung on for three days till Izdoh.

Frank (laughing): Jackie, you shoulda seen this guy - sort of a carcass. And when Jimmy connected the electrical wires ...

[Excitedly]: He struggled on the hooks, Jackie. You sprinkled a little water on it to feel better electrical discharges. Jackson screamed ... (read FBI) [First one title]

ACT I

DIABLO: What a great night to drive out evil spirits!

PATRICK: What you want with that?

DIABLO: Something - more than electrical - more than neon - a capacitor.

PATRICK: Will gamblers pay for it?

DIABLO: Electrical current unites us all. You - *us*. So let's return to the craps tables.

PATRICK: If you're the devil, make the tables disappear, erase them from my retinas.

DIABLO: Wanna leave a message? I think you get it, Father. Stop behaving like an insular infidel.

PATRICK: Mother said it's of particular importance to avoid hanging out with the devil. I can ask you what's important so long as nothing turns dangerous. You're a liar. You mix lies with truth to attack islanders, continentals alike. Mental attack's powerful. I remember that much.

DIABLO: I love your attitude.

PATRICK: You don't love coffee though, and don't allow remarriage. [Cellphone starts ringing.]

DIABLO: You need reassignment to get outta this line of undercover work. It's wrong, not doing you any good.

PATRICK: I'm one of the best the islanders got.

DIABLO: It's psychiatry. You know that, Father. You need to get out. You're invalid, like a lost parking ticket.

PATRICK: Should've known better.

DIABLO: I think you should.

PATRICK: How's your own experience back there?

DIABLO: Down there, you mean. Continentals better start looking for a new psychiatrist-god.

PATRICK [laughing]: Mother used to say faith can make something satisfactory into an extraordinary power or a fast-track engine performance. Depleted, you raise the wheels half a leg off the ground - you hear the stories - same thing here, same principles.

ACT II

DIABLO: What's wrong with your son?

PATRICK: Temporal lobe I think.

DIABLO: What do you mean, for Christakis? You *see* me or not? You're acting crazy ridiculous, psychological. A split personality or ...

PATRICK: I know the temptation to leap into psychiatry. Any reasonable psychiatrist will exhaust the potential of the physical first.

DIABLO: What's next?

PATRICK: A pneumo-encephalogram to pin down the lesion. Perhaps include another electrical cord into the arrangement.

DIABLO: Oh dear God.

PATRICK: That should eliminate other possibilities.

DIABLO: If you pay the electrical bill, sure. Why the candy? Someone else's boy sharing your boy's room?

PATRICK: In some cases.

DIABLO: Who is it? Captain Beginsu?

PATRICK: His roommate's name's Costa Move.

DIABLO: If you ask him to speak to me, would he answer me?

PATRICK: No

DIABLO [pretending to be a psychiatrist]: Why not?

PATRICK: My boy's afraid of you.

DIABLO: That's shock therapy talking. You heard of confession? A ritual manner whereby rabbis and priests derail the Spirit of the Species. It's ignored these days except by Catholics who take the Devil into the closet as an embarrassment, but uh, it works as a proposal-force.

PATRICK: You tell me I should take my boy to traditional healers?

DIABLO: I don't care much about healing except when it starts with conflict or guilt and leads the patient into illusions of his body being invaded by alien minds, or souls, if you wish.

PATRICK: I tell you again so you'll be sure - I'm not gonna put the boy into a damned confessional.

DIABLO: I'm sorry your mother's buried inside there.

PATRICK: Christ you apologize yet you tell me ... garbage.

DIABLO: Think of it more as shock therapy. As I said, there's a little chance yet.

PATRICK: For God's sake what is it?

DIABLO: Religious beliefs.

PATRICK: *No.*

ACT III

DIABLO: Where *is* your boy?

PATRICK: In a special hospital not far from here. Why?

DIABLO: If you ever go to that hospital again, take me with you.

PATRICK: Why?

DIABLO: I'm like the first missionary on the surface of Mars.

PATRICK: You wanna pretend again, yes?

DIABLO [pretending to be a possessed entity]: I'm Captain hello. What is not.

PATRICK: Captain who?

DIABLO: Captain hello.

PATRICK: Captain hello?

DIABLO: You know I'm not on the issues. The Captain answers *no.*

PATRICK: Oh, hello, Captain hello.

DIABLO: Damn bloody slaughter pigs Nazi! Jesus wants dick though he went through you!

PATRICK: Rage is driving us. Throw it through the gates of heaven to the depths of hell.

DIABLO: Shove it up your parrot ass!

PATRICK: Of this creature of God …

DIABLO: Damn. Hell with him.

PATRICK: Show me double the same person, same voice, everything. I know in my heart I wanna tell you what you don't know. Nothing wrong's with my boy, just in his head - you said so.

DIABLO [pretending to come to his senses]: It might be helpful if you provided some basic information about your boy's different personalities. So far, I'd say there are three I'm convinced of.

PATRICK: I see only one.

DIABLO: The writer one in Paris crucified on a red cross?

PATRICK: Oh, no, nothing like that, but a more docile personality.

DIABLO: You keep narcotics in the house?

PATRICK: Doctor told me I shouldn't but thank God my will is weak.

DIABLO: Christ you don't smoke grass.

PATRICK: Hide from the law? I don't know anyone who doesn't feel illegal sometimes.

DIABLO: Stay away. We've sowed the seeds!

PATRICK: You? An alien pubic hair's in my trap - have not seen THAT before in my life.

DIABLO: The face of me - lick it!

PATRICK: You know what you look like? - a wertlos John Garfield.

DIABLO: вы Schwanzlutscher sans valeur!

PATRICK: You speak Latin?

DIABLO: I AM Latin.

PATRICK: You didn't go bowling with Goebbels' Nazi bastard. So leave Mother alone to die.

DIABLO: Shut up. Keep your fingers from her cursed vagina!

PATRICK: Why her? Why that woman? Mother? What happened to me?

FINAL ACT

DIABLO: Gory violent continentals.

PATRICK: Absolvo T-ego. It's feared the priest ...

DIABLO: A Los Angeles de ma Tante.

PATRICK: Oh no this isn't squirming. My boy sits on the bed a total anomaly. Floor's shaking. He's got legions of lesions.

DIABLO: Problem with your boy's not his bed. It's his BRAIN. [DIABLO pretends to remove his hand from the sick boy's head.]

PATRICK: I'm not alone.

DIABLO: You cannot go to the cinema, Father. You wanna be happy?

PATRICK: I've seen, yes of course, evil versus evil.

DIABLO: You cannot help your boy to the altar, you Metro bum.

PATRICK: What are you doing here? The diner's closed.

DIABLO: Now *my* bed's shaking. Can't sleep.

PATRICK: You gotta clean the sheets.

DIABLO: Uh huh. 'Fraid so.

PATRICK: Hello captain - health of capital's not very nice.

DIABLO: You're gonna die upstairs.

PATRICK: You noticed the attic? I think you ought to clean it.
DIABLO: I found your boy up there … in small pieces.

coil-reliance: time of rendering is 16.

Strip the news - step on the mouth! Beyond those beaches
　　　blasphemy cohabits with the Christian impregnation.
Bravo! *high, high* Bravo! *high, high*. Hang your carriage with a
star!
Tremble, support the permanent war for the main-line haulage
system, but *conceal you.*

　　　Толпа — слепец Толпа — варвар (selected text) (*в/цензурой*) Разврат
　　　(selected text) Раздор (*в/цензурой*) Разврат (selected text) Террор
　　　(*в/цензурой*) Раздор (selected text) Террор (*в/цензурой*) Разврат
　　　(selected text) Внутренний враг (*в/цензурой*) Раздор (selected text)
　　　Террор (*в/цензурой*) (selected text) Раздор (*в/цензурой*) Разврат
　　　(selected text) Террор (*в/цензурой*) (selected text) (*в/цензурой*)
　　　Террор (selected text) Разврат (*в/цензурой*) (selected text) Раздор
　　　(selected text) (*в/цензурой*) Толпа — слепец Толпа — варвар -
　　　Дай мне жить! Дай мне жить! Дай мне жить! Дай мне жить! Дай мне
　　　жить! *Waaaahrrrrr-r'waaahrrr-r'waaahrrr-r'waaahrrr-*
　　　r'waaahrrr-R'WAAAHRRR!

Tellus Mater

- What you want, ole islander? ... search for explanations of new
realities through sequences of continental history? activate
deposits of mitológicas forces lest they # - - a-refl mng
themselves? Well, yes *and* no. Rather, yes *with* no.

　　　To pretend I'm the son of a neoyorkino banker, exorcist-
acolyte improbado: Sir Automaton Mostruso, Man ünico &
Necessary, initials *F & &*.

　　　This confession will be a labyrinthine one, full of hiding
places, transformed into a monólogo of incomprehensible length.
Imagine layer upon layer of superficial occidentalismo: a Czech
season in France: tassels of a Damascus lampshade: thunderclap
of door knockers: troublesome curtains of glass beads: nailed
leaves of walnut fitted to their marks: centuries of floor tiles. I
will go on of course.

I don't hear you - you're in Dubrovnik!

I make conversation left shoulder right shoulder left shoulder right shoulder left. That's as far as I go without a green light.

The high pressure area causing this ninety-nine-degree heat ...

Will be staying with us throughout the week.

That's Las Vegas.

You people leaving the city should find it hot. High pressure heat's why.

We'll stay here all week then.

The chance of thunderstorms this evening is Yin clean in the desert.

The weekend should be real warm for leaving the city too.

You hear our boy crying?

Why no I don't dear. Now that we're in bed it's time for you to put questions to me.

Turn off the air conditioner.

Ah so dear it shall be done.

Dead in fact it's so hot. You got cold milk?

Why was your tablet dismissed?

Hello boys. 95 mgs.

You care for my boy?

How'd you know that?

For I heard screams.

Oh wait a minute. -

That was a failure. -

Why?

Ah little scattered, nothing more, simple, easy.

Very high.

Oh hell. Fun to me, size to us.

Your legs are dragging.

What are you doing? My eyes what?

How to say? Your eyes abnormal.

You wouldn't know.

Hey, man. - Hey, MAN. You've chosen.

No, I cannot. *No* -

Go look around at your hand. - At the bottom of your foot.
Oh my God -
Your respect. Come on, man, I want your respect.
I not be the same?
Sit *down*, Costa Move!
You mean sit with other patients.
I mean drink the milk. - Get it down your throat. Cold milk
won't kill you.
That drink's long, straight, ordinary as Lipton tea.
Don't you taste my boy's blood, Costa Move!
My own mother's trying to beat me.
So where's the place you belong?
Only a mother can beat her baby boy.
Not true. I once shook my son too quickly.
Think about it. Take a look at your child. I promise not to
harm him right away.
So who's this mother you speak of?

Las Vegas is not circular (or, My stinky baiginio years)

SO -- before the inception of our heavily cultured Time Of
Beloved, Joey Scattergood had $300 in his right trouser pocket
that night. He watched as the cop teams (lawyer teams in tow)
examined the floors, counters, walls, ceilings, tables of the Las
Vegas Corner Bar.

If you wanna hear the first thing I know, it's where I was born,
my childhood, what's wrong with Mother, how she caressed
me, my feelings of wanting to know the truth about things.
Next after that I got bored a lot. Thirdly, my parents had two
hemorrhages apiece, from colon cancer. Fourth, I took
personal time off for sensitivity training, to relate better to my
mother who's insightful, I mean, she's fragile as hell. I won't
speak a total shit auto + biography or something. I'm not *that*
crazy.

Unknown how far me & Diablo will go to reach the
eastern edge of the continent. I recall the old-fashioned
spiral-arms of a galaxy turning … ignoring the little

yellow globes, the jaundiced-yellow sun. Not referring to orbital distances here, God no, rather ninety-one-thousand-million miles to reach a blue-green planet bearing undescended primitive life forms, digital watches, surprising pictures of pedestrians walking, thinking, talking - to themselves.

"This has nothing to do with stashing sleeping pills in the bar nuts," Scattergood said to the mangy-looking cops, "uh, my credit here's endless, limitless, I mean, the tab I run … Look - there's reason for each financial ingredient. *Look*." [He points at the gratuity he left on the bar right beside the bar nuts.]

I got time to think about what happened last time we spoke. I feel ragged. I'm alone. I don't have to mean what I say, though I do anyway, out of politeness. Ask Diablo: Las Vegas is not so contemptible these days, *and* less circular. That's why I can't help returning, visiting casinos over and over again each and every weekend. Onwards from my hotel - a place they sold to a film producer last fall. All's I got left's this Jaguar, some English ale, one hundred-thousand dollars. Learning how to gamble in Las Vegas is costing me another four hundred-thousand dollars. Damn that's a lot of dough - - don't help me measure the ordinary against the extraordinary (as I learned from those splendid books (novels?) you reviewed last year in the *LA Times*).

If God's a problem here [gesturing to the city's westernmost region at the verge of a crumbling sidewalk], that's good - if not, I say let's make the errors impossible to hide (impossible to avoid what fails to succeed). Pedestrians are calm in the continent's western cities outside the reach of available travel agencies rather than within the warehouse level of knowledge. This training must avoid shortcomings, doubts, errors at least, losses, misguided results of an undercover detective looking for *what?* - two important ways (more problems?).

"I assure you we'll do what we wanna," [exclaimed?] [expostulated?] the cops - in unison. "Jesus you're white as a sheet, Scattergood. The way you hold yourself - *act* - like a foreign consulate from New York City. Possession of drugs don't matter here. It's the car we mean, the car we *need*, magnetic tape inside the car, your whereabouts last Friday 6:00 pm. Don't you get it, Scattergood? Las Vegas is *not* circular."

Matanza Me! Your screenplay adaptations are best when you keep the goldfish hidden inside the bowels of small children. That's the right position if you want the audience to enjoy the movie using their own money. Sure, they have to. In any case Hollywood's a bitch. Don't let anyone tell you otherwise. Las Vegas is a bit different - visible hotshots and all. Still, Hollywood writers put advertisements in a thousand different magazines. I saw your ads, counted them, saw lunatics with cameras leaping over backyard fences everywhere around here. I haven't seen horses except at the racetrack.

Planet nonetheless - or elsewhere - so the problem (issue? directive?) is most of those pedestrians find their strolls a bit disappointing most of the time. I've proposed many solutions to that disappointment (again, who's *they*?). Yet nothing relates to the exact movements of small green pieces of paper, strange papers those (reading the fine print, mind you). Those small green pieces of paper leave them *what*? Problem's the pedestrians aren't malicious or virtuous enough (2 sides of 1 coin), haven't made the necessary sacrifices, lack the daily discipline. They're miserable (even the ones wearing bright red digital watches with angry scarlet faces).

The Stone Brothers sat there at the long bar silent as a stoned weekend - silent as bankrupt in [INTERFERENCE] - silent as the curse of a vacant Las Vegas office building.

A thousand magazine advertisements. Hotshot guys leaping over backyard fences with expensive-looking photographic equipment. If all goes well, most of those guys'll be playing ball with lawyers and cops over there at the country club [pointing outside the moving car window]. Haven't seen thoroughbred horses anywhere. Now, check out that gentleman up there [pointing outside the moving car window] - that billboard picture advertisement. Reads something like *Since 1948 Hollywood's molded your children into attractive young teenagers thinking they ought to see a movie this weekend (got nothing better to do)...* Local pigeons pause afore taking a shit on that likeness. "Serial form's higher than high school yearbooks around here" - to quote - unsure - unclear - clearly confused- that's all. If two, again we got both sides of one coin.

> Mimi, I don't know if me & Diablo will reach the eastern side of the continent. I remember strange spiral arms of a galaxy spinning, … remember ignoring little yellow globes - (Hey there, Huang Xiao!) [waving to an old friend in the front row] - jaundiced-yellow sun. Hardly tracking distances here, rather debating God for some $100,000. I see our slightly inclined Earth enter the blue-green Clear Land that holds earlier forms of life, digital clocks. Unsurprising how the images of pedestrians walking and talking carry their own ideas.

"I help people work out their obsessions with the Americanized dream," said Scattergood: "They need that training - I need my car."

In *one* sense I came to Las Vegas as if I were attending a Saturday night high school football game with someone half my age bereft of realistic expectations. On the other hand (opposite case) I got lost in the Games Room, struck up a conversation with an Anglo-Saxon proto-suicide, couldn't find my way out, spent years of hard work without a win. That's evident. I remember three suicides. Saw a few skinny, effeminate producers who wanted madness, such weapons, freedom from age, from having to blow your nose. In return I kept everything hidden from them including the bus schedules. Now you know the call. To this day I enjoy the scratchy giggles, the fake bleeding gums I meet on the Strip. It's great to be lost in Las Vegas. What the hell - everything you hear, the cries, deep terrible cries from hot-&-sunny platforms (similar to what you hear in Laurel Canyon). My nails aren't bitten down to the quick like that guy's over there [pointing outside the moving car window].

> Many pedestrians believe - one day - a big round mistake arrives (from Outer Space) to set the autumn trees swaying, to lavish windswept heavy-set colors on those leafy branches. You take the wrong step (off a sidewalk), however, you'll never wanna leave this city on the shores of the desert. This is the continental West End, ceremonial West End. That's right. The time you're struck by a car (metal carriage of Fate with its windows rolled down) on your way to the music shop, struck by anything resembling a stupid catastrophe … occurred … gone forever: history itself.

"Some *what?*" The cops laughed - in unison. "You'll be driving the whole way making *foooooolish* …"

Unfair to pretend these continental cities were driving me crazy. I was always at my best. Yet I had no time for sitting down beside sweethearts at the bus schedule kiosk. We struck up a conversation. I loved it. Her big nose, nails bitten down to the quick. She had a future - though it was hemorrhaging at a place where the Whole Damn Future was forgiven for advertisements of fertilizers to fathers of boys with terminal illnesses. You know the call. You're not an idiot. You know I'm not from New York City. I wasn't on the fencing team. I refused to play with video equipment. I kept to my faults like a roadmap keeps to its scale. Another cold morning Mimi requested inspecting the New York City subway map. The times were fun. I trained myself for ostracism.

> Despite this planet or any other place (even a planet here? - your criteria?), most of the pedestrians find *what?* They're not hopeless most of the time. Tabling proposals to solve their problems (again, *by whom?*) - making no mention of the small movements of a mysterious green book filled with strange files (the print's small, remember). This small piece of green paper won't leave injuries. Problem's insufficient to the proper ways of sacrifice and discipline. I enjoy every

day I can (while dressing as a bright red digital clock with a red angry face).

One way Scattergood prepared for his journey was to find Bobby Bortolotto soon as possible. Bobby Bortolotto, with his shirts of peacocks, his special tape recorders - - - - the two of them - Scattergood & Bortolotto - screaming their cover stories through the Nevada desert, replacing primary responsibilities with seventeen years of used-up horsepower plus Belgian heliowatts.

Look at this wrinkled subway map *then* make the comparison [pointing outside the window of the moving subway car]. Mimi don't know where to look first, where to go last. We gotta return to a time of family dinners at family diners - no influenza. Taking the subway reminds me of another reason for ostracism. A *train* of ostracism. My serious high school literary instructor told me we should train ourselves to return home. Like me, that instructor didn't speak a total shit auto + biography. Anyway, Mimi forgot to explain when Christmas holidays begin. How many holidays this year? She wants to return home for the holidays. Hollywood's not circular either. Ask the *craaaaaazy* producer who banned four writers from the set, gave them warnings afore giving them the ax handle across the forehead. Me? I gave myself multiple warnings afore I arrived in New York City on Thanksgiving weekend to freeze my ass off.

One Thursday - at the continent's West End - 2,000 years after (they?) nail one man to an oak tree, President Dr. Rikmansuort announces how nice for those pedestrians to change (adapt?). President's own little girl sits in a diner - with yours truly - on the other side of (the plate-glass window) awaiting an audience in a theatre. We understand what we got here - a theatrical piece. What went wrong Last Night? How to correct the planet, make its continents better happier places?

"Who cares? No evidence here," said ole Scattergood, adjusting his support for free enterprise. "I'm not *craaaaaazy* about gambling in Las Vegas. Don't sleep much either."

Me? Just received personal warnings. Mimi? Mysteriously homeless dude stole her camelhair coat from the cloakroom. Leather gloves right in the pockets. I'm not joking. This city's full of thieves and more crooks. Everything's cold. Streets sound like magic. Difficult studying the pedestrians [pointing out the diner window at the mobs of people on the sidewalks of lower Manhattan]. Their performances leave me cold. Sure, this diner's heated. That's why I'm freezing my ass off. Not joking. Me? I feel like saying farewell, returning to the place I love. Mimi?

> Believes more pedestrians - one day - will make bigger mistakes. Following year (in space anything's possible) *they* reduce the trees to swaying in the wind, very strong wind, leaving some colors on the leafy branches. But you take a wrong step (along the same distance of the sidewalk), you won't leave this city by the sea, city at the verge of the continental shelf-banks. That's right. You're hit by a car (with a metal transfer-pass lodged, like fate, in the windows of time). Loss of metaphorical coherence strikes anyone as stupid, a terrible disaster - my signature. So I return to the story itself.

Oh but Scattergood was flagrant *not* chemical - that's who cares - 00 00 00 - plus the socio-psychological factors. He "participated in the glass," as we say in our friendliest West Coast voices.

Very dark right afore dinner. Very disturbing to watch these … I know where the taxicab's going. Dunno who's saying goodbye to me when I arrive there though. Don't care if the place is sad or good, if it smells like November or December. Getting darker, much darker. Need a roundtrip ticket back to sunny ole hell, something worse than failing to remember a freeway going round and round a rectangular piece of asphalt. Need to see the traffic lights bounce their multicolored balls better. Mimi don't get it.

> Our story's scary, stupid, its special effects disastrous. Here's a storybook tourist-guide called *Galaxy Pair*. Mind you, not the Land Book - (unpalatable on this planet), rather the terrible calamity of a book *occurring*

(otherwise invisible, inaudible to pedestrians). An unusual book, a remarkable tome locked in the jaws of the great grizzly bear of International Publishing (IP). That book's not quite unique, somewhat unsuccessful, less popular than last year's literary time-bomb *Kodukeemia Heavenly Bus*. But the book sells more than fifty-thousand copies (most things eventually do) - weighs more than lots of lost copies of that most controversial of trilogies *Philosophical Blockbuster*.

Life's difficult for weasels. Pigs don't rise from shit. Men, of course, come out brandishing *what*? Toilet paper? Those are credit cards, people!

Damn I forgot *how* to say goodbye this time of year. At least Mimi gets it. I find goodbyes difficult. Sky's getting darker, much darker. Put my head out the taxicab window. Gulp the cold air. Out here I see the multicolored electric balls better. Having a good time if you wanna know the truth. I *am* the wind. I quit smoking. Got strong. Thus the curse. Tonight I'm going beyond the damage soon as I resume breathing again. Mimi? She grew up six hours from here, practiced flute over there. Another thing disappears from my view of the crossroads. Dunno what'll happen to me. I have in the past *known*. I'm the wind if you wanna know the truth.

One Thursday, on the continent, two years later, a man spikes a forest through the trees. He's chairman Dr. Rikmansuort. He's nice to passersby so long as they're willing to exchange their children with the sitting president and provide him support - I - in some parts (windows, I mean) sitting in this public theater. To learn more about us here in this theater - errors occurred in the past - keep reading. You'll learn how to change the world, make it a better happier place.

What I mean's Scattergood deceived a prostitute out of a few days baby-rest from a malfunctioning uterus. Now she sits in a Las Vegas solarium listening to screw music with a gun trained on a white man draped in olive oil.

I close the taxicab door behind me. "How are you? Well, but Mimi acts the ideal, you know ... "Your room's upstairs. Turn to the right." If you wanna know the truth I hung the phone up, turned around, left. You still living in San Francisco?

> If God's wrong about this [gesturing at the sidewalks of the great city], so be it - if He's right, I say let the greatest number of errors remain with Him. Let Him escape with what he's set in motion. Many communities are more calm on the western outskirts of the continent, outside the realm of Tourist Capture - replaced by the standard repository of knowledge, with its flaws, many doubts, wrong numbers running loose (wild?) *where?* More pedestrians looking for *what?* in two important respects (aspects?).

Outside the Las Vegas Corner Bar an out-of-work screenwriter hurries away from the sunset, while city councilmen reduce the roads to a few belts of understanding interspersed with a series of six-party talks on order & creation.

> History's crazy, awesome. Its special effects have consequences. Scripts serve as travel guides. Indices call out the right galaxy. Please note our world's not posted on a wall. Please note a terrible disaster occurs in this book. You can't see or hear the infantry approaching. That's okay too - a wonderful book, astonishing, locked in the jaws of Large International Gray Print (LIGP). This book's not quite funny nor excessively successful. The popularity of last year's literary time-bomb - *Kodukeemia burning bus* - won't prevent this book from selling more copies. (In tomorrow's editorial meeting, what should I tell the editor-and-chief?).

[x]

MAIN CIRCUIT CABLE

ACT I

PATRICK [to the AUDIENCE]: When I grew up on the island to become something of an adult, I didn't say a word to Mother till I said no to divorcing my first wife. Then I turned up here, on the continent, though I wanna return to the island when I'm not back there. Tonight I can't think of going back. Decades I'm here. Secret missions to look forward to - how fearless of me. Moments I stand afore the diner's restroom mirror I get weak. Every minute the devil squats in the stall behind me. He's too strong. Every time I turn around the restroom's walls move in a little tighter.

DIABLO [to the AUDIENCE]: That's the horror of what you see on the continent. You got no right calling me a murderer if you got the right to kill me, got no right to judge me either. I express IN WORDS what's important for you who don't *see* what horror means. Before you got a friend in horror you got enemies in fear. Then terror turns those friends into enemies. A thousand years ago I came to the continent to inoculate our ancestors against fear. Then I left the island. *Then* this man, Father [pointing to PATRICK] - a seminary dropout - comes running after me shouting. He doesn't *see* me here yet Father returns, hacking my hand away from every inoculated arm - packs of small arms I remember. In, uh, … tonight I'm shouting to keep from weeping like some grandmother tearing her teeth out. I wanna remember, wanna forget, don't wanna realize if I'm shouting at the diamond chandeliers above your heads - like bullets through my eyes - I think, oh my God ... a genius, a genius, I'm a genius ready to work, a full true complete genius, pure, crystalline as those diamonds up there, stronger than anyone out here. I stand on this stage to say I'm NOT a monster, while you in the audience, in a receptive frame of mind - hearts of men and women in the audience - fighting - families, children getting lots of love - your abilities - the power to do … trained to listen without feeling compassion, without decisions affecting the fate of each one of you.

PATRICK [turning to DIABLO]: Said as you like it. Your home's here on the stage - that you threaten to kill them, incinerate them all. Pigs pig - cattle's cattle - village after village. To say what? - you're more than a man, more than a *wise* man? If the plan's you're a genius, that's bullshit, man.

DIABLO [turning to PATRICK]: Are we, uh … Hey, man, you're talking to the [INTERFERENCE] here. *Listen.* This here's a poet-philosopher in the classical sense. It's, ah ... well, you can say *hello Captain* to the devil, right? He leaves the auditorium but you don't notice him. You can grab him - you did too - but he throws you into a corner. [Turning back to face the AUDIENCE] The devil asks this of his audience - learn the WORD at the center of your world. If you can't, you've come lost 'neath the blame of your misfortunes. You're mistrusting yourselves when all's left to doubt. I'm not, cannot ... I'm a younger man than I look. What a young man I am, a large man too, with large hands - though I wish a few ragged nails would scuttle cross this auditorium's floor.

PATRICK [turning his back to the AUDIENCE, speaking to the back of auditorium] This performance is my dream, *my* dream of the worst place in the world - I just don't know it yet. Weeks off the island, thousands of miles across the continent connected directly to a dream. This is no coincidence. This is *my* dream. I'm manager of these memories. More backward from the island than forward into a series of lost incidents, more possible to relate a story in private than speak out about it. If this story's a true acknowledgment it's also *me* [turns back around to face the AUDIENCE].

DIABLO [turning to face PATRICK]: Tell me how many people I've killed if that's what you actually know about me. Near enough to beat the last breath out of every person on the continent. Shouldn't be any different now. Damn, when one murder changes the speed of delivery through … You accepted a secret mission.

Hell are you doing accusing *me* of recruiting assassins? The way you fight, I'm thinking about how special you are *against* me yet insufficient to frighten everyone on the streets out there.

PATRICK: Oh your shit's piled up so high so fast!

DIABLO: No wonder.

ACT II

DIABLO [gesturing at the streets outside the diner's window]: Tough to weed through what's out there. Bundles of four-star clowns hired to complete the whole circus tent. Damn, man, it's better than Disneyland. I see 'em more, more, more often. Never grin at the other half. Give' em Band-Aids instead.

PATRICK: Man, you're insane!

DIABLO: Look around you. What compares to how they live around here? It's wacko, worse than bad. It's nasty without idols. Look around you. I'm not afraid of continentals. Skulls, altars, whole damn things. If those pedestrians died in bed, their souls would fail to do in hell what they're terminally incapable of doing in heaven.

PATRICK: Right now I don't care if you continue on but if *not* … so whaddya *want*? Scary as shit, if you ask me, if continentals can't learn - learn from our mistakes. *Mon Dieux!* A weapon's power is a power you can win if you want. You *can* win but *they* can win too. That's the main thing.

DIABLO: I work with continentals as much as I work with islanders. That's something else - something out of anything. I stay here because this is my … it's *me*. This life keeps my insular instincts intact, reminds me what I once fought for. If you were a continental, you'd fight every major battle in history too.

PATRICK: The dream's close, real close, too close. I can't see the outline but I know people are being sucked upriver. I see the water's flowing right back into the sewers.

DIABLO: Hell, I can't *not* care where the current takes them so long as they remain on the continent. Looking at you, I know you'll light their world on fire.

PATRICK: Light - space - truly one zap.

DIABLO: As you live.

PATRICK: I can see the dream yet cannot yet believe it. One zap.
DIABLO: Typical islander classification.
PATRICK: Shit you're insane.
DIABLO: You're on a mission. For your sins I'm giving you a mission, a real choice mission.
PATRICK [laughing]: To surf or fight.

ACT III

DIABLO [gesturing at the streets outside the diner's window]: Look at the old-world monkeys bite. One through nine - no maybes, no cellphones or fractional fictions. You can't travel in space out there, can't go *into* effect, not like in your dirtiest dreams. There's no fractional fictions to provide a ground, no three-quarters to eight. What are we doing when we go from here to there on this broad piece of land? - that's the materialist dialectic of physics.
PATRICK: Your job's to drive me crazy. Otherwise what?
DIABLO: No. I train young islanders who need to STOP people dead in their tracks. I'm their commander. I won't allow them to scrawl the word [INTERFERENCE] on a diner's restroom walls - it's obscene.
PATRICK: The smell of that. You smell *that*?
DIABLO: Shit?
PATRICK: Napalm, sir.
DIABLO [sniffing]: When this episode's over, I'm walking. I'm no one's pawn.
PATRICK: You know that smell?
DIABLO [sniffing]: They told me it's no longer classified.
PATRICK: Who?
DIABLO: We launched a classified mission.
PATRICK: Who?
DIABLO: They didn't say why.
PATRICK: *Who?*
DIABLO: The island. Thought you looked promising, thought you knew what to do. How could this happen?
PATRICK [gesturing at the streets]: Look at the pedestrians. They don't bang but whimper and whine their parts - *our* parts, sir.

How many of them would return home if they wanna know the truth and experience it *hands down*. How far they *wish* to go to get *at* the truth?

DIABLO [gesturing at a man on the sidewalk]: Akayavunja he broke his arm. Never seen such a man broken up, ripped apart after what I said to you. They *think* they wanna banish me? More than ever, it seems.

PATRICK: Hell you know about anger? You're not from New Jersey.

DIABLO: Hand me that sampler platter. I see everything, everything you see outside this windowpane. Nothing I detest more than the wrong smell of a disinfectant. If you understand me, Father, you'll do the same for me.

PATRICK: I know my mission.

ACT IV

PATRICK [to the AUDIENCE]: The day he freed us from the diner I imagine he knew we weren't returning to the island soon. He knew more than what I was gonna do. He wanted that - then more. Now I know he's out there waiting for me to draw pains from people on the streets - to go after pedestrians - at first - standing them up, in long rows, not unlike a weak-old rag-assed renegade. He doesn't want me dead yet. His orders aren't strictly correct.

DIABLO [to the AUDIENCE]: If Father goes mad I kill him.

PATRICK [to the AUDIENCE]: But how would he know that?

DIABLO [turning to PATRICK]: As you say, sir. Rock & rollóirí in the grave with one foot.

PATRICK [to the AUDIENCE]: Tell me what you think is good. What's wrong with you out there? You know why you can't step in the same river twice?

DIABLO [to PATRICK]: They know it's moving.

PATRICK [to the AUDIENCE]: Sho 'enuf - war starts tomorrow on Buddha's time.

DIABLO: You're the asshole of the world, Father.

PATRICK [turning to DIABLO]: I'm fighting for something great in history that scares the crap outta you. I'm not afraid of *me*, of what I'll accomplish when I arrive at the East End of the continent. I know the danger. I feel something more than desire to deal with …

DIABLO [turning to the AUDIENCE]: You know what's in order here? Wonder this shit's not found its way into the media.

TV in the corner replies: - "O People of our nation, civil war can be difficult - the stories, the wilderness, the cries to be strong and belong. Appeal to your sense of justice, of jetsam, sunken rocks, looters, blood-spattered fibers, unrest in palaces, monuments to sand. Clamoring for truth in a revolutionary way. To see your error disturbances on the day of wrath your enemies call Revolution."

    Commands we're not afraid of. Our country has those. Full of our misery - *you* - of our joy & faith, our respect & gratitude. You refuse to accept our defamation of the economic man. Cannot put away our curses now. Should that please you, let us begin with our thoughts, with a maximal nod, a shrug when we - both sides - each time we discover we believe in a collusive victory.

"Your apparent disorder I'm unafraid of. Many places to be, once was there. I owe respect & gratitude for my own tragic, so full of you, joy & confidence in me. If you won't embrace me successful in the men you've slandered, I won't curse it up. Why should I look like you if you're not *with* me? A few men brawdol."

    Oh you make our world hard. Wild stories crying to be strong. We know we fear in the dark ways to see errors of disturbance on that day of wrath called Revolution. We're not afraid in many places as once we were. We know the fear of dark tragic improvements in distress around the world again. International meetings intervene on the major powers of the dark crying out in continued hold on a Republic universal in waste at the vicinity of arrival of a prevention-case unannounced.

"Impending tragedy fills you with joy & confidence in me. I urge what you want. Give it once to me as a command-in-prayer to achieve this at favorable odds - not you wanting it, no, fixing your lives back together to make it right -. Again.

Let us return to thoughts on excellence just as we see resources on right principles - justice, logic, equality. If differences in divine realities of ordinary people are against us, it's heartbreaking - attaining a prayer contrary to our lives back together made just.

"Oh people of our nation - top significance in your future! Only a few ugly fraternal men left untouched, nice legs coming forward with statutes, rights, duties. This evening, I think - no, I'm sure - new rules you people build on this island. We look forward to ideas to strengthen, shock(en) the heart. More people growing without pain is too great if the national self-centered jerks let the world go free."

This evening, we think - no, we're sure - new rules people build on this island - *No*. Others, like the rule again, we're not men, men like you. We start with minds on highest, nod, shrug - two each time - take note of victory. The importance of future national - *go* selfish jerk!

"On to ways, revolutionary ways, facts seen wrong in riots raging today. Ah people of our nation you can be difficult. Afraid of many places. The loud noise of your wild stories leaves me in the dark. One way to fear, the other days of anger. I know the darkness of evil, misery of your world, fear growing on an international scale, disorders, dark powers crying out to continue prevention of our Republic's attempt at universal achievement without laying waste."

We demand everything you want become a tragedy filled with joy & confidence in us. Grant a contradiction if that's not something you want. A way to command the resolve to pray - not implying you prefer in our lives one chance to bring it back together. This evening we like that too - no, we're sure - new rules are not the old ones our people built upon this island.

"The future's hot - nice legs can't be spared. Rights & obligations of the legislation afore this night, I think - no, I'm sure - new rules you people soon will build upon this island."

-. Our stories inherited from the continent - deserted, strong voices appeal to your sense of central state justice -

logic, justice - dark abandoned goods, crates of sunken
rocks, robbery, blood spatter, fibered-over chaos, palaces,
monuments shorn from an island of sand.

Striding right out the insular organization

" the offender - the offender: - he, however, … creative."
O Mainland Grundpositor! O long narrow piece of
bare earth upwards to the left slowly! O Sandbank
Psychagogue, head bowed, hair streaming there in the sea,
numbers drawn in sand wet with sticky toes.
Stand at the edge of the Flood itself -
Stand for this moment - face the vastness of your promise-
monstrous!
Oh Vorsee bass separated by water wide as the deepness-point
on your knee-joint's knot -
O Mainland how impulse turns your torso -
How glancing at the sand you show deep expressions of
deepness-sleep -
As in memory.
As if your front stuck limitless on the threshold of sea-wind-
&-fog -
Oh use your character proud -
Turn yourself over to look over your shoulder,
Sit there on the beach,
Hip, beautiful, head raised in your chair.
- go where I want.

Connection-appearance, with hair streaming there

"To attract a lot of cattle - for this I left our island and came to the
continent?"
Oh brave new woman sitting at your easel with exclamations,
entertain, please me like never before -
The edges of your element
Perpendicular to the rest of this series -

Long-legged, swimming, living figure - hands behind your
head - capsized - laughing.
Fruity knees spread their goods -
"Critics should be angry with me!"

firm in the white sand people

"Whom do they hate most?"
>Men with big beards, big teeth:
>Ugly children surrounded by hags:
>Sandburgs, sellers shelling cakes on pages:
>Whole families emerging from women,
>Those gray shallow lakes inhabited by children
>Who talk
>Hemdgewändern wide starkfarbigen.

Interruption-tables of values

displaying many opinions that oppose each other in general.
"They found a chemist wild with white hair."

Morgeneleganz careful with nudity

Of chorus these little rooms house our individual brothers: most
interesting part of my journey. They share cells we cannot enter.
The disorder, the blank walls within those walls where brothers
unite on the floors of two rooms: wood, coal - before the second
room: bench with lathe set against one night's journey. No oven
though.
When I express surprise the leader replies, "Smile at your
leaders. They must work very hard."
Of chorus the entrance to the first room is equipped with a
slide-opening for serving food. Next we ascend the residential
scale to sleep among living room furniture: tables, chairs, a
wardrobe, bedroom with a real bed, access equipment, lectern.
Agendas depend from bare walls we watch every hour (and after
Bella). Those agendas depend from the wall for very very long.

Very strict too: Halb Morgens 5 hours. You must get to the middle of the day passing through the middle of prayer: physical work, meditation, church attendance, more food. Food is scarce, meat is not, but there's fish here, sir.

Leader introduces me to numerous posts. I see the brothers receive visions (though not the poor) from 10 o'clock to noon.

Outside the monastery walls, shops or restaurants share common sidewalks. You wouldn't know it by looking.

One day last week becomes available to free speech between 5-6 hours afore sleeping till the 11 o'clock bell summons us to stand at prayer. After a short break in the common path, brothers retire to the yards at one point about 2 o'clock in the morning. At 5 o'clock again Halb-bed. It's inappropriate in a Charterhouse to be, … including 7 years of cooling.

Later, after the brothers leave, will sessions of the cubic type leave no doubt "back there" for more.

Das kolloide Gold, Liquor Cerebrospinalis (Or, an Indonesian in a pink rabbit-bunny suit stalks Tompkins Square Park)

1.
Now I *live* on the continent. No crumbs or dirt anywhere. No chairs. No clarion bugle-calls. We're alone. We die there, over *there* [pointing].

Last night, in the women's room, Mimi Kuishi discovered she's disgusting. I trimmed her armpits to stop the itching. Now the question obtrudes: how can you get so bad in such a good situation? No matter. We never perceive the details, me & Mimi - we're not like Veronica over there [pointing at a young lady scrubbing the diner's (terrazzo?) floors].

Last night Mimi provided me a summary of her views. She's the messenger of time (at least in poor weather countries). She savors disasters more before than after dreading them (death + despair she still don't understand). I'm captivated by her charms. Nor the slightest signs of change occur anywhere else on Mimi's broad body - even when cancer's eating away at her (pelvis? … pancreas?).

"Waliwaua - our private heroes!" she shouts at me across the table this morning - or shall I kill herself? Answering that question's like trying to predict the position of an unknown planet.

Short time later we delve into the gory details. For now we got step, step, step, step, slot, step, slot, slot - right up to the process of cellular death known as 'apoptosis.' Inevitable. Time's not changing here, people - take my fatherly hand.

It's next fall: continental year penultimate 1. Me & Mimi are (sent?) to //--//-- for reasons we don't understand. We got no money, no resources, no hope. We're not the happiest people in the world, not as happy as we were less than a year ago, six months ago, living on Manhattan Island, spending our days and nights in diners and cafes. We were artists back then. Don't think we are anymore. On the continent, serious literature gets in the way of living (well, surviving). No more how-to books for writing thank God. What's this you're holding then? - not a book. That's defamation, slander, libelous behavior. Not a book. That's a maze in a mind the size of … no, not that either. It's an insult lasting for a very long time, a sea of green in the face of the arts, a kicking in its pants. God I'm a man of God, Love & beauty, commercial crises, sunspots. What? That's right. I'm singing to you [pointing out at the AUDIENCE]. I'm a bit more important than I used to be. In that case I'm not ready to sing. Ah ~ ~ Ah ~ ~ Foot wicked powerful ei 啦 … asthma at Kitty Hawk … I'll sing when I croak - dance my body dirty.

Poetry's something we eat for breakfast. Edema comes later this afternoon. Plus I have a little extra information on music - no accordion or guitar stuff here. Main thing's singing. This is a song I'll be singing - not yet. This song's for you, Mimi, in memory of you, Veronica. Wish I could sing it better, make it more melodic - but you'd disagree to hear me then. You may have heard (from others) that when I sing I leave others out in the cold. Mimi sings too, very nicely or not nice enough.

Though I turn thirty-something in October, I can't tell you why these leftover dreams from last year's November 15 are leaving me insufficient time between the *new* dreams to learn how much time I got left on the continent. If I find here a world of solutions, I forget where I left the matches last time I left the island for the continent. Imagine a cancer's eating away at? Silence falls over the music wherever … My stomach (or the breakfast hidden within it) retreats again into chaos, confuses my mind - a total forgetfulness of facts I've written. Me & Mimi are filing away at our private chaos. That's why we sing. Not even Walt Whitman shed the fields of death from the skins of time. In fact he's alive - in the womb. That's our usual practice of writing.

Later this morning I take a nap and dream of love's pathology. In China I'm a six-foot male. In Canada? Hello there - penis for free - bones of an animalistic man - one of his legs. This literary framework's irritating to continentals. Impatience? Yeah that too - good luck. My kangaroo has a double-bar: once a week, once to rest. Man, it's hard to awaken from a nap. Information from a woman asking if you found the Address Book. Address? No doubt: 'beautiful lesbians big,' as we used to say.

Pathology? That's the function of the main installation on Stage 1. Out of fear of those 3 enemies in spandex suits, I'm performing this one on a big 'uppercase' Thursday night. I got earplugs and I'm approaching 10. My long black curly hair looks strange - intense - severe. Those 6 amps over there [gesturing to the back of the auditorium] allow us to establish the sound around here. I'm afraid though: beyond those walls of amps, the phase field poorly covers the outer world (including that ornate lobby). The devices don't allow me to *see* the extra-audience, as it were. I'm afraid. You're a different crowd tonight. Crazy, fun, random. Strange. Very impressive. This ain't Duluth. This ain't 2005. This is 3 times the 2nd branch of chemistry - influenza strains too, each thing easier to see than anything else you can imagine: I see the pain inside. Can't you shut up? - I *am*. The likelihood of a wedding's very high tonight.

Few exceptions to the number of countries listed throughout heaven & hell. You won't find them in this theatrical piece. They might be part of someone else's performance so we won't rule that out. I wanna maintain a clean-line story here - describe a continental life in lifeless sections, a large part of any literary mission being to wipe the past + future clean of the present, render memories mummies and dreams rumbling tummies. That sounds strange and distressing. Things I'm embarrassed to write about - success of my work, for example, or the colorless texture of money. If I send readers into the confines of a mental hospital - no problem. Or credit card debt - no problem. Unlike shooting a film in the middle of an of ice storm - lens freezes over. (Intriguing?) how things I've written this year are crowding out, kicking out last year's problems from my mind - psychological indeed participatory. As if I wanna get married *one last time*. Or a child appears, or a brother vanishes, or a sister *then* a brother, or a sister dies leaving her own two sisters with their own four children and divorced husbands. I'm half dead myself (like Nathanial Hawthorne). Who's my favorite, the best writer of prose after Herman Melville died?

2.

I said I *live* on the continent. Not a crumb of dirt anywhere (or recognizable forms of presidency, for that matter). We're left alone to die here. The question obtrudes: how will the story end?

This is where I make first mention of Minnesota. As a drunk patron of bar life I'm excited to begin a strong relationship with that state. Regardless of your own state of worldly knowledge, first time we meet I'll ask if you've heard of Minnesota, an astonishing state filled with imagery pulled from a vast array of family photo albums. Welcome to Minnesota - one of the Great Lakes States (like Michigan used to be). I'll answer your questions soon enough. I won't actively or disruptively describe Minneapolis. (We have our fair share of worldly concerns here.) Sometimes, in Minnesota, people meet in downtown Minneapolis. On the other hand I could hand you a copy of a map of that city, leave it at that.

You know who my islander brothers are? Where they are? (Saturated?) A drowned truck-driver collapsed in

the Nevada desert (*of* the sand?). You know what melts
iron into glass? You know how porcelain runs through
the sides of this coffee mug? If I throw it at you? Know
the sounds of zithers, tambourines, fiber-reinforced
plastic recombined? It's not at all modern. Film's still
more ridiculous. You know why an acrobat bisects his
horse? All's in his eyes. (Incandescent eyes are rubbish.)
You know how flowers cling to that rectangular poster?
More in the nature of indifference - almost idiotic -
almost. You heard about the Chinese Parasol Messenger
Injury? All so modern. You know how I know these
things? - shittiness shorn of its riddle, a vessel less than
a blossom plunging through space, sycamores of
destruction, cables of coincidence, Atlantic messengers
of death, a fat-fat rat-mouse thick, the rat-a-tats rat-a-tats
rat-a-tats. Don't make no sense. 几乎. Chinese advice
through an injury in your head. I'm dragging the shit
right behind me: matchsticks from the stone age,
economic catastrophes, gospels of terror, films of folly.
That's what we need - bondage as reaction to liberty
over the course of the whole cosmos. It's two o'clock -
night's in no hurry. Editors keeping you fed? Got a great
haircut from stone - flying prehistoric lizard - giant jaw
cut from the sides of rock - bondage as your reaction to
liberty. Why trouble waking you if you'll throw the book
at me? You'll stuff your fists right back into those
trouser pockets. Your company's known for shit. You
know why I insist on the work of that rectangular poster.
Me? I'm on fire. Insomnia's an absurd passion of mine.

Last night, in the women's room, Mimi said she wasn't happy
with how I shaved her armpits after the itching stopped. How can
she feel so lousy in such a beautiful place? Ah that's unimportant.
She'll never admit we live (make love) so close to the bone, me &
Mimi. She pretends the lice have left us forever.

I believe Minnesota's got the same kind of creative arc as
Indiana and Illinois, where accuracy counts as bravery, and
confidence integrity. In snowy Minnesota, the visual arts

inspire unlimited creativity, summoning a complete lack of interest in despair. Minnesota's purpose is to be good, inspiring, regardless of whether its citizens pursue musical activities or, let us say, "cut bent twisted roads through the heart of Michigan's Upper Peninsula."

How these solutions work for *my* work! Memorial writing's what I've done for such a long time. Wrote my sixth story in the sixth grade. That work was cold, too cold, its words *beyond* money & fame, as if I had a sense - gobs of common sense - that my writing life would become less than what I think it is today. All those things I did to experience humiliation. You may remember my artist family on 46th Street. They liked tragic things a lot - like speaking long sentences into portable recording devices. Man, your parents' depressing marriage can be so hilarious. You know what's important to me to *this day*? - portable recording devices. How's that for a specific period of time I need to work out a life philosophy? You may be right. I may be God. Elected. Yet something's sad + depressing if far too interesting to leave to the filmmakers. We writers can replace those images with these things [pointing at the beautiful prose on this beautiful page].

This morning Mimi's giving me a summary of her views. Not bad. She's a prophet. She predicts the weather will continue: more disasters, death, more despair - not a hint of change in the world. Cancer will eat us alive, kill our heroes afore they have time to kill themselves - a hero not once but forever, step by step, block after block, a deathly prison sentence of fame & wealth. No escaping changes in this harsh continental weather.

Minnesota landscaping brings to mind lots of snowplows, frozen lakes, disturbing dreams of snow atop snowbanks. Yet the summers are serious works of art (literally). Mass unemployment's one way to confuse the public. Another way is "first ten years of the millennium of independence."

You're here for more information on the snow, right? All the same all or nothing's the same. Speed's unnecessary.

Creatures see the great outdoors. The sun & moon & stars. Bright eyes agleam with bullshit. Tell me about the risk of a long knife beneath the skin - red blistered night - red sparkling at night. More big literary relief - silly - *almost* - like the mysterious Tip at the end of the Line. A simple option. *Zerotoreransuporishi New*. Musical soundtrack to an ordinary man's life. I gave up the green light, entered the iron ore fields. A gun - a loud voice - a great sense of responsibility. God's form of penetration of experts into the world (though the social facts of pestilential horror are busted). Low-wage Asian immigrants trapped in the paths of capitalism, the rice fields over there. So let's do things other than kill mosquitoes.

Now's my third autumn on the continent. Islanders sent me here for reasons I cannot fathom. Got no money, no resources, no hope. I'm *not* the happiest man in the world. Many years ago, six months ago, yeah sure, I thought I was an artist. I disrupted economies of scale necessary for creative work. Now something's fallen away from me. No other books to read - thank God. This? This is *not* a book. This is libel, an insult to character. This is not a book in the usual sense of 'book.' It's Kick Ass, so to speak, a mélange of God, people, fate, time, love, beauty, straw hats, trouser belts, Mr. Edison & the electric light, superabundance of silver, beer-drinking - what I call Kick ASS. Call it what you want. I'll sing about it in a voice a little fake-sounding, sure, but let me sing afore I croak. I'll be the dirty dancing corpse. To sing you should open your mouth, right? Don't require an accordion or guitar or … Ah ~ ~ Ah ~ ~ Foot wicked powerful ei 啦 Main thing's you sing what you wanna sing. First two songs you sing should behave like a pair of light little birds who know nothing about scales & harmony. This story depends on *you* Mimi who sings. Pity I can't sing more melodically. Never convinced you to listen to me. My singing's beautiful, beautiful enough.

As someone who loves to cook, loves to eat, I appreciate the variety available here in Minnesota. Takes everything I got to survive a plate of southern Louisiana cuisine - though surviving High Pronk without a conventional landing strip is obvious in Minnesota. I'm here, on a job, in the middle of a meeting, in a tradition passed down generation to generation. Look at me, how I chop vegetables, cook pasta in salt water (though I don't eat cabbage: it's like glopp to me). In Minnesota, Christianity's a religion of universal orthodoxy, yet I feel like I'm in a Dallas kitchen. *Almost*. I should register these theological arguments with the elders. This is Minnesota. No one's home, or if she is, her grandmother will eat us alive. That's how it works. When you eat more than your dinner table allows, grandmother gets pregnant.

> Combinations + permutations involved in this process, messing around with paragraphs, sentences, picking through prose - ... - hitting my characters hard over their heads with metaphorical skillets not hammers. I call it "continuous follow-up literature." That was another world another 20 years ago. I wasn't attending parties in Paris. God no. I was watching the *Romanization Show*. Odd TV channel. Wide range of human emotions there - convergence of the world - defense mechanisms against dark matter. Interesting channel, incredibly bleak. Entertaining. Today they're calling it "girls-and-punishment black comedy." Flann O'Brien's important to me. John Steinbeck's not. Who the hell's Donald Antrim? Line up, people, line-to-line, make yourselves out to be surprising prose writers, best writers of prose. People forget. Readers forget. I'm the champion of forgetfulness. I own these bookshelves.

By this point in the narrative my dreams are realizing their left side. I watch the world around me dissolve. Here and there, spots of time, an earth cancerous from overeating. (That means you're getting high off calories.) Everywhere music prevails, chaos restored. That's the reason I sing - not for me if the world dies. I'm alive & kicking in the womb, in fact, writing from behind.

("She's neither [INTERFERENCE] nor Greek nor ...")

> What should I say about the outskirts of this westernmost of continental cities? Short answer's 'no

guessing.' You agree? What else? Adjustment's the idea here. Ten cassette compilations of my favorite songs. Near the end, yes. Press Play? Lord, let's say I told you the password to my digital music library. Let's say I reversed (revered?) the chronological order of music that accompanies an ordinary human life. I'd allow for strange new artistic benefits - *italics* for example. What happens? That's right. An angel of light from heaven - a detailed auto + bibliography of my reading history. Something like that's real fun.

Some sleep - a Chinaman with six legs enters Penis World [AUDIENCE laughs]. That man over there's penis-free [AUDIENCE laughs louder]. Animal penis bone! [AUDIENCE applauds.] Thus the bone ... Hurry up you little fool. I'll bite your hands off, chew the bones right through. Better yet I'll roll your hands till there's blood everywhere, in your mouth, on the ground. Slowly you'll die, your eyes too, pain subsiding grayish black. From the ground you'll never rise to heaven - there's no God - hah your body will rot right there if there's the remotest chance of it. I know you must stop this eternity lest you never see me again. No wonder your parents divorced. What? They said it, not you? Stop your damn crying - tears are a loss of precious water.

How did this happen? How *could* this happen? Do I have to listen to stuff like Deep Purple's *Machine Head*? I sense something strange is about to change me here. I start deleting songs from my digital music library to help identify the right music for an account of the spirit of God. At the end of this long summer I'll be damned by the publication of my first 'nonfiction novel.' I didn't invent that form. Forgot how to laugh or cry. Afraid I feel drunk too. (Heeee.) So, a few things count as a literary crime here. Good luck. Misdeeds painful to us, intolerable burdens, groups of lies whispered to friends in unbridled envy: we hate people who love us lazily, their stolen office supplies, bloated expense accounts, concerns that all forms of violence reduce to the reckless speed of highwaymen. Look at the buffers of Bandar:

right down to the belt, man, one site at a time, one loop, loop-d'-loop (that's easiest). So we copy out Montaigne from the 19th century French verso, take that man's prose right back to the Liberty Library. Our friends (others?) steal their kisses *from?* (lies of togetherness). Last night, let's say, in a state-run motel rank with the tanning power of adultery: convincing (at first), till we learn how to bury the ashes, how to hide our partners behind gifts of money, gifts in memory of wives and husbands once loyal beyond non-recognition now hidden behind the cruel bad luck of strangers who themselves act cruelly towards hidden friends and lazy waiters. Who's blaming us for turning over the wrong cards, turning a cold shoulder to our favorite tennis players, for laying cards out on the table, for misleading our children in the chess games of their childhood? We must find that man at once - in the market. There he is - waltzing on purpose, doing things unnecessary to our collective franchise before asking us for nothing more than $25 USD to increase the number of serious literary crimes in one paragraph, one chapter, abusing the reader who lacks a standard, who cannot write to the author to berate him for theft of time (+ money) - worse than anal rape of the innocent. We committed the crime - out of anger, lack of sleep, forgetfulness (haven't figured it out), whispering to the author "I'm gonna murder you, you moody bastard - you & your literary sins!" Those are some things we count as crimes here.

[y]

MY FOCUS THROUGH THE BEATINGS

ACT I

PATRICK: On the continent an islander cannot do it how the Boogeyman does it back home.

DIABLO [nodding in agreement]: Over here you're not a human being. If you crack a joke, they know you're looking to disturb them.

PATRICK [laughing]: Born on the island forty-two years ago, Boogeyman said nothing, left nothing to reason or chance, no conscience, no understanding, not a basic sense of life or death, good or bad, right or wrong. He was blank, pale, less emotive than a face with black eyes.

DIABLO: I spent eight years trying to reach him, another seven keeping him locked up in that hospital. I realized the life behind those eyes made his fellow man look pretty damn simple. Spooked?

PATRICK: I'm not frightened.

DIABLO: Lie!

PATRICK: Nor are you, I gather.

DIABLO: God won't take that joke - but I'll bracket your lies. I don't think you need tomorrow.

PATRICK: If you say so. Hey moron, speed kills!

DIABLO: Yes.

[Car screeches to a halt.]

ACT II

DIABLO: Father, tell me, what's Boogeyman to you?

PATRICK: No such thing today.

DIABLO: Look at me.

PATRICK: Don't rip my shirt - it's expensive, you idiot!

DIABLO: Shit.

PATRICK: Boogeyman once showed up in every town. Went to the garage, got a hacksaw. Does it matter if he's described in the local papers or not?

DIABLO: Where are we?

[Car screeches to a halt.]

PATRICK: For heaven's sake you cannot drive - *and* I gave you lessons.

DIABLO: More of your fancy talk. Oh I have a license, but these other people are in the way. I was good at driving last night. What more you need?

PATRICK: Eh? Oh, yes, uh, here ...

[Car inches back into the flow of traffic.]

DIABLO: I got a bad feeling.

PATRICK: What more do you need? I'll prove you wrong.

DIABLO: Hold it.

ACT III

[PATRICK, with DIABLO in tow, walks from the parking lot to the hospital's entrance. The sun sets behind them.]

DIABLO: Oh Jesus ...

PATRICK: You okay? Stop here.

DIABLO: You must believe me, Father, he's ... I know -

PATRICK: I see you're afraid of what's inside there.

DIABLO: Yes, yes I am. If not, it's the funeral of?

PATRICK: I think you got a vision of the Boogeyman, a vision of the thing. I can't stand your patter, ranting on without cause or concern.

DIABLO: I'm [INTERFERENCE] and you're ready to ...

PATRICK: It's the *idea* I mean, the *vision*, the *appearance*. You think you're soooo smart.

DIABLO: And you're soooo serious. You see what you want.

PATRICK: Yeah. I mean, you look ... expect thorazine.

DIABLO: No, no, no - never.

PATRICK: Look - over *there* [pointing].

DIABLO: Where? I can't see anything.

[A shape's hidden in a bush beside the sidewalk.]

PATRICK: Fine, ain't it? That patient wants to talk with us tonight.

DIABLO: I see no one there. You're crazy if you saw a patient under that shrub. Yes, Father, I know you feed off superstitions.
PATRICK [pointing at the bush]: That patient wants to talk with us.
DIABLO: What patient?

ACT IV
[PATRICK, with DIABLO in tow, strides down the shadowy corridors of the hospital.]
PATRICK: You're coming home. How's it feel?
DIABLO: Like I got three choices.
PATRICK: Look in these rooms - the patients sleeping, keeping each other company. Oh it's great to watch these patients sleep and screw around and yell at us as we pass.
DIABLO: I don't care for your reminiscences.
PATRICK: Ummm. You sure?
DIABLO: I'm not afraid.
PATRICK: Not *any* fear?
[DIABLO stops walking, thinks for a moment, resumes walking.]
DIABLO: I saw him - again.
PATRICK: What? What's it?
DIABLO: Boogeyman. Outside in those bushes. We walked by - I admit I saw him.
PATRICK: Leave Boogeyman outta this, leave him outside.
DIABLO: Patients got hungry. They ate him.
PATRICK: I saw Boogeyman too. I *saw* him.
DIABLO: What you want now? You thought it would be …
[PATRICK stops walking, thinks for a moment, resumes walking.]
PATRICK: That's all I say here.
DIABLO: Look - Boogeyman's not in his cell! He stepped out for the night.
[PATRICK stops walking, thinks for a moment, pulls off the clown mask.]
PATRICK: Okay, meat-head, joke's up. Where'd the doctors put my son?
DIABLO: Dunno. Here, take this. You can pass the time reading a magazine.

Then he blew his brains down

This is *not* a case where the American writer Tomas Upchinon notes more than 90 indie rock bands in these words: "Rock 'ñ'-not only role of a group's everyday life's become a basic miracle."

As proof: music critic Manager Joe wrote *this* for awhile last season: "One is about the intriguing I. Here's a group with what I think 32 is old still counting. They do? Yes. 25 years they did eight to the core - 27 in fact."

Upchinon agrees, noting a common vessel for money is what makes a great group at 32 survive beyond bands relegated to a corner of the old. "This is beautiful as it is, a group built on a kind of personal life. They like it more than anything they do as a permanent group. This commitment is true."

Instead of a psychedelic vein, Manager Joe puts the group's works in the category of documentaries on the latest advances beyond Serekushonribenji Cucolarus (truer words cannot be spoken). "Refer to this group as interesting before learning to trip over their rhythms. They play the role of every sort, ensuring the tonic settlement occurs within the group improvisational dynamic," says Manager Joe.

Indeed their music's described as a 'nearby community approach.' "The lead singer makes steps backward as 'leader' per se, while the interesting strategy, I must add, is acting one day like the fact of the world doesn't register on you. The group puts punk in the minds of an audience without taking its spirit away. That's like saying, 'Anyone here can do this no different from the audience out there,'" continues Manager Joe.

The audience *is* no different, writes Upchinon. "Spectators may not find the material interesting, but the fact the group has a long British punk heritage turns the performers away from the first wave, makes them into a show impossible to ignore on the filmic level. The mystery of this one, considering the group's place, is: with what or how to preserve their live sound - the individual notes of the group - while maintaining the wax & reduction of musical commitments."

Upchinon notes that a direct determination of the meaning of the blood vessels can become a little vague. It's clear each member's honest enthusiasm will provide for the group, though expression of their individual creativity, where music becomes available if you don't dream too hard - money too of course - cannot block a lack of recognition. Common sense says respect yourself before taking anything from the world.

Upchinon: "Groups, as we know, define their successes by those of another band. They live in hope for their group to make money from their music, everyone does, including Saritimuzuaidia [the replacement violinist]. That suits our collective reality."

The group plans to stay together until there's economic success far more involved than any single stage show. "To fight for the group's survival's nothing. That's what I find attractive about their performance on film - what many expected them to offer on stage: life plus those groups appear to *this* or *that* person. That's the approach of their stage show - strange lighting and those interesting projectors," concludes Manager Joe.

I love pigs, plus pigs - here come make a bad hairy chiny chin

Next: San Diego - amazing story of this family: 28 years behind the elderly, he's the cousin of a year-old 77-upstart (little salty), a wild warrior with wisdom on people, man who challenges and criticizes trends on no one else's account. The upstart - [INTERFERENCE] waiting in the wings - after screaming, caught the attention of Hollywood (representing youthful society connected, fresh, happy, with hundreds of thousands of believers who see their own positions in a growing phenomenon). Next, upstart's relatives plunge into the hands of a series of pilot adaptations optioned, made available by producing team Jay & This Story, Finalist Pulitzer Prize winners, heads of Raw Media Trends, creators of Another Set of Annual Awards.

The cousin - golden dog [INTERFERENCE] - asked questions about what an upstart's required to compile.

1. So you cannot hear your upstart uncle's presence - this is not stupid?

A geuneundoejii - his name's not Samuel. It's shorter. For many years, in the fields of nuclear medicinal energy, University of California, San Diego, Los Angeles Times - those outlets based on individual configurations visible to the naked eye - except one day Samuel comes home - he's refused a job interview. Look at that Simpson voice live.

二. Note: That saemipinikka remark comes at the end of our summer interview. Cousin calls him Uncle Samuel Geugaganeum - 10 seconds with a smile on the mobile phone - Is this what?"

三. You say he's a success?

According to recent chatter, yes. Ah ... Samuel's in his head so much, unwilling to grow, says: "This Note: You lucky I got warts. Members of the public - if you got a big penis start noticing I *don't* remember.

四.但是 - salty dialogue -

He starts complaining about realizing anything interesting. According to Mr. Cancel, Uncle Samuel used a computer several years, wrote, however, less compelling voices ("You're more than two hours into the bathroom scene ... no, we don't have specific requirements. Don't *need* to flush the toilets should be used. This is my linoleum-and-tile closet."). Another embarrassment-variant: ("I'll give you the time, lend you gym equipment - I need to sweat out these bird droppings. Fanny-pack's where this work belongs").

五. That's interesting?

In Uncle Samuel's life yes. In mine? - 28-year-old cousin filled with initiatives to find factors underlying perceptible things - gets a new line on a grumpy old man, makes contract offers when he sees lines of agreement expose an interest in removing elements unsuitable for important big laughs. Uncle Samuel comes to the Kamerakomedisukuriputo, composing it by 'right of feeling.' For example: "Oh, come here, practically invented the delay. Audience before the call for use of the lazy."

六. What has a chance in the television series? What *is* this?-?

Dog feces in silence. Bad thing, if you will :) Lord's Grace for Uncle Samuel, Good Morning Miami, 4 King of the Test - all due to failure on the part of my uncle's autobiography. See above: In a conversation with Raw Media Trends, Uncle Samuel lifted speaking restrictions - an anonymous man who sounds like deprivation of a 77-year-old uncle.

(Photos LaPresse) - Headline injuries

United Tajik Opposition theft - Oct 24, 6:14, line on motor N. Fair Oaks Blvd. Machine left running red Acura stolen 10 days ago.

Trailers - Oct 24, 7:04, 100 Strand, George Street at Evelyn. Three cars in the area. "No Parking" near trailer. Area used for urban village farmers market.

Sabotage - Oct 24, 6:38, 700 Avenue Block Dallas. Graffiti found in toilet, entertainment in the park.

Theft - October 23, 4:36, 1500 block Samedra Street. Toyota Tacoma CATALYTIC converter stolen - hacksaw left on engine.

Theft - Oct 22, 5:37, 1100 Ayala Drive. Keys, chains cut to steal a bicycle valued at more than $900.

Theft - Oct 22, 11:06, 1100 at Block Reid Avenue. At night, an unknown subject in washing machine. Hair falls in wash basin. Crumpled cash in that machine.

Find a Car - Oct 22, 8:42, 700 block machine Chopin. Acura abandoned in tudung, closed the window, filled with many things close to the car. Iron filings on engine-block.

Theft - Oct 22, 9:40, 1600 block of Meadowlark Lane. Man returned to car, found his missing money in the trunk.

Find a Hotel - Oct 22, 9:21, 700 block machine Lakebird. Computer located on the front page of a residency permit.

- Oct 22, 6:33, 1400 Block S. Wolf Road. Palu pneumatic truck hijacked.

Theft October 21 -, 5:25, 1000 block of Bryant Road. Residents indifferent to rusty mowing machines worth more than $400.

Theft October 21 -, 10:25, 1100 Block N. Mathilda Avenue. Black reported lost or stolen. Laptop bag containing business or personal products, also passport.

Vandalism October 21 -, 8:44, 900 at Poplar Avenue. Window smashed in a blue Toyota car. Two toolboxes missing from bed of trunk. Estimated losses more than $ 400.

Theft - October 20th 3:49, 600 block of S. Bernardo Avenue. Man dashed out of grocery store with meat value-pack totaling two sachets.

Hit-and-run - October 20, 12:21, 800 housing in Lake Haven. Bertabrakan car with a Ford Mustang diparkir at night.

Theft - October 20, 11:15, 1200 Block Old Mountain View - Alviso Road. Two stolen PORCELAIN industries behind business. PORCELAIN OVENS valued at $40,000.

Theft - Oct 19, 9:37, 1600 block of St. Martin. Red Honda motorcycle anti-theft remains sabotaged.

- October 20 6:25, 800 block machine Lakechime. Scrawls on the wall - find the man sprawled in the middle of the toilet.

As a result of new flu shot is 17

Editor's Note: Whether or not our news magazine provides a sense of personalized instability, it occurs to this editor our mission's to emphasize, starting with presses around the world, how a waterfall leaves its fish out to dry on the sandy shores of history. Like asking you to imagine the Rolling Stones *with* Mick Jagger as lead singer. Or in Italy, where everything's gone Tarallucci & Wine - words of rumor, speculation, official statements from fellow reporter-adventurers. Those are pitfalls of the joke.

Consider the Moroccan man of 35 who suffered through a "news opera" - he died one Sunday in hospital San Sebastian when he attended the launch of a bilateral pneumonia conference. Victim suffered serious heart disease. He won't go alone. Performance ended with hugs.

Two more dead for several hours in Maharashtra liver transplant center resulting from brand-new influenza virus. Of the other victims none is in Caserta thank you God.

Points out objective criteria for assessing the results of placing 'sticks' clear of interfering in our health policy. "Take the road, take it high," according to Deputy Minister for Health speaking at a conference sponsored by the scalpel, "plus reconcile the health with policy in the name of meritocracy. That's the strategy we want - in the convergence regions of stock liquidation, with high levels of confidence-building measures, thus guaranteeing our national health service."

The priest has humor. Plus severe heart disease

"He's the father of the child representing the impoverished folks floating away in their helium balloons," said the priest's ancient mother to a customer-support/case-cost worker at a local religion-inspired hospital. The lawsuits agreed to provide the criminally poor-insane with two test-sentences. Jobless claims lowest since January.

"I don't wanna leave [I work in this hospital], but I won't be kidnapping patients again either. If they wanna rob someone's smile, much less a person, it's impossible to accelerate their healing work - often much less useful than a long walking distance."

Now that man is craaaaaazy

I don't understand *what* happened. You can ensure I don't understand more than what the President didn't understand what happened.

Well, Mr. President, what's with the shirt/tie combo? Dealer for part-time? For males' participation in the evaluation of a "doll road" revival show? O God, voters, it's 2009 not 1948.

Even more - Jialipulei's selling books, writing mad claims. Mr. President kept asking stupid legal solutions - how, who cares for control of scale? Told again forever. That's inappropriate - this is Onbha.

No. 3 ([) suitable for expressing what's impossible to speak in English or understand linguistic punishment for all.]

A [, family photo album - or I shall say Detroit? - Mr. President's shirt inappropriate/ tie combination?]

He doesn't love her - strange - Mr. President likes shiny white girls. He's married about 8 of 'em.

But I'll leave that problem - more interesting ...

In any case, Mr. President requested - then stopped, asking ... addresses the voter sitting there hooked up to the microphone. Dumb. Any other word? No. Dumb.

Strange …

[More fun, without video verification, as shown below.]

Of course I can't stop myself.

CUSTOMERS' HEAD INJURIES

ACT I

DIABLO [putting down a magazine, rising from the bench, … hurrying down the sidewalk]: We Winnie or Freddie tonight, Father?

PATRICK [following DIABLO]: Mmmmm … Linde Wendy. Gimme a cigarette.

DIABLO [ignoring the request]: Oh you're more than gentle. [DIABLO reaches out for PATRICK.]

PATRICK: Stay away from me. Stop pulling at my sleeve.

DIABLO: Why?

PATRICK: Let's get back to the diner. It's cold out here.

DIABLO: Why?

PATRICK: I'm puzzled by something, need time to think about …

DIABLO: Things, … about your life? You gotta think you're virtuous for at least a few more minutes. Any [INTERFERENCE] left in you?

PATRICK: Please. Hurt!

DIABLO: I do *not* hurt.

PATRICK: Stay away from me. Stop pulling at my sleeve.

[PATRICK swings his fists, delivering overhand rights, lefts.]

DIABLO: Father, light of my life, I'm not gonna hurt. You won't allow me to end the sentence. I said - do not harm you. Just gonna steal your ideas.

PATRICK: Stay away from me. Hurt!

[PATRICK turns around, trying to retrace his steps on the sidewalk back to the diner.]

DIABLO [sarcasm]: Work to crush. Damn right. Mmmmm ha ha ha.

PATRICK: Stay away. *Stop.*

DIABLO: Stop the bank-swingin'. Fists down, Father. Father? Tender bat.

ACT II

PATRICK [crossing the street against traffic]: There's a big party, right?

DIABLO: Four presidents, movie stars - all good continental people. Don't live within them. They can't live without it.

PATRICK: Words of wisdom, sir, words of wisdom.

DIABLO: No, *you* sir. They're temporary words. I'm professional. I know why I'm here. So let's make a new rule for the rest of the night: when you listen to me, reach to print [sarcasm], or reach out to me, or write across me [sarcasm], what I'm here for is listening to you. I'm *not* trying to experience what time means to you. I know you can deal with that.

PATRICK: I got no idea what's moral and what's unethical anymore. Small difference ain't it?

DIABLO: All I'm saying's move your fingers to hold talks with me.

PATRICK: I don't wanna talk with you.

DIABLO: Now, why not start right here, right now?

PATRICK: His Majesty opens that door? I'm not going inside there.

DIABLO: Of course the noisy crowd will be fun. We're gonna have a good time.

PATRICK: I'm stepping inside a stranger's apartment to spend the night the way *you* want? Shit, I look forward with pleasure to something else.

DIABLO: Take this as a sign [gesturing to the partygoers in their gay partygoer uniforms]. Why do you drink, sir?

PATRICK: Hair of the dog bit me.

DIABLO: Let me tell you something. If you get worried, come into the back-room, interrupt my focus through the beatings - call out to me. There'll be time to return unmolested to the diner. Understand?

[On a nearby TV screen, Jack's trying to murder Wendy.]

PATRICK: I bet everyone in the audience will find it difficult to accept this kind of playacting.

[AUDIENCE laughs.]

DIABLO [turning to the AUDIENCE]: Yes, I know every time new performers show up the performance takes a turn for the worst.

[AUDIENCE laughs, louder than before.]

DIABLO [turning back to PATRICK]: Now, Father, come out, come out with your stupidity.

PATRICK: How?

DIABLO: Don't wonder about it.

PATRICK: What are we doing at this party? What should be done here? I don't remember. I was on the verge of ...

DIABLO: Why you don't wanna talk?

PATRICK: Can't remember ... travesty [INTERFERENCE] soon as possible - when 'my' must be taken to a linguist soon as possible. I'm worried for the audience - of course, not for *me*.

[AUDIENCE laughs louder than ever, applauds.]

ACT III

DIABLO [to the AUDIENCE, with hands upraised to shield his eyes from the lights]: One of my responsibilities ... tonight's never a dull moment. Work's *my* responsibility - I alone. First time standing before you, I agree to delete what's never happened here, but my request to you, the audience, the ticket-owners, is to have full faith and confidence in my performance - signed as a contract to accept full legal responsibility. Sidewalks, streetlights, ideas of ethical and moral principles. If you stop watching this performance according to your moral responsibilities to your colleagues, nothing else can happen. Got it?

PATRICK [directly to the AUDIENCE, hands at his sides]: Of course he never thinks about *my* responsibilities?

[AUDIENCE laughs.]

DIABLO [turning to PATRICK]: Oh Jack are you talking about *what*?

PATRICK [turning to DIABLO]: I'm leaving now [turns his back to the AUDIENCE to face the rear of the auditorium].

DIABLO [turning to the AUDIENCE]: Graceful. He looks good. [No response from PATRICK, who stands unmoved, his back to the AUDIENCE.]

DIABLO: Well it's unpleasant for me too. This here's hard work, a little, uh, a great sense of isolation up here on the stage - like a Kazan hotel where heating occurs daily in different areas on rotation of damage. Thus we cannot generate the elements for radical social reforms.

PATRICK [turning around to face the AUDIENCE again]: There'll be somewhere ... but what about my sick little boy? How does the audience think about him?

DIABLO: He's not for them.

PATRICK [turning to DIABLO]: Oh.

[AUDIENCE laughs.]

DIABLO: [turning to the AUDIENCE, shielding his eyes]: I'm not suspicious. I've seen Father on TV.

[AUDIENCE laughs, applauds.]

PATRICK [directly to the AUDIENCE]: I remember when I was a child Mother taught us how to open our mouths without holding any speeches. For a long time the two of us made it bright. As you see from the devil's mindset, other people now do it too, though most don't know or believe in it. What extent can accomplish what? - won't talk about it.

DIABLO [speaking directly to the AUDIENCE but gesturing at PATRICK]: How can I reply *that*?

ACT IV

PATRICK [sipping coffee at the diner table]: Tell me something. Tell me, who lives in the mouth of my son?

DIABLO: Your boy?

PATRICK: Yes.

DIABLO: Who says that's what you're afraid of?

PATRICK: Unafraid - things are how they are. I think hard now. *Think*. Keep on thinking but I don't find anything there.

DIABLO: You're trying to think of your son in his hospital room?

PATRICK: Anything wrong there? I think of the past as something here in this diner, how the whole of it's better …

[DIABLO shrugs his shoulders, says nothing.]

PATRICK [gesturing to a building across the street]: You never said anything about this place. Signifier for a hotel?

DIABLO: You enjoy strange hotels, yes? Well stay away from that one. Don't try to extract a funny game from that architectural situation.

PATRICK: Maybe I'm afraid I'm having the worst nightmare. This is a horrible dream. Cut my son to small pieces. God O … must be losing my thinking capacity. God O … my little boy's crying.

DIABLO: Who? Your boy's a very bad boy if I can be so bold. He's a great talent too.

PATRICK: Why?

DIABLO: Stubborn child, a very bad boy with serious problems, and stupid, cannot be relied upon.

PATRICK: Uh, to prevent …

[The waitress turns the pumpkin-colored little knob closer to the center dot.]

DIABLO: Away, away, wherever you are, there'll be resentment. Not blow your home.

[A piþirin NEGRO enters the diner.]

PATRICK: That's strange, sir. I got no memories invested in what you say.

DIABLO: This place is a little slow tonight. Hahahaha. Here - gimme that.

[DIABLO starts flipping through the stale newspaper.]

[z]

Girls had stolen Costa Move's pulmonary artery from the depths of orange on his head

Children

1. Costa Move's demented mother described him as a victim of violence at age 10 years, putting that state of mind into his hands & head with 3 pillars of evidence: bed-wetting, zoosadism, pyromania. Deeper genealogical inquiries were never … after the (alleged) [*What?*]. In his youth, Costa Move was intrigued by alcoholic beverages, drug abusers, chronic suppressors. We believe his anger derived from erectile dysfunction and psychological deregulation. [Yes?] "To" he suffered from. [Quote Honourable Mention here?]

> Imagine: a small rocky island palace - a young woman of rock waist thigh hidden blade-deep whispering of colored skies prior to downloading digital images. Imagine a giant old thing failed an instant afore the eagle habitat took home with the more active fish - now *with* those fish. Imagine my voice is God. Imagine a train. Cars in arteries. Imagine any exception to shadows - spread wings in November. Or a dog depending on how long ago 5 skulls went universal. Oh, dear, those continental soldiers were brave shooting hostile fire at our island. Their future's today's pulpy star: our sun's now an intellectual hole.

DIABLO: A right way doesn't prevent the wrong way.

PATRICK: Yet that way stops the bad way from trampling out the name of wisdom.

DIABLO: Keeps things on the right track yeah - never stopping / ' in the name of logic' / stopping - no, I can't stop these people from doing what they're doing to the continent.

PATRICK: So what? These people? Just to …

DIABLO: Once, back on the island, three councilmen failed to account for what the divers were suspended to find, and suicide became … Occasional stories, opportunities, intersections, odd things that look … I wanna know what'll happen. I, eh - it's like watching movies. Not anything I *say* like Who or What is that or let's meet those people with a handshake and open the continent up to new forms of social humility. What can you say when what happens remains unsolved? The books say: "We cannot go *through* the past, only *around* it, not through it."

PATRICK: I'm tired.

DIABLO: You're here to stay.

PATRICK: I'm tired - of *that* [gesturing to the dark streets outside the diner's window].

DIABLO: You know the elements common to all groups?

PATRICK: This problem …

DIABLO: We share a common factor

PATRICK: Everything's connected. You guys heard that one before? Useless asking a demon or devil to say thank you while your books say: "We cannot go *through* the past, only *around* it, not through it." You said that. *I* didn't.

DIABLO: Try to look. It's dangerous confusing angels with devils. Attempts can make you into a silly idiot, into *two* silly idiots. I'm thinking you secretly loved me when I set up the ethical brackets here.

PATRICK: How? No matter what I do, I get loved. Where are you coming from?

DIABLO: If I drop-shit the kicking dog, you want me near you?

PATRICK: I'm tired. I used to be smart - now I'm sitting here acting silly.

DIABLO: See how we're meeting at this diner again? You never opposed it. I'm judging you. In silence. I'm the selector.

PATRICK: Selector?

DIABLO: I know a night like this don't mean shit to you. Over there, that man [gesturing out the window] - cops find him dead, his money stolen. He was living for that money but his father and mother lived their lives for *him* - a genius, man, with shit like a child. It hurts - *hurts*. Statistics are a flash in the pan. It hurts when the past never happens once more. In the trade we call that sensation "Vietnamese electricity." That's not a figure of speech in most parts of the world, no way. Your body and head slip down … destroyed. Such is life in the time of family freaks. What can you do if you don't do *that*?

Early adult

2. Costa Move developed into a most mysterious hypochondriac, often in the middle of illness though time-to-time suspending illness to commit violence, as "the neighbor girls stole my car battery." He expressed discontent over the depth of orange on his head. When he discovered vitamin C failed to absorb and disseminate throughout his brain, he chased his skull with a razor, believing that by shaving his head he would see his own "belief activity" - [There's dissatisfaction here.]

> Yes. Signifikansi. Autumn: a revolutionary mind. Green tea aneath the paper. Fall season: half-awareness. Helium rare. An ocean glass of fraction within a voiced bell. Unforgettable skies cave in. Ha. Miliaran-millions of stars. No. Autumn: nature's accessories linked to crime. A windy gap. Quail. Ironi encoiled mystery. Parents are spectacular. Yes. Signifikansi. He babbles on about bleeding problems.

PATRICK: You mean what? - to say the man out there's *not* on the wheel of existence?

DIABLO: Look at the things around him on the sidewalk. Try at least.

PATRICK: Ah, that looks bad. His eyes are bad. Twelve years of school. I, uh, schools are … What's the point? I used to be intelligent. Now I'm stupid. How sad.

DIABLO: Well, yes. Degrees … and classes. Get your eyes outta that newspaper. Look out *there* [gesturing to the streets outside the window]. Need more coffee or water to drink? Try something, anything else. If you're like a child, you're stupid as you keep saying - a beautiful porcelain doll, porcelain buttocks, hips of a child so beautiful at birth.

PATRICK: I think [INTERFERENCE] … therefore the mind's stupid. God, what, what am I thinking? I go out, wanna curse myself. I return to the island but I'm stupid there too. I need to go home, get some sleep.

DIABLO: I, uh, I forgive you. One more thing - blah, blah, blah, something, something. Him, out there, watch the man die. Once a small child. Now death's addressing that man millions of years ago. Yet *you* - right *now* - can do better.

PATRICK: What *don't* I do? What the hell? I'm like him. What *he* says out there to the other pedestrians is what I'm saying to you right now. I know I can't be stupid. I love ... What's more powerful than imagination? Damn shame. Most of my life ... What is it? I'm ashamed that shameless guilt won't help me regret something I shouldn't allow myself in the first place.

DIABLO: This isn't the end. These aren't closed dimensions you asshole - *no*. You're a sorry individual. You say a little parable, you lose your mind. Life's [INTERFERENCE]. Oh so hard to achieve, so long, short life for so long, so long, oh … God created the word 'goddammit' for a number of reasons.

PATRICK: What is it? How? What is it then? What is it?

DIABLO: In this big game, you got something you must have. Make your moves. Damage the system.

PATRICK: Are you hungry? Line down? Muffin?

DIABLO: This is a game with children. Surprised? Yes I said it - *now*. In the human world, evolution's anthropology. It's not organic - ask the animals.

3. Not long afterwards, Costa Move burned down his mother's home (much as I did), then tried to poison each neighbor who rented storage lockers from his father. Costa Move began climbing *through* his bedroom door into the near future, right *through* the wall of his closet onto the roof his father created when he built that house. ("I can't make enough money to move beyond the next town.") Costa Move chased after alcohol, marijuana, acid, often in states of intolerable intoxication, lying naked in his bedroom even when company arrived. His roommate was unable to translate Costa Move's behavior into anything more than a refusal to vacate his unkempt bedroom. [Oh I get this.]

> All to see. Close. Find a reversal away from what stories can scrape off metaphor. That's the case. Easy. Same soft curly hair. Crying. All to see. Close. Dependence on open systems. I'd imagine an asphalt playground if I were you. Big Bang.

Milkmen descending on Hound's Tooth Road. Descending basket rotations, prophets, Imams iron-fisted with guns. Piegi clothing productions. Pressure explosions destroyed Praise Hills. That's the way to our grave. Positioning our colors. Our guardian contacts passing through the age of democracy. Grandfather's very angry.

PATRICK: Shame taught me the skills to look for work. But I say no, I'm not seeing this - *no*. You're *not* a reflection of my soul - no - I won this game. Teachers, students will support my aching heart. "Sinus Mary Jane, sincerely cock," as I used to say.

DIABLO: More embedded ideas. I told you it's dangerous to confuse angels with children.

PATRICK: You said demons.

DIABLO: Demons?

PATRICK: Or devils.

DIABLO: Now that we ah listen - I wanna know your answer to the question .... In this life, if this is not what you expected, if one thing's unworthy, you still have to *do* something.

PATRICK: I get to live the biggest regret of all - dreaming of returning to the island.

DIABLO [in a deep bass voice]: Everything's worth telling everyone! We have to go pee, have to poo. Killing others is one of the ways we take part in the distribution of men and women.

PATRICK: Men ... Shit, those are bad things, right? Heinous things.

DIABLO: Yes sir it's true I said the proper distribution of men and women. If that's a terrible disappointment ...

PATRICK: Excuse me. What was it I asked?

DIABLO: Bullshit! You're apologizing for things you never had occasion to say. No need for that. I don't apologize for what I describe. You think you got friends out there? [Gesturing to the city outside the diner window.] Are those *your* friends? They're gonna be okay when you start abusing them, mocking their problems. Uh-huh. But when things start going wrong, think again.

PATRICK: I wanna ... feel good about this performance. I wanna ...

DIABLO: Your being nervous won't make you hate everyone. Many attractions [gesturing at the city streets] - many good things to seek in a series, it seems, with the police in tow, helping you collect on it without problems. Now imagine you lose an appendage - an arm, for instance, or a leg.

PATRICK: I lost my arm?

DIABLO: Today, early this morning, before sunrise, you lost your arm. Tell me what I wanna know - what's on your mind?

PATRICK: What?

DIABLO: I don't see a fool sitting across from me at this table. I don't feel stupid being right here with you. This is how we ask questions around here. Why you think I'm lying when it's unnecessary?

PATRICK: So, today I lost my arm.

DIABLO: Yes, you can do that today - like yesterday I lost my shadow. Today you lose your arm. *Wait.* I know you fear you might … That's right - your stupidity's your problem alone. Everything you hear is a good listen. The problem's yours alone.

PATRICK: I started, I … no … eh …

4. When exclusive apartments opened up across the street, Costa Move chased and killed those neighbors' pets as if his behavior were a proxy for committing suicide. He daydreamed about various livestock, raw materials, devised means of mixing those raw materials in a milkshake mixer that included swallowing a "Coca-Cola body." Such was the joy of his life - "to stop the heart drop."

> Red, at the bottom of the jamb. Drunk in a foreign palace. People like that. Scattered pearls. Houses at lower levels. Hills - off perutku. I hope it's *good* butter. Good for me. Stroberi. Amazing for you. We have the speed of our weight tonight - laws of inertia are indifferent. So tell me - this would happen without you? Yes or no? Desires sense what comes later. Print queues up the old. Drainage printing machines frame (we investigate) the roots of gold.

DIABLO: You lost your arm today.

PATRICK: I lost my arm today.

DIABLO: That's your problem alone.

PATRICK: Happened like you said - the smell.

DIABLO: So what went wrong? You're a good person.

PATRICK: I'm no more popular than you thought I am, though my physical condition's a bit worse than you expected.

DIABLO: That's a myth. I see you're still nervous. From the coffee?

PATRICK: Don't know. Biological factors - worse than vague weakness, worse than unemployed women.

DIABLO: Why are you depressed? You lost your arm. That's an opportunity, right?

PATRICK: The problem's I'm a regular user of arms. I'm an arm addict.

DIABLO: Hero by default, your brain's fluffy-blond, chock full of nothing. You're big but you're - tell me - incredibly boring. This continent's existential spiral offers you a love interest. That's disgusting, disturbing - the trail of a refugee reduced to … something you cannot reach. Get behind me, Father. I can say anything I want about you.

PATRICK: *No* - you know nothing about navigation. If you did, we wouldn't be stuck here in this low socioeconomic perspective.

DIABLO: This is a combination of what's wild. This is what the Nazis failed to do. So why do you use the last full …

PATRICK: Local punks are a good match for us. They know how to download their hormones - like idiots in movies - sleazeballs, thieves, flunkies. I love what these idiots around here do for the movies.

DIABLO: You're saying vulgar? I'm teasing you a little, not bullying. Strange for me to sit so long without drinking a vodka and tonic.

PATRICK: This isn't a bar. I'm not cringing.

DIABLO: You don't think the opportunity to drink's important?

PATRICK: Well, maybe. … Yes, yes …Well, aesthetically.

DIABLO: Other than politics we got little in common.

PATRICK: Why are there so few customers at this hour?

DIABLO: We got nothing in common, not even a common place of reaction.

PATRICK: Well, I too was a virgin at our first meeting.

5. When an underground mental hospital recruited Costa Move for its studies on "healthcare blood infusions," he began receiving plasma injections from the vessels of rabbits. Hospital staff shared their own fantasies about killing rabbits with him. Soon Costa Move discovered a distribution of blood around his mouth twice every morning. When the hospital staff started drinking "bird liquids," one of its employees turned up murdered in the basement with the blood of a razor cut. Costa Move claimed dead birds were being thrown from the upper windows of the hospital - inspiring the personnel to dub him Dracula.

Common ruin of gold. 3 people in each party. Tteomilryeotgohapnida. Robes of scarlet fever. Secrets in those rooms. Here *later* is a better community - teen indefinitely. Harmonic variations. Waving heroes dazzle the savages.

DIABLO: I got no plans for mass murder except to be open for business.

PATRICK: I got no plans on how to instigate more than 13 killings to get the attention of the road not taken.

DIABLO: I'll tell the managers to expect mild treatments - to help the patients achieve the best in adult life. Tell them to be God's servant.

PATRICK: Or soldiers of God.

DIABLO: Yes, careers in God's army, confident loyalists exchanging positive energies. I can picture it. Six years spent sent to war zones. Military maps and other signs.

PATRICK: Though not great terrorists, nor disturbed ketidakcocokan cranks.

DIABLO: God no.

PATRICK: Nor religious extremists attacking soldiers who no longer *see* the enemy.

DIABLO: God forbid.

6. Growing older, Costa Move learned how to reduce his total dependency on the pressure of blood vessels, inducing episodes where he replaced oxygen with carbon dioxide or nitrogen, in effect becoming a "therapy dog." He claimed a retired pharmacist had cracked open a vault of glass syringes for community use. A

few weeks later, many local drug addicts were reduced to the
level of basic animal care.

Side by side just fine. Quiet outside the open window. Ginkgo
branch. Host country to their insular forces [leave this section
blank]. Funds evaporate. Rejections alone. Skiing from side to
side. By the end of the first act of indifference, dissolved,
integrated into infinity, the Birth Star, I think.

PATRICK: Or both?

DIABLO: Horrible wounds of the past six years spent …

PATRICK: You'll see the alleged motives for murder, including his
thoughts, ideas, contacts. You'll see measures taken and that he's
held accountable - right up to the time of the shoot.

DIABLO: His steps look confused to me. When if ever is the death
of an innocent permissible?

PATRICK: God you know how to cut to the chase. This war's on
the verge of producing peace. Whence this productive academic
interest?

DIABLO: Seems to solve the problems we discussed between the
11th and 12th Centuries.

PATRICK: Depression, even stress trigger fatal attacks of
intellectual ... *What?*

7. By that time, Costa Move was suffering from mild forms of
drug psychosis or schizophrenia. [Who am I? Why am I here?
Why do I do what I do? Need clarification.] His claims were
becoming outrageous. He told a drug counselor that
"psychotropic compounds are no longer as dangerous to society
as they were in 1976." Another time he demanded his demented
mother be "released from the state under written obligation that
she be weaned off antipsychotic drugs requiring her to behave
like her son's pet zombie [*sic*]."

Fear of animals indicates the limits of a brain that cannot
appreciate loneliness is a member of the headache clan.
Menggambar the first element of blood. Biting nails scrape
mengilap iron. My clothes horrible in horrible disorder.
They're stupid to see the world through the sides of their
skulls. Cities, foreign countries - what fun.

I pull the ticket from my briefcase and shake it at the bellboy who shakes his head at me. What pitch you mean? - What limes? That fruit's all you got? - Well then, explain Mr. Rousseau's Mafioso-style name scrawled across the cover of those two overlapping manuscripts. The frog-eyed bellboy refuses to understand me. His reality's too twisted relative to mine. I grab his bicep, squeeze. Still nothing. Dead silence. I see he's on edge, spooked. It's serious now. You Luzon? That's a focused parabolic? What number you looking for? I explain we're leaving for Minnesota, leaving Nevada far, far behind, checking ourselves out of the twisted wreckage of this Las Vegas suite. At the hotel's entrance, thugs are waving around five-dollar bills, yelling at a prostitute. They're ready to romp her, as we used to say, run her down on the curb in a position hard to explain. Who *are* these people? Where did they come from? Minnesota too.

8. One evening in the summer of 2002 Costa Move was seen in a car wearing a blood-soaked nightshirt, driving buckets of blood along a "weapons drive" near a military installation.

I'm hungry. I'm thirsty. In this gold medal palace. Here's the second hand. The face-off. With geometry. I have hair on the field I'm gonna detect. An unusual experience to do at first. A universal language. I swear. Meeting here at the edge of Truth Regardless Of Desire. Smell? Petrified wood out of season. Fewer than 100 women on their heads. Free chain moyangku grandma 9. Eternal youth of the world - again, purity - again the garden turns imprisoned. Every 4.10 years. Las Square. Sharp nose. Short thick legs. Son operates Machine Black One. Waste paper blue. Inside a small white temple.

Yes he never did a thing like that before - Mr. Riordan didn't. A young man with a prostitute embarks on a journey beyond the horror. The journey drags on into cinematic history (drags across the carpeted lobby past plastic palm trees, past overwhelming odors of cleaning fluids). An unbearably virtuosic film, thrilling experimental experience of the physical limits, hypnotic trip sticky, tiring, *topo*, most innovative & exciting of the year. - Oh, don't get me too excited (I'm paring corns with this here razor). Exact opposite. The young man with the prostitute takes his breakfast in bed. Prostitute's name's Penelope. Two of them talk about politics, earthquakes, end of the world, God-the-Failure. Violence explodes into monstrous nightmares, fogs of green steam, smutty photos, odd meal of oysters, potatoes, potted meat, drinking water. It's serious now. Very heavy gig, Mr. Riordan. End's inevitable, yes, as in classical Irish tragedy, indeed a relief. (Those strange vibratory glows are keeping the reader from falling asleep.) - Conclusion? - You think he sodomized her? Go check yourself in the mirror if you dare. Mmmmm good. Discipline *that* - rejoice! Islanders still like Jesus in Dublin - trust me.

9. Later, following his arrest, Costa Move would tell investigators he was "convinced the military police are not *right* for taking animals captive without extending forgiveness to me."

What happens without savages? Hah - view Divine. Laying violent winds out before the indifference of animalistic fear. The Department of Imbalance without sensation of movement. What's left to me? Among the many useless things. Memorabilia from a collection. Communication-connections. Insulator set-pieces. Extensive legal fiction - no inspiration. Damn, the idea, the term's not reached the drive or desire to love what I do. Enact?

Mr. Riordan, remember last week when we pretended to be laid up sick, chatting about Hell-slash-Heaven in this mega-hotel of a thousand odors? Outside that window [gesturing] headlights of cars passing - flickering lampposts - track rumblings boosted infra-low (like Gibraltar thunderbolts) - fake-plastic prostitutes attached between the commuter-train seats - Mr. Riordan with the prostitute squeezing into the train's W C - lack of light penalties - general B-movie atmosphere - pasties off the

nipples. Mr. Riordan's in bandages. Prostitute's
methylated, let us say, big baby-faced prostitute with a
nosebleed, sprained foot, old maid's voice - anything to
slip into a lonely man's hotel room, wheedle him out of
money, crawl up his legs with a knife between her teeth.
At the hotel bar they take yellow expensive drinks not
whiskey or stout - (You sure this ain't Dublin?) - 2 Cuba
libres with beer, mescal on the side. Prostitute blows her
nose into the cocktail napkin. Mr. Riordan drinks
heavily. You think he sodomized her? Why not? He's
kidding.

Murder

10. Costa Move shot, killed his first victim while driving drunk.
After the shooting, several neighbors witnessed Costa Move in
his own backyard firing the 22-caliber rifle doing ballistics tests.
When one of the larger more intimidating neighbors asked about
his disturbing behavior, Costa Move allegedly replied, "Making
sure there's no trace of the murder weapon left."

Your help's not sentimental. It's ridiculous. (The island's
capital city's more out of control.) Why's a stronger rejection
of Alzheimer's so fantastic? - even if I like a drug craze. Ha.
How I enjoy the wings of these pseudo-continental habitats.
The small delicate bones, the symptoms. I like the breast of an
almost motionless woman, the loose thighs - of the first half
anyway. The cold working of a big mouth. The pores.
Umskorinn. Inside a giant box.

Stable? Able to talk? Having survived five days in the
ICU we regain consciousness decades before the dark.
We speak when spoken to. We're sleep professionals
sleeping on the opposite side of those elegant sliding
glass doors [gesturing to the glass, man]. Look outside -
a big machine hangs in the sky with strange symbols and
filigree. The patients (that's us) snooze through the
alarms, forget to read our Bibles. Cycle repeats. More
blood poisoning. We ignore the effects of these
expensive drugs, pretend nothing's happening. Thirty
minutes. Gonna be a close call. Dr. Menton knows this -

kill the body, the head will die. He paces around nervously. It's serious now. He cannot let himself hear the sound so he screams at the bartender. Nothing. You see what they did to him. Memories of the rest of that night are hazy.

11. Two weeks later Costa Move returned home one morning after a night of drunk driving to find the front door locked. "Not good," he said, before smashing in the door with his boot-clad feet, then urinating on his former girlfriend's tobacco-cigarette products wrapped in defecation-stained bedding along with personal items plus a "hardcopy-shoe."

Surfing the windows of the neighborhood in the evening light I shall love. Einróma destiny. You, why Ayun scream? Here they're placed atop an empty platform. Manager so. Very dangerous. A woman becomes the central axis of each performance she learned through the magic word. She must pay. Tomorrow? Breakfast in the morning. With each case enthusiast. Discussing heresies in May. The world stops in the area I've added. A curling Planet Channel. Power means we're unclear how many times we turn on a certain point in time.

I'm baby too lazy to read long books. Dr. Menton says my ailments are a pack of lies. He's the dirty barefaced liar here. His eyes narrow. He's on the edge. He's wearing a .38 revolver on his belt. I lunge at the doctor, begin babbling. You bastard! Paranoid scum! What scene? Turn that shit off! You're scaring the shit outta the patients! - Let me study *your* habits. This ranting scares the piss out of Dr. Menton. Now I know he'll remember my face. I'm thinking wait till he sees what's happening in the elevators. Hell, only reason the patients are using those elevators to flee in terror is to escape the hospital *right now*. This ain't the Nevada State Prison - it's damn close. I been to Carson City, Nevada - went crazy there in a racist frenzy. Hell of a long night. Gravel roads. Hunched low over the wheel. Concrete-block houses. Tattoo parlors. Moneychangers. Cotton-candy booths. Dust clouds over parking lots. Cop cars. Bike trailers. A fine sunrise over deserted casinos.

12. Sucking the blood of a dead woman didn't revolt Costa Move (as some movies depict). He proved it too, first to himself, later, after his capture, to the entire world - look within the walls of his home. [Lack of public sympathy there?] He purchased two kittens, killed them, drank their blood. He planned a blood-drinking rampage but failed to follow through on it. He never ingested the brains of children or set foot in a church afore taking antidepressant medication. (I'm the one who ate children's brains *next* to a church, well, across the street from a church, in a Wal-Mart parking lot.) - [I tried to confuse them using poisoned food I pulled from a trouser pocket.] - [I can slip past anyone.]

Yes I come from a good stock. Mixed. Now change your body. Relax - make your legs stick to the seabed. Those tight little naked feet. The new Adam: sun & sea: a type solution - though in reality: closed systems.

Lost control of the situation (like hanging on the rim of an indoor merry-go-round). What the hell's going on down there? What's that shooting sound? Across the aisle a large reptile gnaws on a woman's neck. I try to focus on my club sandwich. I try to stare out the hospital window at the midnight sky. I try to see myself lying in bed with Penelope the prostitute. Not a wise move. Feel like I got a bone caught in my throat. That lizard's a very special breed. That woman's sinking to her knees. Loss of basic motor skills leaves her screaming gibberish at the world, howling anything comes to mind. Reptile's found the main nerve, main circuit cable. It's serious now. This train car reeks of hellish … Watch out. *ZANG!* That's right - go ahead, reader, - laugh about it. Where'd you get that hunting knife?

Capture & Aftermath

13. After knocking on the back door, cops released an invitation to enter, only to discover "a blood clot the size of a persecution image" in Costa Move's kitchen. In the refrigerator unit: few dead hot dogs, macaroni-&-cheese provisions. Scrawled in canary

blood over the sink, the insanity plea: *Cheisufuruhandopurinto Danimeredisu [Channel 4] [trust] payment will not be made WALLIN I continue to chase my innocence.*

Unforgettable hole in the sky. My clothes, this terrible mess. She's got mighty blood problems. Yes. Signifikansi. ○ every 4.1 years. Las Vegas Plaza. Spicy nose. Short thick legs. Yummy little bone. I hope one's a *good* oil. Good for me. Stroberi. Surprise me. Your gait - the weight of the night - the laws shall redeem us. Tell me - that's not you? Yes - *no*. Under the definition of lust. Red, under the door frame. State: how funny. Big box inside.

Room service sent her up. This book's author thinks drinking whiskey lacks vanity - a good thing - plus adds two inches of edited copy to your auto + biography (on par with surviving five days in the ICU). He'll bother you 10 years outside his Brooklyn apartment, standing there in a Harley-Davidson T-shirt, giving you a lotta crap about, you know … not listening … sidewalks full of noisy drunken shouting in three different directions. Hell of a long night. Nobody notices the book's author says one thing about sex is a child locked in a dark room for nine years. Another thing is this fearful Jesuit's monkishly mimant property.

14. Ole Costa Move had failed to take flight or appear amazing in a final car chase. He lay across the mattress in a blood-soaked nightshirt, adopting the standard suicide position where breathing has stopped while the mobile phone keeps ringing. He forgot to feed the puppies. [5 source] - [be trusted?] (I ate him?)

Your help's not painful - that's absurd. A grave dissolved in a minor star where I was born I think. Let's put our logo on the ginkgo industry. Contact us, Guardian Angel, please, for the sake of the democratic era. My grandfather's angry. Contact us for a later better society - a childhood forever. Harmonic changes. Taj Mahal heroes. Steam funds. Trouble tickets. Chemical burns. Times for multiple transfers. I'll show off to the barbarians one final time. Yes, I arrived in a good condition. Now my body changes. *Release.*

When the stakes start getting too high I start to hear myself mumbling. Weird watching myself behave in this terrible way without controlling it. The ground floor's full of gambling tables, craps tables, blackjack. This place is getting to me. Where have all the flowers gone? Next hour's waiting, cursing the creeps who burned me with their bizarre shucks, their drunken voice-messages screaming gibberish at the world.

Rub out ole dog-fox

God - can I *say* that? Am I supposed to *think* it? Me? Hear me out. I'm waiting for my grandson lawyer. I understand he's elsewhere - on a journey in search of a red shark with an indifferent face painted on its cheeks. That shit's important.

> Yes, man, islanders are beginning to question their personal interests, furiously attacking their own existence, snuffing out pride while pretending to forget about everything else. Their friends are taken to one side, their abstract interests to the other, leaving behind reconciliations, agreements, commitments. Nor are those islanders any longer a part of the continental government. Their secret motives - ask me about their motives - ask me if some - *any* - words of betrayal occurred in their speeches or were caught up in slights of passion. Ask me if the villain's become the Continental General Assembly. IF - *IF* - soldiers in war turned on soldiers free at war's end, valiant, noble, …
> Benefits of interest to the assembly of gifts or privileges
> .

Well, you should explain things better, speak to the reader like a child, prove (verify?) you can exist at the level of a dumb animal with a rotting mind. Flash the reader a grin right here, admire the shape of her skull.

> Standing on the highest steps of the altar, I tell the islanders we need to *act* smarter, *appear* more awesome - IF the whole of the island can ever disentangle its

chains of reason from the weakness of confinement, sir.
You hear me? I don't know how we got buried up to our
shoulders in mixed metaphorical beach sand.

This is not the enemy one hundred times more -
whispering: - "Yes, I want so much trouble -
everything."

You're grinding your teeth at me - understand: that's not me -
those are *your* teeth - your gums. I got a response to your stories.
That's me glaring at your flashlight in hand. Man, your vibrations
are ugly tonight. I'm so sure of that I can taste it.

Hear *me*? Catch *that*? One way to do it - understand?
Me? Impure fear, confusion sickeningly - automatically
- biasing the Continental General Assembly. Rounding
up the nonsmokers, accusing each of us of "immersion
in the struggle to yank the island away from the
continent."

So deep that one hears the distant sound of sea
whispering: - "Why prize money for these
people?"

Better 10,000 acts of cruelty than destruction
failing to meet the bar.

Give me that pink phone. Hold my neck in your callused
hands. You need less arrogance to support each other in your
misfortunes. Let words resign -

Then beat your chest - wear out the coastal waters. I'm
not ashamed by this aquamarine mess. Islanders ever
refused your money? How would we pay for our
defenses otherwise? Good thing it don't matter we got
our own *private* limits - we don't ignore anything. Good
thing elephants are afraid of the sea.

"If they can escape, let's allow the moment to
become available …

You're turning. Again I say less arrogance. Your coconut
trees. Driving force winds. Drums beating. Here. Sit down. Boy,
you got a beautiful facemask right there. Rays of lit candles
running through your upraised hands.

That leaves a 'left defense,' lots of legal advice afore this thing's over - a 'rhinoceros detection of violation,' a 'damage to the winter rains,' a 'tear flowing from her face to the wall' a … garbage & hope - the Screaming Eagles of Carthage.

A

AUDIENCE applauds, stands up, leaves the auditorium.

www.ingramcontent.com/pod-product-compliance
Lightning Source LLC
Chambersburg PA
CBHW072209170626
46813CB00003B/858